S

WASTERS

SPACE WASTERS

David Garnett

orbit

An *Orbit* Book

First published in Great Britain by Orbit 2001

Copyright © 2001 by David Garnett

The moral right of the author has been asserted.

A CIP catalogue record for this book
is available from the British Library.

ISBN 1 84149 012 1

Typeset in Imprint by M Rules
Printed and bound in Great Britain
by Mackays of Chatham plc

Orbit
A Division of
Little, Brown and Company (UK)
Brettenham House
Lancaster Place
London WC2E 7EN

For Frances
for ever
and ever
and
for the title

CHAPTER

ONE

1

Wayne Norton pressed the palms of his hands together, lining up his thumbs and fingers. He turned his left hand towards him, and his right hand was completely covered. Then he turned his right hand towards him, and there was no longer a perfect match. Because his right index finger was missing, completely gone.

'Stop it,' said Kiru.

Her eyes were closed, so how did she know what he was doing?

'Stop what?' he asked.

'Looking at your lost finger.'

'It's not lost, it was stolen.'

'Stop looking at it.'

'How can I look at something if it's not there?'

'You can't,' she said. 'So stop it.'

He kept staring at the place where his finger should have been. There was no scar and the flesh between his thumb and middle finger was so smooth it was almost as if the finger had never existed.

'You want a drink?' he asked.

'No.'

'Something to eat?'

'No.'

'Anything?'

'No,' said Kiru. 'I've got everything I want, every-thing I need.' She raised both her hands, wiggled her fingers. 'Everything I was born with.'

'More than you were born with,' said Norton, as he studied her nude body. Kiru lay supine on the beach, hands folded across her stomach. She was wonderful, beautiful, a fantasy come true. And they were on their honeymoon.

Norton looked away from her, glancing around the island. The crescent of red coral was no more than two hundred yards across, and it was set aside for their private use. The skimmer lay half in the water, half on the beach, ready to take them back to the tourist zone whenever they wished, back to their suite at the top of the highest skytel on the entire planet. Whatever they wanted, it was theirs for the asking, compliments of the resort management.

If Norton had ever been asked his idea of heaven, he couldn't have described anything better than this. Alone on a desert island with the most fantastic girl in the universe. He might not have thought that the waves which lapped rhythmically across the warm sand would be pink, or that the whole world would be vari-ous shades of red, but that was only because he could never have imagined that he'd spend his honeymoon on an alien planet.

He gazed at the horizon, out where the scarlet sky melted into the crimson sea, watching through his out-stretched fingers.

'Stop it,' said Kiru again, although her eyes were still closed.

'How long before we grow webbed fingers?' he asked. 'How long before we grow webbed toes?' He reached down and grabbed one of her ankles and slid his fingers between her toes.

'Don't!' she laughed. 'It tickles.' Kiru pulled her leg free and rolled away. 'You'll have to do a lot more swimming before you grow flippers.'

It was she who had taught him to swim; she who had taught him so many things. On Caphmiaultrelvossmuaf swimming was almost essential. Only one percent of the planet was land, and it wasn't necessarily dry land. It rained almost all the time over most of the planet. The exception was the pleasure islands, where the climate was as controlled as the casinos.

'If we stay here too long,' said Norton, 'our bodies will start to adapt.'

'We'd have to be here years and years for that to happen,' said Kiru.

Away from Earth, the world where their ancestors had lived for countless generations, humans began to change. No two planets were alike. Even if the gravity and atmosphere were identical, the basic chemical composition of every world was different, as were the physical and psychic influences on its inhabitants. It was a slow process, very subtle, but if a person spent too much time on an alien planet, beneath the light of an alien star, then finally they would no longer be totally human.

Kiru had put her arms behind her head and her long, wavy hair cascaded across the sand, the shells and the tiny pebbles. It was as if she was already part of the island, part of the planet, her hair as red as the world where they had each found themselves – and where they had rediscovered one other.

'Years and years?' said Norton.

'Years and years and years,' said Kiru.

What did that mean here? The planet didn't even have days. This half of the world was always turned towards its distant sun. It never grew dark, there was never any night. Time seemed not to exist on Caphmiaultrelvossmuaf, which was one reason why it had been developed as a vacation planet. Visitors came here to spend, to gamble and to buy. Because there was no sunset, their spending, gambling and buying never had to end.

'Whatever you say, Mrs Norton,' said Norton.

Kiru pushed herself up on one elbow and made as if to pull off her wedding ring. The ring Norton had originally slipped onto the third finger of her left hand was nothing more than a circle of shell, polished by the sands and tides, coruscating with every possible shade of red, as if the essence of the entire alien planet was trapped within its delicate orbit. Since then, the shell had been fused inside a ring cut from a single, lucent diamond.

'I'll keep this,' said Kiru, with a smile, as she twisted the wedding band around her finger, 'and you keep your name. Is that a deal?'

'But what do I get out of the deal?' asked Norton.

'Depends what you want,' said Kiru, and she smiled again.

Kiru said she'd only ever had one name, that one was all she needed. He called her 'Mrs Norton' for fun. 'Mrs' seemed so strange, so anachronistic.

Norton knew nothing about Kiru's family, and very

little about her past. As far as he was concerned, her life had begun the day that they met. Because in a sense, his certainly had.

Kiru was naked the first time he saw her. So was he, he remembered. She'd burst into his room on Hideaway and threatened him with a gun. That was the kind of thing criminals did. Norton knew because he was a police officer. And Kiru was an ex-convict.

Opposites attract, and Norton had certainly been attracted to Kiru. The most amazing thing of all was that she had felt the same about him. The ex-cop and the ex-con were the first couple to be married on Caphmiaultrelvossmuaf – or Café World, as the holiday planet had become known.

Kiru was still playing with her wedding ring, and she frowned. It seemed the ring wouldn't come off.

'You must be putting on weight,' Norton said, trying to provoke another reaction. To his surprise, Kiru merely nodded.

'If you want to sell the ring, you'll have to chop your finger off,' he added. 'Then we'd be equal.'

'You think you could be equal to me? Never!'

Where Norton came from, the diamond would have been worth a fortune. But on some worlds, diamonds were as common as sea shells on Caphmiaultrelvossmuaf. They must have been, because the jewel which encased the broken shell had been another gift from the resort owners.

'If it bothers you that much,' said Kiru, 'get another finger. You can have one grown.'

Without realising, Norton was looking at his right hand again. Rationally, he didn't mind too much that his index finger was gone. It was no great loss, he could manage without, and it was like his own war wound.

He was a warrior who had sacrificed a part of himself in the eternal battle for truth and justice and liberty.

But the bastards had still taken his finger away.

'As long as I've known you,' Kiru continued, 'you've been minus one digit. That's the way you are, Wayne, and that's the way I like you.'

'But you'd like me even more if I was complete, if I was perfect.'

'Perfect? Let's face it, no matter how many fingers you have, you'll never be perfect.'

'You know what I think?'

Kiru yawned.

'I think,' Norton continued, 'we should go back to Hideaway and get my finger. It must still be there, because they said I could have it back when I left.'

'You should have asked for it.'

'Asked for it! How could I have asked for it? Thanks to you, I was arrested and locked in a cell.'

'I know,' said Kiru. 'I was there.'

'Why don't we go back?'

'You should never return to the scene of the crime. Haven't you heard that?'

'That's for criminals, Kiru, not cops. I didn't commit a crime. I was innocent.'

'That's what they all say.'

'Is it what you said?'

'Yes,' said Kiru. 'But what good did it do me? They locked me up with you. It's amazing what you can do in a cell, remember?'

'Yeah.' Norton nodded, remembering. 'Let's go back to Hideaway, get my finger.'

'It isn't your finger that's there, Wayne. Why did they remove it?'

'Yeah.' Norton nodded again, remembering again.

Without him knowing, his index finger had been replaced with a non-lethal digital defence device. No weapons were permitted on Hideaway, and so the NLDDD had been detached from his hand. It was back on Earth that his finger had been swapped for a gun implant. 'Okay, let's go to Earth.'

'We can't,' said Kiru. 'I'd be arrested.'

Norton looked at his right hand, looked at Kiru, then looked at his hand again, as if wondering whether her arrest was a price worth paying to be reunited with his finger. Kiru wasn't an ex-convict. She was an escaped convict.

'Why do you want to go anywhere?' said Kiru. 'Don't you like being here?'

'Yeah.'

'Don't you like being here with me?'

'Yeah, sure, yeah. I love being here with you. Sure, yeah, sure.'

He kept gazing up at the sky. The alien sun was always masked behind a veil of cloud. Over most of the island, these were scarlet rain clouds. Above the holiday isles, the pink clouds were the resort's sunscreen, engineered to protect the tourists from the heat and radiation of Caphmiaultrelvossmuaf's star.

'I wonder what the sun's called,' said Norton. It was something he'd thought of before, but never got around to asking about.

'The sun. That's what the natives call it.'

'It must have another name. What do we know it as?'

'We don't,' said Kiru. 'Obviously.'

'Yeah, I suppose not. If it isn't visible to the naked eye from Earth, it probably only has a catalogue number.'

'Imagine this whole beach as stars,' said Kiru, as she allowed a handful of sand to trickle through her fingers. 'There aren't enough permutations of the alphabet to name all of them.'

'Someone must have started doing it,' said Norton. 'Why else call this planet Caphmiaultrelvossmuaf? Or was he the person who discovered it?'

'Why "he"?' said Kiru. 'It could have been a "she".'

'Or an "it".'

'In any case, the people who evolved here discovered the world first.'

'Is Caphmiaultrelvossmuaf their name for it?'

Kiru shook her head. 'You know what the Caphafers call this planet?'

'What?'

'Water.'

Norton nodded, because he should have guessed. It was the same as naming a planet Land or Soil or Dirt . . . or Earth.

'Speaking of water,' said Kiru, as she stretched, ran her fingers through her hair, then stood up, 'let's go for a swim.'

'You go,' said Norton. 'I'll guard the clothes.'

'That's a pathetic excuse. We haven't got any clothes.'

'They're on the skimmer, so I'll guard that.'

'Guard it from what?'

Norton shrugged. 'Who knows?'

Although he could swim, that didn't mean he enjoyed it. He was always nervous when he got out of his depth, and he was convinced that the waters of Caphmiaultrelvossmuaf were not as devoid of slithery, slippery, slimy sea serpents as the resort operators claimed.

'Are you coming for a swim?' asked Kiru.

'No.'

She walked to where Norton was sitting, then stood above him, her feet either side of his legs. Putting her hands on her hips, she raised her right foot and rested it on his left thigh, slowly sliding it higher.

'Anything I can do to persuade you?' she said.

'Maybe,' he said.

'Too bad,' said Kiru. She quickly lifted her right leg over his head, spun around and strode away. 'Because I can't be bothered.'

She walked towards the edge of the warm red sand and stepped into the warm red ocean, wading out until she was waist deep. Then she dived forward, splashing through the foaming waves. She glided across the surface, arms and legs outstretched but not moving, and then rolled over onto her back, lifting her head slightly so she could see Norton. He waved.

'You can change your mind,' she called.

'I didn't bring my swimming trunks,' he shouted.

'What?'

'And I haven't got a towel.'

'What?'

Kiru stood up. The waves broke around her waist, the sea covering and then uncovering her hips. She shook her head, and her hair swirled out around her shoulders, sending drops of spray flying. Her body was speckled with beads of water which dripped down her naked skin. She put her hands to her ears, wanting Norton to speak again.

He said nothing, all he did was look. It was as if Kiru had stepped from a painting by one of the ancient masters of the art. She was a sea nymph, a mythical goddess, a fabulous beauty. All that and more. To Norton, she was everything.

They had been together for such a brief time on Hideaway, and then he thought he'd lost her for ever. Finding her again, here on Caphmiaultrelvossmuaf, had been a miracle.

Kiru fell back into the waves, allowing herself to drift further and further away from the island until she kicked her feet, twisted over, and dived beneath the surface. Several seconds later, one of her arms reappeared, rising vertically out of the water. She waved her hand, once, then her arm sank back in to the sea, and nothing was left except a ripple on the ocean.

At first, Norton had thought he was in paradise. The honeymoon had been wonderful. And it still was. He and Kiru were on permanent vacation. The way things were going, it could last for ever. His life was full of superlatives, and he had all he could ever possibly have wished for. But . . . but . . .

He just wished something would happen.

2

He dreamed of the dark, of being trapped in eternal blackness, unable to move because the walls were so close, and they were coming closer, closer, squeezing down, crushing him.

It was a dream he'd had before, although not for a long time. He knew it was a dream, because he was aware of his true surroundings. This was Caphmiaultrelvossmuaf, and it was the first time he'd endured the nightmare since being on the red planet.

He felt cold, icy cold; he hadn't been this cold for ages. And at one time, he was cold for ages. Literally ice cold, cryonically frozen for over three centuries.

Even after his revival, it had taken a long while to get warm again. In fact, he still hadn't fully recovered even when he first met Kiru. She was the one who had finally thawed him out and brought him back to total life.

Wayne Norton opened his eyes, blinking against the light, and glanced to either side. Kiru wasn't back on the beach yet. He sat up and gazed out over the sea. There was no sign of her, she must have been hidden behind the swell of the breaking waves. He stood up, wondering how long he'd been asleep, how long Kiru had been in the water. Even at this angle, he couldn't see her. She often swam around the small island, so perhaps she was on the other side.

As he walked across the atoll, he kept glancing all about. There was nothing to obstruct his view. This was no tropical isle dotted with swaying palm trees. Except for the rocks and pebbles, sand and shells, the island contained only a few isolated clumps of vegetation. Nothing more than weeds, he supposed, red weeds.

Kiru wasn't on the opposite side. He walked around the edge of the island, heading back to where he'd started, looking out to sea all the time. At first, he hadn't been too concerned. Now, he picked up speed and jogged back to where the skimmer was beached. Could she be on board?

'Kiru?' he called. 'Kiru!'

The craft was empty.

He stood above the cockpit, which gave him the highest vantage point, and scanned the ocean.

'Kiru!'

His mouth was dry, his heart pounding in his chest.

'Kiru!'

Was she hiding from him, playing a trick because he'd refused to go swimming with her? It was impossible. There was nowhere to hide, nowhere except in the water, and she couldn't stay beneath the surface for long.

Something must have happened to her.

'Kiru!'

He knew the ocean was dangerous. The tourist resort had to claim it was safe, or else no visitors would risk coming here. What kind of alien sharks and piranhas inhabited the deeps? The Caphafers might be able to deal with such creatures, but what chance did a human have? What chance did Kiru have?

'Kiru!'

Or maybe it was the Caphafers. Norton had never trusted the natives. He never trusted any aliens. They were almost as bad as humans.

'Kiru!'

She could have got into difficulties swimming, caught cramp, or been swept away by a treacherous current. Perhaps even now the tide was carrying her helplessly away, far out into the endless ocean.

'Kiru!'

Norton jumped down from the skimmer and into the water. He had no idea where she was. There was nothing he could do – but he couldn't do nothing. He waded out, splashing through the waves.

'Kiru! Kiru!'

The surface of the water a few yards ahead of him suddenly swirled and erupted, and he caught a glimpse of red emerging from beneath.

'Kiru!'

'What's up, mate?' asked a deep voice.

It was a Caphafer. They were amphibious, but lived

most of their lives in the water because their planet had so little land.

'I was looking for someone,' said Norton. 'Have you seen her?'

'Someone like you?' asked the Caphafer.

'Yeah!'

'You aliens all look the same to me.'

'But have you seen anyone, any alien – any human, I mean? Anyone swimming around here who isn't a Caphafer?'

The natives were humanoid, with webbed fingers and toes. Their bodies were covered with scales and their skulls were ridged, with fins on either side of their heads and a series of gills down their necks. They were red, of course, and approximately the same size as humans.

'Swimming?' said the Caphafer, as though it was a word he had never heard. He gazed at Norton through large crimson eyes, water dripping from massive sharp teeth.

Norton had learned not to think of aliens as 'it'. Most were 'he' or 'she', although it might be impossible to tell which. Two was the usual number of different sexes required for the continuation of the majority of species, but in some cases one was sufficient. Even then, it wasn't appropriate to consider a sentient alien as an 'it'. Correct, but not appropriate.

He could recognise male and female Caphafers, but only if he saw them below the waist, which he preferred not to do.

Probably because of their aquatic environment, the Caphafers had never developed much of a clothing or fashion industry. But since part of their world had become a holiday resort and they had met other species from different solar systems, many of the natives had begun adopting alien ways. This one was wearing a sleeveless lime green top, the neck fringed with ribbons of blue lights which kept flashing on and off. He looked like a tourist on his own planet.

'Yeah, swimming,' said Norton, and he moved his arms to mime a breaststroke.

'Sorry, mate,' said the Caphafer, 'can't help you.'

Norton realised the Caphafer was using his own native language. Even naked, there was one thing Norton had on him: around his neck was his slate. A simultaneous linguistic and tonal equaliser was the only way of communicating with obstinate aliens who insisted on speaking their own language. (Not necessarily their own tongue, as many races didn't possess that anatomical feature.)

Norton could see himself reflected in the Caphafer's big, watery eyes. Or one of them. The alien's left eye was dull and cloudy. It seemed the creature was half blind, perhaps losing part of his sight to some savage fish.

'Got to go, mate,' said the Caphafer. 'Things to do.' He started to turn away.

'But what about Kiru?'

'Kiru?' The Caphafer looked back at Norton. 'You mean *the* Kiru?'

'Yeah!' said Norton, nodding for emphasis. 'Kiru. You know her?'

'We all know her, mate.'

'Do you? How?'

'Because of what she did for us, the people of Caphmiaultrelvossmuaf.'

When Norton first reached the planet, a number of the natives were working as resort staff. They had to say 'sir' or 'madam', although naturally enough they had trouble identifying when to use the right word; they also had to wear a ridiculous uniform. Not any more. Those who worked for the vacation complex were no longer virtual slaves. They were employees of Café World, paid a regular wage, only had to wear a uniform while on shift, and the obsequious 'sir' or 'madam' wasn't required when they were off-duty.

'Kiru told us we were being exploited,' said the Caphafer. 'Kiru was the first alien to talk with us instead of giving orders. She is our friend. Is she a friend of yours?'

'More than that,' said Norton. 'She's my wife.'

'The word doesn't translate.'

'Kiru is . . . er . . . she's my mate.'

'We're all mates in the ocean of life, mate.'

'Good, I'm very glad. But what about Kiru? She went into the water and didn't come out.'

'What's wrong with that?'

'We're not like you.' Norton put his hands to his neck, where he didn't have gills. 'We need air all the time. Kiru hasn't come back, so she must still be in the water.'

'I'll find out.'

With that, the Caphafer sank beneath the waves. The sea was only up to Norton's waist, and he took a deep breath before he also ducked down. He always closed his eyes when he was under the surface, but he forced himself to open them. The water was clear, but there was nothing to see, the alien had vanished. He stood up again, wiped his face, and glanced back towards the island. It was still deserted.

'She's gone, mate.' The Caphafer was back.

Norton looked around. 'Gone? Gone where?'

'Don't know.'

'How do you know she's gone?'

'I asked.'

'Who? Who did you ask?'

'Everyone.'

'Everyone?' Norton gazed across the empty ocean. The surface was empty, but beneath the waves lived an entire alien race.

'No one knows where she is,' said the Caphafer. 'Which means she's not on the world.'

'Not on the world,' said Norton, slowly. 'You mean she's . . . she's . . . ?'

'Yes. She's left the planet.'

Norton looked up. There was a distant flash of light across the sky as another tourist ship streaked through the atmosphere, heading for the infinite darkness of interstellar space.

He didn't know how there could have been enough time for Kiru to leave the planet, but he did know that she hadn't left voluntarily. She had been abducted.

But who could have done it, who would have done it?

There was only one possible suspect . . .

3

'Where's Kiru?' asked Wayne Norton.

There was no reply. He could have been speaking to a blank wall. In fact, it appeared that he was speaking to a blank wall.

But behind the wall was the resort's observation centre. Norton was being watched by a microcam above the entrance. The camera was hidden, so was the entrance. The whole of the vacation complex was covered by secret cameras. Because most of the off-worlders who worked on Café World seemed to have a criminal background, it was as important to watch them as the customers. The employees were aware of the spycams; this prevented too much theft, both of property and of time. What they weren't aware of was the location of the security centre.

'Let me in,' said Norton.

'Go ahead,' said a voice.

Norton held out his right hand. As if it was made of water, the wall parted where he touched it. His fingers vanished, then his wrist and his arm. Norton moved forward, and the wall absorbed him for a second or two until he stepped into the hemispherical room beyond. The inner wall was almost completely covered with monitor screens, all the images changing every few seconds as the entire tourist zone was constantly scanned.

'How's things, old boy?' said Jay.

It was Jay who was the old boy. What was left of his hair was grey and his face was lined and gaunt. It was about time he had a rejuve. Unless he'd already had one, in which case he would keep on looking older and older.

'Bad,' said Norton. 'Kiru's missing.'

'The lovely Kiru?' said Jay. 'I warned you, Wayne, you've got to keep an eye on that wonderful girl all the time. You know how much she fancies me. And who can blame her?'

'This is serious, Jay. I've lost her.'

'Keep your hair on. She can't be far away. Let's run a trace. You want a snifter?'

By that, he meant a drink. Norton shook his head.

'You sure? You look like you need one.'

'No,' said Norton. 'Just find her.'

As always, Jay sat in a floating chair in the middle of the command room, a row of buttons on the armrest by his left hand. By his right hand was a row of tiny bottles, each containing a rare liqueur from the most exotic worlds in the galaxy. Jay claimed he would only drink alcohol from planets he'd visited during his spacefaring career. He reached for one of the bottles, opened it, lifted it towards his mouth.

'Trace –' he said. Then he tilted the bottle to his lips and drank. '– Kiru.'

Every screen in the room blinked, and a moment later Kiru's picture was displayed on them all. She was identical on each monitor. Her face was in close-up, eyes wide, smiling, framed by a mass of wild, red hair. She was looking forward, but slowly her head turned until her right profile was on display. A web of lines appeared on screen, as if holding her head rigid, and every detail was carefully mapped. Then Kiru was gone, and all that remained was a matrix which exactly matched her features. This was the image which would be scanned as every security camera checked every person – whether alien or human – on every pleasure island. The comscreens changed, each of them rapidly going through a sequence of heads and faces, all searching for the precise match.

'When did you last see her?' asked Jay.

'About an hour ago,' said Norton.

'Is that all?'

'It's an hour too long.'

'Young love,' sighed Jay, and he smiled as he shook his head.

Since Norton and Kiru had been married, this was the longest time they had spent apart. It had taken him half of that hour getting back to the resort by skimmer. For the first half, he'd kept going around the island in wider and wider circles, hoping he'd find her. But that was irrational, he realised, he was acting the way a civilian would have done. Norton was a cop. Once a cop, always a cop, and the best way to locate Kiru was by behaving like a cop.

His personal involvement with the case should not be allowed to cloud his judgement. He'd only been a rookie when his original police career was interrupted, and even then most of what Norton knew about detective work was what he'd seen on television. Detectives spoke to witnesses, found evidence, gathered clues, pieced together what had happened.

What was needed was an eyewitness, and the observation centre had eyes everywhere. If Kiru could be found, then Jay would find her. Just as Kiru had originally found Jay.

Norton continued to resist thinking of the present and future, which left only the past, and he remembered how he and Kiru had first entered this secret sanctum. They had been exploring, always amazed by how rapidly the complex was growing and changing, and were walking past another new, anonymous, and inevitably red, building. There were no doors, no windows, nothing to indicate its function.

'I wonder what it's for?' Norton had said.

'Let's go in and find out,' Kiru had said.

'How?' he had said

'Like this,' she had said, as she stepped towards the wall and melted into it.

That was Kiru's special skill. She could open doors.

First, she could find them; second, she could get through them. Even doors which didn't apparently exist.

She had stood half within the wall, half out, and she'd reached for Norton's hand, then pulled him through. They found themselves inside the optiscan centre.

'Blimey,' said the man in the command seat. 'How did you do that?'

That was how they had met Jay. He said he was from Earth, an old space bum who had ended up on Café World and found himself a job controlling the surveillance network which ensured that no one, either guest or employee, could cheat or rob or defraud the resort. The only ultimate winners at the gambling tables were the casino owners.

Jay never wore one of the various uniforms of the Café World workers. That was probably because none of the guests ever saw him – although he certainly saw them. He never seemed to leave the observatory, which was how he referred to his hidden domain. It was almost as if the room wasn't on Caphmiaultrel-vossmuaf, that it was in another dimension, perhaps because the colours within were not skewed towards one end of the spectrum.

'Trace Kiru,' said Jay.

'You already said that,' said Norton, snapping back into the present. 'What's wrong?' he added, although he could guess. 'You can't find her. She's not here, is she?'

'It doesn't,' said Jay, slowly, 'look like she is.' He scratched at his stubbled jaw. 'Where were you? On that island you go to?'

'Yeah. Kiru went swimming and . . .' Norton shook his head, not wanting to say any more.

'You go there for privacy, and unfortunately that's what you get. The atoll is below the horizon from here, which means it's not within line-of-sight observation.'

'What about satellite vision?'

'I'm checking,' said Jay, 'but there's no permanent watch beyond the tourist zone. No. No. No. Getting no current location for her. Last sighting was . . .'

Every screen in the room showed Norton and Kiru on board their skimmer, heading away from the holiday islands.

Jay said, 'And your last sighting was . . .'

The hundreds of images changed. Kiru was gone, the skimmer was gone. The picture showed Norton standing in front of a blank wall, then stepping through the wall, dissolving into it.

'Nothing can have happened to her on Café World,' said Jay.

'Something has happened to her! She's not here.'

'If something had happened, we'd know. She went swimming, and there are still enough Caphafers in their territorial waters to report if she'd got into difficulties.'

'Still enough?' said Norton. 'What do you mean?'

'A lot of them prefer to spend their time on land.'

'Working on the resort islands?'

'They've got their own resorts now, old chap. Whatever Café World offers for tourists, it provides the equivalent for Caphafers.'

'I don't see many of them here off-duty.'

'They aren't rich enough for the central islands. They have their own places to go, places where they can gamble too much, drink too much, get into fights, enjoy all the benefits of civilisation.'

'Never mind that. What about Kiru?'

'If there was an accident, if she was hurt, or worse, we'd know about it.'

'What if it wasn't an accident?'

'Who would want to hurt her?' asked Jay.

'She's disappeared, we know that. If she didn't go voluntarily, then someone has taken her.' Norton gestured towards the screens, all of which had returned to routine scanning. 'What areas of the pleasure zone are not monitored?'

For the tourists, there was no such thing as privacy. Every one of them could be watched all the time, wherever they were, whatever they were doing, and whoever they were doing it with.

'Here,' said Jay, as he gestured around the domed room.

'Apart from here,' said Norton. 'Because Kiru isn't here.'

'The management office.'

'Never heard of it.'

'You're not supposed to.'

'Where is it?'

'No one knows.'

'But you do.'

Jay nodded.

'Could Kiru be there?' asked Norton.

'How could she have got there?' Jay nodded towards the rows and rows of comscreens. 'Her last sighting was with you on the skimmer.'

'Whoever set up this surveillance system can control it, you know that. You think you're not being watched, but you probably are.'

'No. They think I'm being watched, and it seems as if I'm being watched, but I've taken myself out of the circuit.'

Norton gazed at the comscreens, at all the people, all the aliens. 'Have there been any Algolans on Café World recently?'

'No.'

'How can you be so sure?'

'Because I know. There have never been any Algolans here. Or not since opening day.' Jay paused and looked at Norton. 'From what I've heard, that would have been worth having on archive.'

'Can you check?'

'There's no need. Café World isn't their kind of holiday destination. Algolans don't have holidays.'

'How do you know? Have you been there?'

'Me?' Jay laughed. 'No.' He laughed again.

He was lying, Norton realised.

'No outsider has ever been to Algol,' Jay added. 'Or if they have, they've never come back. Why are you asking about Algolans? You think they have something to do with Kiru being missing? Okay, let's check. Total time trace Algolan.'

Every comscreen blanked for a second, two seconds, three, four. Then they all blinked back to life, all resuming their previous security imaging.

'See?' said Jay. 'No sign of the blighters, and there never has been.'

'If your cameras only cover the central zone,' said Norton, 'that means they could have landed somewhere else on Caphmiaultrelvossmuaf?'

'It's not that easy to find somewhere to land, not on this planet.'

'But a lander could have come down without being observed?'

'That's not my department, but I doubt it. Everything that lands is authorised. Anything unauthorised would be noticed and challenged. Are you sure you don't want a drink?'

'Yeah. No. I don't know.'

'What do you know?' asked Jay, as he unscrewed the cap from a small bottle.

'I know that Kiru is gone, and I know that a Caphafer told me she'd left the planet.'

'A Caphafer told you?'

'Yeah.'

'Are you sure,' said Jay, as he took a drink, 'it wasn't a red herring?'

Norton looked at him. 'Is that meant to be a joke?'

'A very good one, I thought.'

'I'm going,' said Norton, and he turned around, looking for the exit.

'No, don't,' said Jay. 'I was being a cad, I'm sorry. But I want to find Kiru almost as much as you do.'

Norton turned back, folding his arms and waiting.

'If Kiru has left the planet, that's why you asked about Algolans, because you think they might be involved?'

'Yeah.'

'Why would the Algolans want Kiru?'

'It's not them, it's someone who's with them.'

'Who?'

'Grawl.'

Jay choked on his drink, coughed, spluttered, wiped at his mouth, then coughed and coughed again.

'You know him?' asked Norton.

'No,' said Jay. 'Why should I?'

'He's from Earth.'

'It's a big galaxy, you know.'

'He's small but very broad, all muscle. Doesn't say a

word, ever, because he can't speak. His actions speak
for him. He's tough, ruthless, dangerous.'

'What was his name?'

'Grawl.'

'Never heard of him.' Jay shook his head.

He was lying again.

4

'Hello? Anyone in?' said Wayne Norton.

If Kiru had been with him, she could have opened
the door; but if she'd been with him, he wouldn't have
needed to open the door. He assumed there was a door,
just as he assumed there was a building. Since his original time, the whole concept of buildings and rooms,
walls and floors, windows and doors, had completely
changed.

A building used to be a solid construction, which
stayed in the same place. It was divided into rooms by
walls, which were also solid and also tended to stay in
the same place. In this era, none of that was necessarily
true. Walls could be transparent, as if made out of
glass, and so could roofs and floors. But he had never
come across a building in which everything was transparent, including the contents. He still hadn't, because
he'd been unable to find the management office. It was
totally invisible.

He only had Jay's word that the place existed, but he
had refused to leave his observatory and take Norton to
the exact location. Instead, Jay had shown its position
on every comscreen in the centre. And every screen
had been empty.

'There's nothing there,' Norton had said.

'That's because it's secret,' Jay had said. 'There's nothing that can be seen. That's where it is. Just follow your nose.'

Norton kept his hands held out in front of him, as if feeling his way in the dark, because he didn't want his nose to find the place first.

This might not have been its true location, Jay could have been lying again – although it was only because of him that Norton knew the office even existed. But Jay could have been lying about that, too.

'Hello?' said Norton. 'Anyone there? Hello?'

The tourist zone of Caphmiaultrelvossmuaf had originally been established on a group of islands, none of them more than half a mile wide, all within a radius of about ten miles. The seabed had been raised until, by now, the islands were only separated by narrow canals. All of the initial construction work had been done in less than a year, Terran time. Norton had watched many of the buildings grow, but they were not constructed brick by brick, put together by hand and by machine. They had grown themselves, almost as if they were organic.

The complex was still expanding, the shoreline reaching further out into the red ocean, the buildings rising higher into the red sky. The only time construction work had ever halted was during the opening ceremony.

Where Norton stood was at the centre of the central isles, the busiest area on the entire planet, the last place to hide anything. Which must have been why head office was hidden here. If it was hidden here.

The area was bounded by water on three sides, caught within the loop of a meandering canal. There was an elaborate bridge behind him, which seemed made out of spun copper. Ahead of him the canal was carried across an aqueduct built with crystal prisms, and this curved back and around until it was higher than the filigreed bridge. The course of the canal seemed like an optical illusion.

Water always found its own level, or so Wayne Norton had learned at school, and it didn't flow uphill. But that had been a very long time ago, and evidently it was no longer true. Or at least on Café World.

Tourist gondolas sailed leisurely along the canals and up waterfalls, ferrying holiday guests between the different islands and to all the amusements and entertainments available to them. From funfairs to enviroscapes, casinos to sensynthsations, skytels to pleasure malls, Café World had everything for the tourist to spend their money on.

'Hello, anyone?'

Norton felt an idiot wandering around and speaking aloud like this, but no one was taking any notice of him. They were on vacation, all high on some kind of physical or mental stimulant.

He had walked from the bridge to the aqueduct, and now he turned to go back. As he did so, he counted the number of paces. Eighty-seven. He returned again. Sixty-five paces. It was further in one direction than the other. Considering the surrounding topography, he wasn't too surprised.

As he halted and turned his head, he heard a sound close to his right ear. It was as if a wasp had flown by. But there were no wasps on Caphmiaultrelvossmuaf; no insects were permitted within the vacation zone. Tourists didn't come on holiday to be bitten or stung by alien bugs.

Norton began to look around, and he heard another wasp buzz past, this time near his left ear. He waved his hand across the side of his face, trying to keep the insect away from him. But it was already gone. It wasn't a wasp, he realised; it wasn't any kind of insect.

He was being shot at!

Out in the open, with nowhere to hide, all he could do was throw himself to the ground. But if he kept still, that meant he was an easy target. He rolled away, over and over and over, then realised he might have been rolling towards his unseen assailant. Norton stopped, and he raised his head slightly as he glanced around him. Close by was the canal with the tourist boats cruising past. Above and beyond the waterway, looming high over everything, were dozens and dozens of red edifices of every shape and design: pyramids and turrets, pagodas and columns, pillars and towers, poles and spires, polyhedrons and ziggurats, pylons and slabs and structures which didn't have a name because they were geometrically impossible.

Any one of them could have been the book depository in which lurked the lone gunman.

Stranded in the most open, most empty, most exposed place in the entire central isles, Wayne Norton didn't stand a chance.

He wished he had a gun. It wouldn't have done him much good, he knew, because he had no idea where his assassin was. But he wouldn't have felt so helpless, so vulnerable. Even if he was.

There were no weapons on Caphmiaultrelvossmuaf; they weren't conducive to a holiday atmosphere.

The ground near to Norton's right hand suddenly vaporised, and a crater an eighth of an inch wide appeared in the dirt.

No one, it seemed, had told the sniper that guns were not permitted.

A moment later, another crater erupted next to Norton's left hand. He watched as red dust drifted down onto his fingers. An eighth of an inch. That wasn't much of a hole, not if it was in his hand. In his head, however, size wouldn't matter.

He sprang to his feet, zig-zagged towards the edge of the canal, leapt up over the ornamental parapet to dive into the water –

– and landed in a heap. On dry ground.

'Do you have an appointment?'

Norton stood up and also looked up. He seemed to be at the bottom of a deep, round shaft. It was so bright that he had to cover his eyes with his hands. The voice had come from above, but he could see nothing because of the intense white glare.

'I'm looking for my wife,' he said. 'Her name is Kiru. Is she here?'

'Did she have an appointment?' asked the voice.

'No, I don't think so.'

'Then why would she be here?'

'Because she's nowhere else on Caphmiaultrel-vossmuaf.'

'How do you know?'

'Because Jay told me,' said Norton. He tried looking down, but the floor was as dazzling as the rest of the place.

'How does he know?'

'Because he operates the surveillance centre.'

'And you want to find someone, do you?'

'I already said that. My wife, Kiru, is missing. I think she's been abducted. You've got to help me.'

'Why should we do that?'

'Because you owe me.'

'Do we? Are you talking about the winnings in a

game of chance? How much do you mistakenly believe
we owe you?'

'You owe me everything.'

'Everything? Isn't that rather a lot?'

'I've done a lot for Café World.'

'Such as?'

'For one thing, I thought of the name.'

'Did you? What is your name?'

'I'm Wayne Norton,' said Wayne Norton.

'Are you?' asked the voice, and all the lights went
out.

A second or two later, the light returned, but it was
no longer as harsh. Norton blinked, gazing around.
Although he'd felt no movement, he was no longer in
the same place. He hadn't moved, he realised, instead
the deep shaft had been transformed into a small room.
It looked familiar, the kind of room he hadn't seen for
years and years. There was a desk with a typewriter
and telephone and lamp, a row of filing cabinets
behind it, charts pinned to the walls, a carpet on the
floor. Because there was a closed venetian blind over
the window, most of the light came from a fluorescent
tube on the ceiling. There were two wooden doors,
both shut, one of which must have been the exit while
the other led further inside.

It was a typical reception office from the time of
Norton's first life, three hundred years ago. What
wasn't typical was the receptionist behind the desk.
An alien.

The alien spoke, and an instant later the slate began
the translation. 'It's an honour to meet you, Wayne
Norton,' he said. 'My name is Dulsedech. How may I
help you?'

He was the most common shape for an alien, with

two arms, two legs and one head. The galactic standard seemed to be: matching anatomical features on either side of the body, and one of everything down the centre. Slender and small, dressed entirely in black, this was the first time Norton had seen one of these aliens since the official opening of Café World. They were probably the most secretive race in the galaxy. If, that was, they came from this galaxy. But whether they did or not, by now most of it was under their thumb. Or their many thumbs.

Each of Dulsedech's hands had five fingers and two thumbs, covered in black gloves. His eyes were masked by huge goggles, the dark lenses of which showed no glimmer of reflection, absorbing every trace of light. The only flesh visible was that of his face, which was so pale and colourless it seemed virtually lifeless. The skin was translucent and Norton could almost see the veins and the blood within. If the alien had veins and blood, of course. Norton couldn't imagine Dulsedech's race as being red-blooded, or even hot-blooded.

They already owned Hideaway, the galaxy's most famous pleasure satellite; and now it seemed, as Norton had already suspected, Café World also belonged to them. The Caphafers probably had to pay rent for living on what had recently been their own planet.

That was what Dulsedech and the rest of his species did. They collected money. Because they were the Galactic Tax Authority.

'Please take a seat,' said Dulsedech.

There was a chair nearby, all plastic and chrome. Norton stared at it, then looked at the alien, sitting incongruously behind the polished desk.

'Where did you find all this stuff?' he said, gesturing around the room.

'It's designed to put you at your ease. I hope you find these surroundings familiar and reassuring.'

Norton still hadn't moved, not since being at the bottom of the shaft, not since the shaft had changed into a twentieth-century Terran office. This certainly wasn't the usual locale of a galactic tax official. He realised exactly where they had found all the furniture and fittings: from his memory . . .

He felt both sick and dizzy, and he sat down in the chair which had been copied out of his brain.

'I apologise,' said Dulsedech, 'for your initial placement in our primary interview room.'

'Interview room?' said Norton. It had been more like a floodlit hole in the ground.

'It's the ideal location for interviewees to give the correct answers to carefully selected questions.'

'How did I get there?' asked Norton, thinking back, then remembering. 'I was shot at! Someone was shooting at me!' He started examining himself for holes.

'That's not a very nice thing to do. Are you sure? You appear to be unscathed.'

'Only because I escaped. I ran and . . .' Norton gazed around the room. 'What's going on?' He looked at Dulsedech.

'You're making inquiries about your missing wife.'

'How do you know that?'

'Because you told me.'

'Yeah, but you already knew. You can read my mind. You can read everyone's mind.'

'I wish we could. It would make our work a lot simpler. What makes you believe I can read your mind?'

'This,' said Norton, and he gestured around the fac-
simile of a reception office.

'You are mistaken,' said Dulsedech. 'Although this
area has been created to put you at your ease, its
imagery comes from our observation records. We cor-
related your personal file with the details of your
native planet to produce a simulated location with
which you are familiar.'

'But there's nothing like this on Earth, not now. It's
all ancient, completely out of date, it's from the time
when . . .'

Norton paused, looking at the alien. He couldn't see
the eyes, but he presumed Dulsedech was looking at
him.

The room was a reproduction of a twentieth-
century office, which meant the aliens had been
watching Earth three hundred years ago. Were they
the ones in the flying saucers, the little green men . . . ?

The telephone rang.

Norton looked at the phone, the alien looked at the
telephone, at the typewriter, then at the lamp. He
picked up the lamp, and the ringing stopped as he held
the bulb to the side of his head. A few seconds later, he
replaced the lamp.

'Excuse me,' said Dulsedech, and he stood up. He
was hardly any taller than when sitting down.
Although he was little, he wasn't green. He went
through the door to the side of the desk.

As the door closed, Norton rose to his feet, slipped
his hand through the shutters of the venetian blind and
peered through the gap. There was nothing to see. The
blind didn't cover a window, it covered a stretch of blank
wall. Norton looked at the second door, wondering if it
really was one. Then the first door opened again and

Dulsedech returned. He sat down behind the desk, and Norton returned to his chair in front of the desk.

'You're Wayne Norton?'

'Yeah.'

'Your wife is missing, I believe?'

'Yeah. I've told you.'

'No, you haven't told me. You told my colleague.'

Norton glanced at the door. One alien had gone out, another had come back? He had no way of telling whether it was true or not. The ones he'd seen previously had all looked alike, and not because his human perceptions couldn't tell the difference. The seven aliens he saw the day of the official opening had been identical. As well as identical to the one which had left the room. And to this one.

'You're not Dulsedech?' said Norton.

'Yes, I am. For security reasons, we are all named Dulsedech.'

'Isn't that confusing?'

'No, why should it be?'

'Because . . .' Norton paused. He was getting sidetracked, and going this route could only lead to a dead end. Norton pointed to the door and said, 'He—'

'She,' said Dulsedech #2. 'We are all female.'

Little, but not green – and not men.

Dulsedech #1 must have been replaced because she'd revealed that her race had been watching Earth for centuries, waiting for the opportunity to make a takeover bid.

'Let me say how sorry I am about your wife leaving you,' the second alien continued. 'It must be quite distressing.'

'She didn't leave me! She was taken from me.'

'Oh, dear. What a shame. You must be quite upset.'

'Quite upset?' said Norton. 'I'm more than dog-gonned quite upset!'

'Naturally you are, how unsympathetic of me. Without your wife, you lose the reduced taxation allowance we granted you as a wedding gift.'

'Tax? Tax! This isn't about tax.' Norton glared at Dulsedech, which was difficult without seeing her eyes. 'I don't pay tax. You don't give me any income. All I've done for you, for Café World, and I haven't seen a single red cent!'

'All you've done, Wayne Norton? What would that be?'

'This!' Norton's gesture encompassed more than the room, it took in the entire planet. 'Café World. It was my idea.'

'That's a matter of debate, but there's no copyright in ideas. Do you have legal title to the name "Café World"?'

'No.'

'Did you register any prototypes?'

'No.'

'Or trademark any logo designs?'

'No.'

'What did you do?'

'I saved seven of you from being killed.'

'Yes, but that was after you were granted your reduced taxation status. You must have been aware that the agreement would become invalid if the life functions of all our delegates had prematurely ceased.'

'What?' said Norton. 'You think I only stopped the killings to get into a lower tax bracket?'

'It must have been a factor in your decision,' said Dulsedech. 'We were grateful for your assistance and—'

'Assistance?'

'As I was saying, we were grateful for your assistance, and because of that you and Kiru have been our
honoured guests on Café World. We've covered all
of your expenses ever since, which are naturally considered as taxable benefits.'

'Stop,' said Norton, and he held up his right hand
the way he'd been trained as a traffic cop back in Las
Vegas. 'No more about tax, okay? All I want to know
is: do you know what happened to Kiru?'

'No.'

'Will you help me find her?'

'Naturally, we'll help you,' said Dulsedech. 'If it's
cost-effective.'

'Is that all that counts to you? Money?'

'Counts, yes, exactly. Price is the only objective
standard of comparative value.'

Kiru was priceless, but Norton knew it would be a
waste of breath to say so. Breath, air, oxygen, they were
also beyond price – but on many worlds they had to be
paid for.

Dulsedech said, 'You've only known Kiru for a
short while, is that correct?'

'Yeah.' Norton wondered what was coming. 'Why?'

'And it's quite rare for you humans to complete a
marriage contract to its full term, is that correct?'

'What are you saying?'

'Can't you find another wife? There must be several
suitable candidates on Café World.'

'No! Kiru's been missing for a couple of hours, and
you already want me to find someone else?'

'I apologise for my insensitivity,' said Dulsedech.

'Good.'

'Later, when you've forgotten about Kiru, you can
find someone else to fill the vacancy.'

Norton jumped to his feet. 'I'm going. Let me out of here.' He'd rather be shot at than spend another minute with Dulsedech, any of them.

'Tell me all you know about Kiru's disappearance,' said the alien. 'We'll do whatever we can to assist.' There was a pause. 'Whatever the cost.' There was another pause. 'Within responsible financial constraints, naturally.'

'Naturally,' said Norton, and he sat down again.

5

'Because this is an extraordinary general meeting of the board of directors, we'll dispense with the usual protocol of reading the minutes of the previous meeting and go straight to the business in hand.'

An 'extraordinary' meeting Dulsedech had said, and Wayne Norton was inclined to agree.

'You will have noticed,' the alien continued, 'that our quorum has a supernumerary, Wayne Norton, of whom I am sure you have all heard, and I should like to thank him on behalf of the company for attending this board meeting. Before we proceed any further, I take this opportunity to remind you of our special guest's actions immediately prior to the company's successful aquisition of Café World, when he prevented the termination of the life functions of seven management executives, all of them expert personnel whose skills and training represented a significant amount of corporate investment. I propose a vote of thanks.'

'Seconded,' said a second alien, a second Dulsedech.

'All in favour?' said the first. 'A show of hands, please.'

Seven alien arms were raised, seven alien hands, forty-nine alien digits.

'Carried unanimously,' said Dulsedech, the one at the far end of the table.

Norton was sitting directly opposite her. The table was rectangular, and there were three more representatives of the Galactic Tax Authority sitting on either side. He wondered if they could have been the same seven who had been at the official opening. Or perhaps seven was their lucky number. It had been that day; they were lucky Norton had saved their lives. Or their life functions, as they termed it.

Humans had four fingers and a thumb on each hand, making a total of ten digits – except in Norton's case, although he'd had the correct number until relatively recently – and ten was the basis for human arithmetic. Because Dulsedech's race had an additional finger and thumb, it was often said this was to make it easier to count the vast amounts of money with which they dealt. Perhaps the number seven, or maybe fourteen, formed the basis for their system of mathematics. That was why there were seven of them here now, sitting around the table with Norton.

'Well . . . yeah . . . thanks . . . er . . . for your thanks,' he muttered.

'I suppose you're all wondering why I've called you here today,' said the chairman – or chairalien.

Norton presumed this was the one he'd spoken with half an hour earlier, the second one. The second one with the same name. From what he'd been told, all seven had the same name. At least that was something, because he didn't know the name of their race. That was another secret, like the location of their home planet.

The boardroom was a bigger version of the reception room he'd been in previously. There were more blinds on the walls, presumably without windows behind them, there were more fluorescent light strips and there were more doors. The receptionist's desk had been replaced by the large wooden table around which Norton and the seven aliens all sat.

He was sure none of this could have been their normal procedure, and that they were going through the whole charade simply to reassure him. In which case Norton felt very unassured. He'd never been in a room like this, although it did seem familiar, as did the formalities; but that was only from having seen so many television dramas where actors played businessmen gathered around a similar table.

Suddenly, he realised this was exactly where the aliens must have picked it all up from. They had been watching TV back in the twentieth century, surveying the human race, waiting for mankind to venture into space, to the Moon and the planets, then out amongst the stars. Waiting to tax them.

'Wayne Norton's wife, Kiru,' Dulsedech continued, 'of whom you may also have heard, disappeared a few hours ago. From all the information available to us, it seems she is no longer on Café World. Wayne Norton has reason to believe that the Algolans may be involved in her abduction. Yes, Algolans, I knew that would give you cause for concern.'

Although it was difficult to tell, the other six didn't appear concerned. In fact, none of them moved a muscle. They all remained motionless and silent.

'At approximately the same time that Kiru vanished,' continued Dulsedech, 'an unauthorised vessel entered the atmosphere. Simultaneously, data from the relevant observation satellite was nullified and we have been unable to make a positive identification of the ship.'

'That proves Kiru was kidnapped,' said Norton. 'A ship came down and took her away. It was the Algolans. It must have been.'

'There's no official documentation to confirm Algolan involvement in your wife's disappearance.'

'Official documentation! You want it in writing, you mean, everything indexed and filed in triplicate?'

'That would be most helpful,' said Dulsedech. 'At present, however, the Algolans are beyond our remit. That also means they are almost certainly responsible for violating the landing regulations of Café World.'

'Then you agree?' said Norton. 'It was the Algolans who came for Kiru?'

'It seems unlikely that an Algolan ship would have travelled to Café World for the sole purpose of taking your wife.'

'But she's gone. And there was a ship, you know there was. You said it was probably an Algolan ship.'

'Quite,' said Dulsedech. 'But the operating costs of even the smallest interstellar craft are very substantial, and although your wife may be of value to you, it seems unlikely that the Algolans would consider it economic to send a craft from their home world for the sole purpose of her abduction. The ship did not come here for your wife, although that appears to have been an incidental effect. The Algolans came to pro- voke us.'

'Why would they do that?' asked Norton.

'Because they are dangerous and aggressive and ruthless, and also treacherous and irrational and a menace to the entire galaxy.'

'Oh.'

'This is the latest in a long series of incidents. The Algolans want war, and they have been looking for an excuse to attack.'

'To attack Caphmiaultrelvossmuaf? What for?'

'Because it's there. And not just Caphmiaultrel-vossmuaf. They want to attack every planet which is part of the galactic tax alliance. Although we're doing everything possible to prevent hostilities, all our over-tures have been rejected. We are a peaceful people. We don't want war. It's not our way. Unlike the Algolans, we know nothing of weapons and violence. Death and destruction, invasion and annihilation, is that any way for a civilised species to behave?'

'Probably not,' said Norton. Dulsedech kept looking at him. 'Definitely not,' said Norton.

'The lights are going out all over the universe. The Algolan Empire casts a long dark shadow across every solar system. They won't talk, they won't negotiate, they refuse to make trade agreements. It's as if there's a barrier between Algol and the free galaxy.'

'Like a curtain, you mean?'

'A curtain?'

'An iron curtain?' suggested Norton.

'How could a curtain be made of iron?'

'Er . . .'

'And how could there be a curtain across the galaxy? What would it hang from?'

'It wouldn't hang from anything,' said Norton, 'because there's no gravity out in space. But it's just a figure of speech. You were talking about light and dark, and you said "barrier" so I said "curtain". Because a curtain keeps out the light.'

'A curtain keeps out the darkness.'

'Okay, okay. Not a curtain, a venetian blind. That keeps out the light. But there's no giant venetian blind dividing the universe in half, not really.'

'What's a venetian blind?' asked Dulsedech.

'That is.' Norton pointed at one of the shades covering a non-existent window. 'Do you know how to make a venetian blind?'

'Is this relevant?'

'No,' said Norton. None of it seemed relevant. 'I have to find Kiru. You said you'd help me. Will you? I have to go to Algol.'

'And we want you to go to Algol. We can help each other.'

'How?'

'You will be our ambassador to Algol. What do you say to that?'

Norton said nothing. He didn't know what to say. Not yet.

'It is an immense honour and privilege for you to be given this role, Wayne Norton,' said Dulsedech. 'There is absolutely no precedent for an alien such as yourself being awarded the status of a senior diplomatic representative, but we have already decided that under the circumstances you will be granted the exalted position of ambassador to the imperial court of the Empress of Algol.'

'The Empress of Algol?' said Norton: 'You mean Janesmith?'

'Her majestic highness, Janesmith of Algol, that is correct.' Dulsedech paused a few seconds. 'Ah, yes! You know the Empress, I remember now. What a coincidence!'

'It sure is,' agreed Norton.

'Knowing Empress Janesmith is the best possible

reference for the job. She also believes you are an aristocrat, is that correct?'

'I'm not an aristocrat, I'm an American!'

'The Empress, however, believes you are of noble birth, is that correct?'

'Yeah, but that was a mix-up over names. She thought I was a duke.'

The most difficult words to translate from one language to another were names. 'Janesmith' didn't sound very alien, but according to the slate that was the name of the Empress of Algol. Norton had known her when she was just a princess.

'That's an example of how ignorant and backward the planet is,' said Dulsedech. 'It's a dictatorship ruled by a feudal monarchy. Politically, Algol is still at a primitive stage of evolution. No wonder they are so savage and barbaric.'

'Savage and barbaric?' echoed Norton. 'Is working as ambassador to Algol very . . . er . . . safe?'

'There's no guarantee of long-term job security. But that's the universe we live in. Even Café World isn't completely safe. Someone was shooting at you, you said. At least on Algol you'll have diplomatic immunity.'

'And that will prevent them arresting me, torturing me, murdering me?'

'We hope so. Although if they do kill you, be assured it will prompt a stern diplomatic rebuke from us.'

Whatever the risks, he had to go to Algol. And being a diplomat might help him find Kiru.

'The Algolans are easily impressed by titles,' said Dulsedech, 'so you should continue your masquerade of being a duke. Your personal contact with the

Empress will prove very advantageous in your diplomatic capacity.'

'Yeah, maybe, but . . .' Norton shrugged. 'How can I be your ambassador? I don't know anything about it.'

'You'll be given expert advice on how to be a diplomat and influence people,' said the alien. 'The whole art of diplomacy is communication and dialogue.'

'Talking, you mean?'

'Quite. What to say and what not to say. All we need is for you to talk with Empress Janesmith. Once we can enter into discussions with the Algolans, it reduces the possibility of war and increases the possibility of trade. It's very simple.'

'If it's that simple, why can't you talk to them?'

'They refuse all contact with outsiders. You, however, have already been introduced to the Empress and can act on our behalf. If we cannot negotiate with the Algolans, then sooner or later there will be war. You're our main hope of preventing such an apocalypse.'

'Me?' said Norton, and he smiled. 'It's up to me to save the universe from a galactic war?'

'Yes,' said Dulsedech.

Norton began to laugh.

'You find it amusing, do you? Countless billions of people killed, whole planets destroyed, entire species annihilated?'

Norton stopped laughing.

'Why are you here?' said Dulsedech. 'Think back over your life, Wayne Norton, your long life. Remember all you've done, all the events which have led you to be in this exact place at this precise time. You've come so far, in both time and in space. There's no one in the galaxy who has experienced what you have. You are unique. Have you ever wondered why you exist, what is your purpose in life? Most people never know their reason for being, perhaps because most people have none. But you do, Wayne Norton. This is your destiny. To bring peace and harmony to the universe.'

'Gosh,' muttered Norton. He'd thought it would be tough enough to save Kiru. Now he also had to save the universe. 'Do I get a uniform?'

'What?'

'Do I get an ambassador's uniform?'

Dulsedech looked at another Dulsedech. All seven of them looked at each other, exchanging silent glances.

'Can't you go as you are?' said the one at the head of the table, the one who had done all the talking.

'Like this?' said Norton, glancing down at himself. He was wearing a faded teeshirt, frayed shorts and a pair of battered sandals. 'What about something, er, befitting the dignity of the office?'

His outfit was what he usually wore; it was too warm on Caphmiaultrelvossmuaf to wear anything more. All his life, Norton had never been fully at ease in casual clothes. He preferred to be smartly dressed, but he refused to wear any of the uniforms available on Café World. They were what the resort's employees wore and he didn't want tourists asking him directions all the time.

'We can't justify any unnecessary expense,' said Dulsedech. 'Our budget doesn't include a tailoring allowance.'

'You want me to save the universe dressed like a beach bum?'

'It's what you say that's important, not how you look.'

'That sounds fine in theory, but it's not true. First

impressions are very important.'

'The Algolans won't care what you wear or how you look. Do you notice what other races wear?'

'Yeah, I do,' said Norton. He looked at each of the seven in turn. 'I admire the way you take care of your appearance, it shows your professionalism.'

'You have one hour, Wayne Norton, in which to acquire something to wear in your role as ambassador to Algol.'

'An hour? Is that all?'

'We believe there is a certain degree of urgency about the situation. You seem to think differently. Your wife has been abducted and you want to go on a consumer quest?'

'Only as a distraction.'

'You may have one hour of retail distraction. Your ship leaves for Algol in three hours, two of which are needed for your basic training in interplanetary diplomacy.'

'Two hours?' said Norton. 'Is that long enough?'

Instead he opted for the advanced course, which took every minute of the available three hours. Then Wayne Norton left Caphmiaultrelvossmuaf and boarded the orbiting ship which would carry him to the very heart of the evil empire: the court of Janesmith, Empress of Algol.

He was still dressed in his teeshirt, shorts and sandals.

CHAPTER
TWO

1

Swimming deep below the surface, watching all the shoals of exotic red fish darting between the weeds and rocks, it was like being in another world. Probably, thought Kiru, because this was another world. Or at least it wasn't Earth, wasn't her home world. But home was where the heart was, and her heart was here, here with Wayne. This was home.

Caphmiaultrelvossmuaf was her third planet, but Kiru had never been happier. Earth was nothing but bad memories, years of a desperate struggle to survive. Arazon, the prison planet, had been a holiday resort in comparison with Earth. Now she'd ended up on Café World, the ultimate vacation planet. Married to Wayne and enjoying an endless honeymoon, Kiru had thought life couldn't get any better. But she'd been wrong.

She knew that Wayne was restless, wanted to be going somewhere, doing something. They had the rest of their lives to do that. For now, she was more than content to remain on Caphmiaultrelvossmuaf. And soon Wayne would feel exactly the same.

As always, Kiru felt she could have spent forever in

the warm ocean. Water was the source of life, and it was where her distant ancestors had evolved – although on a far distant planet. When she was swimming, time had no meaning, she was at one with the water, the planet, the galaxy. This was her place in the greater scheme of things. She was a part of the universe and the universe was a part of her.

Floating on her back in the alien sea, gazing up at the alien sky, Kiru came to a decision. Her life here with Wayne had been perfect, and now was the time to tell him the impossible: it was going to get even better.

The small island was behind her, and she kicked her legs languidly, slowly gliding back to the beach. When she reached the shallows, she stood up, wiped the water from her face and swept her hair behind her neck. Then she turned around towards the atoll. She frowned.

Although she'd swum completely around it, this should have been the same part of the island where she'd entered the water. But Wayne wasn't on the beach. Perhaps he'd decided to go for a swim after all, and she glanced back out to sea.

Then she realised it wasn't only Wayne who was missing. There was no sign of the skimmer. Even if she'd come ashore at the wrong place, the island was so small, so flat, she could have seen the skimmer from any point. It wasn't there. Neither was Wayne.

He'd gone. Gone and left her on a deserted island.

But he couldn't have done. He wouldn't have left her alone, not without a word. There had been no reason for him to go. They hadn't been arguing. Even if they'had, Kiru was certain Wayne would never have abandoned her. Nor would he have gone off as a practical joke. Had there been some kind of emergency, a reason he suddenly had to return to the central isles? If there was, he'd have looked for her first. She wasn't difficult to find.

Something must have happened to him. He'd been taken, that was the only answer. Who would have done that? And what about the skimmer? It wasn't the quietest of craft, and she was certain she'd have heard it. They'd taken him and the skimmer.

Despite the heat, she shivered for a moment. She was still standing in the water, and she waded through the shallows and up onto dry land. That was when she saw a distant figure lying on the amber sand, and she smiled with relief. She ran up the beach.

'Wayne!' she called.

He was almost in the centre of the island, as far from the sea as he could get.

'Wayne!'

But it wasn't Wayne.

Kiru halted, gazing at the figure twenty metres away and wondering who it was. It took her several seconds to realise it was a Caphafer, one of the natives of the planet. She'd never seen one like this before, and she walked slowly towards him.

The alien was lying on his back, slowly clapping his webbed hands together, his red head swaying from side to side. His heavy jaw moved up and down, showing his sharp teeth. He must have been singing, but there was no noise. All was silent, because the Caphafer was at the epicentre of his SoundAround system.

This was the first time she'd noticed a Caphafer listening to music. Because they lived mostly underwater, they had never got around to making musical instruments – or even making music. This was also the first time she'd seen a Caphafer lying down on dry land. It was as if he was sunbathing, except he was dressed. And this was the first time she'd seen a Caphafer dressed this way.

Before outsiders had reached their planet, they never wore clothes, they had no reason to. Because they were always in the water, clothes would always be wet. When part of their world became a tourist resort, a number of the Caphafers were given jobs – and given uniforms to wear at work.

Kiru and Wayne had gone native. They never wore anything when they were alone together, and they didn't dress up to go swimming. The same was true for many of the alien races who came to Café World on vacation. They wore as little as possible on the beach or in the sea, and often that meant nothing.

But it seemed this native had gone tourist. He was wearing a loose green shirt which was decorated with pulsing blue lights, and a pair of tight yellow trousers. At least his feet were bare, but he'd have needed a huge pair of shoes to cover his massive webbed toes. The top half of his face was masked by a mirrored blue sunvisor. He continued soundlessly clapping his hands and singing, rolling his head as he did so.

'Hello?' said Kiru.

The Caphafer became immediately still. He levered himself up on his elbows, looked at Kiru, then nulled his SoundAround.

'Hello, mate,' said the alien. 'Isn't it a beautiful day?'

Kiru didn't need a slate to hear what he said. It was a standard greeting, and she knew enough Caphafese to understand.

'Yes,' she agreed, also in Caphafese. 'It's a beautiful day.'

But it wasn't. Without Wayne, it was the exact opposite. Neither should the Caphafer have thought it was a beautiful day. They preferred it to be raining, which it did over most of the world most of the time.

'Are you Kiru?' said the alien.

She also knew her name in the local language, although it bore little resemblance to her own pronunciation. Caphafese was soft and sibilant, not at all the kind of sound one would have expected from such an apparently fierce species. Kiru had tried to forget her Terran prejudices, but pre-judging was almost inevitable. The Caphafers were very relaxed and easy-going, and they didn't seem to care that their planet was being stolen away from them and transformed into the galaxy's top vacation resort.

'Do I know you?' asked Kiru, and to say this she needed her slate.

She looked closely at the Caphafer. There were a number of them she knew, but this one was hard to recognise with his clothes on.

'No, mate,' said the Caphafer.

'But you know me?' said Kiru.

The word 'day' on Café World was theoretical; but the day the vacation world was officially opened was very eventful, one of those events being that all the Caphafer workers went on strike.

When she first arrived on Caphmiaultrelvossmuaf, Kiru had met many of the natives while she was swimming, and she'd told them that working as unpaid labourers and cleaners wasn't the great honour they'd been led to believe. As a result of taking industrial inaction, the Caphafers won better conditions and were even paid for the first time.

'No, mate,' said the Caphafer, again.

'Oh,' said Kiru. She glimpsed her reflection in his sunvisor. Although she wasn't bothered at being naked, not in front of an alien, she began to feel uneasy. He was here, but Wayne wasn't. Did he have something to do with the disappearance? The visor made him look sinister, and she took a step backwards.

'I know your name because I was asked to give you a message,' said the Caphafer.

'Who from? Was it Wayne?'

'It was like you, a human creature, and it said it was your mate.'

'Yes, that's Wayne! And he's a "he", not an "it".'

'You said "it" first.'

'Alright, alright,' said Kiru. 'What was the message?'

'He said he had to go somewhere, and he wanted me to give you a message.'

'What message?'

'I told you: he had to go somewhere.'

'Where? Where did he have to go?'

'He didn't say, not exactly.'

'What did he say?' asked Kiru, becoming impatient. She took a step forward, then another. 'Exactly?'

The Caphafer said nothing. The sunvisor didn't make him appear sinister, not when she was staring down at him; his clothes and eyeshades looked ridiculous.

'Why are you wearing that visor?' said Kiru. 'And why—'

'Because,' said the alien, and he took off the mirrored lens, 'the light hurts my damaged eye.' His left eye was cloudy and lifeless.

'Ah,' said Kiru, and she decided not to ask about his clothes in case he had a skin complaint.

'He told me his mate was called Kiru,' said the Caphafer, as he replaced his sunvisor, 'and asked me to give her a message. He said he had to go somewhere. His exact words, if I remember, were . . .'

Kiru waited while the Caphafer remembered.

Slowly, the alien recited, '"I have to go somewhere and do something. Tell my mate I like her and I'll be back tomorrow."'

The wording definitely lost something in the translation. It was a double translation, in fact, through two simultaneous linguistic and tonal equalisers. From Wayne to the Caphafer, then back from the Caphafer to her. She was glad that Wayne liked her, but she presumed the original word was 'love'. She hoped it was. And as for him being back tomorrow, in Caphafese there was no word for 'day' – because on Caphmiaultrelvossmuaf there were no days. The natives were very vague about the whole concept of time. To them, the future was always a non-existent 'tomorrow'.

In other words, Wayne had gone somewhere, to do something, and he'd be back sometime. Or so the Caphafer said. It seemed a very unlikely story, but Kiru believed it.

She'd known Wayne was becoming bored because he had nothing to do. Recently, he'd kept going on and on about his missing finger. It had become an obsession, but she never imagined he would do something as extreme as this. How could he have gone away, leaving her stranded on an island on an alien planet?

Kiru glanced out to sea. Beyond the red horizon was the tourist zone. There were numerous small islands in between, and many areas where the ocean was shallow enough to wade through. Even so, the journey back would be a long one.

But not as long as Wayne's journey, across the universe and back to Earth.

2

'Thanks,' said Kiru to the Caphafer, as the skimmer slid to a halt on the beach. She jumped down and began walking.

Because of the ride, her journey had been much easier and shorter than she'd first feared. It wasn't chance that the skimmer had picked her up. The Caphafer had been sent out to find her, and she hoped it was Wayne who was responsible. When she'd heard the craft speeding across the waves, she thought he must have come to his senses and was returning for her. She was wrong. Once Wayne made up his mind, very little could dissuade him.

That was one of the things Kiru liked about him, his determination, the way he set out to do what he planned to. She also liked the way he could always be persuaded to do what she wanted, usually by her convincing him it was really his idea. Unfortunately, by now Wayne had worked out this tactic – which was why he hadn't told her of his plan to leave Caphmiaultrelvossmuaf.

As the skimmer approached the tourist isles, Kiru's first idea had been to make for the skytel to see if Wayne was still there. It was too late for that now, she realised. He had a few hours' start and there was no reason for him to be hanging around. But if she'd gone to their suite, Kiru could also have put on some

clothes. Clothing wasn't always essential on Café
World, although the more exclusive restaurants did
impose a dress code. In any case, she had other pri-
orities.

Her second idea was to head for the landing zone,
where she could try to find the ship Wayne was taking.
Café World was becoming busier and busier, and as
more tourists from more solar systems arrived, the
spaceport was expanding ever further over the ocean.
In the time since she and Wayne had left for the atoll,
the port area would have grown larger. Even if it
wasn't too late, locating one particular passenger would
be impossible.

Impossible for Kiru, but not for someone else.

That was why she'd chosen the third option, and
the skimmer had set her down on this side of the central island. It was a pity the amphibious craft weren't
more manoeuvrable, or it could have taken her directly
to her destination. There was no other transport,
because that was one method of discouraging the
tourists from this area. They were not forbidden,
because in theory they could go anywhere and do anything on Café World.

There were a number of people around, most of
them resort workers, Caphafers as well as off-worlders.
A few tourists could also be seen, those who liked the
safe adventure of exploring behind the scenes.

All the species which came for a Café World vacation had two basic similarities: they could breathe
the air, and they could tolerate the gravity. But the
planet was beginning to attract aliens whose respira-
tory systems were not designed for an oxygen/nitrogen
atmosphere or whose unprotected bodies would have
dramatically increased or decreased in mass. Despite

having to spend all their vacation within an envirosuit, they came because the resort had already gained an inter-galactic reputation.

Kiru reached her destination. Aware that she was expected, she could have gone straight in, but it was polite to knock on doors first. Wayne always insisted that politeness cost nothing, which was just as well because neither of them had any money. They had no money, and the building had no door. The red walls of the observation centre were completely blank.

'You know I'm here,' she said. 'Let me in.' She paused, then added, 'You want me to be polite and say "please"?'

'That'll be the day,' said a voice, every syllable of which seemed to come from a different direction. 'Or night. Sunset on Café World when you're polite. In you come.'

Kiru stepped into the wall, which melted and flowed around her. After two or three paces she was inside. She blinked, getting used to the different light. Outside, the building was low and rectangular; inside, it was high and domed. That was the way of the galaxy, Kiru had learned. Nothing could be trusted, not what she saw, not what she touched.

And not, it seemed, even Wayne.

'What's going on, Kiru?' asked Jay. 'Where's Wayne?'

'That's what I was going to ask,' said Kiru. If he didn't know, no one did. 'You mean you haven't checked?'

'Not in the last couple of hours.'

'You sent the skimmer for me?'

'Yes.'

'I thought so.' Kiru nodded.

'Can I take that as a "thank you"?'

'Up to you.'

Jay's face crinkled into a smile. He was staring up at the banks of screens which completely covered the inside of the room. She realised he hadn't looked directly at her yet. He sat in his command chair which hovered in the centre of the hemisphere. She'd never seen him anywhere else; it was as if he was never off-duty.

'You want a drink, my poppet?' he asked. 'You can probably use one.'

'Not probably,' she told him, 'definitely.'

This was the best bar on the whole planet, and it was the most exclusive. Jay had a selection of exotic liqueurs from across the galaxy, all of them genuine. Or so he said, having collected them all during his travels around the universe.

'On one condition,' said Jay.

'What's that?'

'Put something on.'

'Why?' Kiru glanced down at her naked body, then held out her hands questioningly. 'Is there something wrong with me?'

'No,' said Jay. 'Not at all, I can see that.' But he couldn't see, he'd closed his eyes. 'At my age, Kiru, I can't take it. I could have heart failure. You don't know the effect you have on an old codger like me.'

That wasn't true, because for a long time Kiru had known exactly the effect she had on old men, young men, most men. And being nude just meant the effect was even quicker.

'Here,' said Jay. Without looking, he threw her a coverall. He'd had it draped over his chair, waiting for her to arrive.

'But it's not cold in here,' said Kiru, pretending not to understand. Nowhere on Café World was cold.

'No, it's not,' agreed Jay, and he wiped his brow. 'Just get dressed.'

'Why? You must have seen me like this before.'

'What makes you think that?'

Kiru glanced around the command centre. Everywhere she looked, there were screens which monitored each part of the central islands, both outside and within all the tourist facilities. Because there were far more microcams than screens, the displays kept changing as a different series of images appeared. She was always amazed by how much detail each screen could show. Everyone within the leisure zone was under constant surveillance. Including her.

This was all done 'in the best interests of customer safety and security' – although the customers didn't know about it.

'It's my work,' said Jay.

'Do you like your work?'

'Some of it.' Jay shrugged. 'I'm only human.' He scratched at his stubbled jaw, then smiled guiltily – and guilt was a good way of persuading him to help her.

'Or so you say,' said Kiru. She also smiled, and she began pulling on the coverall.

'Not many of us here on Café World,' said Jay, as at last he spun his gravchair around to face her and brought it down to her level. 'And looking at aliens is no fun.'

'Naked aliens, you mean?'

'You think I'm some kind of pervert?' Jay held up a hand. 'No, don't answer that.'

He glanced at the armrest of his command chair,

studying the array of small bottles lined up there, selected one, produced a glass, decanted half the purple contents, passed it to Kiru. Usually, she asked what he was giving her, and Jay would narrate a history of the planet the drink came from, tell how he'd found himself on that world and that a very strange thing had happened to him while he was there; she'd also hear what the drink was made from, how it was produced and how long it had been aged for. That was the price of a glass.

There wasn't time for any of that. She swallowed half of it in a single gulp. It was sweet and syrupy, aromatic and very potent. Only the last really mattered. She shuddered for a moment as the fiery liquid burned her throat, then she felt the warmth flowing throughout her whole body.

'Down the hatch,' said Jay, as he swigged from the rest of the bottle. 'What's happened? You and Wayne had a kerfuffle?'

'A what?'

'A bit of an argy-bargy.'

Jay claimed to be from Earth, but some of his words and expressions seemed totally meaningless. When Wayne used an obscure phrase, at least he had the excuse of being born three centuries ago. Jay was also old, but not that old. With him, sometimes it was as if he was talking through a broken slate.

'Translate,' said Kiru.

'A row, an argument,' said Jay. 'It must be serious for him to leave you. What a rotter to do a thing like that. Now's your chance, Kiru. He's gone, but I'm still here. You were too good for him. Why not make an old man very happy?'

He always said this whenever Kiru was with him. It

was a running joke, because Wayne was usually there as well. But this wasn't something to joke about, not now that Wayne was really gone.

'Where is Wayne?' Kiru gestured around the room, taking in all of the comscreens. 'Did you see him leave the island we were on?'

'No,' said Jay. 'Unless any tourists go there, that area is beyond the permanent surveillance limit.'

Not many visitors strayed from the holiday zones of the central isles. Those who did needed protection, mostly from themselves. Café World may have been a pleasure paradise, but Caphmiaultrelvossmuaf was still an alien world and had not been totally tamed. A few casualties could be covered up; but if too many visitors went missing, it might be noticed. The planet couldn't afford the notoriety of being unsafe, the only risks guests should have to face were in the casinos. That was one reason why the main form of tourist transport was by gondola. It was slow and, if anyone did fall into a canal, the water was very shallow and would immediately drain away to prevent drowning.

'But you saw me,' said Kiru. 'That's why you sent the skimmer?'

'Yes. When you came within range, an abnormality was signalled. Only Caphafers should have been swimming way out there. When I checked, I realised it was you and dispatched a skimmer.'

'You couldn't have got to me any faster?'

'If it had been an emergency, if you were in any danger, yes.'

'Or if I'd been a tourist.'

'Of course. Can't let anything happen to the paying customers.' He took a swig from his bottle.

Kiru drained her glass, then said, 'Okay, where's Wayne?'

'After sending the skimmer for you, I ran a trace on him and discovered he'd already returned. He came back in the boat you'd both gone out on. Another drink?'

'No. Where is he now?'

'I haven't checked. But you shouldn't go chasing after him, petal. If he left you, wait for him to cool off. It's just a storm in a teacup, it'll all blow over. He'll crawl back to apologise.'

Kiru shook her head. 'I don't think so. Can you try finding him?'

'What are his other names?'

For a moment, Kiru wasn't sure what Jay meant. She thought he was asking about aliases.

'It's Norton,' she answered, 'Wayne Norton.'

'Trace,' said Jay, 'Wayne Norton.'

Wayne's picture flashed up on every comscreen in the room. It was a close-up of his face, looking forward. His head then turned until his right profile was on view, and a criss-cross of lines appeared on each screen, analysing his features. Then the multitude of faces blinked out, leaving only a scanned pattern of his image. This was what all the cameras on Café World would now seek to match. Every screen flickered, countless different faces, faces from all over the galaxy, appearing in rapid succession.

When Kiru had first met Wayne, he was using another name. As long as she could remember, she'd only ever had one name, one word. One was plenty. For most of her life, she hadn't even needed that because nobody knew she existed.

She only knew Jay by his one name, which could

have been short for something; or maybe it wasn't 'Jay' but 'J.' which meant it was even shorter.

Names were easy to change, easy to add to. In his long life, during his travels across the galaxy, it was likely that Jay had used other names, other identities. (Or maybe he was neither 'Jay' nor 'J.' but 'J' and was working his way through the alphabet.) Names could be changed as easily as clothes — although judging by Jay's coverall, his outfit could be even older than his name. The fabric was virtually indestructible, but his coverall was worn and torn, faded and stained. Kiru watched him studying the screens, his face becoming more lined as he frowned.

'Did he tell you where he was going?' asked Jay.

'He didn't tell me anything,' Kiru answered. 'I went for a swim, when I came back he was gone. Can't you find him?'

'No.' Jay shook his head. 'He's nowhere, nowhere on the planet.'

Kiru clenched her fists. Although this was what she'd guessed, she had still hoped it wasn't true.

'But you don't watch the whole island,' she said. 'He could be where there are no cameras.'

'He came back to the central islands. There are only two places not under surveillance. This is one of them, and he's not here. The other . . . the other is the management office.'

Jay had frequently talked about the observation network he operated, but he'd never mentioned a management office before.

'Could he be there?' asked Kiru.

'I'll check his last sighting.'

'There he is!'

Wayne appeared on every screen within the dome,

all around and above. He was at the spaceport. Boarding a shuttle.

Kiru shivered, her whole body instantly frozen.

He'd gone. It was true. He'd abandoned her. She didn't want to believe it, she couldn't believe it, but she had to believe it.

'I'll be jiggered,' said Jay. 'The bounder's leaving. I don't understand. It doesn't make sense.'

Kiru put her hands over her face, trying to block out all the images of Wayne's desertion. Her eyelids felt wet. She must have got something in one of her eyes, in both of them, pieces of alien grit while swimming.

'How could he do it?' whispered Kiru. 'How could he go and leave us?'

'Us?' Jay sounded puzzled. 'You and me?'

'You and me?' Kiru repeated. 'No!' She shook her head, keeping her face covered. 'Me and . . . me and . . .' She dropped her right hand and rested it on her belly. Her belly that was no longer as flat as it had been.

'A baby! You're having a baby?'

Kiru wiped her eyes with her left hand, then she nodded.

'Crikey!' said Jay. 'Congrat . . .' His voice trailed away as he looked back up at all the screens. Wayne was no longer in sight. 'That's why he left? What a heel. What a . . . what an utter scoundrel!'

'No,' said Kiru, 'that's not it, that's not the reason he left. He doesn't know. I was about to tell him. As soon as I got back from swimming, I was going to tell him about the baby. But he wasn't there. He'd already gone.'

'I don't believe it,' said Jay, softly.

'It's true. Wayne didn't know. If he'd known he was

going to be a father, he'd never have gone back to Earth.'

'Earth?'

'That's where he's gone.'

'Are you sure?'

'The Caphafer wasn't very precise, but I'm sure.'

'What Caphafer?'

Kiru told Jay about her meeting with the native and the message Wayne had left for her. Jay ran his fingers through his hair, what there was left of it, in bewilderment.

'How long since Wayne boarded the shuttle?' asked Kiru.

'Ninety-two minutes. That's what it says here.'

'The shuttle would have taken him out to an interstellar ship. Was there a ship for Earth in orbit?'

'I'll run a datascan,' said Jay. 'Yes, apparently there was a ship bound for Terra. But that doesn't mean he boarded it.'

'What else does it mean? We saw him leaving. He must have gone somewhere.'

'Why's he gone back to Earth? Who in their right mind would go to that dump?'

'I wouldn't, you wouldn't, and Wayne wouldn't if he'd known about the baby.'

Why hadn't she told him before? At first, she'd wanted to be certain she was pregnant. Then, she'd wanted to wait until exactly the right moment. She wanted to surprise him, amaze him, delight him. Instead, he'd surprised and amazed her. But she certainly wasn't delighted.

'So it wasn't planned?' said Jay.

Kiru laughed briefly and shook her head. No, she hadn't planned for a baby. Nothing in her life had ever been planned, probably not even her own conception before it. She'd always been adrift, floating whichever way the tides of the universe had swept her, until finally she was cast ashore on Caphmiaultrelvossmuaf and reunited with Wayne. She should have guessed it wouldn't last.

'No one else knows about the baby,' she said. 'And I don't want anyone to know.'

'A baby isn't the kind of thing you can hide. How long before . . . ?' Jay gestured towards his own stomach, his hand outlining a much larger waistline.

'I know, but I want it kept quiet.'

'Yes, I understand that. You've got to decide what to do with it.'

'Do with it? What do you mean? You think I'm not going to have the baby, is that what you mean?' The idea had never crossed her mind. It was her baby, her child, hers and Wayne's. Did Jay think she might not want it?

'No, not at all.' Jay raised one hand in denial, then lifted his other hand to drink from the bottle it held. 'But you don't need to have the baby yourself, do you? Imagine the whole process, think about your body and what's going to happen to it, and finally when . . .' He closed his eyes, preferring not to think about it, and took another drink.

'The traditional way of incubation and birth is the best for the child,' said Kiru. 'This is my baby and I'm having her or him myself. And for now, Jay, no one else is to know anything. Promise?'

'I'll keep it under my hat. You have my word as a gentleman and a scholar.' Jay looked at Kiru and he nodded solemnly. 'But what I still don't understand is: why did Wayne leave?'

'Because of this.' Kiru raised her right index finger. 'That.' She touched the finger with her matching left one. 'His missing finger.'

'I didn't know he had a missing finger.'

'He does, and he's got this crazy idea that he can go back to Earth and find it.'

'No.' Jay shook his head. 'That sounds complete balderdash. Are you sure he didn't leave because he knew about the baby?'

'Wayne would not,' said Kiru, emphasising every word, 'do that.'

'You're certain?'

'I'm certain.'

'You're probably right. He's straight as a die, that young fellow m'lad of yours.'

'I need your help, Jay.'

'You've got it. Anything. Just name it.'

'I've got to go after him. Help me get back to Earth.'

Jay shook his head again. 'He's gone, Kiru. Maybe not because of the baby, but he went and left you for some reason or other. Are you sure you want to go after him?'

'I have to,' said Kiru. 'And he hasn't left me. In the message I got, he said he'd be back.'

'In that case, have you thought this through properly? No, daft question, because you haven't had time to think. Listen, Kiru, think about this, think very carefully: Wayne has gone, but he says he'll be back. If he'd wanted you to go with him, he'd have taken you. You should stay here and wait for him to come back. You shouldn't go off on a wild goose chase across the galaxy, not in your condition.'

'I'm not. I'm following Wayne and I know where he's gone. Can you get me a passage on a ship to Earth?'

'Can you pay for a ticket?'

'Pay? You mean with money?'

'That's the usually accepted method.'

'No, I can't pay,' said Kiru. 'But Wayne didn't have any money, and he boarded a ship. Explain that.'

Jay scratched at his stubble. 'Wayne has done a lot for Café World. They owe him. So maybe they paid him.'

'I'm his wife. They can pay me, too.'

'I don't think they'll see it that way.'

'Maybe I could send him a message, tell him about the baby, then he'd come back.'

'Contacting a ship in falspace is impossible. Even if it wasn't, how could Wayne get back? A ship full of passengers isn't going to turn around in mid-voyage.'

'How much time will it take him to get to Earth?'

'How much time?' Jay shrugged his shoulders. 'It's all relative.'

Because Kiru and Wayne had deliberately avoided mixing with most of those who ran the pleasure planet, Jay was the only other person she really knew on Caphmiaultrelvossmuaf. Without Wayne, he was the only one. All they had in common was that they were both human, both from Earth. But it was clear Jay couldn't or wouldn't help her. As she'd been for most of her life, as she'd been before meeting Wayne, Kiru was all alone. Alone against the universe.

Or almost alone. Inside her, another life was beginning.

'You think I should stay here?' she said.

'Yes. You mustn't go off-planet, not in your condition.'

This was the second time he'd said something like that.

'What condition?' said Kiru. 'I'm not ill. There's nothing wrong with me.'

'No, no, I know,' said Jay.

'In fact, I never felt better in my life.'

'Good, great.' Jay nodded. 'Even so, you ought to take it easy, and this is the ideal world to do that. You should just tootle around and wait for the baby to arrive.'

'Then wait for Wayne to arrive?'

'Yes.'

'You're right, Jay.' Kiru nodded her head. 'I suppose I knew it all along, but I needed you to convince me. I'll stay and have the baby here. It's the best thing.'

'Good show. If there's anything I can do, popsy, just say the word.' Jay reached for another bottle. 'Let's toast your happy event.'

Kiru held out her empty glass.

'Not for you,' Jay told her. 'Can't have you getting blotto. Alcohol is bad for the baby. Alien alcohol is probably even worse. You shouldn't have had the first drink. You're going to be a mother, Kiru, that means you have to behave responsibly.' He tilted the bottle to his lips. 'Bottoms up.'

'Don't you have anything non-alcoholic?' asked Kiru, as she watched him drink.

'Non-alcoholic?' Jay sounded very offended. 'No.'

'I'm going.' She turned and began to walk away.

'Where to?'

'Back to the skytel. I'll have a shower, I'll wash my hair, get changed, then I'll watch SeeV for . . . what's nine Earth months in hours?' She tugged at the coverall. 'You want this back?'

'Keep it,' Jay said. 'See you later, blossom. Toodle-pip.'

'Uh-huh,' said Kiru.

She left the optiscan centre, walked back to the shore, found a skimmer, and headed straight to the spaceport.

3

Kiru and Wayne had lost each other once, then they had found one another, far away on a different world. They could do it again.

She had to find Wayne for his own good. He wasn't safe to be out in the universe alone. And he wouldn't be safe once she found him. Abandoning her the way he had, she'd teach him a lesson he would never forget. Once she'd tracked him down, maybe she should walk out on him. That would show him.

Kiru had never given even a moment's consideration to Jay's suggestion of remaining on Café World. Without Wayne, she had no reason to stay. At first thought, the baby might have seemed like a reason; but on second thought, wherever she went her unborn child went with her. She had no intention of letting any baby of hers gestate in an exo-womb – and by keeping it within herself, she'd know for certain it was her baby.

Boarding a shuttle out to an orbiting ship would be no problem. She could easily mix with the hundreds of tourists who left Café World every hour. Visitors were only checked on arrival. As long as they had money to spend, everyone was welcome. When they had spent up, they were encouraged to leave as fast as possible.

The problem was finding a ship bound for Earth. There wasn't one, not so soon after the flight Wayne had taken. But if Kiru didn't leave quickly, Jay might run a trace, discover what she planned and try to stop her. Her only choice was to board a ship to a different destination, then transfer to another vessel which would finally take her to Earth.

Like it or not, it had to be done. She boarded a shuttle and rode up into orbit.

Her chosen destination was Hideaway: the most exclusive and expensive pleasure satellite in the galaxy. It was the ideal place to find passage to Earth, because it was a focus for vessels from all over the galaxy.

Kiru had no ticket. Although that had also been true on her previous voyages, it was different now. This was the first time she was travelling as a fare-paying passenger. At least in theory.

All she had as she left the surface of Caphmiaultrel-vossmuaf was the coverall she wore, but that was more than she'd arrived with. Then she noticed there was something else, the ring Wayne had given her during their wedding. As well as another gift from Wayne: a new life within her.

Like all the other passengers on the shuttle, Kiru stood within a solo niche for the express journey. She watched the datascreen as Café World receded below. Her hands rested on her stomach, and she twisted the red ring around and around her finger. She remembered the wedding ceremony and realised there was even more she was taking with her from Caphmiaul-trelvossmuaf: her memories. They were good memories, almost all of them, unlike those of her previous journey into space.

This would be her fourth voyage, and statistically it was impossible for it to be any worse than the other three. Although in her case that didn't mean much.

For a start, the flight would be shorter, which meant there was less time for anything to go wrong. Unless something did go wrong, in which case . . .

Kiru preferred not to think about it.

One reason for choosing Hideaway was because it was relatively near to Café World, which meant her time onboard would be brief. After leaving the shuttle, she was sure she could hide herself somewhere on the interstellar ship; she'd done it before.

Kiru had also been to Hideaway before, and she had both good and bad memories of her visit.

She'd first met Wayne there. That was the good part.

But it was also on Hideaway that Grawl had tried to steal her body and suck her brain from her skull, eliminating Kiru's self and replacing it with someone else's identity.

And that, she seemed to recall, was the bad part.

4

Kiru fell. She kept on falling, falling, falling . . .

She knew it was a dream, even asleep she recognised it as the nightmare she'd had for most of her life. But knowing it was only a dream didn't make it any better; and while she was sleeping, trying desperately to wake up, she was still falling, falling further and further, faster and faster. One day she'd never wake up in time. One day she'd fall all the way. One day she'd be dead.

'Uhhh!'

Her eyes opened, but she stayed still as she stared around in the gloom and wondered where she was.

This was Hideaway, she remembered, and she was hiding away. Kiru sat up and leaned against the curved wall of the narrow alcove. She was aching, and it was almost as if she'd injured herself during the fall. But it was only a bad dream – *the* bad dream – there had been no fall, there never had been. Or not for her.

It was her father who had fallen, having jumped to his death. An economic crisis had wiped him out financially; the fall had wiped him out physically. Like most people on Earth, Kiru's father had lost everything he had during the planet's worst ever crash. Her father had lost more than most people, because he'd lost his life.

Kiru had no memory of him, no real memory, because it was all mixed up with her perpetual dream. In the nightmare, a red devil had tried to kill her, to throw her from the top of a building. Her father had fought with the demon, and instead it was he who had plummeted to his death. Although she'd long realised it couldn't have happened like that, that was still how she remembered it.

Because Kiru had never known her father, she was determined it wouldn't be that way with her child, and that was why she had to find Wayne. He was crazy to have left her. As she sat huddled in a cramped service tube deep within the guts of the artificial satellite, Kiru wondered if she was even crazier.

What if Jay was right, and Wayne had left her, left Caphmiaultrelvossmuaf, because he'd known about the baby?

In that case, she was glad he'd gone, and the other side of the universe wasn't far enough away for him. But she'd also left the paradise of Café World, and she wondered if she should return. Anywhere had to be better than where she was now, cold and uncomfortable and hungry. It reminded her too much of her life back on Earth. That hadn't been life, though, it had been existence: struggling for survival, foraging for food amidst the economic ruins of the Crash.

Then she'd made a mistake: she got on the wrong side of the law. Literally. For Kiru, no door was ever locked. She was always opening doors to see what she could find. And this time she'd found herself inside a police base.

That was why she was given a five year sentence on Arazon and transported across the galaxy. Once on the prison planet, known as Clink to its reluctant residents, she discovered there was no way off. Every sentence was for life, and life on a world full of convicted criminals from all over the universe was usually very short. Kiru had escaped from Arazon with a gang of outlaws, which was how she'd reached Hideaway the first time.

Stretching out her arms and legs, Kiru winced. She was getting too old for sleeping rough. Either that or Café World had made her too soft. She'd spent too long in luxury, doing nothing, thinking nothing. Even before becoming pregnant, she'd started putting on weight – and she hadn't even cared. Wayne was right, it had been time to move on, and she wished she'd listened to him.

She wished he was with her now. It had been a long while since she'd last had her falling dream; since she'd been with Wayne, the nightmare had gone away. It was no coincidence that now she was alone, the dream was back.

But she wasn't alone, there was someone else with her, inside her, and Kiru had somehow to get them both to Earth. It was the only possible destination, because that was where Wayne had gone. She knew him too well, and he'd never have left if he had known about the baby.

She'd told Jay that nothing in her life had ever been planned, and that was true. From now on, everything would be different. Reaching Hideaway had been relatively simple, because the two worlds were commercially linked and relatively close, and there was a regular service from Café World. The next stage of her journey, an interstellar voyage to Earth, would be more difficult. She needed a plan.

What Kiru needed before anything else, however, was food. From now on, she had to eat for two. She started to stand up.

'Stop! Not move!'

Kiru didn't hesitate. A warning to stop, not to move, meant she could only do one thing. She did it: she sprang out and ran, keeping her head down and her body low, away from the voice, away from the dark shape looming towards her in the tunnel.

She didn't get far, she slipped, fell, saw another dark figure above her, realised she'd been tripped, and she rolled and rolled, over and over, then stopped abruptly as a heavy foot thudded hard against the small of her back, forcing her face down to the ground, and something cold and sharp touched the side of her neck.

'Slate not working?' said a voice, a different voice. 'This is what "stop" and "don't move" mean.'

It didn't matter whether her slate was working or not, she could understand the voices without it. They were both speaking a version of Terran.

'Who you?' said the first voice. 'Where you from? What you want?'

Kiru was wondering the same thing about her

captors. All she could see of them was one and a half pairs of feet. The other half a pair was still on her back, pinning her down. Each foot of the full pair consisted of four massive claws, while the single foot was hidden inside a very worn shoe.

'Answer!' said the other. This was the one with the blade against Kiru's flesh.

Remaining silent was not an option, nor was giving the right answers. Kiru had learned never to tell the complete truth – and never to tell a total lie.

'Am I under arrest?' she asked.

A good delaying tactic was replying with another question.

'It speaks, it understands,' said the second voice. 'And if it doesn't answer, I'll slit its throat.'

'You speak,' said the first voice. 'He like killing.'

'I adore killing. I worship killing. Without killing, life isn't worth living.'

Kiru suspected that most killers wouldn't waste time talking about how much they loved it, although there were bound to be some alien races who were the exception. But if they had wanted her dead, she'd never have woken up. They must have been watching her, waiting, wondering what to do. Because of their uncertainty, they were unlikely to be a Hideaway security squad.

'You speak soon,' said the first voice. 'Very soon. Very now.'

'Yeah,' said Kiru. 'I'll answer. What was the question?'

'Where you from? Who you?'

'No,' said Kiru. 'It was the other way around. You said, "Who you?" first.'

'You certain?'

'I think so,' said Kiru. 'You with the knife, what question was first?'

'This isn't a knife,' said the one with the knife.

Because of the angle it was held against her neck, Kiru couldn't see the weapon very well. 'Seems like a knife to me,' she said.

'You're wrong. It's a cutlass.'

'Is it?' said Kiru. 'That's interesting. I've never heard of that before. Tell me again what it's called.'

'A cutlass.'

'Cutlass,' said Kiru. 'Cutlass. What kind of knife is that?'

'It's not a knife. I told you that. It's a type of sword, a pirate sword.'

For a moment, the edge of the blade was gone from Kiru's neck. She jerked her left side, from shoulder to hip, forcing the foot on her back upwards, then she swept out her right hand, pushing the leg she could see away, and she sprang halfway up before thrusting her whole weight against her captor, knocking him off balance, slamming him against the tunnel wall, kicking out at the torso while punching the limb holding the sword. The sword fell, so did he. Kiru was on her knees and grabbed the hilt, held the tip of the blade against the alien's throat. But he was no alien, even in the half-light he looked human. Almost. His back was bowed and his neck bent forward as if his body had become twisted to fit within the narrow tunnels. Small and slender, dressed in rags, he was no more than a child.

Kiru looked around, watching for the other one, the one with clawed feet, the one who must have been an alien. Too late. All she saw was a shadowy shape rapidly disappearing along the gloomy tunnel. She turned quickly back, and the boy was already leaping at her. Kiru dodged aside, ramming her elbow into his belly as he flew past her.

'Ohhhhh!' the boy grunted. He crouched on all fours, as if all his limbs were legs, his big eyes glaring at her. 'Give me –' he was winded and gasped for breath – 'my cutlass!'

'It's a knife,' said Kiru. She practised swinging the curved blade through the air. There wasn't much room in the tunnel. She was kneeling, and the roof was only a few centimetres above her head. 'A long, fancy knife. Pirate weapon, ha! What are you doing with it?'

'I'm a . . . pirate.'

Kiru laughed.

'I am!' said the boy. 'My father was a pirate.' He took a short breath. 'And I'm a pirate.' He breathed in again. 'That was his cutlass.' Another breath. 'Give it me back. Now!'

Kiru was impressed by his confidence. She glanced from side to side, gazing along the tunnel in both directions, wondering if his confidence was about to be justified. There was nothing to see, nothing to hear. She studied the boy, who no longer seemed as young as she'd first thought. He could have been around her own age, perhaps a few years older. The size of his warped body was deceptive. The whole universe was deceptive.

Away from Earth, everything changed, including time itself. Age could no longer be counted by years, and even years couldn't be measured in years. Every world had different ways of calculating the passage of time. On Caphmiaultrelvossmuaf, for example, there was no such thing as a day; not twenty-four hours, not any number of hours. Seconds and minutes and hours were the same wherever humans went, because they took those measurements with them; but weeks and months became obsolete in, well, a fortnight or so . . .

'Say "please",' said Kiru.

'What?'

'You heard me. If you want your sword, your *cutlass*, then say "please".'

'You want me to beg you?'

'Saying "please" isn't begging, it's being polite. Politeness costs nothing.'

'This is a trick. Even if I say "please", you won't give it back.'

Kiru settled down on her haunches, holding the sword across her knees, and she kept looking across at him. He leaned back against the tunnel, wide eyes staring at her, and said, 'Please, please give me back my cutlass, please.'

'How could I refuse such a polite request?' said Kiru. She set the blade on the ground in front of her. They faced each other across the tunnel, the sword lying between them.

He moved his hands back, demonstrating that picking up the sword was the furthest thing from his mind. 'Who are you?' he asked.

'Who me?' said Kiru. 'Where me from? What me want?'

'Yes. Who are you?' He kept looking at her. 'Please.'

Kiru laughed again for a moment. 'My name is Kiru. What's yours?'

He opened his mouth to speak, then paused. It could be that he was inventing a name, or it could be that it was so long since he'd used it that he was trying to remember.

'Terry,' he said, 'because I'm from Terra.'

Kiru's second impression had been that he was human, although by now she was no longer so sure. His eyes seemed too large, and the way he balanced his weight on his hands was almost simian. But it was possible he was genetically human, anything was possible.

'So am I,' said Kiru.

'Are you?' said Terry, and he stared at her more intensely than ever. 'Really?'

'Yes,' said Kiru. She'd doubted him, and now he was doubting her. 'I'm human, can't you see that? It's a bit dark in here, but I don't look all that bad, do I? We talk the same lingo. We're from the same home planet. I'm glad not everyone from there is called Terry.'

'Why? Something wrong with my name?' One of his hands had moved fractionally closer to the sword.

'No, it's a good name. Terry. A very good name. But it would be confusing if everyone from Terra was called Terry.'

'Would it? Why?'

'Because . . .' Kiru hesitated as she tried to think of a simple explanation. 'Because if a group of Terrans meet up, and they're all called Terry, when someone says "Terry" they wouldn't know which of them it was.'

'I've never met anyone called Terry,' said Terry.

Neither had Kiru until now, but she decided it was best not to say so.

'I've never met anyone from Terra,' added Terry.

'I meet them all the time,' said Kiru. Most recently, there had been Jay on Café World; most importantly, there had been Wayne here on Hideaway; most dangerously, there had been Grawl on Arazon. 'And you're another one.'

'I've never met anyone,' Terry said.

'If you behave the way you did to me, I'm not surprised,' said Kiru. 'Attacking and threatening me like that. Who did you think I was?'

'A stranger.'

'Do you threaten and attack every stranger?'

'I've never seen a stranger.'

'We're not strangers any more. I know your name, you know mine. I'm from Earth, like you.'

'Not like me. I've never been there.'

'You should go.'

Terry looked down, he looked up, he looked along the tunnel to the left, he looked along the tunnel to the right, then finally he looked at Kiru and said, 'How?'

'Can we go somewhere else and talk?' said Kiru. 'Somewhere more comfortable?'

'Com . . . fort . . . able?' said Terry, as if pronouncing a word he didn't know.

'Yes. Where do you live, where are you staying?'

'I live . . . here. I stay . . . here. What are you doing . . . here?'

Sometimes the truth was the best answer. 'Just passing through,' said Kiru. 'Unofficially, that is. I've been on Caphmiaultrelvossmuaf for a while, which you might know as Café World, and I'm on my way back to Earth.'

Terry rubbed at his jaw, scratched his scalp, frowned. 'You're not from here,' he said, slowly. 'But you are here. How did you get here?'

And sometimes even the truth was disbelieved. 'I told you, I came from Café World.'

'By spaceship?'

Kiru nodded. 'It's the best way to travel between the stars.'

'You wouldn't be here, not in this part of Hideaway, if you came by ship. Passengers can only arrive through the main entrance, and crews aren't allowed because they don't have enough to spend.'

'I'm not a passenger. I'm not one of the crew. But I don't have enough to spend. Look at me.' Kiru gestured towards herself. 'This is all I have, just this coverall. But I'm here, I came from somewhere. You're here, how did you get here?'

'I was born here,' said Terry, and by now his hand was resting on the hilt of the sword.

Kiru was beginning to feel uneasy, but not because of the blade. If there had been any risk, she wouldn't have given it back to Terry; and although she didn't have a weapon, she was far from defenceless. What bothered her was what he'd been saying.

'Your father was a space pirate?' she said.

'Don't you believe me?'

'I believe you,' Kiru said, and she did.

Hideaway was an artificial planet, its origins a mystery. Every planet, every natural planet, orbited its own sun, a star massively larger than the planet and also a great distance away. But Hideaway's sun was deep within the artificial asteroid. At its very heart was a tiny star, and this solar core made Hideaway independent of the rest of the galaxy: a self-contained world, a world which could travel across the cosmos.

Hideaway's builders were unknown but presumed to be a long-extinct race from another universe. What Kiru knew for certain, however, was that Hideaway's most recent residents had been space pirates. For them, the planet had been the ideal hideout, a secret headquarters from which to raid the interstellar spaceways –

until they realised their greatest asset was the base itself, that they could make more money at much less risk by transforming their unique world into a pleasure planet. Hideaway had become the universe's number one sybaritic satellite, a place where the richest of the rich from every inhabited world could find every pleasure which was unknown or illegal on their planet.

The elite of the galaxy headed for Hideaway, and the pirates made a fortune. Every world was different, every alien race had its own taboos. What was forbidden on one planet was mundane on another; the most decadent and unspeakable vice for one species was boring and routine to others.

Previously, space pirates had made a living through looting and murder. After the success of Hideaway, their only killing was financial – and it was spectacular. But then they made one mistake: they didn't pay their taxes. As penalty, they were dispossessed and Hideaway was taken over by the Galactic Taxation Company. It was they who still owned and operated the asteroid.

The pirates had gone back to their traditional trade of hijacking, abduction and ransom, until their new secret base was discovered and destroyed. Unlike Hideaway, their replacement headquarters couldn't be moved around the galaxy – although that happened to the survivors, when they were transported to Arazon. Kiru had met some of them on the prison planet, which was how she knew Hideaway's history.

'Why didn't you leave Hideaway when the pirates were evicted?' Kiru asked.

'My father was away,' said Terry. 'I was very young

and I don't really know what happened. My mother stayed behind, I stayed with her.'

'Where is she now?'

Terry looked down, slowly. The sword was across his lap by now, his right fist tightly gripping the hilt. He either didn't know the answer or didn't want to say.

'I was abandoned,' he said. 'Down here, we're completely cut off from the rest of Hideaway. We live on whatever we can find.'

With Terry, evolution seemed to have reversed. His body had become deformed through existing within the labyrinthine tunnels; he went on all fours because that was the fastest way to move; his eyes were big so he could see in this twilight underworld. He and the others must have lived like vermin, scavenging for survival deep within the fetid bowels of Hideaway.

'How many of you are there?' Kiru asked.

'Why?' Terry glanced at her suspiciously.

'Forget it,' said Kiru. It didn't matter how many there were, or what species they were, or how they came to be here. All that mattered was finding a ship to Earth, and for that she needed Terry's help.

'If you were born here,' she said, 'you must know everything there is to know about Hideaway.'

'I was born here. And I'm going to die here. There's no escape for the likes of me.' He looked at Kiru. 'Or you.'

Kiru shuddered for a moment as she glanced along the dark, narrow tunnel. Was this where she would spend the rest of her life, trapped within a maze of forgotten service ducts? Was this where her baby would be born and always live, bent and weak, never seeing natural light, never breathing fresh air, never experiencing real gravity, never setting foot on a true planet . . . ?

'You got here,' said Terry, 'but you'll never get away again.'

CHAPTER
THREE

Someone knocked on the door.

Wayne Norton turned his head and stared. Back in the old days, back in the twentieth century, doors were made of wood. People knocked on doors to let the person inside know they were there. Doors were no longer made of wood, nothing was made of wood. He wasn't sure what the cabin door was made of, or what the cabin was made of, or what the spaceship was made of. It was all some kind of plastic. Perhaps. During his first life, plastic and other man-made materials had begun replacing wood and metal. By now, plastic itself had probably been superceded – and not necessarily by something man-made, human-made.

Because the comscreen wasn't working, Norton couldn't see who was in the corridor outside. The door began to move and he saw four fingers appear around the edge, sliding it open.

'Fancy a snifter, old fruit?'

'Jay!' said Norton. 'What are you doing here?'

'Working,' said Jay, as he walked in with a tray of bottles and glasses, setting them down in front of where Norton was sitting. 'What else? It's the story of my life.'

Norton looked at him, wondering what was different. It wasn't his clothes, because he was still wearing the same outfit as always, which looked as old and worn as he did. Then Norton realised. Jay had legs, he was standing up. Until now, he'd only ever seen him sitting in his command seat in the optiscan centre on Café World.

'But . . .' Norton shook his head in bewilderment.

Jay surveyed the cabin with a slow glance. Norton knew that space within a spaceship was always at a premium. Because of the cabin's size, it had probably once been a luxury suite; but it seemed to have been unused for a long while. Whatever materials it was made of, they hadn't stayed clean and untarnished. Some of the fittings had been stripped out and dumped on the ground, as if refurbishment had started but then been forgotten.

'As knackered as the rest of the ship,' said Jay, and he sighed.

Norton could guess what Jay meant and he agreed. Considering it was carrying an ambassador – in other words, Wayne Norton – the vessel was less than impressive. It had seen better years; it could even have seen better centuries.

'Looks aren't the main thing,' he said.

'In your case, Wayne,' said Jay, 'that's true.'

'A spacecraft is a working vessel, and it's performance that matters, not appearance. Some space ranger told me that.' Norton looked at Jay. 'Must have been you.'

'Space ranger?' said Jay. 'I like that. You do come up with some corking phrases, Wayne. But it's this ship's performance that bothers me.' He looked at the door and ordered, 'Shut!' The door stayed open. He shrugged. 'You want a small tincture?' he asked, nodding towards the bottles.

'Is this what you mean by "working"? You're the ship's steward?'

'Got to do something to keep myself busy.'

'I was a steward once, on a ship to Hideaway.'

Jay glanced at him. 'Strike a light,' he said. 'Something else we have in common. In that case, we can take it in turns.'

'Acting as steward for the others on board, you mean?'

'What others? It's just you and me. This old crate flies itself. What do you want to drink?'

'Anything. You're the expert. When I was a steward, it was a cover for my real work.'

'Stewth, another coincidence! Every job I've ever done has been a cover for my real work as a steward.' Jay was examining a turquoise, pyramid-shaped bottle, trying to see which of the corners to pour from.

'What?' said Wayne. He didn't understand, but that was not unusual when Jay was talking.

'Hey!' said Jay, as he succeeded in finding the opening. He poured two glasses, handing one to Norton, then raising his own in a toast. 'To Kiru.'

'Kiru,' said Norton.

The two glasses clinked together. The sound was exactly right, and he realised they must have been made of the real thing: glass. He took a sip. Liquid velvet caressed his tongue, tickled his tonsils, then stroked his throat as he swallowed.

'I wonder what's happening to her?' added Norton.

'I try not to think about it.' He took another sip. 'But I think about her every moment.'

'Kiru's safe,' said Jay, as he sat down, 'I'm sure of it.'

'Safe? How can she be safe on Algol? They've sent you to check up on me, I know. But I don't care about being an ambassador. All I want to do is find Kiru. And if I have to start a galactic war to do it, that's okay by me.'

'No one's sent me. It was my own idea. I heard you were leaving, and I thought you'd like some company during the voyage.'

'So you're here for my sake, not yours?'

'Well . . .' Jay shrugged his shoulders. 'When I found Café World it seemed the ideal place to hang up my space boots, and it was for a while. But I grew bored, the gravity was getting me down. I'm a spacer. This is where I belong.' He looked around the cabin again, and shook his head. 'Although maybe if I'd known it was this ship . . .'

'You don't want to go to Algol, I don't blame you.'

'Algol's a spiffing place. There are plenty of worse billets.'

Norton stared at him. 'Hold it. When I asked if you'd been there, you told me you hadn't.'

'Did I? Must have slipped my mind. I've been to so many worlds, although I didn't set foot on most of them. Those where I landed, I usually never got further than the first sex salon or bar – which was often the same place.' As if that reminded him, Jay drained his glass. 'Drink up. I hate drinking alone.' He paused. 'No, that's a lie.' He poured himself another drink. 'A bottle lasts longer if you're alone.'

'Not in your case,' said Norton.

Jay laughed. 'That's better. See? One drink and you're cheering up.'

'I'm not cheering up. How can I cheer up when Kiru's been kidnapped?' He set his glass down. 'You think drinking will make me forget?'

'Drinking always makes me remember. Alcohol is good for the brain, it's a well-known preservative.'

Jay sat with his glass held halfway to his lips, as if he couldn't take a drink until Norton did.

'If you've been to Algol,' said Norton, and he reached out to wrap his thumb and three fingers around the glass, 'you can tell me all about the place, yeah?'

'To help you with your diplomatic role, you mean?'

'To help me find Kiru.'

'I'll do anything I can for Kiru,' said Jay. 'Although not much for you, of course.'

'Likewise,' said Norton, and he managed a half smile. He lifted his glass. 'Cheers.'

'Cheers,' said Jay, and they both drank. 'What's all this effluent about you being an ambassador?'

Norton began to tell him about his visit to the management office, then remembered what had happened immediately before, how he'd been shot at.

'Were you killed?' asked Jay.

'Killed?' said Norton. 'What do you mean? Killed! I'm here, I'm alive.'

'If you weren't killed, you weren't shot at. Or not seriously.'

'You mean . . . it was some kind of warning? I was being warned not to look for Kiru?'

'The opposite. Our friends from the Universal Taxation Agency probably wanted you to think it was too dangerous to stay on Café World. They were giving you another reason to be their envoy to Algol.'

'No.' Norton shook his head. That wasn't the way tax authorities operated. They didn't shoot at people. The Internal Revenue Service may have ended Al Capone's career, but they trapped him with filing systems and cross-referencing, not by ambushing him with sub-machine guns. 'The taxliens . . . I mean the tax aliens, they—'

'What,' said Jay, 'did you say? Taxliens? Is that what they call themselves?'

'No,' said Norton again, and again he shook his head. He looked at his glass, aware the alcohol had made him run the words together. 'I just . . . er . . . made it up.'

'Taxliens,' said Jay. 'Top hole, Wayne. You've done it again. They've been given lots of names, most of them obscene, but no one's ever really known what to call them. Nameless aliens, from a nameless world, they hide behind names such as the Galactic Tax Organization to disguise what they really are.'

'Which is?' said Norton.

'A galactic tax organisation. They use false names which tell the truth. What an absolute shower. But from now on, you and me know who they really are – Taxliens! This calls for a drink.'

'No more for me,' said Norton, putting a hand over the rim of his glass. He couldn't see why inventing a name was such a big deal, although with Jay everything called for a drink.

'If you're the ambassador,' said Jay, 'you've got to practise drinking. It's a diplomatic skill.'

Jay filled another glass and gave it to Norton, which meant he had one in each hand.

'To galactic bastards everywhere,' said Jay, raising his only glass in a toast. 'And the Taxliens are everywhere. Here's to their downfall and demise, death and destruction, disintegration and every other "D" in the dashed dictionary.'

'Nobody likes paying tax,' said Norton. He looked at his two glasses, then put them both down. 'But tax money pays for public services.'

'What's a public service?'

'Schools, roads.'

'Roads?' Jay scratched his stubbled jaw.

Norton realised that roads was a bad example, and he was about to mention the police and the military, but Jay went off on another rant.

'Income tax, travel tax, sales tax, gambling tax, birth tax, death tax,' said Jay. 'The perishers even have a tax tax. And what do they use it all for? I'll tell you. To buy more planets, more solar systems. The Taxliens don't conquer by force, they just buy up everything. Any opposition, they buy it. Governments, armies, warfleets. They buy them all. They own them all. Café World, for example. And Earth.'

'Earth?'

'I'd guess so. They don't announce these things. Everything is a secret with them. Most of the universe doesn't even know they exist. Not many people have ever seen them. You have, I have. Or have we? Their appearance could all be a front. The ones we've seen are a race which works for them or masquerades as them. They aren't the real Taxliens.'

'There are no "real Taxliens",' said Norton. 'It's only a name.'

'They've got to have a name, so does their planet.'

Norton picked up one of the glasses in front of him,

swirled the clear liquid around, then took a sip. 'Revenue World,' he said.

Jay looked at him, open-mouthed, then filled his mouth with a gulp of alcohol. 'Perfect,' he said.

'It's only a name,' Norton said, again, and he drained his glass. Revenue World. It sounded good, he was pleased with it. Maybe he did have a talent for this. First Café World, now Revenue World.

'You're right, Wayne. It's all cobblers. Revenue World isn't on any star chart.' Jay poured himself another drink. 'They're so shifty that instead of pretending not to be who they are, they could really be who they're pretending to be.'

'What?'

'The ones you've met, they could be the real Taxliens. And now you're working for them. Ambassador to Algol. What did they say to make you agree?'

'I'd have agreed to anything, all that mattered was getting a ship to Algol so I can find Kiru. About Algol—'

'Plenty of time to talk about that,' said Jay. 'Did the Taxliens say you were uniquely qualified to be their ambassador?'

'Yeah. How did you know? Are you one of them?'

'I don't think so. But the "you are uniquely unique" is one of the techniques they use. It makes a change from bribery and blackmail. They told you this was what you were created for, that it was your destiny to be their ambassador to Algol?'

'Yeah.' Norton nodded his head. 'And to save the universe from annihilation.'

'Sounds easy, but not everyone can do it.' Jay laughed for a few seconds. 'They can be frightfully convincing, Wayne. That's how they've taken over so much of the galaxy, through deceit and treachery.'

'Like I said, all I wanted was a ship to Algol.' Norton picked up his second glass. 'But what they told me, it did make me think maybe there was a reason for my life. Here I am now, far from the world where I was born over three hundred years ago, and perh—'

'What –' Jay spluttered and coughed up some of his drink. He wiped his mouth with the back of his hand – 'did you say?'

'About what?' asked Norton.

'Three hundred years, you said. You were born over three hundred years ago? Is that right?'

'Yeah.'

Jay stared at Norton for several seconds before nodding his head, evidently convinced he was telling the truth, then said, 'But . . . how? No, I don't mean "how". I mean, how come you've lived so long? You look good for your age, Wayne. What year were you born?'

'1947.'

'What year is it now? I haven't been back on Earth for a while, and I've lost count. Must be around 2280 or so. Which means you're . . .' Jay paused, calculating.

'I haven't been alive and kicking all the time,' said Norton. 'There was a long period of hibernation, three centuries' worth. I was revived about a year ago.'

'You were in a time freeze? Why?'

'It wasn't voluntary.'

'Ah,' said Jay. He waited for Norton to explain, but he didn't. 'Why did you never tell me? But why should you have done? Never tell anyone the truth about your past, that's the best policy. And you've got more past than most people.'

'The twentieth century doesn't often come up in conversation, so I don't usually need to mention it.'

'But the Taxliens know all your details. They know everything. Does Kiru know?'

'Of course.'

'Maybe there's hope for me yet. I'm younger than you . . . old man.' He smiled and sipped his drink. 'When we find her, you won't stand a chance.'

'You're going to help me find her?'

'I'll do everything I can to reunite you.'

'Why?'

'Because . . .' began Jay. 'I dunno.' He frowned. 'Why should I? No idea. But I do like Kiru, I like her a lot. She's fun and she's smart. Good-looking, too. When you get to my age, Wayne, that's all there is to do: look. Although considering *your* age, I'm amazed that . . .' Jay suddenly broke off.

'Amazed that what?' asked Norton.

'Amazed that . . . that Kiru sees anything in you, that's all. But I suppose it's my humanitarian duty to help out an old buffer like you.'

'Maybe that's what the Taxliens thought, and that's why they're sending me to Algol.'

'If you think they might have a trace of altruism somewhere in their alien bodies, you must be bonkers. They make space pirates seem like saints.'

'They can't really expect me to be their ambassador. They wouldn't even give me a uniform.'

'A uniform?' said Jay. 'Did ambassadors wear uniforms back in your time?'

'Er . . . not a uniform, not as such. But they would wear something dark and dignified and . . .'

'. . . diplomatic?'

Norton looked at Jay's shapeless, faded coverall, and

realised it might not be a good idea to discuss the importance of proper attire with him.

'How about,' said Jay, 'something with gold braid around the lapels and cuffs, epaulettes on the shoulders, and lots of shiny buttons? Is that the kind of thing you mean?'

'Could be.'

Jay drained his glass and stood up. 'Don't go away,' he said, and he walked out of the cabin.

Norton didn't plan on going anywhere. In the hour or two since boarding, he'd already discovered there was nowhere to go. Although he was pleased that Jay was on board, because it meant he had some company, he wondered why he was really here. Despite his denials and what he said about them, he must have been working for the Taxliens. On Café World, he'd spied on the entire resort for them; on this ship, he only had Norton to watch.

'How about this?' said Jay, when he came back. He was carrying an outfit which was exactly as he'd described, with plenty of gold braid and shiny buttons: navy-blue tailed jacket and pressed pants, ruffled shirt and buckled shoes, stylish cravat and matching cummerbund.

'Wow!' said Norton, reaching out to stroke the velvet collar of the jacket. 'What groovy gear.'

'That means you approve? That's the ticket. You can tell I'm a professional steward because whatever you want, I can get it.'

'I'm impressed, Jay. Where did you find it all?'

'Just a little something I knocked up.'

Although Norton knew clothes could be made very quickly, he doubted it was one of Jay's talents or that the ship had the specialist facilities.

'You found this on board,' said Norton. 'And you knew it was there. You've been on this ship before, haven't you?'

'You got me. It's a fair cop.' Jay poured himself another drink and sat down. 'It was called the *Demon Star* in those days. Could still be, but I always say: what's in a name? I was the ship's steward then, and I am now.' He glanced around the shabby suite, sipping at his glass, then he sighed. 'You can't escape fate, Wayne. I thought I'd escaped, but I'm back here again. It's as if I've been going around and round, walking a mobius strip, trapped helplessly on a whirling cosmic roundabout, never able to get off.'

'Uh-huh. These are great,' said Norton, examining the clothes. 'I wonder what Janesmith will think of them?'

'Janesmith?' said Jay. 'I knew a Janesmith once. She was an Algolan, a princess.'

'So was the one I met on Hideaway. She ran a fashion boutique and designed me a new suit. And that's one reason why the Taxliens want me to be their ambassador to Algol, because I know her.'

'Must be the same Janesmith. She was on the *Demon Star*, but jumped ship when we berthed at Hideaway. I wondered what had happened to her.'

'She's the Empress of Algol.'

'Is she?' Jay nodded, impressed. 'She's done well for herself.'

Norton looked up from examining the embossed buttons. 'Janesmith was on this ship? With you?'

'Yes. You bought a suit from her, but I spent a voyage from Earth to Hideaway with her. I must know her better than you. The Taxliens could have asked me to be their ambassador.'

'She did try to seduce me.'

'And me.'

'You?'

'Yes, me. What's so odd about that?'

'Er . . . nothing, nothing at all. Are you sure you didn't misunderstand? The traditional Algolan greeting is, "Show us your genitals".'

'I think, Wayne, it's safe to say I've met more aliens than you. I know what Janesmith said and I know what she meant. But then she met Grawl, and he was the one she really fancied.'

'Grawl!'

'He was also on board the *Demon Star*. I know what I told you back on Café World, that I hadn't heard of him, but that was a load of old tosh.'

'You know Grawl *and* Janesmith?'

'I've been around. I've met lots of humans, lots of aliens.'

'Of all the trillions of people in the universe . . . ?'

'Did you ever hear of Parker's Paradox?' said Jay. 'It's the reason why wherever you go in the cosmos, you meet people you already know, or people who know people you know. It's because there aren't, in fact, trillions and trillions of people in the galaxy, there are relatively few, which is why you keep running into the same ones.'

'Where did you hear this?' asked Norton, and he poured himself a drink.

'Some geezer. Some bar. Some planet. Never met him again.'

Norton drank.

'Perhaps it's linked with the idea of solipsism,' continued Jay. 'You know, that things only happen where you are, and that wherever you are is the centre of the universe. And what if a star blows up and no one's there, can it be heard? Well, no, because nothing can be heard in the vacuum of space. And if anyone's near a star that goes nova, they'll never hear anything ever again. That's without considering the unspeediness of the speed of sound.'

Norton drank some more. He was no longer so pleased that he had Jay to talk with, because he didn't like what he'd been saying: not the garbage he was now spewing, but one word in particular.

Reluctantly, Norton spoke the word again:

'Grawl,' he said.

And Jay asked, 'Did you ever hear of a chap called William Ewart . . . ?'

CHAPTER
FOUR

'And who might you be?'

Kiru froze. She'd hardly set foot in the central gaming room, and already they knew she was an intruder. Spinning around, she jabbed her cigarette holder towards the guard's face.

'Let me guess,' continued the voice. 'You're an angel, and you're here from paradise.'

He wasn't a guard, Kiru realised, and she stopped herself from poking out any of his various eyes. She presumed he was male, although with an alien it was often difficult to know — and always irrelevant. He stared at the cigarette holder a few centimetres from his face.

'Have you a light?' she asked.

'But you are the light,' he said, 'the light of the universe.'

He was tall, dark and hairy; purple in flesh and dark blue in clothing; two short arms, two long legs; his oval head was completely covered in thick hair except for the eight crescent-shaped eyes which were evenly spaced around the cranium; his mouth was invisible, only detectable when he spoke and the thick hairs around it rippled; his outfit was made of fur, its texture matching his hirsute flesh. And he seemed exactly what Kiru needed.

A flame flashed, and her cigarette was lit. Because she wasn't used to smoking, she inhaled carefully. The holder was meant as a fashion accessory, to complement her long dress and the purse she clutched in her other hand.

Kiru had seen his species before, although she'd no idea what world he was from. Neither did she care. But it was polite to ask, and the first step on the route away from Hideaway was being polite.

'What's your name?' she asked. 'Where are you from?'

'Permit me to introduce my humble self,' said the alien. 'I am Lord Ozen, fifteenth potentate of the glorious planet Seltar.' He turned his head to the left and then to the right, so that all his eyes could examine her. 'From my experience in these matters, I believe you are a female person. Am I correct in my surmise?'

Kiru nodded, but because body language differed so radically amongst bodies which were so radically different, she said, 'Yes.'

'Most excellent,' said Lord Ozen, 'because I am a prime male example of centuries of selective aristocratic breeding. I believe our bodies to be physically compatible, so may I indulge in the preliminary mating rituals of your species? Do you desire a meal, purchase of which is often a demonstration of a suitor's wealth? Or would you prefer an alcoholic beverage or perhaps some narcotic stimulant stronger than the mild herb you are now inhaling? Or is there anything else I may offer so that you will consider intercourse with me? Otherwise, would you allow me to caress your secondary sexual characteristics, or shall I proceed immediately to your genitalia? This may be done in a less public venue, if you prefer.'

'You are too generous, Lord Ozen,' said Kiru, doing her best not to step back as he loomed over her. 'A drink would be most exquisite.'

There was something about hearing an alien voice through a slate which made her reply in a similar way. It was almost as if she was helping to translate her own words.

'Let us proceed to the refreshment emporium,' said Lord Ozen. 'What liquid intake would you prefer?'

'Something from your home world would be most intriguing,' said Kiru. 'I'd be very appreciative if you could make the choice, because you are indeed far more expert than me . . . er . . . than I.'

It didn't matter what Lord Ozen chose. Kiru now had a bugcollar, and she could safely swallow any alien food or drink. The collar had been provided by Terry, as had her outfit, the purse and its contents: plenty of gaming chips – and a knife. They had all been lost or discarded over the years, ending up in the asteroid's underworld, and Terry had stored them in various hiding places. He was human, he was male, and he hadn't needed much persuading to show Kiru his various collections and to loan her a few items.

Kiru had arrived on Hideaway barefoot and penniless, but to leave required money. Money was the sole reason for Hideaway's existence. Anyone who could afford the journey was presumed wealthy enough to enjoy its esoteric pastimes. Because Kiru was here, she was assumed to be rich. What she needed was someone who really was wealthy, someone who could buy her a ticket to Terra. It was too far to Earth to be a stow-away.

During her previous brief visit to the pleasure satel-lite, she had been too busy saving her life, her mind, to explore any of Hideaway's luxurious attractions. The contrast between this and Café World was incredible. The latter was always crowded and bright and loud, but here it was quiet and subdued, much more subtle and far more exclusive. All around her, fortunes were being won and lost, and the winners were as inexpress-ive as the losers – although because there was such a variety of different expressions on Hideaway, 'inex-pressive' was the wrong description. Every race, every species, was uniquely different from every other.

Café World could accommodate only a narrow range of aliens, those who could breathe the atmosphere and take the gravity; but they were the vacation-going majority, and Café World provided for the majority. Hideaway, however, pandered to the minority: the richest of the rich. And they were all trying to become richer. The asteroid was a magnet for greed.

'Would you prefer to sit, to stand or to recline?' asked Lord Ozen.

Although the bar had seemed a long way from the entrance, Kiru and her alien escort had reached it very quickly. Perspective and distance had no meaning on Hideaway. Before going into the gaming room, she had walked all around it as she weighed up her alternatives, and the casino was smaller on the outside than it was within. Inside, everything was designed to appear larger. The ceiling seemed far above, but it was an illusion, probably not much higher than Kiru could have reached.

'Whatever your lordship prefers,' said Kiru. 'I am in your hands.' She glanced at his hands, which were like huge hairy mittens with fur so thick she couldn't even tell how many fingers he had.

The bar area was in the centre of the gambling room. All around were different gaming tables, games of chance from across the universe, and all around these were different types of people, mostly alien, some human. Unlike Café World, where most gambling was done on fast, random (or not so random) automatic equipment, here everything was controlled and operated manually – by hands which dealt cards, or tentacles which threw dice, or claws which spun wheels.

'What planet are you from, may I enquire?' asked Lord Ozen.

'I'm from Terra,' answered Kiru.

'That is a shame,' he said. 'Please excuse me, I must go find a female from some other planet.'

'Why? What's wrong?'

'Wherever one travels in the cosmos, it's a well known fact that there is no one less sexually satisfying than the Terran female. Fare thee well.'

With that, Lord Ozen turned on his long legs and started to walk away. He moved quite slowly, and the eyes at the back of his head stayed focused on Kiru. She watched him go. Creep. He hadn't even bought her the drink he'd promised. For that, she knew, she was meant to defend the sexual reputation of half the human race. And he hadn't even bothered to ask her name. He didn't care what she was called, but at least he could have pretended.

It took a long time for Lord Ozen to reach the casino exit. Although the doorway seemed huge and distant, it was small and relatively near. He hesitated, then was gone.

Kiru looked around the bar and noticed someone watching her. The figure raised a hand in her direction. Kiru recognised the gesture as a greeting, because she recognised the figure as human and female, and she walked over towards her. Although she looked human, nothing could ever be accepted at face value, particularly faces. Some humans were known to alter their appearance, believing that by looking like aliens they would seem more enigmatic and exotic. Presumably, the opposite also occurred. There must have been aliens who had changed themselves to appear human.

Human or alien, the figure looked like a Terran woman. It could have been a long time since she was on Earth, however, or she could have been Terran by descent and might never have been there. Everything about her may have been different from what was on show, from her age (around twenty Earth years), body-shape (very curvaceous) to her eye colour (emerald green). She was dressed in a spectraflesh suit, which shimmered in harlequin patterns, its various colours changing every few seconds, random panels briefly becoming transparent and exposing her real flesh beneath.

When Kiru gestured to the seat next to her, the woman made the human affirmative signal of nodding her head, and Kiru sat down.

'Totally good *move*,' said the woman, in Terran.

'What was?' asked Kiru.

'Spurning the Seltan's *amorous* advances.'

'He wasn't my type.'

'*She*.'

'She?'

'Did she ask what *sex* you were, and when you said "female" she *told* you she was male?'

'Something like that,' said Kiru. 'But male or female, what difference does it make? They're still *alien*.' She hadn't meant to emphasise the final word, and hoped the woman didn't think she was imitating her.

'What was her seduction *technique* with you?' the woman asked, as she twisted the stem of her glass around and around.

'That human females are so sexually unsatisfying,' said Kiru.

'What *a* nerve!'

'I know. Who'd fall for that?'

'After *all* I did for her, she *dared* to use the same line again on you!' The woman drained her glass.

'You mean . . . ?' Kiru looked away from the woman and towards the exit, then back to her new companion.

'You didn't miss *anything*. Believe me – what's *your* name?'

'Kiru.' She'd considered using an alias, as almost everyone else seemed to; but giving her real name was probably even more deceptive.

'My name's *Candy*. Believe me, Kiru, one thing I've *learned* about people, about humans, about aliens, when it comes to sex there's *one* golden rule: the more they talk about it, the more *pathetic* their *performance*.'

'Maybe,' said Kiru, 'she realised you were so good, that's why she wanted to have sex with another human female. Me.'

Candy laughed briefly. 'How *about* a drink?'

'Thanks,' said Kiru, as she took a final drag on her cigarette. 'But that doesn't mean I'm going to have sex with you.'

Candy looked at Kiru, saw her smile, and she laughed again. 'It's *not* compulsory. What *would* you like?'

'Something very long, very cold, zero alcohol.'

'*Very* wise. Must stay *alert* here.'

The gaming room was a casino with a bar in the centre. If customers wanted anything except gambling or a drink, there were other areas of Hideaway to provide whatever they could wish for – and probably more than they ever dreamed of. This was only one of the casinos on the asteroid; there were more on other levels where the gravity was higher or lower, meeting the physical requirements of various alien races. Different sections of the planet provided atmospheres for species who couldn't breathe a nitrogen/oxygen mixture. Hideaway claimed to be the ultimate resort: every race in the known galaxy could be accommodated in luxury, and every hedonistic fantasy made real. Or apparently real.

'To Earth *girls* everywhere,' said Candy, and she clinked her glass against Kiru's.

'Earth girls,' echoed Kiru, wondering if Candy would qualify in the second category. There was something about her face that hinted she'd had an early rejuve, and enough about the rest of her that more than hinted she'd had plenty of bodyfix. 'I like your hair,' Kiru added, when she realised she might have been staring at Candy too much.

Candy's hair colour matched her eyes. It was emerald green and woven into countless tight plaits which spun and twisted together on top of her head and then flowed down across her shoulders.

'*Thanks*,' she said. 'I haven't seen *you* around before.'

'I've just arrived. How about you? Have you been here long?'

'I come and go, *passing* through. Hideaway is a *great*

place to pick up data, find out what's *really* going on in the galaxy. So *where* have you come from? It must be a totally remote planet if *that* dress is still in fashion.'

Ever since trying it on, Kiru had felt uneasy about her outfit, but it was the only thing remotely suitable for venturing into Hideaway's guest zones. It probably was ancient, which was why it had been dumped and ended up in one of Terry's collections. Clothing trends came and went, then came back again, but Kiru stopped herself from saying that doubtless Candy could recall when the dress had last been very fashionable – and also remember the time before that.

Although Kiru was wearing more than she usually did on Café World, she felt more exposed. The flared skirt of her long dress hung down to the ground, which was fine because it hid her bare feet. (One thing Terry's wardrobe hadn't been able to supply was shoes which fitted.) It was the top part of the dress which bothered her. The way her breasts were only half-covered, the whole outfit kept threatening to slip off. If it did, she'd be exposed as an impostor: no one was nude on Hideaway.

Kiru was in the midst of a galaxy of extreme colours, creatures with bizarre shapes and limbs of weird proportions, their flesh covered with fur or feathers, scales or shell. But they were all clothed, to some extent or other, because clothing was the universal mark of civilisation. No matter on what world they had evolved, any species which wore clothes proved they were no longer primitive and savage.

Back on Earth, Kiru's early life had been relatively primitive and savage, and keeping up with fashion had been low on her priority list. An outfit had to be functional, to protect her from the weather and have enough pockets to hold her things. Not that Kiru had ever had much to carry. She'd never owned anything valuable except her wedding ring, and that was only of value to her. Now, it was all she had to remind her of Wayne. That and the baby.

'I never think clothes are very important, Candy,' said Kiru. 'It's the person within that matters. And once you meet the right person, who needs clothes?'

Candy smiled. 'I agree *totally*,' she said. 'Who are you *looking* for?'

'I'm not,' said Kiru.

'You *keep* looking around. Am I *that* dull?'

'No, no, no,' said Kiru, quickly. She realised she'd been gazing around the casino, checking out everyone, wondering who she could put the squeeze on.

'Yes, yes, *yes*!' Candy laughed. 'I don't *blame* you, I do the *same* myself. Whenever I'm on Hideaway, I always like to *expand* my horizons, if you get my meaning.'

Kiru frowned, not understanding.

'I'm heading back to Earth *soon*,' Candy continued, 'but I'd like *another* experience under my belt before then.'

'Ah!' said Kiru, as she suddenly realised Candy was talking about intimate alien encounters. But that wasn't the important part of what she'd said. 'You're going back to Earth?'

'Yes,' said Candy, 'only a *few* more hours on Hideaway, then back into the *real* universe.'

Her emerald eyes were gazing across the room, scanning the entire casino, but Kiru's attention was focused on Candy.

'Another drink?' said Kiru, and she slid her hand inside the purse to pull out some gaming chips. 'What is it you do, Candy? If you keep visiting Hideaway, what line are you in?'

'*Information* and *communication*,' said Candy. 'News *and* views. I'm *chief* executive and *lead* reporter of Sol Galactic Network, Earth's biggest comservice, which you've *certainly* heard of.'

'I certainly have,' agreed Kiru, although she certainly hadn't. But she had to find out everything she could about Candy and her job. 'I see why you do so much travelling. It must be *very* interesting work. What's the latest big news in the galaxy?'

'It's only *big* if you're from Earth.'

'That's me, Candy. I take a personal interest in the old home planet.'

'And I take a totally *personal* interest in this story. I've been *following* it for years, following *him* across the universe for *years*.'

'Who?'

'William *Ewart*,' said Candy, and she almost spat out the name.

CHAPTER

FIVE

'William Ewart?' said Wayne Norton, and he shook his head.

'No reason you should have heard of him,' said Jay. 'It all happened near the end of your three hundred year kip.'

'What happened? Who was he?'

Jay scratched his stubbled jaw. 'Hard to know where to begin. William Ewart was my brother, my half-brother. We had the same father, we grew up together. We were good chums in those days. I loved cooking, he loved eating.' He smiled at the memory. 'We used to talk about leaving Earth, going out into space.' He sipped at his drink. 'Soon as I made some money, I headed off to see the universe. Started as a paying passenger, became a spacer, ended up on this old kite.' He looked around the cabin and shook his head. 'The ship was in orbit around Earth, waiting for the new owner to arrive on board. Turned out it was William Ewart. If I'd known, I'd have jumped ship when I had the chance. Everything would have been different.'

'Does this have anything to do with Janesmith and Grawl?' asked Norton.

'Only peripherally. They were there, but like me they were only minor players, not part of the main drama. Grawl was one of Ewart's bodyguards. Princess Janesmith was doing something similar, she was chaperoning her sister, Princess Marysmith, who was Ewart's latest wife. We left Earth, popped in at Hideaway, I know that much. Janesmith was on board when we reached Hideaway, but she was gone when we left. Not that it mattered at the time, because by then we had other things to worry about.'

'Like what?'

'Like: where were we and who was controlling the ship?' Jay poured himself another drink. 'If you're the steward, you never know anything, so I was almost used to it. What I wasn't used to was losing such a huge slice of my memory.' He looked at his glass. 'Losing it for no apparent reason.' After studying the cabin for a few seconds, Jay said, 'It was in this state-room. There was me and Ewart and . . .'

CHAPTER

SIX

'. . . You and me, Zena, Grawl and your wife.'

'She's not my wife!' said William Ewart.

'You married her,' said Rajic Jao Rajic, as his brother was now calling himself.

'That's a technicality. You think I'd marry an alien?'

The wedding had been by proxy, arranged purely for commercial convenience. Ewart and the Algolan weren't really married. Which was just as well. Because she was only four years old.

He'd been told that Marysmith was nineteen, and in Algolan years she was. According to the wedding contract, they should never have met; instead, she was on board the *Demon Star* with him. What was she doing here? That was something else he could remember nothing about.

'She's a lot less alien than some of your other wives,' said Rajic.

Ewart ignored him. 'Only the five of us on board?' he said. 'What about the captain and crew?' As owner, naturally he had nothing to do with the crew of the *Demon Star*, but he wondered if he'd ever dined with the ship's master. One of the worst things about his memory loss was that he couldn't remember eating any of the sumptuous meals which had been specially prepared for the voyage.

'There's no captain,' said Rajic. 'As for the crew – here I am.'

If Ewart had to name the one person he most detested and loathed and hated, it would have been his brother. What was he doing here? Rajic claimed he was a member of the crew, that it was just luck he was on the ship when Ewart had bought the *Demon Star*. Ewart didn't believe him. He never had, so why should he begin now?

'Luck?' he'd said to Rajic.

'Bad luck,' Rajic had said to Ewart.

William Ewart gazed at the infinity of stars on the viewscreen. It was an amazing sight. Out in space. A voyage across the galaxy on his own spacecraft. It was what he'd always wanted.

He was in his stateroom on board the *Demon Star*, the ship in which he'd escaped all those completely ludicrous, totally bogus, absolutely trumped-up charges of tax evasion and avoiding alimony payments to his four ex-wives. Leaving Earth far behind, he had headed for the stars. And then, then . . .

He couldn't remember. Not a thing.

'What's going on, Zena?'

'I do not know, sir,' said the bodyguard. 'The gap in my memory is still there.'

Rajic also claimed to be unable to remember, but whatever he said was always unreliable. Grawl could say nothing, because he had no voice. He was Ewart's other bodyguard. (A man in Ewart's position needed all the protection he could afford.) Zena and Grawl appeared to be the exact opposite. She was tall and lean, very attractive. He was small and wide, very ugly. And Ewart owned them both.

He hadn't bothered asking Marysmith if her memory had also been affected, partly because the memories of an alien infant must have been very insignificant, and partly because what he wanted was as little to do with his alien bride as possible. Ewart had assigned Grawl to take care of her. It was very strange to see them together. Marysmith seemed the same as any other blonde, blue-skinned four-year-old, and she obviously liked having someone her own size to play with, but Grawl also appeared to be enjoying himself. He was violent and ruthless, and had never shown a trace of expression until meeting the Algolan girl. When Ewart saw him *smile* for the first time, it had made him shiver.

'But I have been able to access the ship's memory files, sir,' added Zena, 'and they have either been deleted or are encrypted in unauthorised code.'

If she, too, couldn't remember anything about the voyage, it meant Ewart wasn't going prematurely senile. At sixty-five, he was still in his prime. That was one thing to be grateful for, and about the only thing. If the ship's data had been corrupted, it proved his memory loss was due to external influence.

He was in the owner's suite of his own spaceship, but he'd no idea where the *Demon Star* had been, or where it was heading – or even where it was now.

'Pour me a drink, old bean,' said Rajic, as he sat down.

'That's your job, you're the steward. So you say.'

'You invite me to your quarters, and you don't offer me a noggin?'

Ewart sighed. 'Give him a drink to shut him up, Zena.'

Before she could move, the door sounded. Ewart and Rajic and Zena gazed up at the comscreen. It showed the corridor outside, but no one was there. And no one could have been there, because only five of them were on board. Three in the stateroom, Grawl and Marysmith along the corridor.

Zena reached for her infinite repeater. She walked slowly towards the door. Opened it.

'Mr William Ewart?' said the man who stepped inside.

'Er . . . right,' said Ewart.

'Delighted to meet you.'

Ewart found himself shaking hands with the smiling stranger.

'I'm sorry I haven't been able to make your acquaintance until now,' the man continued. 'Allow me to introduce myself. My name is *******.'

'What?'

'*******.'

Which was what Ewart thought he'd said.

He was of average height, average build, with no distinguishing facial characteristics; he was so ordinary that he seemed almost like a composite human. What was he doing here?

'Please let me apologise for not explaining everything earlier,' said *******. 'My only excuse is that I've been so very busy. I realise this must be quite unnerving for each of you.' His deferential smile took in Ewart, Rajic and Zena.

'It was you,' said Ewart, as he realised. 'You've done all this.'

'You're correct, of course,' said *******, nodding

his average head, 'and I sincerely hope you'll forgive me.'

Ewart said nothing for a moment. He wasn't used to such a naked display of total politeness.

'Would you like a drink?' he asked.

'That's very generous of you, although I feel I've already imposed myself far too much on your hospitality.'

'Not at all.'

Ewart only realised what he'd said when Rajic muttered, 'Flaming Nora!'

'What would you like, Mr *******?' asked Zena.

'Whatever there is. I don't wish to put you to any trouble.'

'It is no trouble,' said Zena, fluttering her eyelashes.

'Are you going to let him get away with this?' said Rajic. 'What game are you playing at?'

'It's no game, Mr Rajic, but I'm extremely sorry if I've inadvertently offended you in any way. Please don't take umbrage.'

'*Umbrage!* How can I take umbrage? I don't know what it means!'

'It means "offence",' said Zena.

'Offence?' said Rajic. 'This ruddy twerp commandeers our ship, takes us who-knows-where. Why should we be offended?'

'Our ship?' said Ewart. 'My ship, you mean.'

'I hate to give even the slightest offence,' said *******, turning to Rajic and smiling. 'To anyone. It creates such a bad atmosphere and is completely unnecessary.'

'Ha!' said Rajic.

'I agree entirely,' said Ewart.

'Double ha!' said Rajic. He held out his hand for

the glass Zena had poured. She ignored him and gave it to *******.

'Thank you,' he said, and he sipped his drink. 'That's absolutely delicious and so, if you don't mind me saying so, are you.'

Zena had crippled the last person who'd made a similar remark. But instead of breaking *******'s legs, she modestly lowered her head, blushing shyly at the compliment.

'I owe you an explanation, Mr Ewart,' said *******, 'as well as my personal thanks and eternal gratitude for your cooperation.'

'Cooperation!' said Rajic.

'I'm sure you have a very good reason for what you've done,' said a voice, and it took a moment for Ewart to realise it was his own.

'You're too kind, Mr Ewart.'

'My friends call me "Bill".'

'You haven't got any friends,' said Rajic. 'You've never had any friends.' He glanced over at Zena. 'Am I getting a snorter?'

'No.'

'Then I'll get myself one.' Rajic started walking towards the cabinet which held the ranks of bottles. Zena looked at him. He stopped, backed away and sat down again.

'I suppose you're wondering why I brought you here,' said *******.

'Right.' Ewart glanced towards the huge viewscreen, wondering where exactly 'here' might be.

'I realise I should have asked your permission, Bill, but necessity took priority over courtesy.'

'Get on with it,' said Rajic.

'I'm hunting space pirates,' said *******.

'Space pirates?' said Ewart. 'They really exist?'

'They do, alas.'

'Isn't it – er – dangerous to hunt them?'

'That's very astute of you, Bill. You're absolutely correct, of course. It is dangerous, very dangerous, and I regret that I've had to place you, your ship, and everyone on board in such a precarious situation. If there were any alternative, please believe me, I'd have chosen it.'

'Humbug,' said Rajic.

'What bug?' said Ewart.

'Humbug, sir,' said Zena. 'A hard boiled sweet or candy, often with a striped pattern and usually flavoured with peppermint.'

'Really?' Ewart licked his lips.

'May I proceed?' said *******. 'If, sadly, events do not go to plan, I can sincerely say no one will regret your unnecessary deaths more than myself.'

'I'll regret my death a lot more sincerely than you,' said Rajic. He stared at *******. 'Unless you're the only one left to do the regretting. Is that what you mean? We're all going to die except you?'

'The greatest misfortune of life, Mr Rajic, is that it's terminal. We're all going to die sooner or later. I'd prefer to survive this mission, and I'd prefer everyone on board to survive. If necessary, I will die. If necessary, I'm afraid you will all die.'

'I don't plan to die,' said Ewart. 'Ever.' He gazed at the screen again. Somewhere out there, out in the endless depths of infinite space, he hoped to find his own eternity.

Suddenly, the image on the viewscreen changed. Instead of a starscape, sparkling with bright points of stellar light and the glow of distant galaxies, the screen was focused on a single planet.

Until now, Ewart had thought the screen only showed a simulation of the universe. This, however, was real: a dark, lifeless world encircled by a halo of derelict spacecraft.

'The pirates' secret base,' said *******.

Until now, Ewart had thought ******* was as plausible as Rajic.

'If it's secret,' said Rajic, 'how did you find it?'

'That's my job.'

'But it's not my job. What am I doing here?'

'You're here, Mr Rajic, because I need you. I also need Mr Ewart and Princess Marysmith.'

As well as being four years old, an alien, with blue skin, Ewart's latest bride was the daughter of the Empress of Algol.

Ewart looked at Rajic. Rajic looked at Ewart. Then they looked at *******.

'Why?' they both asked.

'Because—' said *******. Something caught his eye, and he glanced towards the viewscreen. There was a flare of light as one of the ships encircling the planet ignited its engines. 'You must excuse me.' He turned and walked towards the door. 'We're about to come under pirate attack.' He left the stateroom.

Rajic looked at Ewart. Ewart looked at Rajic. Then they looked at the screen, at the craft which was accelerating out of orbit and heading directly towards them.

'Space pirates?' said Ewart.

As a child, he'd dreamed of flying between the stars and setting foot on alien worlds; he'd imagined discovering an unknown planet and naming it after himself.

He and Rajic had grown up together, shared the same dream together, but Rajic was the one who'd achieved their childhood ambition of escaping Earth and globe-skipping across the spaceways.

That was only one of many reasons to hate him.

'Space pirates,' agreed Rajic.

Zena was staring at the warship. As it came closer, she drew her infinite repeater and aimed it at the screen. She became aware of being watched, glanced back at Ewart, shrugged, then lowered the gun.

'We are dead, sir,' she said. 'The pirates have a weapon which will kill everyone on board but leave the *Demon Star* undamaged. That is how they operate. They only want the ship.'

'When did you become such an expert?'

'Grawl and I watched a very entertaining drama about space pirates, sir. You can learn a lot from SeeV.'

Ewart doubted it. Ewart Communications Corporation had produced countless, and endless, SeeV programmes. Their educational function had never been a priority.

'When did you and Grawl find screen time together?'

'I . . . I do . . . I do not know, sir.'

Ewart stared at Zena. It was the first time he'd ever heard her hesitate. He guessed the reason immediately.

'Why are you lying, Zena?'

'I do not lie, sir. Not to you, sir.'

Rajic laughed. 'She's been with you so long, she doesn't know the difference between the truth and a lie.'

Perhaps she wasn't lying, she still retained a memory trace of the time erased from their minds.

'If we're going to die,' said Rajic, as he stood up, 'I'd better go prepare a last meal.'

'For me?' said Ewart.

'Not on your nelly. You're too fat already.'

'I'm not fat!'

'From now on, you're on a diet.' Rajic glanced at the screen. 'The ultimate diet.'

'So are you.'

'At least I'll die happy, doing what I like most: cooking. As for you, what do you like most?'

They both knew the answer and Ewart tried to think of nothing, of everything, of anything except food. He failed.

'I'm going to rustle up a meal for someone who really appreciates my cooking.' The door opened. 'Princess Marysmith.' The door started to close. 'Toodle-oo.' Then Rajic was gone.

CHAPTER
SEVEN

'It's like seeing the whole cosmos in a single room,' said Kiru, as she gazed around the casino on Hideaway, watching the alien elite squander their wealth.

'It was *always* my ambition to see the universe,' said Candy, as she twisted the stem of her glass on the bar, 'to travel to other planets, meet the people, interview them, help bring *understanding* and *peace* to the galaxy. And I've *done* it.'

'That must be very rewarding.'

'I deserve *every* rupan.'

'That's not what—'

'I work hard,' Candy interrupted, '*and* I play hard. I only wish I had more *time* so I could visit more worlds. But the universe is *infinite*, the number of alien races is *infinite*, and no amount of time would ever be enough.' She sipped at her drink. 'Most alien species are on such a different *level* of existence, so far away from what humans can *recognise* as sentient creatures, that we have more in common with terrestrial *invertebrate* gastropod *molluscs* than with the evolutionary pinnacles reached on most worlds.'

'What molluscs?' asked Kiru.

'*Terrestrial* invertebrate *gastropod* molluscs,' said Candy. 'More often known as *slugs*. Which reminds me: William *Ewart*.' She grimaced. 'He *destroyed* my career.'

'What career was that?'

'News *presenter* and investigative *reporter*.'

'I thought that's what you did now, Candy.'

'It is, but no *thanks* to William "Fat Man" Ewart.'

Kiru nodded as if she understood – and as if she cared. 'What's made you such a success in your profession?'

'I am always totally *truthful*, because if I'm not completely *honest*, how can I expect to find the truth on any assignment? And I'm totally *interested* in other people. I was first *interested* in people on Earth, of course, then I became *interested* in people all over the galaxy. I'm a very good *listener*, which is essential. Everyone in the universe has a *story*, and I have to persuade them they are the most totally important person *in* the universe. Whenever I'm with *someone*, I let them do all the talking, keeping myself almost *silent* and self-*effacing* except for subtle questioning. I *learned* this when I worked for Ewart Communications Corporation.'

'Ewart?' said Kiru, in what she thought was a subtle questioning tone.

'Myself and my *friend* Mandy, we were media students,' said Candy. 'William Ewart *arranged* our first job, our new names, and our first new bodywork.' She looked Kiru up and down, as if wondering what work had been done on her, but she didn't ask. 'I owe him my *career*, and we were both *more* than grateful, but that didn't give him the right to try to totally *ruin* me.'

'It's because of William Ewart you're going back to Earth?' This was what Kiru really wanted to find out.

'He *vanished* from Earth years and years ago.' Candy paused and sipped at her drink. 'Years ago, I *mean*. I was very *young* at the time. The *Candy* and Mandy Doubletime News Show soon became Ewart Communication Corporation's *top* rated programme, but then we were offered a *much* better deal by Hiroshi Larnvik who *owned* Sol Global News. Ewart didn't like *that*, not at all. He tried to *buy* out SGN so he could have my show back again.'

While she listened, Kiru noticed a broken thread hanging from the top of her dress. She gently tugged at it, hoping to pull it free, but the thread quickly unravelled. In a moment, she had almost a metre of it gathered in her hand – and the top of her dress hung fractionally lower. Kiru tried to snap the fine thread with her fingers, but it wouldn't break, and it probably wasn't a good idea to take out the knife to slice through the line. In any case, she realised the thread wouldn't be easy to cut. If the fabric was as strong as it seemed, the dress might have been really ancient. But there was a basic design fault, because the whole thing would completely unravel if she kept pulling on the loose end. She tucked the long thread down her cleavage.

'Your show?' she said. 'What about Mandy?'

'I was the *star*, I was everyone's favourite. When Ewart *failed* to win me back, he became angry and irrational. If ECC couldn't have me, then *no* one else could. He committed commercial suicide by *wrecking* his own comservice, and the disintegration of Ewart Communications also dragged down and totally *destroyed* Sol Global.'

'But you're here now,' said Kiru.

'I am,' agreed Candy, 'but only because of my *unique* personality and *extraordinary* talent.'

And modest self-effacement, thought Kiru. But Candy was right. The only way to achieve anything, Kiru had discovered, was to set a target and pursue it with single-minded determination. Candy had decided what she wanted, had set out to get it, and she'd succeeded. For as long as she could remember, Kiru had let external events control her life. Now she had a goal of her own, to reach Earth and find Wayne, and she would do everything in her power to achieve that ambition. Nothing, absolutely nothing, was going to stop her.

'Sol Global was destroyed?' said Kiru. 'I thought you said you were working for them.'

'Sol Global News was *annihilated*,' said Candy, 'but out of the *ashes* arose Sol Galactic Network. And I don't *work* for them. I *am* them!'

'How did that happen?'

'I *married* the owner, Hiroshi Larnvik. Business was *tough* at first, when there was only myself and him.'

'What about Mandy?'

'Why keep *asking* about Mandy?'

Candy didn't seem to want an answer, so there was no need for Kiru to invent one. Wayne had mentioned someone called Mandy. When he'd been revived from his cryonic sleep, she had interviewed him for an info-slot.

'You want something *in* that?' said Candy.

Kiru realised she had the empty cigarette holder to

her lips. She took it out and shook her head. 'You're going back to Earth in a few hours?' she said.

'It's still *home*, and I like to return now and then. I'm also chasing a *lead* on William Ewart. There's a rumour that he's *back*, trying to start up a new com-service. There have been so *many* stories over the years, that he was *dead* or that he'd been sighted on some *distant* planet or other, but there's something about *this* story that rings true. He's probably become someone *else*, it's easy enough to do, but I'll recognise him no matter how *extreme* his bodymod.'

'It's easy to become someone else?'

'Totally *easy*,' said Candy. 'I've had *numerous* ident-ities, I need to for *security* reasons. It doesn't *have* to be anything extreme. To *most* of the galaxy, one human looks the *same* as any other. A change of *name* is often enough of a disguise. And because there's no *secure* method of bodycoding, anyone can *be* whoever they want.'

Kiru nodded her head, wondering what else she needed to know. Candy wasn't looking at her, which was nothing new. She was staring into the distance, as if beyond the casino, beyond Hideaway.

'What I *really* want to find out,' she said, 'is how he vanished.'

'Ewart?' said Kiru. 'When he left Earth, you mean?'

'No.' Candy shook her head. 'Ewart had been *arrested* and was in court. I was the one who'd *served* the summons, which was a totally unique *live* news story. Then Ewart *escaped*. His bodyguards *broke* him out of court. The others got away, but Ewart was soon arrested again and *locked* up. He was in a zerozone *cell*, totally secure. Then he –' Candy snapped her fingers – '*vanished*, literally *vanished* into thin air. It was all recorded, and I've *studied* the datafile over and over again. One moment he's in the cell, the *next* he's gone.' She snapped her fingers again. '*Vanished*.'

'Totally secure?' said Kiru, as she considered the concept.

'Totally, but Ewart got *away*,' Candy continued. 'He had a ship waiting in orbit, and he escaped *Earth* and escaped *justice*.' She finished her drink. 'But I've always *known* I'll meet him again.'

'Another?' asked Kiru, gesturing to Candy's empty glass.

'We *shouldn't* be doing this,' said Candy, as she shook her head.

'Doing what?'

'Buying *drinks* for each other. This *wouldn't* happen on Earth, would it? It's our *right* as totally fabulous females to have everything paid for by someone *else*. Would you *like* to eat?'

'Yes,' said Kiru, who hadn't had a proper meal since leaving Caphmiaultrelvossmuaf. What Terry had offered her could hardly be classified as food, although to be polite she'd nibbled at the least inedible morsels.

'Let's find ourself a couple of *dates*,' said Candy, as she surveyed the people in the casino more intently than before. 'It's amazing to think that Hideaway existed when our *ancestors* were living in *trees*, and it will probably still exist when the human race is *extinct* or has evolved totally *beyond* all comprehension.'

'Yes,' said Kiru, who would herself become extinct unless she ate; and her own contribution to the future of human evolution also needed sustenance.

'There are stars, planets, alien species which developed *aeons* ago, long before Earth was even created. Some of those races have survived and continued to *evolve*, going on beyond the primitive life-cycle of birth and death, on into *realms* of pure thought. They have *surrendered* all bodily needs, because they no longer have bodies. They are as far above us as we are above terrestrial *invertebrate* gastropod *molluscs*.'

'Speak for yourself,' said Kiru.

Candy smiled. 'They are totally spiritual, without any of the atavistic *desires* or *cravings* of the flesh.' She paused before adding, '*Imagine* how boring and dull it must be! No sex, no food, that's *not* what I call living!'

Without a physical body, thought Kiru, could it even be called life?

'It's ironic,' continued Candy, 'that the two things which are *vital* to the survival of the species – sex (to create life) and food (to sustain life) – *started* as essential but have *become* luxuries.'

'I wouldn't call food a luxury,' said Kiru. 'While we've still got bodies, we need to eat.'

'But there's a vast difference between *needing* to eat and the divine, sublime, sensual *delight* of an exquisite meal. When I was young – *immature*, I mean – I used to think that food was fuel for the body. Eating, like breathing, was *simply* something which had to be done. It was William Ewart who taught me how to *appreciate* eating and also how to *enjoy* fine wines and liqueurs. He totally *spoiled* me, which is *another* reason to hate him, because now I can't *bear* to eat dull food. Ewart initiated the *education* of my palate, and I've continued to learn. Wherever I go in the universe, I like to *meet* other races, *talk* with them, *eat* their food, and then . . .'

Kiru finished the last mouthful of her own drink. 'And then?' she prompted, although she already knew what was coming.

'Then do *sex* with them,' said Candy. She smiled, and continued to survey the casino, then she gasped, her eyes focused on the entrance. 'I *don't* believe it. Look *who's* arrived! An *Ipralan*!'

Kiru kept looking at Candy, making it clear she wasn't at all interested in the alien arrival, and Candy kept on talking.

'Some people are *very* old-fashioned, and they'll only do sex with one person of the *opposite* gender, human or alien. Not *me*, of course. The Ipralan is *male*, by the way. I've checked the *references* with great interest.'

Kiru was even more old-fashioned. She'd only do it with someone of the opposite gender, from the same planet – and preferably of the same species. Even so, she finally looked at the Ipralan.

He was multi-limbed, very tall, his segmented body shape resembling an insect. His head, however, was more like that of a sheep – perhaps because of the tufted wool which covered his face and the curled horns on either side of his head. He was wearing a black suit made of feathers, his many-fingered hands, and also his many-toed feet, all covered by many pairs of white gloves. And Candy fancied him . . . ?

'The one with four arms and four legs?' said Kiru.

'Isn't he *gorgeous*?'

That wasn't the word Kiru would have chosen.

Candy continued, 'He has *double* the usual number of arms and legs of most species, and that isn't the only thing he has *double* the usual number of.'

'What's it got to do with me?'

That was when Candy turned her gaze away from the Ipralan and towards Kiru. She ran the tip of her tongue over her green lips, then raised both green eyebrows questioningly.

And Kiru suddenly realised what she was suggesting.

'No!' She shook her head. 'Never!' She kept on shaking her head.

'This is a *unique* opportunity. I've been *dreaming* of this for ages. Ipralans are reputed to be *insatiable*. On their own world, there are *two* females to every male – and that's the *ratio* in which they mate. I've *lusted* after an Ipralan male for so long, but they will only do sex with *two* partners. Now there's two of *us*, two human females!'

'There's one,' said Kiru, as she slid from her seat. 'You.'

'This could be the sensuous *experience* of your lifetime,' said Candy. 'Ipralans are *legendary* lovers. You'll *always* regret throwing away the chance.'

'I'm not going to have *sex* with *anyone*,' said Kiru, 'except my husband. I'm a married woman.'

'So *am* I. But I'm a *free* woman, not a sex slave. Where's *your* husband now?'

'He's . . .' Kiru shook her head.

'You don't *know* where he is. But wherever he is, he's either *doing* sex or he's *done* it or he's going to *do* it – and not with you. It's all that human males *ever* think about.'

'I'm going,' said Kiru, and she turned and began walking away.

'Where *to*?' asked Candy.

Earth. That was where Kiru was going, where she had to go. But she couldn't get there by walking. She paused and glanced over at the Ipralan.

Sexual attraction was no more than a chemical response in the body, Kiru knew. Close up, it was a reaction to another person's pheremones. That was what had happened between her and Wayne Norton. But what had started with primitive lust had become a more complex and higher emotion: love.

Candy couldn't have been attracted by the alien's pheremones, because humans and Ipralans had evolved on different worlds, under radically different conditions. They had no biochemical connection – although Candy obviously hoped to make a physical connection.

If it was sexual gratification that she was after, she could easily have found it on Hideaway. Candy had mentioned how boring it would be not to have a body, because without bodies there could be no sex. Hideaway, however, offered its guests the ultimate in simsex: unlimited by the restrictions of the flesh, the mental pleasures enjoyed purely within the brain were almost infinite – and the ecstasy was absolute.

But Candy was on a different mission. She didn't want safe, cerebral sex. It was too easy to turn on an instant, touch-of-a-button mindfix. In the pursuit of new physical sensations, new thrills, new dangers, Candy had become addicted to strange sex, deviant sex, alien sex. And it didn't seem to have done her any harm.

Kiru watched as the Ipralan walked around the hyperchance table on his double quota of legs, scattering gaming chips with his double quota of arms, and she wondered about his other double quota under his black feathered clothing – *somewhere* under his black feathered clothing . . .

The most evident feature of any alien was that they looked different. And the parts of them which couldn't be seen were usually the most different of all: in size, shape and also location.

When Kiru had first entered the casino, she'd been approached by an alien claiming to be Lord Ozen of Seltar; but according to Candy, the Seltan had been Lady Ozen. Not that alien versions of male and female necessarily corresponded with the human ones. As far as Kiru was concerned, an alien was always an alien. Female or male, it didn't matter because it had no relevance to her.

The majority of advanced races had two sexes, because under most circumstances that was the ideal number for reproduction and the continuation of the species. As translated into Terran by a simultaneous linguistic and tonal equaliser, the two sexes were normally called 'female' and 'male'. The 'female' usually gave birth, but sometimes it was the 'male' who adopted that role. The methods of conception, gestation and birth were as numerous as there were alien species. Some reproductive processes were so complex and bizarre and extreme, it was amazing that the race had ever survived a single generation, let alone evolved into a space-faring people.

The universe was infinite and everything was possible – with only, it seemed, one exception. There could be no inter-racial breeding, no new alien created by the fusion of conflicting chromosomes, no natural birth from unnatural selection, no hybrid child with parents from two different solar systems, different planets, different species, different genetic lifeprints. This had been proved by countless experiments, most of which had been conducted by enthusiastic volunteers – although seldom under strict scientific conditions.

The sexual act – and in Kiru's limited experience (limited to humans), she'd realised that much of it was an 'act', that lovers often put on a 'performance', and that women in particular were always very good at 'faking' – even the sexual act itself, who did what to whom, and with what, varied with every variety of alien. And the range of biological equipment with which it was done was extensive, sometimes almost impossibly so.

But amongst so many species, there was a certain amount of compatibility – a projection from one species might fit within the orifice of another species, for example, perhaps because the physical attribute of either or both of the participants was very flexible.

Kiru clenched her teeth, her fists, and everything else she could clench. She thought of Wayne, who was on Earth, she thought of the baby, who was inside her, here on Hideaway, then she went and sat down next to Candy again.

'*Good*,' said Candy. 'Let's *analyse* our tactics. First, we *introduce* ourselves, because he *may* already be as interested in Terran women as we are in him, then we *offer* him a drink, *flatter* him with compliments and *invite* him for a meal.'

'We wine and dine *him*?' said Kiru.

'We *must*, because on Ipral the female *pair* has to pursue the male. There's totally intense *competition* for his attention, and it's the supreme *honour* to be selected as his wives.'

'Wives? We have to get *married* to him?'

'No, no, no, no no, *no*.'

'Good. Because I have to be in *love* to get married.'

Candy looked at her, perhaps wondering if Kiru was deliberately talking like her. Kiru wondered the same.

'No *jokes*,' said Candy. 'Ipralans are very *serious* people, so no references to his *four* arms and *fore*play.' Candy smiled at her own attempt at humour.

Kiru wasn't in a joking mood. She felt very queasy.

'It makes me feel ill thinking about it,' she admitted.

'Don't *think*. Doing sex has *nothing* to do with thinking. It's the *body* talking. Matter *over* mind.' Candy looked at her, a long, deep look. '*Ah!* I *see!* This your *first* time with an alien. You're a *virgin!* How I *envy* you! Your first alien *encounter* and it's with an Ipralan!' She sighed. 'Let's go do *dialogue* with him.'

Kiru reached into her purse, stroking the firm handle of the knife for a moment, then gently caressing the reassuringly sharp tip of the blade.

'I need a drink and a cigarette first,' she said.

'First, a *drink*,' said Candy, 'then a cigarette *after*.'

CHAPTER
EIGHT

The door to William Ewart's stateroom closed, and Rajic was gone. If Zena was right, if they were all about to be killed, at least Ewart would never have to see his brother again. Every Magellanic Cloud had a silver lining.

'This may not be the right time, sir,' said Zena, 'but if I do not ask now it will be too late. Before we die—'

'Zena, we're not going to *die*!' Ewart looked at the screen, at the menacing ship powering its way towards them. 'I won't allow it.'

'If you say so, sir, but I still have a request.'

'What is it?'

'I would like your permission to get married.'

Ewart looked from the screen to his bodyguard.

'Married? That's crazy. Why do you want to marry me?'

'I do not, sir. I want to marry Grawl.'

'Grawl? You mean . . . Grawl?'

'Yes, sir.'

'You can't marry Grawl.'

'Why not? Because you want to marry me, sir?'

'No!'

'Then why not?'

'Because you can't.'

'That is not a reason, sir.'

'I don't have to give you a reason, Zena. You can't get married, right?'

'Why not?'

'Because you're an android!'

'I know that, sir. But why can I not get married?'

As Ewart tried to think of an answer, he remembered the salesman saying, 'A zygotically engineered neoplasmic android will maintain the same youthful appearance until you trade it in.'

Zena was always 'she', never 'it'. At first Ewart had envied the way she'd never grow old, but that was as pointless as being jealous of a building just because stonecrete and glasteel lasted longer than flesh and bone. Machines didn't age, they became obsolete.

He hadn't bought Zena because of her looks, of course, although she had been constructed to his own precise physical specifications. She was a machine and, if he was ever in danger, she would sacrifice herself without a moment's thought. The same was probably true of Grawl, if only because he probably never thought.

Because Grawl was human he couldn't be on duty twenty-four hours a day, and so Ewart had needed another bodyguard. Zena, however, could have been on duty all the time. Out of his natural generosity, Ewart had retained Grawl's services. The psychopathic dwarf had hated Zena at first. And now they planned to get married. Ewart had hated all his wives, but not until he'd married them.

'Does Grawl know you're an android?'

'Yes, sir. Because he is dumb does not mean he is stupid.'

'Humans don't marry androids.'

'Why not? You married an alien, sir.'

'That's different. And I didn't.'

Zena raised an eyebrow.

'Right, right. Tell me one thing, Zena. Why do you want to get married?'

'Because we are in love, sir.'

'Love?' How could she be in love? Ewart managed not to ask. 'That's no reason to get married. Marriage isn't a good idea, believe me. Look what happened to my marriages. They all ended in disaster, and perfectly good friendships were ruined.'

'This is different, sir. It is not you who is getting married. There will be no time to ruin our friendship.' Zena gestured towards the viewscreen. 'We already know it will end in disaster. And very soon, sir.'

Ewart tried to ignore his approaching doom by focusing on the only distraction there was.

'Grawl is very ugly.'

'Beauty is only skin deep, sir.'

'When did you decide to marry?'

'It was . . .' Zena frowned. 'I do not remember, sir. It must have happened during the time which is missing from my memory.'

'Do you remember Grawl's proposal? Did he go down on bended knee and ask to marry you?'

'You know he could not ask, sir. But when you are in love, words are not necessary. Love is more than words.'

Perhaps, but they could often help. Grawl had refused Ewart's offers of a voice implant. He must have preferred being the strong, silent type.

'But why marriage?' asked Ewart.

'Then Grawl will be mine, sir, all mine.'

Who else would want him? But Ewart said: 'Have you slept together?'

'I do not sleep, sir, you know that. Or do you mean "slept together" as a euphemism for sexual intercourse?'

'Right. Have you had sex with Grawl?'

'That is no concern of yours, sir. I am entitled to my private life.'

'Private life! Zena, you're an *android*. I *own* you! You *don't* have a private life.'

'I may be an android, sir, but genetically I am human. If you prick me, do I not bleed?'

'No,' said Ewart, 'you don't. You're not human, Zena, and you're not female.'

'Is that why you have never slept with me, sir?'

'I always sleep with you.'

'I am speaking euphemistically.'

Ewart was at his most vulnerable when he was sleeping, which was why he needed a bodyguard. Perhaps it had been a mistake choosing one as attractive as Zena. But what was the alternative? Grawl . . . ?

Even though she was designed for total physical compatibility, he had never had sex with Zena. How could he ever do it with a bioelecrondroid? He was no pervert. In any case, sex was a very over-rated pastime. The phrase 'sexual appetite' had always seemed inappropriate, because satisfaction could easily be reached in a minute or two, whereas a good meal would take well over an hour, a banquet even longer.

'When you should have been guarding me,' he said, 'have you been slipping away to have sex with Grawl?'

'No, sir!' Zena paused. 'I do not remember.'

'So it can't have been that ecstatic. The earth didn't move?'

'Earth has not moved, sir, we have moved away from Earth.'

'Right. You're saving yourself for your wedding night?'

'There will not be time for that.' Zena was watching the screen again. 'I will die a virgin, sir, but I would like to die a bride.'

'Who's going to perform the ceremony?'

'Ship's captains can officiate at weddings, sir.'

'That's from the old days, when they had ships that went on the sea. What were they called?'

'Seaships, sir.'

'The *Demon Star* doesn't have a captain.'

'Perhaps not as a separate entity, but the ship and its captain may be one and the same. If there is no crew on board, sir, it must be because they are not needed. The ship is a symbiotic organism, capable of many functions, its own master as well as astronavigator.'

'And licensed to perform marriages?'

'It is too late now, sir,' said Zena.

She was staring at the predatory shape which almost filled the viewscreen. Ominous orange lights lanced from the prow of the corsair. It was firing at them.

Ewart's heart suddenly stopped. Was this the pirate weapon in action, the one Kiru claimed would kill everyone on board but leave the vessel intact? And what about her? Did the buccaneer's beam destroy androids? Then his heart began beating again, very very fast. But he wasn't breathing. He would suffocate to death. Then he coughed, breathed again, and wondered if it would be his last breath.

'All I ask is your blessing,' said Zena, 'that you would have given permission for me to marry Grawl.'

Watching the fatal beams from the attacking ship slice through the cold vacuum of space towards the *Demon Star*, Ewart managed to nod.

'Does that mean "yes", sir?'

'Right,' he whispered, as he waited for his whole life to flash before his eyes, 'it means "yes".'

'Thank you, sir. Goodbye, sir.'

There was a flare of white, a silent explosion of absolute brilliance. The *Demon Star* shook from stem to stern as the ship was engulfed by total light.

CHAPTER
NINE

'The *Demon Star* wasn't destroyed,' said Wayne Norton.

'No.'

'Because it's here. Now. We're in it.'

'Yes.'

'And you weren't all killed.'

'No. Not then.'

'Not then? What do you mean? Some of the others were killed later?'

'Others? What about me?'

'You weren't killed.'

'How do you know?'

'Because you're here. Either that or I'm talking to myself.'

'How do you know you're not?'

'I don't. I don't know anything. So what about the *Demon Star*? It was being attacked by death rays. What happened?'

'Lots. Let's have another drink first.'

'Not for me.'

'No,' said Jay. 'For me.'

'Your name used to be Rajic Jao Rajic?'

'Yes.'

'What do I call you?'

'Call me anything you like, Wayne, just don't call me late for tiffin.'

Norton didn't bother asking what that was. He put a hand over each of the two glasses in front of him. One was empty, so he up-ended it.

'Call me Jay,' said Jay, as he poured himself a drink. 'But with just us on board, we shouldn't get too confused about who we're talking with.'

This was all Norton had to look forward to during the voyage: Jay, his conversation, and his endless flow of alien alcohol.

Once, the stateroom had been fully equipped with full-specification SeeV equipment. Now, there was nothing. Nothing to do to pass the time, and on ship that was what was needed most. Norton wished one of Café World's tourist attractions was on board, even the most mindless; in fact, preferably the most mindless. He didn't plan to spend the whole voyage drinking, although that seemed to be Jay's intention. Jay had drunk his way around the galaxy, and been drunk all over the galaxy. Norton wasn't going to end up an old wino like him. And the way to stop was never to start.

'You brought these bottles on board with you?' asked Norton.

'That's right. Twenty years ago, plus or minus two, Terran time.'

'Twenty years? I thought you'd brought them for this voyage.'

'What, as hand baggage? Bottles are *heavy*, Wayne. Full ones, anyway, and what's the point of empty ones?

Some of them are minor masterpieces, I admit. Maybe I should have started collecting them years ago, souvenirs of my travels across the spaceways. Look at this one.' Jay gestured to the pyramid-shaped bottle. 'The planet where it was made is now a wasteland, almost deserted, its few inhabitants back in the pre-brewing age.'

'What happened to them?' asked Norton. 'War? Natural catastrophe?'

'Unnatural catastrophe,' said Jay. He tilted the turquoise bottle, emptying it into his glass. 'This is probably the last bottle in the universe.' As the final drop dripped out, all the colour drained from the whole bottle. Empty, it no longer had a purpose, and it became dull and grey. 'Wow!' said Jay, then threw it over into the corner amongst the other piles of debris.

Bottles were no longer made of glass, and they no longer broke. As the bottle hit the ground, it folded in on itself. Its bright colour was already gone, and now its unique shape collapsed.

'To the last of the Silish,' said Jay, raising his glass. He drank. 'Poor, miserable buggers.'

He hurled his empty glass against the blank viewscreen which filled most of one wall. The glass shattered. The screen remained intact. Intact but useless.

'Some species survive,' said Jay. 'Some don't. Natural selection. Some planets survive. Some don't. Unnatural selection.'

Norton picked up his own glass. It was still half full. He swirled the clear liquid around and around, then held it to his nose, inhaling the alien aroma. Alcohol had always seemed an anaesthetic, but the strange liquor appeared to have heightened his awareness and he felt totally alert. The taste still lingered in his mouth, its warm glow igniting his whole body.

'This is the last of it?' he asked Jay.

'The last,' said Jay, 'ever.'

'To the Silish,' said Norton, raising his glass to a distant planet. He took a sip, allowing the cold liquid to turn his tongue to fire, then trickle down his throat. Another swallow, and the glass was drained.

His resolution not to drink hadn't lasted very long, he realised. He studied the empty glass, then threw it against the viewscreen. Again, the glass broke; again, the screen didn't.

'Although,' said Jay, 'I might have another bottle or two down in the cellars.'

'These are from when you were on the *Demon Star* last time?'

'Yes. Good bottles improve with age. Like me.'

Wayne Norton was twenty-one years old when he went into suspended animation. He'd lived about another year since then, making his elapsed time twenty-two years. Jay must have been well into his seventies, maybe even older. The evidence was in his lined face and sparse grey hair, but he was as fit as someone three decades younger. Like so many things, age didn't mean the same as it used to. Life expectancy was much longer, a century of Earth years was easily achievable thanks to genetic biomed. And for those who could afford it, a complete rejuve could add another thirty or forty or fifty years. But for the longest potential lifespan, a rejuve had to be done as late as possible. At whatever age a person was rejuvenated, that was when the possible extra years began. Someone having it done at forty might live another half century, although it might only be thirty years or even less. They would look younger but they would die sooner. The human body could only take one rejuve; if another was attempted, the body became a corpse.

'We're not going to run out of bottles on this voyage,' said Jay. 'But we'll have to make the glasses last longer, even if smashing them does save the cleaning.'

He reached for another bottle. This one was about a yard long, an inch in diameter, metallic, golden. It could even have been real gold. There was a black band near the neck and the base, which Norton presumed was the maker's label. Neck and base looked identical, both very narrow, both with a black cap. Jay removed the cap from one end, then held the bottle upside down. Nothing happened.

'That's how you can tell it's genuine,' he said.

'Because it's empty?'

Jay turned the bottle until it was horizontal, then twisted the cap at the other end and pulled it off. 'Two glasses,' he said. 'One at each end.'

Norton took two new glasses from the tray and held them to either end of the bottle as Jay tilted it, first one way, filling one glass, then the other way, filling the other. The liquid was as gold as the bottle, very thick, like molten ore.

'You want the caps?' asked Norton.

'Not likely,' said Jay. He glanced around for a level surface, then carefully put the bottle on the floor. 'It shouldn't be closed. If it is, it becomes sour and undrinkable within minutes. Once a bottle is open, it all has to be drunk.' He accepted one of the glasses from Norton. 'Here's to the Russthuan genius who thought of that. Cheers!'

Norton knew he was beaten. 'Cheers,' he said, and sipped his liquid gold. It felt like crushed ice on his tongue, cold and heavy, which suddenly melted, and his mouth exploded in a spectacular eruption of flavours he'd never experienced before. Taste wasn't the only sense which was heightened. He could almost feel the liquor flow through his veins, to his ears, to his eyes, to his nostrils, even down to his fingertips.

'Not bad, is it?' said Jay.

'No,' said Norton, slowly, 'it's not.'

Jay nodded his head and smiled. 'I drink,' he said, and took another golden gulp, 'therefore I am. Alcohol is the best high in the universe. Forget all the drugs, all the stimsense and simsense and nonsense of neuroscapes and hypereality. The effects of drink aren't imposed on you, they all come from within you, inside your own head, your own mind. Alcohol is a natural product, the fermentation and distillation of grape or grain or its equivalent. What's the best thing about drinking?'

'You tell me,' Norton said to Jay, because he knew he was going to.

'Getting drunk,' said Jay. 'What's the worst thing about drinking.'

'A hangover?'

'It's so long since I've had one, I can't remember what it's like.'

Norton wondered if that was because he'd never stopped drinking long enough to have a hangover.

Jay continued, 'The worst thing about drinking is getting drunk. The best and the worst are the same thing, they balance each other out. Perfect harmony. But because getting drunk can be reversed with instant detox, there is no worst thing about drinking.'

'Glad to hear it,' said Norton, and he took another taste of Russthuan liquor.

'If you want to know what an alien species is like,' said Jay, 'find out what they drink.'

'Okay. Let's have a bottle of Algolan . . . what?'

'I haven't got anything from Algol.'

'Why have you got anything at all?' asked Norton. 'Everything else has been stripped from the ship –' he gestured around the partly dismantled cabin – 'so why are the bottles still on board?'

'They were hidden.'

'Like the uniform?'

'No. Who would want that?' Jay glanced at the outfit and shook his head. 'Apart from you, your excellency.' He held up his drink, swirling it around and watching the gold slowly glide down the inside of the glass. 'I'm surprised the Taxliens never found the bottles.'

'Because they would have drunk them?'

'They don't drink. They probably don't even eat. The bottles are valuable, not a fortune, but a good investment, exchangeable on most worlds. And that's what the Taxliens do – they find hidden assets. I wonder how the *Demon Star* ended up with them?'

In Wayne Norton's original era, he'd driven around Las Vegas in an automobile. Cars were built in Detroit, and cars were sold to drivers all over the States. In the twenty-third century, he travelled by interstellar spaceship. They must have been built and they must have been sold.

'Maybe they bought it,' said Norton.

'Bought it? Bought it! The Taxliens never spend. That's why they own most of the galaxy. They never buy anything. They're as tight as a Caphafer's sphincter.' He started to raise his glass again.

'When Kiru went missing,' said Norton, 'my first thought was: the Taxliens did it.'

Jay lowered his glass without drinking. 'Why did you think that?'

'Because of the strike, when she told the Caphafers they should be properly paid for the work they did on Café World. Ever since then, I'd kept thinking the Taxliens would try to get even with her.'

'Not at all,' said Jay, and he sipped his drink. 'When the Taxliens took over Café World, they were more than happy to pay the Caphafers. To cover their wages, they'll have increased all the tourist prices; they probably put up the prices more than they needed to. When the Caphafers are paid, tax is deducted. That's the whole reason for the Taxliens' existence – to discover every source of income and wealth in the universe. And then tax it.'

Norton still hadn't figured out contemporary money. Maybe because he'd never had any. When he'd been resurrected after three hundred years, a man called Brendan claimed to own the cryonic casket and its contents: Wayne Norton. Brendan said Norton was indebted to him for his revival, which was true; but Brendan was thinking more of a financial debt, and he even hired someone to make an advert so Norton could be sold. He'd become a product to be marketed on SeeV.

Instead, Norton had been 'rescued' by Colonel Travis of GalactiCop and found himself on a mission into space, which was how he'd reached Hideaway. Norton still wasn't sure whether GalactiCop really existed. Neither was he sure whether Colonel Travis did, because Travis wasn't always the same person. Sometimes 'he' was a 'she': Major Diana Travis, who was Colonel Travis's daughter. His own daughter? Her own father? It made more sense than most of what Wayne Norton had encountered out in the galaxy.

Norton was never paid for his GalactiCop work, and on Café World the Taxliens gave him and Kiru everything they wanted for free, which meant he never saw any cash. Although he knew there was no longer any paper money, when he'd first heard of the Caphafer wage agreement he kept imagining the natives swimming home on pay day and all their banknotes getting wet and dissolving in the red waters of Caphmiaultrelvossmuaf.

The unit of currency on Earth was the rupan, which used to be worth far more than it now was. Almost two decades before Norton's awakening, the world had suffered a catastrophic economic depression. Because almost every transaction was made via mazerbanking, and because every branch of the fiscal network was linked, it was meant to be absolutely secure and very fast. And it was very fast. The entire global financial system failed within an hour. This became known as the Crash.

Most of the gambling machines on Café World were coin-operated. Tourists loved to feed coins into the slots, and they loved it even more when more coins poured out. The first ones had been a type of soft plastic, but Norton had suggested that metal would make a more satisfying *clinkclinkclinkclinkclink* sound when they came clattering down the chute at pay-out time. The resort management had agreed – and covered the cost of minting new coins by cutting back on the jackpots.

Most tourists took a few of Café World's coins back

to their own worlds as holiday souvenirs, and the Taxliens imposed an export tax. The red coins had no intrinsic worth, but the visitors paid for them with money from their own planets. The Taxliens also, inevitably, controlled the rate of exchange.

'You hungry, Wayne?' asked Jay.

'Yeah.' Norton realised that he was. He hadn't eaten since before he and Kiru had set out for the atoll together, and that had been a world away. 'You said you were a chef, is that right?'

'Culinary expertise is one of my many talents.'

'Good. The last spaceship food I had was survival rations on board a lifeboat.'

'You've been in a coffin?' asked Jay, using spacer slang.

Norton nodded, but said nothing. He was trying not to think about it.

After waiting a few seconds for an explanation, which he didn't get, Jay said, 'There's no chance of you ending up in another lifeboat.'

'Why?'

'Because the *Demon Star* doesn't have any.'

Norton shrugged and took another drink.

'The other news,' said Jay, 'is that the cupboard is bare. After so many years, there's not much left in the ship's larder, and none of that is edible.'

Norton looked at his glass, then at the long, golden bottle on the floor.

'That's another great thing about alcohol,' said Jay. 'It keeps.'

'You mean,' said Norton, 'there's no food on board?'

'There's food. The Taxliens spared every expense, as you can imagine, but they didn't send you out into space so you could starve.'

'Ah, good. You had me worried.'

'The rations aren't as basic as in a liferaft, and the recycling is far less basic.'

'That sounds okay. What's the problem?'

'What food there is, we'll have to share.'

'Sure. Like we're sharing these bottles, you mean?'

'Almost,' said Jay. 'There are plenty of bottles, but . . .'

Norton finally realised what he meant. There wasn't enough food on board. The Taxliens had intended their ambassador to Algol to be the only passenger. Jay was a stowaway.

'What the heck,' said Norton. 'At least the *Demon Star* is a lot bigger than the lifeboat and I've got some-one to talk with.'

'You were alone, were you? What happened to the ship you were on?'

'I'll tell you about all that some other time, but I wasn't alone in the lifeboat.' He drained his glass. 'I was with Grawl.'

'Oh,' said Jay.

Norton had spent a long, lonely, frightening voyage with Grawl as his only companion. Long because it was on board the escape pod which had taken them both to Caphmiaultrelvossmuaf. Lonely because Grawl was mute and had never said a word. And frightening because Norton knew that Grawl had already tried to separate Kiru's mind from her body – which was some-thing else he tried not to think about. He held out his glass for a refill, and Jay obliged.

'Back to your story,' said Norton, as he glanced around the scattered debris of the stateroom. 'The *Demon Star* was being attacked by space pirates.'

'We bally well were,' said Jay, 'although I was in the

galley at the time, cooking up a last supper. It was a delicious savoury souffle of—' He broke off. 'Sorry, old chap. As I said, I'd left the stateroom by then but . . .'

CHAPTER

TEN

William Ewart wondered if he was dead.

But if he was dead, would he know it?

He could see nothing. His eyes had been seared by the infinite spectral flare which had assaulted the *Demon Star*. He was blind.

Blind, but not dead.

The stateroom door opened.

*******came in.

Ewart saw him.

Which meant he wasn't blind.

'I do hope you're both unharmed,' said *******.

Nor deaf.

'We survived?' said Ewart, blinking. 'How?'

'The ship is fitted with special defences against lethal probe beams,' said *******. 'Perhaps I should have told you, then you needn't have worried.'

'Who was worried?' said Ewart, as his heartbeat slowly slowed. 'Pour me a drink, Zena. To celebrate.'

She didn't move. In fact, she hadn't moved at all. Was she damaged? Ewart noticed she was smiling.

'I am alive!' she said.

Ewart wondered if 'alive' was the right word for Zena.

'This means Grawl and I can get married!'

'Congratulations,' said *******. 'If I may, I'll join Bill in toasting your happiness.'

For a moment, Ewart thought he was caught up in a conspiracy. Perhaps the *Demon Star* had never been in any danger, and it was all a plot so he'd allow Zena to get married.

Nothing was binding. He hadn't signed a contract, and anything agreed when he believed it was his dying wish could not be legally enforced. He needed legal advice, but there was never a lawyer around when you wanted one.

'That isn't what I was celebrating,' he said.

'I don't want to spoil the celebration, Bill,' said *******, 'but we might not survive very long. The pirates will soon realise we're alive, and they may sacrifice the ship to kill us.'

'It'll be too late to celebrate then,' said Ewart. He knocked back the drink Zena gave him. 'And another.'

'I do not think another drink is advisable, sir,' said Zena. 'Let me give you a physcan.' She always carried a medpack as well as a gun; she was both nurse and bodyguard.

'I need a drink,' said Ewart, 'not a biofix.'

'Will there be enough time for Grawl and I to get married before the pirates destroy the *Demon Star* and wipe out everyone on board?' asked Zena.

Ewart looked at *******. 'You're the acting captain, right? So you can marry them.'

'Could you, could you, please, please, could you?' said Zena. 'And would you, sir, give me away, would you, please?'

Although the words 'give' and 'away' were ones

Ewart never liked to consider, he said, 'Pour me another drink, Zena, and I'd be delighted to.' He glanced at ******* again. 'Are you ready for the service?'

Ewart normally had an aversion to marriage, anyone's marriage, not just his own. Under ordinary circumstances, he would do anything to avoid a wedding. But these circumstances were not ordinary, and a ship of such modest dimensions as the *Demon Star* wouldn't allow for avoidance.

'No,' said *******. 'I beg your pardon, but I've got important things to do.'

'What's more important than bringing happiness to a nice young couple?' asked Ewart.

'Exterminating space vermin.'

'That's why you're here, why you stole my ship?'

'I don't like to contradict you, but this was never your ship. You haven't paid for it.'

'Have you?'

'Much as I enjoy your company, Bill, I have urgent matters to deal with.'

'Do you think Mr Rajic would agree to be best man?' asked Zena.

'He'd probably prefer to do the catering,' said Ewart. 'But Marysmith could be your bridesmaid.'

'What a wonderful idea, sir!'

'I hate to interrupt,' said *******, 'but the pirate ship is probably aiming a planet-buster at us.'

'I doubt it,' said Ewart. 'What would you like as a wedding present?'

The marriage wouldn't happen, it couldn't happen, because where would the bride and groom go on their wedding night? Grawl couldn't sleep with Zena, not when she was supposed to be guarding Ewart. And

Ewart certainly didn't intend to share a bed with both of them.

'Why do you doubt it?' said *******.

'Because if there was any real danger, you wouldn't be wasting your time here. Would you?'

'And I suggest you don't waste your time composing a wedding speech,' said *******. 'There won't be time to deliver it.'

'Freedom, sir,' said Zena. 'Give Grawl his contract and myself my liberty, that would be the best wedding present of all.'

'Then what would you do?'

'We would become freelance security consultants, sir.'

'Like you?' Ewart said to *******. 'Or are you a pirate? You've hijacked the *Demon Star*, right?'

'How dare you!'

This was what Ewart wanted, some kind of reaction. With enough provocation, perhaps ******* would reveal why he was really here. Earlier, he had taken command not only of the ship but of the people on board. Now, his attention seemed to be concentrated elsewhere.

Then ******* looked at him. His face was so anonymous Ewart couldn't even tell the colour of his eyes. Cold eyes which bored so deep it was as if – more than if – he knew exactly what Ewart was thinking.

Ewart glanced away, preferring to watch the pirate ship. It seemed far less threatening. Against his will, he found his head turning back towards *******, whose expressionless gaze was still focused on him.

'Zena,' said *******, 'if you and Grawl and I survive this mission, I will personally design each item in your trousseau, I will arrange every detail of your wedding, and I will pay for your honeymoon on the most expensive and luxurious pleasure planet in the universe. But until then, I don't want to hear another word about marriage. Do you understand?'

'Yes, Mr *******,' said Zena. 'Thank you, Mr *******.'

Only then did ******* look away from Ewart. His unblinking gaze passed over Zena as if she didn't exist, and he stared at the viewscreen.

He seemed to do nothing, but the pirate craft vanished from the screen and was immediately replaced by another image: a face, an alien face.

The head was almost rectangular, covered with thick crimson scales. Tufts of ragged hair sprouted from warts all over the scalp and face and neck. Tiny eyes glinted below a protruding forehead. The huge mouth was open, slimy saliva dripping from mottled broken teeth as they slowly munched on something chewy.

Perhaps, thought Ewart, Grawl wasn't so ugly after all. He wondered what the creature was eating, then noticed that the meal was wriggling. It was still alive . . .

The alien was probing one of his wide nostrils with a fat purple finger. He suddenly became still, realising he was being watched, and he quickly swallowed and removed his finger from his nose. His small scarlet eyes gazed out of the viewscreen.

'Who out there?' he asked.

'Doggone it, boy!' said *******. 'What y'all mean by shootin' at me like that? I could have gotten *hurt*. I'll have no more of it, y'all hear me now?'

The alien's heavy face became larger as he leaned towards the screen. Then he drew back quickly, as if he recognised ******* and wished he hadn't.

'Thought you dead.'

Those were the words Ewart heard, but the sounds were not synchronised with the alien's blubbery mouth. Whatever he said was being simultaneously translated.

'Y'all *thought*!' said *******. 'Ain't y'job to cotton-pickin' *think*!'

'Not right code.'

'Hush y'mouth. How *dare* y'all ask *me* for some darn fangled code? I'll have y'*hide*, cheeky whippersnapper!'

The alien glanced down, around, then back at the screen, his eyes blinking rapidly. 'Need authorised clearance,' he said. 'Must be certain. Not enough data. Could be simulation.'

'Son of a gun! I do declare y'all just saved y'self a horsewhippin'. We both know there's only one fellow can vouch for me. Give him a holler.'

'Will take while.'

'Fiddlesticks!' said *******.

The screen blanked.

'You are a pirate,' said Ewart.

******* said nothing. He kept looking at the screen. It was completely clear, without even the pattern of stars that had always been there.

'Sir?' whispered Zena.

'What?'

'Can Grawl and I consider ourselves engaged?'

Ewart nodded.

There was a sudden flash of red across the screen, a zigzag of stylised lightning, and a loud crack of thunder which slowly rumbled away. Ewart was reminded of a station identification signal. But no channel came through, the screen reverted to blankness.

'Who are you?' asked a voice.

'Don't you recognise me?' said *******.

'Visual recognition means nothing, and you and your ship will be nothing if you don't identify yourself immediately.'

'Don't you know your own brother?'

'I don't have a brother.'

'Yes, Kosmos, you do.'

Ewart gasped in astonishment. Kosmos was *his* brother! His and Rajic's.

Their father had got married even more frequently than Ewart had, which meant he had more brothers and sisters than he knew. He wished Rajic was one of those he didn't know.

Could ******* be another of his half-brothers? The name meant nothing, but names never did.

Kosmos was the first person Ewart knew with an invented name. He was their eldest brother, the one who had told them amazing stories of his daring adventures amongst the stars, how he'd battled against alien warfleets and fought off marauding space pirates. Stories, that was all they'd been. Ewart and Rajic hadn't realised it at the time, but Kosmos was too young to have ventured into space and returned to tell the tale.

Then one day he was gone from their lives, never to return, and there were no more thrilling tales of plundering alien treasure ships across the untamed stars. Why did Kosmos never come back? Had he really headed out into the universe and become a galactic buccaneer . . . ?

'We used to play games,' ******* was saying. 'Sometimes we'd fight against space pirates, and sometimes we'd be the pirates. For you, Kosmos, it all came true. Now we've come to visit you.'

'No!' yelled Ewart.

None of that was what ******* had done. It was what *he* had done.

******* had stolen his ship.

And now he was trying to steal his life.

CHAPTER

ELEVEN

Kiru looked out into the corridor and glanced right and then left. There was no one in sight. She stepped from the room and the door closed behind her.

She wished she could seal doors as easily as she could open them, but all she could do was leave it and walk quickly away. It was Candy's room, and she had locked the door as soon as the three of them were inside. On Ipral, the females always took the male back to their place. Because Kiru had no place on Hideaway, although she didn't say so, that meant taking him to Candy's room.

And now Kiru had to get as far away as possible before anyone else tried to go inside – and discovered what she'd done.

The knife was tucked within the sleeve of her spectraflesh suit. It had been Candy's suit, but now it was Kiru's. Everything of Candy's was now Kiru's, the most important of which was her passage to Earth. Candy wasn't going anywhere.

Although she wanted to keep the knife, Kiru knew

she'd have to dump it, and not because it was evidence. Knives were ideal shipboard weapons, and it would be very difficult to smuggle one onto the ship. Terry had claimed his sword was a pirate blade, which could have been true. Guns tended to blow holes in the sides of spaceships, and so knives and swords, even bows and arrows, were often the best weapons for on-board combat. Space pirates had that in common with their nautical predecessors.

Kiru wore the spectraflesh outfit from necessity, not because she was trying to disguise herself as Candy. There wasn't time for that, not even to change her hairstyle and colour. Appearance was only superficial, and Kiru's masquerade would be uncovered by even the most basic questioning. But Hideaway was only concerned with people who arrived, not those who left. As long as they had settled their debts and had a ship to leave on, guests could depart without any formalities.

Candy's bills were already paid, her transfer to the Earth vessel was arranged, and all Kiru needed to do was take her place.

But even when she was on board, she wouldn't be safe. The key factor was how long until her two victims were discovered. If the ship had left truspace by then, it didn't matter. No signal from Hideaway could reach the vessel – and nothing could stop her reaching Earth.

CHAPTER

TWELVE

'Hi, kids,' Kosmos said to his brothers. 'Nice of you to drop by. How's Dad?'

'He's dead,' said Rajic.

'I thought he must be by now. That's life. Here one minute, gone the next. We all hated him, but if it wasn't for him where would we be? Nowhere. Never. Think about that. Still, it's been a long time since we were last together. Fifty years, Earth-time, or is it more? Time flies when you're enjoying yourself. How are you both? Good to see you. I wouldn't have recognised either of you. We've all changed, I suppose.'

Ewart certainly didn't recognise Kosmos, who had changed more than most. Since leaving Earth he'd been biophysically enhanced, building up his stature to match his role as supreme clan leader of the galactic pirates. He still looked Terran, more or less, although there was no way of telling what exotic extras had been added beneath his clothing.

Kosmos had long hair and a thick beard, both of silver. Not the silvery grey of age, but silver that shone and gleamed. A red and white dermisilk scarf was tied around his forehead, holding his hair away from his face. His left eye was covered by a black patch, and a large gold ring looped through each earlobe. His crimson shirt exploded into waves of frills at the neck and wrists, and was topped by a chromohide waistcoat. The breeches were copper coloured, tucked into knee-length boots, also of chromohide, the horned hilt of a dirk protruding from the top of each one. Around his waist was a flexisteel belt encrusted with sapphires. At his left hip hung a scabbard, over a metre of burnished metal, as black as starless space. The cutlass hilt rested across the top of the scabbard, the skull-and-cross-bones emblazoned upon the guard. At his right hip, a small axe was tucked into the jewelled belt.

'You needn't have dressed up just for us,' said Ewart, whose tastes ran to the more conservative.

'Got to live up to my image.'

'A murdering cut-throat?' said Rajic.

'I'm a lovable rogue,' said Kosmos.

If he really was Kosmos, of course. He claimed to be, and ******* had confirmed it. But ******* was no longer around.

When the pirates had searched the *Demon Star*, they found only five people on board: Ewart and Rajic and Marysmith and Grawl and Zena, who were all shuttled down to the underground citadel. After making sure none of them carried a lethal implant, they had been taken into the vast natural cavern deep below the surface of the dead planet.

It reminded Ewart of the headquarters of Ewart Communications Corporation. There, buried beneath the earth of Earth, he had been surrounded by screens, all showing selections from ECC programming across the solar system. Here, viewscreens were wedged into every rock fissure.

Kosmos was seated on a raised chair, like a monarch on his throne. The five from the *Demon Star* were lined up in front of him. No one else was in sight, but it was certain they were being watched.

Ewart and Rajic stood next to each other. Grawl was holding the Algolan princess's hand. They made a strange pair. Grawl didn't look fully human, but some kind of mutant. Marysmith was restless and kept trying to pull away, gazing all around the cavern, pointing at the screens and making strange sounds. When she began hopping from one blue leg to the other, Ewart realised she must have been singing.

Zena was holding Grawl's other hand. They looked an even stranger pair. Zena was tall and lithe, her hair red and gold, tangled and long; but Grawl was the exact opposite. Much smaller than her, he was bald and bullet-headed, barrel-chested and thick-limbed; it was as if he was as broad as he was tall.

They were Ewart's bodyguards, but how could Zena spring to Ewart's defence in an instant if her fingers were interlaced with Grawl's? As for Grawl, one hand in Zena's, the other holding the four small clawed fingers of Princess Marysmith, he might as well have had both arms tied behind his back.

But even a hundred bodyguards wouldn't be much use, Ewart supposed, not here.

'Rajic Jao Rajic, that has a good sound to it,' said Kosmos. 'But William Ewart, why choose a name like that? Never mind, I don't want to know. Here we are. Together again. A family reunion. Isn't that nice? This is your wife, I believe. My sister-in-law. You always did have an eye for a pretty girl.'

'She's *not* my wife,' said Ewart. And she certainly wasn't pretty – not even for a small, blue, humanoid, alien child. Algolans were a dangerous warrior race, which was something else Ewart hadn't known when he married her.

'Love is blind,' said Kosmos.

Maybe, thought Ewart, but Kosmos wasn't half-blind. He could doubtless see perfectly well through his eye patch.

'The galaxy's big,' continued Kosmos. 'Very big. Very, very big. Bigger than that, even. How did you find me?'

'I can't remember,' said Ewart.

'That's the trouble with getting old, kid. You begin to forget. The odd thing is, it's the recent things you forget. What happened yesterday? Don't ask me. Yesterday, today, tomorrow, what's the difference way out here? What I remember best is the old days, when we were kids. Come on, how did you find me? Was it when you were on Hideaway?'

'We were on Hideaway?' said Rajic.

'What's Hideaway?' asked Ewart. The name sounded almost familiar.

'It was where your ship last was,' said Kosmos.

'Was it?' said Ewart.

'Hideaway is a pleasure asteroid,' said Rajic.

'Hideaway is *the* pleasure asteroid,' said Kosmos. 'We made it what it is today. No, I shouldn't be so modest. *I* made it what it is today. As pirate headquarters, the satellite was never used to its full potential. Every successful business has to expand and diversify. Under my guidance, Hideaway became a world where every dream could come true, every fantasy become real. Then it was stolen from us. From *me*.'

'I know the feeling,' said Ewart, because he'd been robbed by that thieving liar, Hiroshi Larnvik.

Larnvik was the owner of Sol Global Network and the richest man on Earth, and Ewart had been poised to take his place. But when he should have been leading his assault on Larnvik's financial citadel, he was in court; and when his tactics had begun to go wrong, his corporate troops had no general to oversee their retreat. Instead, they'd been massacred and all of Ewart's assets annihilated.

'Who stole it?' asked Ewart.

'The enemy,' said Kosmos. 'Everyone's enemy. They said Hideaway was confiscated to cover tax liabilities.'

Ewart felt as if a ghostly spirit had walked across his wallet, and he shuddered.

'Hideaway will be ours again,' said Kosmos, clenching his huge bioenhanced fists. '*Mine* again.'

'It isn't so bad here,' said Rajic, gazing around the subterranean chamber. 'You've got a cosy little place.'

'Cosy!' said Kosmos. 'It's *dark*, it's *damp*, it's *cold*. You know how much it costs to *heat*? Nice? Look at it. You see any fabulous antiques, any great works of art from the infinite corners of the galaxy, any carvings or sculptures, any murals or mosaics, any magnificent paintings hanging from the walls? There aren't even any *walls*! I'm living in a *cave*!'

'Lots of viewscreens,' said Ewart. 'Plenty to watch.'

'Take a look at them,' said Rajic, his voice low. 'More blasted bumf than ECC shows.'

Every screen displayed a different spacecraft. An exterior view of the hull would change to a different angle, then show the craft shooting through the stars, before the image switched to an interior, a cabin or a propulsion unit or a command deck. After a minute, the whole sequence would repeat itself.

'What is it?' asked Ewart.

'It's our stock in trade,' said Kosmos.

'Would you buy a second-hand spaceship from this man?' said Rajic.

'He did,' said Kosmos. 'The ship you came on used to be one of ours. Defensively modified since, it seems. Old but unreliable. Why buy something powered by the Rollein-Twist? You know more ships using those engines go missing than any other?'

'Isn't that your fault for stealing them?' said Rajic.

'Not by choice, they're very hard to shift. I think that one was a trade-in. Even on the most remote planet, they haven't installed the Rollein-Twist for a long time. You've got a vintage classic there. Can't be many of them left in commission, if any.'

Ewart hadn't known this when he acquired the *Demon Star*, and neither had he known he was buying the ship from one of Hiroshi Larnvik's companies.

'A rusty old tub with dodgy propulsion,' said Kosmos, and he chuckled. 'I hope you got a good price on it.'

'The best price of all,' said Ewart. 'Not a single rupan.'

Kosmos nodded his approval. 'There's nothing like closing a good deal, but business isn't so good out here in the wilderness.' He sighed. 'Would you like something to eat? A terrific meal?'

'Right!' said Ewart.

'So would I. We'd starve to death before we reached a halfway decent restaurant. It takes weeks to go for a good night out, and you know how far it is if we want to go shopping?'

'Shopping?' said Rajic.

'Okay, okay,' said Kosmos. 'Looting. Never used to

be like this on Hideaway. I should have kept it that way. When we tried to go legit, to give up on theft, we were robbed. Now we're stuck in this dump, too far away from the spacelanes. Our income has nosedived. We've got to take three times as many ships to make as much money. That's gross income, of course, and you wouldn't believe the overheads we have.'

'If you need any business advice,' said Ewart.

'From you!' Kosmos laughed and laughed.

'What's so funny?'

'Things are bad here, kid, but at least we're not on Earth. You were in debt. Your companies were in debt. When you left, there was no one to pay the bills and then – *crash!*'

'I don't believe you.'

'How shall I put this? The failure of Ewart Communications Corporation to take over Sol Global News caused a series of financial ripples,' said Kosmos. 'You're with me so far? These ripples swelled into a tidal wave which flooded the banks and investment houses and trust funds. They didn't have a lifebelt between them, and the entire financial system was drowned. Debts went unpaid, companies went bankrupt, and the whole economy of Earth spiralled down and down into the depths of depression. Already it's known as the Crash, with a capital "C". You destroyed the whole planet, kid. I'm proud of you.'

'Really?' said Ewart.

'Would I tell a lie?' said Kosmos. He laughed again, then suddenly stopped. 'Enough of this. Much as I'd like to listen to you chattering on about the bad old days, I'll have to postpone this trip down memory alley. Very urgent business needs my attention. I've got to decide which one of you to kill.'

Kosmos looked from Ewart to Rajic, from Rajic to Ewart.

'Kill?' Rajic said.

'Us?' Ewart said.

'Why?' they both said.

'Because you came here uninvited,' said Kosmos. 'Because the crew of the sentry ship have been executed for not destroying you. Had to be done. I have to think of my reputation. I may be tough, but I'm also unfair. The punishment caused some bad feeling among my merry men, and they want reprisals. Can't say I blame them. One of you has got to die.'

Ewart and Rajic looked at each other, then at Kosmos.

'Let me explain,' said Kosmos. 'I'm the hardest, toughest, meanest, cruellest bastard here. That's how I got to the top. That's how I've stayed at the top. And I can show I'm still the hardest and toughest, meanest and cruellest, by killing my own brother. I can't play family favourites. There's no room for nepotism in business. Promotion has to be by merit. And death is the ultimate demotion.'

'You said you were a lovable rogue,' said Rajic.

'Never believe your own publicity,' said Kosmos. 'I am, it's true, a murdering cut-throat. Some would blame my parents. It's all Dad's fault! Or maybe it's the company I keep. My associates want you dead. Both of you. All of you. More than dead, in fact. Tortured. Mutilated.'

'So that we'll tell you how we got here?' said Ewart.

'No, we'd use a mindprobe for that. But who cares how you got here?'

'Then why torture us?'

'For fun. Why else?' said Kosmos. 'I won't be

dictated to, however, and I've made an executive decision. I'm only going to kill one of you. Quickly and painlessly. Is there a volunteer?'

'Him,' said Ewart and Rajic.

'I thought you might say that,' said Kosmos.

'Isn't there a saying: the greatest sacrifice is to lay down your life for your brother?' said Rajic. 'But you could top that, brother, you could sacrifice yourself for both of us.'

'Self-sacrifice has never seemed very attractive to me,' said Kosmos. 'Either in business or my personal life. And if something happened to me, I wouldn't be here to protect you. You'd both be killed. What's the point of us all dying?'

'If someone has to die . . .' said Ewart, and he tilted his head a fraction.

'You want me to kill one of them?' said Kosmos, looking at Marysmith and Grawl and Zena. 'Which one would you prefer? Your wife? You'd love that, wouldn't you? A lot quicker and cheaper than a divorce. She's only a kid, but so what? There are plenty more of them; they're the easiest and cheapest things to make in the entire universe. But this one is an Algolan princess. She's worth too much to kill. A queen's ransom.'

Ewart had thought he was marrying the daughter of an Algolan tycoon, and they would never meet. The marriage had been an integral part of a bilateral investment transaction negotiated between Ewart Communications Corporation and a company on the single planet which orbited Beta Persei. Calling his spaceship after one of the old astronomical names for Algol was the least Ewart could do, as his new father-in-law was funding the *Demon Star*'s purchase.

Or so Ewart believed. But Marysmith's dowry never arrived. Instead, she did.

She also turned out to be the second youngest daughter of the Empress of Algol.

A planet ruled by women. What an insane way to run a world. No wonder the financial side of the deal had completely collapsed. Women were the same throughout the galaxy. They couldn't manage money. All they could do was spend, spend, spend.

Take, take, take. It was as if every female was a tax collector. They were nothing but parasites.

Ewart was lucky he'd married so few of them.

'I'm worth a ransom,' he said.

'You're not,' said Kosmos. 'But I'd probably make a fortune from a sponsored execution.'

'Kill the bodyguards,' said Rajic. 'Two victims are better than one. Then everything will be tickety-boo.'

'Gosh golly wow,' said Zena, 'what a wizard wheeze.'

Ewart looked at her. Rajic looked at her.

'There's no point killing the hired help,' said Kosmos, as he also looked at Zena. 'For a bodyguard, being ready to die is a job specification. Grawl would think it nothing more than a termination of his employment contract. There's no fun in that. And you can't kill an android. It's a machine. You switch it off and throw it away. No, it's got to be one of you two who shuffles off into the immortal soil. I'll give you both a minute to compose your last will and testament. Not you, ah, Billy boy, you haven't got anything left to leave.' Kosmos scratched his beard, yawned, drew the cutlass from its scabbard, and began probing at his cuticles with the edge of the blade.

That was when Ewart laughed. It was all a joke. He

remembered now. This was like one of those tricks Kosmos used to play on them when they were kids.

'I'm glad you think it's funny,' said Rajic. 'Because he's going to kill one of us. Very soon.'

'He's not going to kill either of us,' said Ewart. 'How can he? He's our brother. We're the same flesh and blood.'

'And some of that blood is going to be spilled. One of us is going to die. Whoever it is, there's something you must know, something very important.'

'What?'

Kosmos pointed his sword at Rajic.

'Too late,' he said.

There was a flash of blue light from the end of the blade.

Rajic fell down.

Dead.

CHAPTER
THIRTEEN

'Dead?' said Wayne Norton, formerly of the twentieth century.

'Yes,' said Jay, formerly Rajic Jao Rajic.

'You were dead?'

'Yes. But it wasn't permanent. I'm like a bad meal, you can't keep me down. I was revived, like you. That's another thing we've got in common, Wayne. We could almost be twins!' Jay laughed and drained his glass. 'No, I'm glad you're not my brother. I don't need any more enemies.'

'Kosmos killed you?' said Wayne. 'Your brother, he really killed you?'

'Yes. But we hadn't met for half a century, so we were like strangers. I didn't mean anything to him. I expected to be killed by my brother, but I thought it would be Ewart who did it. He was the one who hated me so much. Can't say that I blame him.'

'But you're not dead, Jay, not now. What happened?'

'It was the Algolans, which was jolly decent of them. They took me back to their planet and did a repair job on me. They've got the best health service in the universe.'

'The Algolans? Where did they come from?'

'You may find this hard to believe, but they come from the planet Algol. There's one planet, but two stars. A bit greedy, if you ask me.'

'You know what I mean. How did they find you?'

'I wasn't hidden.' Jay held up his hands in a placatory gesture. 'I was dead, Wayne, and I can't remember much after I was killed.' He reached down for the Russthuan bottle and tilted one end towards his glass. Nothing came out. He threw the golden bottle over his shoulder, and it landed with a heavy thud. 'Now what?' he said. 'Another bottle, or shall we start on our food supplies?'

'Whose supplies?' said Norton, and he watched as the bottle rolled back across the stateroom floor and came to a halt against Jay's heels.

Jay picked up the bottle again, looked at it, then at the half-full glass Norton still held.

'Our supplies,' agreed Norton. 'Let's eat. After you tell me how the Algolans found you.'

Before Norton reached Algol, he had to find out as much as he could about the world. The first time he'd heard of the planet was from the Empress – formerly Princess Janesmith.

'It seems,' said Jay, 'that an Algolan warfleet attacked the pirate base. They must have come to rescue Marysmith. When they found me, already dead, they realised I'd been killed by the bad guys and that meant I must have been one of the good guys. Which I am. Most of the time. They put me back together again.'

'They put you together again, and you still look that bad?' said Norton.

Jay laughed. 'You should have seen me before I was

dead!' He picked up his glass, realised it was empty,
then put it down again. 'They fixed me up a treat,
nearly as good as new. I can never have a rejuve, but
I've already had an extra life so I mustn't grumble.'

'What happened to Ewart?'

'No idea. Why?'

William Ewart, Norton had realised, was somehow
a focal point in his own life. At this very moment
Norton was on board the *Demon Star*, which used to
be William Ewart's ship, in the same cabin that used to
be his. Ewart had been connected with people who
later became known to Norton: Grawl, Janesmith, Jay.
Norton knew what had happened to those three. Grawl
had been imprisoned on Clink, which was where he'd
met Kiru; Janesmith had become Empress, and she
had taken Grawl back to Algol with her; and Jay was
sitting opposite. Norton felt that if he knew more
about Ewart, then more of his own life would begin to
make sense.

'What were you going to tell him?' asked Norton.
'Just before you were killed, you had something important to say to Ewart. What was it?'

'It doesn't matter, not any more.' Jay shook his head
dismissively. He looked around the stateroom, not
meeting Norton's eyes. 'But . . .' He picked up his
empty glass. 'I've never told anyone this, maybe it's
time I did.' He stood up. 'I'll have to open another
bottle first.' He took a step forward, and his footing
was unsteady. 'Remember this, Wayne: you only get
drunk when you stop drinking.'

Norton watched Jay pick up another bottle. It was
white and it was square, with a small cube on the top
which served as the neck. Jay collected two new
glasses, then sat down again and removed the bottle

lid. Norton admired his energy, because all he was capable of was sitting still and doing nothing. Even holding the glass with the last of the liquid gold took all his strength. He watched as Jay quickly poured, then put the bottle cap back on. The new glasses were square-sided, like the bottle. Norton wondered if this was the professional space steward style, serving drinks in glasses which replicated the bottle – although it would have been difficult to drink out of pyramid-shaped glasses to suit the Silish bottle, and ones with a hole at either side to match the Russthuan bottle would have made drinking very tricky.

'Caphmiaultrelvossmuaf?' asked Norton, because the drink was so red it was almost off the visible spectrum. As he held it, he could feel the glass becoming warmer.

'Inferno,' said Jay. 'Drink it fast.' He took a gulp, swallowing half at once.

Norton sipped tentatively at the warm liquid. It bubbled on his tongue, and he kept it in his mouth for a few seconds to explore the taste. It became hotter and hotter. He looked at Jay, who swiftly drained his glass. Norton swallowed what he had, and he felt the heat flow down his throat. He opened his mouth wide, inhaling to draw in some cooling air. His fingers were burning, he realised, and he quickly put his glass down. The surface of the liquid was steaming, then it began to sizzle and boil. There was a flash of brilliant scarlet and crimson, and the drink was gone, vaporised. For a few seconds, Norton wondered if the liquor would have an incendiary effect on him, then the internal heat was suddenly quenched and he felt very cool, very fresh.

'Ewart and me,' said Jay, 'were half-brothers

because our father kept getting married, and Ewart carried on the family tradition. Before Marysmith, he'd been married five times. Apart from him, I was the only person who knew about his first wife. That was when he was someone else.'

'When he had another name?'

'Of course. He did, I did. Why should you keep the name that's given to you? On some planets, it's the authorities that assign the names people have. You can choose your clothes, so why not choose your name? You don't wear the same clothes for ever –' Jay paused and glanced down at his old outfit – 'so why keep the same name for ever? You've had yours over three hundred years, Wayne. Isn't it time for a change?'

'No,' said Norton. 'So what were you going to tell Ewart?'

'He was married when he was very young, when it wasn't just his name that was different, but his whole character. After what happened, he changed, became another person.'

'What did happen?'

'His first wife was called Myiko. I knew her before they met, but for some reason she decided to marry Ewart instead of me. They had a baby, a girl called Maya. Soon after, there was a deadly epidemic which infected a lot of people. Its origins were a mystery, but it was thought to be an alien virus. I wasn't affected, neither was Ewart, but Myiko and Maya both caught it. He couldn't afford the treatment for them and came to me for money. I had a restaurant that specialised in off-world food, so you can imagine how popular that was at the time. It went bust, and I had nothing. I couldn't help; I wished I could; I'd have done anything for Myiko. Anything. I was still in love with her.

And when she died, Norton found out we'd been seeing each other ever since they were married. Maya survived, but Ewart was convinced she was my daughter, not his. She wasn't, and it would have been simple to prove I wasn't the father, but I let him go on thinking Maya was mine. Why? I don't know. Maybe it was revenge. Maybe I thought if Myiko had married me instead of him, she wouldn't have died. And that's what I wanted to tell Ewart, that Maya was his daughter.'

Norton nodded. He'd never heard Jay speak so softly, so seriously and so soberly. Or so clearly.

'But,' Jay continued, 'maybe the old bastard didn't remember.'

'His first wife, his first daughter, how could he have forgotten?'

'Easily. Painful memories can be mindwiped. What makes us who we are? It's not our bodies, it's what we have in our heads.' Jay picked up his empty glass. 'So what I've told you could be completely wrong, they might be false memories, although I think I'd have chosen better ones.'

'What happened to Maya?'

'Once there was enough treatment, the epidemic didn't last. But a lot of people died, many of them children. Some friends of mine lost their baby, and they took Maya to bring up as their own.'

'Did you ever marry,' asked Norton, 'ever have children?'

'I did the double, married and divorced, but just the once. No children. You?'

'I married Kiru.'

'Before that, back in ancient history, were you married then?'

'No.' Norton shook his head. There were memories he wished he could erase, one in particular: Susie, who must have been dead for three centuries. 'No wife. No children. I never even . . .' He broke off, then changed the subject. 'That's why Ewart hated you, because you had an affair with his first wife?'

'What's an affair?'

'It's . . . er, it's sex with someone you're not married to.'

'Before you married her, you and Kiru had an affair?'

'No. An affair is . . . it's kept secret. It's when you're married to someone else.'

'An *affair*,' said Jay, practising the word. 'Yes, I had an *affair* with Myiko. Then an *affair* with Irina. Then an *affair* with Theresa.'

'Who are they?'

'Irina was Ewart's second wife, who he claims was the first. Theresa was his third.' Jay shrugged. 'By then we'd gone into business together, operating a headware firm, but it wasn't as much fun as running a bar and restaurant. And I wanted to see the universe, to travel to other worlds, so I made a deal with Hiroshi Larnvik and used the money to skedaddle into space.'

'You sold out your own brother to this guy Larnvik?'

'Yes.'

'And cheated on him with three of his wives?'

'Yes. I never knew the others. Pity. I knew Marysmith when she was older, but she wasn't my type.'

'Yeah, because she was an Algolan.'

'No,' said Jay. 'I'm not prejudiced. That Janesmith, she's quality crumpet. She must have been on Hideaway while I was on Algol. Now I'm going back, I'd like to get close to her again.' He nodded slowly and smiled. 'Another drop of molten lava from Inferno?'

'Sure,' said Norton. 'Is it hot there?'

'The opposite. It's one of the coldest worlds in the universe; they spend all their time keeping warm.'

'You mentioned something else in your story . . .' said Norton, watching as red liquor poured into the cubic glasses.

'What?'

Norton picked up the glass and took a mouthful before it became too hot. There were lots of things he wanted to ask, but he was having trouble remembering. Alien alcohol was instant mindwipe.

'The ship you were on,' said Norton, as the heat poured down his throat. 'This ship. The ship we're on. Something about the engines. What was it?'

'The propulsion unit, you mean? The *Demon Star* is powered by a system called the Rollein-Twist. It's old but reliable. Like me.' Jay swallowed a mouthful of red fire. 'No. Unreliable, that's it. Old but unreliable.'

'Like you?'

Jay laughed and laughed and laughed. Wayne Norton didn't.

'It's not that funny,' said Norton.

'I know,' said Jay. 'It's not funny at all. This is probably the last ship in the universe still fitted with the Twist. All the others have been scrapped or lost.'

'Lost where?'

'Nobody knows, Wayne. That's why they're lost.'

'The Taxliens have sent me to Algol in a ship that might not get there?'

'Yes, but they probably don't know. If it doesn't involve money and finance, they don't know anything.'

As the infernal drink cooled him down, Norton

shivered a moment. He hoped it was the drink which made him shiver.

'And we don't know anything,' continued Jay. 'The *Demon Star* could already be lost in falspace, doomed never to reappear. Time and space are different here, everything is stretched and distorted. A million years may have gone by in truspace, but we've no way of telling. We could be trapped on an infinite voyage that goes on and on and on, for ever and ever and ever.'

To Norton, it already seemed like it had.

CHAPTER

FOURTEEN

Zena gave Rajic a physcan, then said, 'He is dead, sir.'

'Your own brother. You killed your own brother.'

'Half-brother,' said Kosmos. 'What's the problem? You didn't like him when he was alive, I know that. You'd rather I'd killed you? You can join him if you want.'

Kosmos was right, Ewart had hated Rajic more than anyone else on Earth. In the whole galaxy. In the entire universe. Or thought he had. But Rajic was his last link with the past. (Apart from Kosmos, of course.) He was his only relative. (Apart from his ex-wives. And his children. And their children. Kosmos, too, of course.)

Ewart hadn't experienced this kind of emptiness for a very long time, and he knelt down by Rajic's side. He looked unharmed, and his eyes were closed as if he was sleeping.

'What are you going to do?' asked Kosmos. 'Pray?' He laughed, his booming laughter echoing around the vast underground chamber deep within the pirate stronghold.

Suddenly, there was a distant roll of thunder. Kosmos became silent, listening. Then another noise came from within the darkness, a noise which grew louder, nearer. Kosmos turned, raising his sword. A heavily armed gang of assorted aliens ran into the cavern.

'What's going on?' demanded Kosmos.

They kept on running, between him and the four survivors, and disappeared on the other side of the chamber.

The thunder was repeated, louder this time, not so far away. It was hard to tell from which direction it came. Then it was heard again. Closer. The sounds merged, rebounded, echoing around and around. Explosions.

Kosmos looked up at the viewscreens. One by one, every ship on every screen was being ripped apart, bursting into a billion fragments. In the vacuum of space, every blast was silent. But the noise within the citadel grew louder, the very rock seeming to tremble as the detonations came closer.

One of the aliens ran back, backwards, firing his weapon in the direction he'd come from. He was tall, the thick grey hide of his tufted face sliced and scarred, clad in a mottled orange and lemon cloak decorated with small black bones which rattled as he ran, wearing a helmet plumed with long feathers, carrying a gun almost as big as himself.

'What is it?' yelled Kosmos.

'Trouble, boss,' answered the alien, firing another volley at his unseen enemy. 'Attacked by a warfleet, invaded by kamikaze kommandos.'

'You did this,' said Kosmos.

'Who?' said Ewart, as he rose to his feet.

'You brought them here,' said Kosmos.

'Me?' said Ewart.

'Kill them,' said Kosmos.

'Yes, boss,' said the lemon and orange alien.

It all happened very slowly, as if in zero gravity. The alien turned towards the four from the *Demon Star*. Slowly. He swung his weapon around. Slowly. He chose his target. Slowly.

Zena moved. Also slowly. Too slowly. She was trying to protect Ewart, to guard him with her own body. Then she slowed even more. And stopped. Which was the slowest of all.

The alien fired.

Hit Zena. Who fell.

She'd sprung in front of Grawl. Saved him.

Saved him when she should have been shielding Ewart.

There was an inhuman cry. Of pain, of anger, of despair.

Not from Zena. She'd fallen in silence.

But from Grawl. It was the first sound Ewart had ever heard him make.

The alien took aim again.

'Excuse me,' said a voice. 'May I interrupt?'

The alien twisted around, swinging his huge gun. Too slowly. His head became an incandescent ball of white flame. He kept turning, trying to shoot. Until his head fell off. Then the gun dropped. And so did the rest of his body. Except for a few feathers floating to the ground. Slowly.

'Sorry,' said *******, as he lowered his blaster. 'Is Marysmith unharmed? Good, I'm so pleased. Everything seems satisfactory. I do apologise for the delay. I hope you weren't put to too much inconvenience.'

Ewart looked at Rajic, lying dead. He looked at Zena, lying destroyed. He turned to look at Kosmos. Who was gone.

'Where's Kosmos?'

'Trying to escape, I presume,' said *******. 'But never fear, he won't.'

'He killed Rajic. He was going to kill me. I was almost killed.'

'You're very fortunate I arrived in time.'

'In time! Rajic's dead. We're here because of you, and he's dead because of you. I could be dead.'

'Rajic's death is regrettable,' said *******. 'My sincere apologies and heartfelt condolences on your sad loss.'

Ewart heard a strange noise, like some kind of whimpering animal. The sound was coming from Zena. Maybe she could be salvaged, although perhaps it was already far too late – the way she'd protected Grawl instead of Ewart, something had gone badly wrong with her programming.

She was lying in a melted heap, her body twisted and smouldering. Grawl was by her side, her head cradled in his lap. What was left of it. Half her head was fused, the other half had been blown away.

It wasn't Zena who was whimpering. It was Grawl. His fingers stroked what was left of the android's ruined face.

'On your feet, Grawl,' said Ewart. 'I need protection.'

Grawl became silent. He looked up at Ewart. Slowly. They met each other's gaze. Every trace of sorrow was gone from Grawl's eyes. They were dark and venomous, full of hatred. When Ewart stepped back, Grawl's attention returned to Zena.

Ripping open her medpack, he examined the contents for a moment before sweeping it all aside. Then he drew back his right hand, straightened his fingers — and drove them deep into Zena's ruined chest. Her pseudoflesh split, and Grawl slid his hand between her ribs, feeling inside. He pulled something out, clutching it in his fist.

'What's that?' said Ewart.

Keeping his prize hidden, Grawl carefully slid Zena to the ground. He stood up, then spun around and strode away.

'Grawl!' shouted Ewart. 'Come here! That's an order!'

The bodyguard kept going. Until now, Marysmith had calmly watched everything that was happening around her. Seeing Grawl leave, she ran after him. He heard the girl coming, looked around, and waved her back. When she stopped, Grawl continued walking away.

Ewart heard another sound, a regular heavy thud. It was coming nearer.

A platoon of armoured aliens marched into the chamber. Invaders. Kamikaze kommandos. Their ridged helmets made them seem taller, but inside their plated bronze carapaces they were not much more than a metre high.

They came to a halt immediately in front of *******, and they all bowed to him. He also bowed, although not as much.

******* said something totally incomprehensible.

As one, the aliens turned towards Marysmith, dropped their weapons, then threw themselves down on the ground. They beat their short armoured limbs against the bare rock, and they screeched and screeched and screeched.

'It's so satisfying to make people happy,' said
*******.

'They're happy?' said Ewart. 'Why?'

'Because they're in the presence of their Empress.'

'You mean . . . ?'

'Yes, Algolans, members of the warrior caste.'

'No, I mean . . . she . . . Marysmith . . . ?'

'Yes, such wonderful news. The Empress is dead.
Long live the Empress.'

'The Empress . . . ?'

'You must be so pleased for her. And for yourself.
You're married to the Empress of Algol, Bill. What an
honour! Aren't you absolutely thrilled?'

'Absolutely,' said Ewart. 'I'm . . .'

'Speechless, I know.'

'I thought she . . . her . . . that . . . but . . . isn't she
the second youngest daughter?'

'She was. On Algol, the youngest daughter inherits
the throne. The youngest surviving daughter, that is,
and there does seem to be a very high mortality rate.
The tragic accident which befell the Empress also
regrettably caused the death of her youngest daughter.
Most unfortunate, although not for Marysmith. It
couldn't have happened to a nicer little girl, could it?
She's now Empress of Algol. That's why the warfleet
is here, to take her back to the imperial palace for the
coronation.'

Ewart looked from Marysmith to her prostrate and
screeching rescuers, still thrashing the ground with
their arms and legs, then turned to *******.

'Who are you?' he asked. 'They bowed to you. Are
you their leader?'

'Do I look like an Algolan?' said *******.

'Not to me.' Even staring directly at *******, Ewart

couldn't have described him. 'But what do you look like to them?'

'I must find Kosmos,' said *******, and he began heading in the direction from which the Algolans had arrived. 'I don't want him to hurt himself.'

'Why would he hurt himself?'

'He's probably a bit upset, which is understandable.' ******* glanced back. 'If you'll accept my recommendation, you shouldn't stay there.'

Ewart felt the rock beneath his feet shake and vibrate. He heard a series of violent explosions. The underground citadel was being destroyed. A cloud of choking dust drifted through the labyrinth, forcing him to take *******'s advice. There seemed to be two ways out of the cavern. The Algolans began to leave in one direction. Ewart went the other way, following *******. He found himself in a twisting, narrow passage, winding his way between sheer rock walls which loomed high above him. After a while, the passage widened. ******* had halted and was gazing in every direction.

'What's going on?' Ewart asked. 'The Algolans are here to rescue Marysmith from the space pirates, but it was because of you she was caught by them. Right?'

'Your analysis is very simplistic, Bill.'

'But I'm right. Aren't I?'

'If you insist on being blunt about it, yes. Excuse me, but I'm afraid we'll have to continue this discussion another time, because I'll be most annoyed if Kosmos gets away.' ******* looked up, looked down, looked all around. 'He's very close.'

'Are you going to kill him?'

'Kosmos has to see the error of his ways, apologise

and show genuine remorse for his wrongdoings, then accept re-education. Execution is no solution.'

Kosmos suddenly appeared behind *******.

And shot him.

******* was violently slammed up against the wall and then dropped heavily to the ground.

'Execution is the only solution,' said Kosmos, gazing at his victim's corpse. 'Don't talk, act. If you want to do something, do it. I can't stand these people who go on and on about what they'll do when this happens, or how they'll do something else if it turns out differently. Talk, talk, talk, talk, talk, talk. The universe didn't get built by people who talked. Imagine if the first explorers had spent all their time talking about what the next star system was like instead of actually going there. No one would ever have gone anywhere. Everyone would still be on their own planet. Where is he?'

'Who?' said Ewart.

Kosmos pointed. Ewart glanced down. *******'s body had disappeared.

Kosmos started shooting again, firing at the ground where ******* had been, then aiming in each direction along the twisting crevasse.

He had a proper gun now, not one masquerading as a cutlass. His own masquerade also seemed to be over, because he was no longer wearing the gaudy pirate outfit. The long silver hair, the beard, the eye patch, they were all gone. Only the axe remained, hanging from a strap over his shoulder. He was dressed in anonymous coveralls, although they couldn't mask his great size.

'Who was that?' asked Kosmos.

'*******,' said Ewart. 'Although he might not even

have been here. He's an expert at deception. His disguises are much better than yours.'

'You think I always wear a buccaneer outfit? You think I'm some kind of idiot? That was for you and Rajic. For a laugh.'

'Right. It was a real laugh when you killed him.'

'You think I'd kill my own brother?'

'Why not?'

'Yeah, well, okay, but only if it was expedient.'

'Expedient!'

'Alright, only if it was necessary.'

'Necessary!'

'Absolutely essential, then. Vital, a matter of life and death.'

'Your life, Rajic's death.'

'I'm good at deception, too. He isn't dead. That was all to fool my co-directors. I didn't kill him.'

'But what about me? Remember your order to that goon? "Kill them," you said.'

'Just a figure of speech,' said Kosmos. 'Let's get out of here.'

'I'm not going with you,' said Ewart.

'Up to you. But if you stay, you're dead. The Algolans are wrecking everything. They're making a real mess.'

'They won't kill me. I'm married to the Empress.'

'That's why they'll kill you. They don't want an empress who's married to an alien. And there's no such thing as divorce on Algol. But if she's a widow . . .' Kosmos shrugged.

Ewart glanced back. The whole place reverberated to the sounds of destruction. He couldn't stay, but neither could he go with Kosmos.

Then there was another explosion, much louder

than all the others, and heavy stones began to rattle down the sides of the ravine.

'If Rajic wasn't dead,' said Ewart, 'he probably is by now.'

'And we definitely will be if we don't get out of here,' said Kosmos. He gestured to the narrow fissure through which he'd appeared. 'You coming?'

Ewart nodded, and the crack in the rock was far less narrow for him. He felt slim in comparison to his brother. Not that he was overweight, of course.

Dust and splinters of rock dropped down on them as they slithered through the passage, and Ewart prayed Kosmos didn't become wedged between the rocks. But very soon he did.

'Oh!' muttered Kosmos, as he suddenly halted.

'What?' said Ewart, pushing at him.

'*No!*' yelled Kosmos. 'Don't.'

He moved forward slightly, then to one side. Ewart stepped after him, left foot, right foot, left foot—

Except there was nothing there, nothing beneath his foot, and he started to fall.

Kosmos grabbed him and pulled him back. Side by side, on a ledge less than half a metre wide, they stood on the brink of a sheer precipice.

'Th –' whispered Ewart – 'anks.'

'Forget about it,' said Kosmos.

The way things were going, Ewart guessed he'd soon forget about everything. It had been dark in the tunnel, but now it was far darker, an infinite chasm of absolute darkness. Below them lay a gaping void which opened straight down to the black heart of the dead planet.

'I'm sure this wasn't here a few minutes ago,' said Kosmos.

'Can you go left?'

'No. Can you go right?'

'No. We have to go back.'

There was a loud crack as the wall of the ravine behind them fractured and split, sending both pebbles and boulders cascading down to block their exit.

'Can't you blast your way back through?' said Ewart.

'No.'

'Why not?'

Kosmos muttered something.

'What?' said Ewart.

'Dropped my gun.'

'You dropped your gun?'

'Yes, I dropped my gun! Okay? Not very professional, I know.'

'Dropped it? You mean you've lost it?'

'Yes, it fell out of my hands. Alright! I've never done it before, but even now there's still a first time for everything.'

'How could you drop it?'

'You shoved me, that's how! Another word, one single solitary syllable, and you're down there looking for it. Understand?!'

'So now what?'

'We stay here. Then we die. Sooner or later. What else?' Kosmos sighed. 'I don't want to be part of a family funeral. This isn't what I'd planned.'

Ewart closed his eyes and leaned back against the cold rock face, trying to mould himself into the contours.

'Have you any funeral plans?' Kosmos continued.

'No.'

'You should make arrangements, because it's not

fair to leave it to your friends and relatives. You're my nearest living relative, kid. Although not for long, I suppose. If you plan your own funeral, you can go out the way you want to go.'

But Ewart didn't want to go. And he certainly didn't want to go now.

'Seems a bit late to make plans,' he said. 'Any ideas? What about you?'

'A traditional pirate funeral. Surrounded by personal mementoes, souvenirs, trophies, my body locked in temporal stasis and sealed within my flagship. The ship cast off amongst the stars on an eternal subspace trip. Drifting across the universe for millions of years, billions of years, finally reaching another galaxy. Slow and dignified, with real style and class. What do you think?'

'About what?'

'You asked about my funeral.'

'Just making conversation. I wasn't listening.'

'What's the point of planning anything? Life is what happens while you're drawing up a business plan. So is death. I'm going to end up in the bottom of a hole. Eaten by worms. How primitive can you get? Food for alien worms, what a way to go. Want to hear a joke?'

'No. I might fall off laughing.'

'That's a good way to go,' said Kosmos, and he laughed.

'Don't.'

'Why me? That's what I want to know. What have I done that's so bad a whole Algolan battlefleet has to come all this way to wipe me out? Why did ******* have it in for me? Did I spill his drink once?'

'No idea.'

'It's odd, isn't it, after all this time apart, all this

way across the galaxy, you, me and Rajic all dying together like this? Fate, is it? Destiny?'

Although he could see nothing, Ewart opened his eyes. A few minutes earlier, Kosmos had said Rajic wasn't dead, that he hadn't killed him.

'Is my talking annoying you?' said Kosmos.

'Right.'

'Too bad. We ought to talk, kid. There's lots to say and we haven't got much longer.'

'How long, do you think?'

'How long can we hang onto this cliff? We could bet on it. Winner takes all?'

Ewart heard Kosmos shift his feet, and part of the ledge crumbled beneath him. Then there was silence.

'You still there?' Ewart asked.

'Yes.'

'Thought you might have fallen off.'

'Sorry to disappoint you. I've been thinking.'

'Right.'

'Isn't much else to do.'

That was true, and it was better than him talking. Kosmos stayed silent. Thinking.

'So?' said Ewart

'So what?'

'So what have you been thinking?'

'I've been thinking,' said Kosmos, slowly, 'there is one way we could both get out of here alive. It's a crazy idea, kid, but it might just work.'

CHAPTER

FIFTEEN

As soon as Kiru boarded the ship, before the docking gate had even closed behind her, she was attacked.

She was already alert and glimpsed a movement in the darkness. Her mental reaction was to nix the gate control and keep an escape route open. She did that first. Her physical reaction was to throw herself aside. She did that an instant later, rolling over and away.

'*Bitch!*' the ambusher shouted, and dived after her.

Kiru saw a shadow rise and knew it was a weapon about to plunge down. It had to be a knife, but Kiru no longer had one of her own, so she threw up her left hand, blocking the arm, forcing it away, then grabbing and twisting with her right, turning it around and bending it back, down, behind, then balling her left hand into a fist and punching out, hard, twisting her wrist at the moment of impact.

'*Ahhhhh!*' screamed the attacker, a human scream, a female scream.

Bending the arm even further, Kiru forced her assailant to drop the blade, then she lashed out with one leg and kept pushing, sliding her opponent away before reaching down to pick up the fallen weapon. It was a short-handled axe, blade and handle fused into a single deadly unit. Kiru jumped up, then planted one of her feet across the ribs of her would-be assassin. She seemed to be what she'd sounded: human and female.

'By *dose*!' yelled the woman, holding one hand over her nose. 'You've *boken* by dose, you *ditch*!'

'And now I'm going to break every bone in your body!' warned Kiru, staring down at her in the gloom, then looking around to see if there was any other immediate threat.

'*You're* not Candy!' said the woman, staring up. '*Are* you? No, I can *see* you're not. Who *are* you?'

'Your enemy.'

'But I'm not *your* enemy!'

'You attacked me. That makes you my enemy.'

'I *thought* you were Candy!' She stared at the open docking gate. 'Where *is* Candy? Let me *at* her!'

'Candy,' said Kiru, 'won't be coming.' She gazed around the deck again. It was a small ship, not what she was expecting, and so she'd been on her guard. 'Who else is on board?'

'*All* the crew. You don't have a *chance*.'

'A chance of what?'

'*Stealing* the ship. You're a *pirate*, you must be.'

'Yes.' Kiru raised the axe. 'How many in the crew?'

'How *many*? Let me *see* . . . er . . . there are . . . I'll have to *count* . . . one . . .'

Kiru lifted the axe higher.

'*One*. There's *one*!'

'Only two of you on board?'

'*Yes*.'

'Who's the other one?'

'The *chauffeur*.'

'The what?'

'The *chauffeur*. You don't think *I* fly this thing, do you?'

'I don't know what you do,' said Kiru. 'Who are you?'

'I'm *Mandy*.'

'Mandy from the Candy and Mandy Doubletime News Show?'

'No, Mandy from the *Mandy* and Candy Doubletime News Show. Were you a *fan* of the show?'

'It was before my time,' said Kiru.

Mandy looked very much like Candy; they could have been sisters. Candy had seemed to be twenty, but she must have been twice that age. Mandy appeared several years older, perhaps because she hadn't had a recent facial update. But she needed some work now, to fix her nose.

'Candy *married* Hiroshi Larnvik,' said Mandy. 'It *should* have been my wedding. *I* was the star. She *cheated* me of so much, taking what *should* have been mine. I lost *so* many years on Earth, trapped there while Candy *datafiled* the galaxy. Then at last, while she was *away*, Hiroshi and I *renewed* our old acquaintance, which means that—'

'Shut up!' said Kiru. 'And stand up.'

Mandy rose to her feet, blood dripping from both nostrils. She was no threat; all she could do was talk.

'Where's the pilot?' Kiru asked.

'In the *command* cabin.'

'Okay.' Kiru looked along the narrow passage towards the other end of the ship. 'You've come to Hideaway to pick up Candy?'

'I've come to Hideaway to *kill* her.'

'You aren't going to kill her. You don't even want to kill her. You want to scratch her eyes out, that's all.'

'One of her *eyes*, yes, the one with the *opticam*.'

'What? Candy had a camera in her eye?'

'What do you mean, *had*? It's her *profession* to record everything she sees.'

'Have you,' said Kiru, stepping closer, 'an opticam in one of your eyes?'

'*No*,' said Mandy, quietly, shaking her head.

'Keep still!' Kiru ordered. 'Open your eyes! Both of them!' She stared at Mandy's irises, her pupils, and she knew she was lying. 'Which eye?' She lifted the axe, pointing the blade at each of Mandy's eyes in turn. Mandy shut both of them again, glittery lids clamped together, long lashes interlocked. 'Which eye or you lose both!' But Kiru already knew that if there had been an opticam in one of Candy's eyes, then it was too late now. She turned her head to one side. 'Left profile.' She turned to face the other direction. 'Right profile.' She turned and looked directly at Mandy. 'I'm an *escaped* convict, I'm *armed* and I'm extremely *dangerous*. Understand?'

Mandy nodded.

'I don't care about you,' said Kiru. 'I don't care about Candy. I don't care about anything in the universe. All *I* care about is getting to Earth on this ship.'

'It's not going *to* Earth,' said Mandy. 'It's just come *from* there.'

'But wasn't Candy meant to return to Earth?'

'She *was*, but there's been a *change* of plan.'

'And now there's another change of plan.'

If the ship had come from Earth, which it had, Kiru

knew it could get back there – which it was going to, she'd make sure of that.

'You're leaving,' said Kiru.

This was going to be a long voyage on a small ship, and there was no way that Kiru could allow Mandy to stay on board. She already knew what it would be like, because even a short time on an asteroid as big as Hideaway had been far too long to spend with Candy.

Kiru put her hand on Mandy's shoulder, turned her around, shoved her towards the docking gate.

'You can't push me *out* into space!'

'Why not?'

'Because I'll *die!*'

'You will if you're out in space,' said Kiru. 'But while this gate's open, the shuttle can't leave. Get in there, open the outer gate. Now! You have ten seconds. Go!'

Kiru let the inner door close, and Mandy vanished inside. She had more than ten seconds in which to transfer. Thirty, in fact. Kiru waited a minute, watching as all the gate lights blinked off. Mandy was gone, heading for Hideaway.

With the axe in her right hand, swinging it back and forth to feel the balance, Kiru made her way along the passageway towards the command cabin. When she reached it, she opened the door and stepped inside.

'Hello, Kiru,' said a voice. 'This is a pleasant surprise.'

Kiru stared at the pilot.

A surprise, yes; but pleasant, no.

CHAPTER

SIXTEEN

Wayne Norton hesitated before jumping down onto the blue grass of Algol. It was only three feet to the ground, but he was wondering about the effect of the much higher gravity. Then Jay pushed him. He dropped and landed on both feet. The fall seemed no different, no faster, no harder than it would have been on Earth or on Caphmiaultrelvossmuaf. Norton lifted his right leg, which wasn't any more difficult than usual. He took a step forward, then lifted his left leg, took another step. Walking was as easy as it normally was, not that he'd done much recently. He raised his arms slowly out from his sides, and they seemed no heavier than before.

Jay jumped from the hatch of the lander, then bent down and tapped his right knee. 'I couldn't have done that before the Algolans fixed me up,' he said. 'Until I was dead, I had a dodgy knee.'

The *Demon Star* had been in orbit around Algol for several hours, during which Jay sent a number of messages requesting landing permission. They had received no reply, which he said might have been because the ship's equipment was faulty. Whatever the reason, Jay suggested they head down to the planet in the lander. Norton didn't like it, but there seemed no alternative. He'd long suspected that Jay had more skills than he pretended, that he wasn't only a ship's steward; but when it took him ten minutes to find out how to close the lander door behind them, Norton began to have his doubts. Eventually, Jay managed to start the craft, disengage it from the main ship and bring them down to the surface of Algol.

Jay tapped the hull of the lander and said, 'A piece of cake.'

The lander was only a thin slice out of the *Demon Star*, far smaller than even a lifeboat. Remembering his own voyage in a liferaft, Norton was inevitably reminded of Grawl. Ever since Kiru had gone missing, he'd tried not to think of Grawl – or even Kiru, because that would have meant wondering what might have happened to her. Until reaching Algol, however, there hadn't been much to do except think – and drink. The voyage had been spent thinking and drinking, and fortunately the latter made the former more difficult. Now that he was on Algol, his mission really began. And he'd no idea where to start.

He started by jumping up in the air, as high as he could, and landed on the balls of his feet.

'You believe me now, old boy?' asked Jay.

'I guess so,' said Norton.

The gravity on Algol was meant to be heavier than on Earth, and he'd wanted to wear an envirosuit. Jay said that wasn't necessary or possible. Not necessary because surface conditions were within tolerable limits for human visitors, and not possible because the *Demon Star* didn't have any. Norton believed the real reason was the size of the lander. It was no bigger than a European automobile, and if they had worn enviro-suits there wouldn't have been enough room in the cabin for all the bottles Jay had brought with him.

'Making out that they come from a world with heavy gravity is just an example of Algolan misinfo-mation,' said Jay. 'According to some infodata, they have tails. That's another example. They want the galaxy to know as little about them as possible.'

'The same as Taxliens,' said Norton.

'No. You can believe half of what the Algolans say. The problem comes with knowing which half. That's misinformation. You can't believe anything the Taxliens say. That's lying. They always lie. But you can't rely on their lies, because they even lie about lying.'

Norton had been taking shallow breaths, hardly speaking a word, but the atmosphere didn't seem to have poisoned him. Jay said he'd been to Algol before, and his visit must have included breathing. Norton opened his mouth wide and took a deep breath. It was great to feel the cool, fresh air in his lungs. He stretched out his arms and legs, looking around at the alien world where they had landed, glad he could focus his eyes on something further away than two or three yards.

Algol seemed to be the opposite of Earth. The grass was blue and the sky was green, but there was no sign of the planet's two suns. A cool wind blew over the plain, which was flat and desolate, without any trees or bushes. In one direction, there was a range of hills on the horizon. With the land so empty, it was difficult to judge perspective and distance, to know if the hills were small and near or high and further away.

Jay had set the lander down far from any centre of

habitation, saying the Algolans would judge this as being less hostile. The next move was up to them.

'What are we doing here, Jay?' said Norton. 'Why am I really here? Why are you here? The Taxliens must have sent you, I know that. You can tell me now. There's nothing I can do about it.'

'They didn't send me, I keep telling you. When I found out they were letting you go to Algol, I decided to join you. It was my decision.' Jay turned back towards the hatch, reaching in for a bottle and two glasses. 'You want an infusion?'

'No.'

Jay poured two glasses and handed him one. 'It's going to be a long wait,' he said.

'What if nobody comes?'

'They will. They know we're here. They'll come to check us out. They want to meet the new ambassador.' Jay smiled and looked Norton up and down, and sipped at his drink.

Norton was wearing his uniform. It was a good fit, and he felt comfortable in the outfit. His only regret was his hair, which was far too long. He'd always kept his hair very short, but Kiru had persuaded him to grow it – and she was very persuasive. He felt it would be unlucky to go back to a crew cut. This was how Kiru wanted him to have his hair, and he'd keep it like this until they met again.

Until? Yes, without doubt: until!

He raised his glass, took a mouthful, then winced. During the voyage, he'd become quite a connoisseur of exotic liquor, and it was easy to tell this was basic rotgut. But he swallowed it down.

Wayne Norton, ambassador to Algol. The idea was crazy. What were the Taxliens up to? He didn't want to

find out, but he knew he would sooner or later. All he
wanted was to find Kiru, and he wished he was more
positive about that.

'I'm sure they don't know anything about a new
ambassador,' said Norton. 'Maybe I should take off
the uniform. If they don't know the Taxliens sent me,
I stand a better chance.'

'A better chance of what?'

'Of not being killed.'

'If they wanted to kill you, Wayne, they'd have
blown the ship to smithereens by now. The Algolans
are a peaceful race.'

'They're not!'

'Says who? The Taxliens? I've told you before, the
Algolans have a great respect for life, all life. They're
vegetarians.'

'They can't be.'

'Why not? The nippers will eat insects and worms,
but that's kids for you.'

'Vegetarians wouldn't have those fangs and claws.'

'You can't judge anyone by appearance. Look at
you, for example. Life evolved differently here than
on Earth, and Algolans developed fangs and claws.
Because of how they appear to us, they've got a reputation for being ferocious and warlike.'

'I've seen their troops. They *are* ferocious and warlike!'

Jay shook his head. 'Algolans aren't violent.'

'Janesmith killed three of her sisters.'

'How do you know?'

'She told me.'

'Did she also tell you she ate their innards?'

'No.' Norton winced again, but not because of what
he was drinking.

'That's what she told me, but maybe she was exaggerating. The same with killing her sisters, perhaps she didn't kill three of them. It might only have been one, two at the most.' Jay sipped at his glass, frowning as he swallowed. 'Come on, Wayne, she didn't kill any of her sisters. She didn't kill anyone. She was making clothes, so you should have realised she was . . . she was spinning you a yarn!' Jay laughed at his own joke. 'The Algolans like to pretend they're violent and tough, but they're lovely people, very friendly and sociable.'

'But when she was on Hideaway, Janesmith was worried about being assassinated by her family.'

'That's what she told you. She was on Hideaway for years and years, and that's about the easiest place in the universe to find someone. You were taken in by her big blue alien eyes, Wayne, and that's one way of spreading misinformation. The Algolans like to present a warlike, ruthless, frightening image. It's the best way to keep the rest of the galaxy at a distance. All they want is to be left alone, left in peace.'

'They attacked the pirate base,' said Norton. 'That's not very peaceful.'

'No, but it was hardly an unprovoked assault. They had good reason to attack, they were rescuing Marysmith. And I'm very glad they did, because they put me back together again, which is what they do with their own troops. Or perhaps Marysmith asked for my reanimation because she liked my cooking. Or they saved me because I was one of the family.'

'What family?'

'The royal family. My brother was married to Marysmith, so I was family. Whatever the reason, I'm alive because of the Algolans. Life is precious to them, and they go to extremes to preserve it. From what I heard, they killed none of the pirates. Or not after they surrendered. They were all transported to Clink.'

'Grawl must have been captured with the pirates, and that's how he wound up on Arazon. But you don't know what happened to Kosmos or William Ewart?'

'I didn't even know about Grawl until you told me,' said Jay. 'And I certainly didn't care.'

'What about *******? What happened to him? And who was he?'

'Or *what* was he? Or *she*. Or *it*. Or *them*.' Jay shook his head. 'I don't know. And I don't want to know.' He raised his left arm, pointing. 'Here they come.'

Norton looked up and saw a single craft heading towards them. It flew low and slow; it had the shape of a helicopter, but the wings of a plane. As it came closer, he realised the wings were flapping like a bird in flight. Then he realised that . . .

'It's a bird,' he said. 'It's a giant bird.'

'It's a technogenetic giant bird,' said Jay.

It was a bird that was an aircraft, so Norton said, 'It's a birdcraft.'

'The pilot sits in the head, and the passengers are inside the body. Algol is a wonderful planet, Wayne.'

'Why did you leave?'

'This,' said Jay, and he raised his glass. 'I couldn't drink any more of it.' He sipped at his drink, then closed his eyes and swallowed what was left. 'Until today.'

'This is Algolan?' Norton studied his glass.

Jay nodded his head. 'Absolutely beastly, isn't it? I'd kept one bottle as a souvenir, although I don't know why I bothered, but I thought it was appropriate for today. You'd better get used to it, Wayne, because it's all they have. You'll soon learn to be very diplomatic!'

'And what are you going to be doing?'

'That's easy, I'll . . . I'll . . .' Jay reached for the bottle and poured himself another shot. 'I'll think of something.'

The giant white bird was only a quarter of a mile away, its giant white wings rhythmically beating. As Norton gazed at its giant black talons and its sharp, serrated, giant black bill, the birdcraft began to circle the lander. It stayed some four hundred yards away and about a hundred feet high, slowly surveying the intruders.

'Hello, I'm back!' yelled Jay. 'Remember me? Rajic Jao Rajic!' He waved up at the creature.

Norton suddenly realised he was hearing Jay's voice through the slate, listening to him in translation.

'You can speak Algolan,' said Norton.

'Very observant, old chap.'

'You could have taught me during the voyage.'

'It's a real stinker of a lingo, but you don't need to learn it, you've got a slate. When I was here last, there wasn't one on the whole planet. That's how isolated they were. They said there wasn't a single slate here, but it was probably a lie. Misinformation, I mean.'

'You could have taught me a few phrases.' Norton kept watching the birdcraft drifting around them.

'The only thing I can teach is cooking, and I taught Marysmith. Lovely girl, she didn't want me to leave, but she said I was welcome back on Algol any time.'

'She's not the Empress any more. She's dead. Janesmith is the Empress.'

'Maybe, maybe not.'

'You mean Marysmith might have been revived?'

'She might not have been dead. This is Algol. Who knows?'

'JAO RAJIC JAO RAJIC JAO!' came a booming voice from the sky. The birdcraft was now stationary, hovering in the air, still keeping its distance.

'Yes, hello!' yelled Jay. He took a step away from the lander, moved back to put down his glass, then began walking out into the open. 'I've come to see the family!' he shouted, cupping his hands to his mouth, then he glanced back to Norton. 'I'll stroll over for a chat. They're good eggs, but you can't blame them for being suspicious. Keep your pecker up, old chum. Pip pip.' He turned and walked out across the blue grass.

'RAJIC JAO RAJIC JAO RAJIC!'

'That's me. I'm here.' Jay raised both his arms and waved his hands.

A streak of cobalt lightning erupted from the birdcraft's beak. It flashed through the air, hitting Jay in the chest.

He exploded. His whole body erupted into an incandescent fireball. A burst of smoke gushed upwards, like the mushroom cloud of an atomic explosion.

Jay was about two hundred yards away, and Norton immediately dropped to the ground as the scorching wave of heat washed over him. He closed his eyes, but the brilliant light seared through his lids. Then came the sound, a single thunderbolt, sharp and loud and deafening.

Norton peered between his interlaced fingers, watching as the pall of dark smoke drifted away. All that remained was a circle of black ash on the ground. The alien wind kept on blowing, and the ashes were soon gone. There was no sign of Jay, not a trace that he had ever existed.

The alien thunderclap reverberated within Norton's

head, and he could hear Jay's voice going around and around his echoing skull:

'. . . *Algolans are a peaceful race . . . they're lovely people, very friendly and sociable . . . they aren't violent . . . all life is precious to them . . . they go to extremes to preserve it . . . Algolans are a peaceful race . . . they're lovely people . . .*'

The birdcraft hovered in the green sky, and Wayne Norton could do nothing but watch and wait to be obliterated from the universe.

CHAPTER

SEVENTEEN

Another world, another group of aliens, another restaurant. After so many years, they were all the same and he never bothered with their names. He'd never be back on this planet, he'd never see these aliens again, and he would never eat another meal in this restaurant – no matter how good it was.

'I'm very pleased to meet you all, gentlemen, and I hope we can reach an agreement which will be to our mutual benefit. The best way to do this is if you start by telling me your current position and how you would like this to be improved.'

They might not have been gentlemen, or even men; they could have been female, or something between female and male; but the slate could translate his words to make the correct gender reference. The correct reference might even have been no reference. And because on some worlds, it was a deadly insult even to say 'hello', it was another of the slate's functions to edit and revise all the formalities. Most star-spanning species had learned that few subtle conversational nuances were available when talking with someone from another planet, although others seemed to believe that if they spoke either loudly or slowly or both, there was no need for any translation. The slate was a bridge across the stellar divide.

In the years since he'd begun his galactic travels, the simultaneous linguistic and tonal equaliser had become much more sophisticated and reliable. A long time ago, he owned a company which made slates. Perhaps even then there were more advanced models than those he produced, but he hadn't been in business to offer products with extra applications. In any case, there was never much profit in manufacturing, the real money was in buying and selling – and the differential between the two.

'Ours is a primitive and backward world,' began one of the aliens, 'we hope you understand.'

He'd heard this so often before, it was almost a standard translation. The phrase 'primitive and backward' was synonymous with 'we don't intend to pay very much'.

The three aliens were humanoid in shape, but disguised their bodies by wearing long, shapeless robes and hid their faces within shaded hoods. It was a very cheap disguise, maybe to prove they really were from a primitive and backward planet and couldn't afford bodymasks. But it might not have been him they were hiding from. They could have had rivals on this planet, even enemies in this restaurant.

The same could be true in his case, which was why his own security was close by. He had his own rivals and enemies, anyone as successful as him always did. This was another reason why he was always on the move, travelling from one star system to another.

'I do understand,' he said. 'Please continue.'

The alien trio sat opposite him, at the other side of a wide table. It didn't really matter what name they had given for their world, because it was accepted practice to pretend to be from somewhere else. They might have been agents for a third party, brokering a deal on behalf of another planet, hoping to make their own profit between buying and selling. None of it made any difference to him, because he always operated anonymously. It was a long time since he'd left his native world; he was a citizen of the galaxy.

Many more galactic citizens were sitting at tables around him – or standing, or lying. He'd been in so many restaurants exactly like this one, with the decor and all the fittings identical down to the very last detail. A random cross-section of the universe, with people from so many different planets eating and drinking and talking, the place could have been on any of the known worlds. All the diverse voices merged into a subdued cacophony of sound, none of which could be isolated and deciphered without specialist decoding. Although he carried his own decoder, which could penetrate the screens of every booth, there was nothing so boring as eavesdropping on other discussions – although listening to the alien opposite him came a close second.

The one in the centre was doing all the talking, and he said, 'Our world is a feudal dictatorship, and its people are virtually slaves. Very few of us are allowed off-planet, and if any word of this meeting were to reach our brutal leaders, we would be executed as traitors. We want to change our world and make a better society for everyone who lives there, a world where everyone has freedom and choice. We want nothing less than a total revolution.'

As he half-listened, he raised his hand and signalled for another drink. Each of the three aliens had a glass of water in front of them, but none of them had touched a drop. Wherever he went, he always tried the water, because the taste varied so much across the galaxy. At the moment, however, he was drinking Terran whisky. If he never went back to Earth, the least he could do was support the export trade. The waiter came across to him.

'Another glass of welsh,' he said.

The waiters (or waitresses) were the only natives in the restaurant. No one who lived on this world could afford to eat here, and this part of the planet was no longer theirs. The locals were humanoid, tall and slender, long-limbed but slow-moving. Only their heads were not covered by their garish uniforms, a patchwork of primary colours, and their faces were so pale the skin seemed almost translucent. They moved from table to table, serving aliens whose worlds they would never see – aliens who did not see them now.

'Please,' he added, looking up towards the deep dark eyes of the waiter. The waiter met his gaze for a moment, then glanced aside. Except for answering questions about the menu, they were forbidden to speak. Taking the empty glass in his gloved hand, he walked slowly away.

The alien sitting opposite was still talking. 'We represent a consortium of dynamic and ambitious venture capitalists who want to bring the benefits of free enterprise to our world,' he said.

As long as all the details were finalised before starting to eat, a business lunch was the most civilised way of making a deal. That meant he could concentrate his attention on what he was eating without too much distraction; and by then he would also know how much his guests were worth to him and how much to spend on the meal. Although business etiquette varied from planet to planet, it was usually the seller who paid for the meal – and the buyer who paid for everything else.

This was his life and what he enjoyed, the wheeling and dealing, the instinctive decisions, calculating percentages of percentages, balancing the intangible against the hypothetical. Any business, any planet, he would have been a success anywhere, from haggling in a street bazaar through to top-tier negotiating in the corporate headquarters of a multi-world enterprise.

Selling was his speciality, and a good salesman only needed to sell one product – himself.

The alien said, 'Our planet is so undeveloped that there is only one comservice –'

He began to pay more attention. This did sound like a primitive and backward world.

'– and this provides us with only one SeeV channel,' continued the alien.

'One?' he said. 'One!'

'Yes, one. It's a state monopoly, and all we get is government propaganda five hours a day.'

'Five? What about the other nineteen hours?'

The slate had a temporal conversion function, translating alien time units into their Terran equivalent.

'Screen time is restricted to five hours a day,' said the alien.

'One channel? Five hours a day?' He'd heard some strange tales of weird worlds, but a planet which only had one SeeV station – and part-time at that – it was barbaric.

'Two hours in late afternoon, for children after school, then a break of two hours for the evening meal and to put the children to bed, then another three hours for adults before it's time for them to go to bed.'

'Thanks,' he said, as the waiter offered him a tray holding the glass of welsh. He took a mouthful immediately, looking at the alien in front of him, trying to see his face within the dark cowl. He looked at the other two, who sat immobile and silent. They had to be exaggerating. 'What kind of programme choice is there?'

'There is no choice. We watch what we are given. Everything we see is educational or cultural, there is no word for   in our language.'

He could guess what the word was. 'Entertainment?'

'What you said did not translate,' said the alien.

'And advertisers sponsor that kind of stuff? Educational? Cultural?'

'We have no advertisements, no commercials, no sponsorship.'

'What . . . none?'

'No.'

'So who pays for it all?' he asked – although 'all' wasn't the appropriate word.

'The government pays. The government owns the comservice. The government owns everything on our planet.'

'Everything?'

'Everything,' said the alien. 'And everyone. We are all slaves of the state. The only media to which we have access is controlled by the government and designed to reinforce the status quo. We're totally indoctrinated, and because we're denied all information about other planets, the vast majority of people on our world are convinced they live in the perfect society. The rest of the galaxy is unknown to us.'

'That's terrible,' he said. And it was. 'It's immoral. It's evil.'

'We need your help.'

'Right,' he said. It was his duty to help them.

'Our world will change, it must change, it is changing, and we're putting together a consortium to establish a brand new comservice. What we want is all the latest equipment, everything we could possibly need, from microcams up to full studio production facilities. We have nothing, and we want everything necessary to service the whole planet.'

He sipped his whisky and tried to appear calm and relaxed.

'Could you arrange this for us?' asked the alien.

'I could,' he said, as he began roughly calculating how much money was involved in such a deal.

'You're the expert, and we'll rely on you to tell us exactly what we need and to get it for us. Does that sound satisfactory?'

'It does,' he said, and he gave up counting because he'd soon lost track of the number of zeroes on the end of the total. 'How many suppliers are bidding for the tender? I'm very competitive, and I can beat any other quote you've been given.'

'You're the only person we've approached so far. We're not experienced in the ways of business and commerce, what would you recommend? Should we also ask some of your competitors?'

'No, oh no, there's no need for that, no need at all, no.'

'We accept your advice. Was there anything else?' The alien paused, as if waiting for one of his colleagues to speak. 'In that case: if you can obtain what we want, the job is yours.'

'Right,' he said, and he raised his glass to his mouth to prevent himself from smiling.

'You agree?'

'I do. Right. I agree. Consider it done. I assure you I can obtain everything you need, all guaranteed top quality, the best value in the universe. I'll need complete details of your world, its geography, demographics, so I can draw up full specifications, and I'll have to know where and when you want it all delivered.'

'There is one more thing.'

He waited. There always was.

'We're not used to these business negotiations,' said the alien, 'and there's one subject about which we're very uncertain. It's delicate, it's embarrassing, and we don't really know how to bring it up without seeming crude and mercenary. It's the . . . the bribe.'

'Ah, right,' he said. This was what it was all about, what they were really after, why they had come to him. At least they were being honest about their dishonesty. 'It's nothing to make a fuss about, I assure you. It can be handled very discreetly. Initiative payments are all part of normal business practice.'

'That's very reassuring. How much would you like?'

He looked at the alien. Could they really be so innocent that they believed the customer paid the bribe . . . ? But the customer was always right, and he didn't want to go against their wishes.

'Commission,' he said, slowly, 'is usually a percentage of the total sum. I'll have to work it all out, and the extra money could be incorporated into the payment schedule, if that's okay by you.'

'These words you mention, *money* and *payment*, they could be a problem for you.'

'What problem?'

'We have no money.'

'That's not a problem,' he said. 'Your money is only legal tender on your world. When you came to this planet, you had to change your currency. Our contract will include all the necessary financial details.'

At one time, and it wasn't very long ago, it was almost impossible for one planet to trade with another. This was partly for logistical reasons, because transporting goods across the galaxy wasn't practical; but once anything became economically viable, it also became practical. Money was the basic medium of exchange, and when the currencies of different planets became exchangeable, there was no longer any barrier to trading from world to world.

And it was all thanks to the Galactic Taxation Agency . . . or the Stellar Revenue Corporation . . . or the InterWorld Levy Adjustment Company . . . or the Planetary Rating Authority . . . or the Cosmic Duty and Excise Collection Board . . . or the Fiscal Assessment Organisation of the Universe . . . and maybe even the Stellar Taxation Levy Rating Assessment Collection Society. Who were all one and the same, different names for the same nameless galaxy-spanning aliens who collected taxes across the universe.

He hated paying tax as much as the next man, woman or alien; he probably hated it far more, because he had far more to pay. But he had to admit, reluctantly, that the enigmatic aliens had begun to establish a financial structure which enabled a galactic entrepreneur such as himself to prosper.

Like all successful businesses, the taxation company had grown through diversification. It expanded into other fiscal institutions, such as investment trusts and mortgage corporations. Wherever money was involved, the anonymous aliens were there: credit and loans, savings and insurance, bonds and securities. Whatever the transaction, there was a tax; and because they handled every transaction, tax avoidance was impossible.

The mysterious aliens were rapidly becoming bankers to the universe. Their business was money. They made money out of money, because there was always a tax surcharge on borrowing, on lending, on inter-planetary currency exchanges, on every transaction. Money was the perfect product. Buying or selling, there was always a profit, never a loss.

'When we said, "We have no money",' said the hooded alien sitting opposite, 'what we meant was: We have *no* money. Money does not exist on our world.'

'No money?' He didn't understand. He couldn't understand. 'How can a planet not have money? It's like . . . like not having air.'

'We have air,' said the alien. 'And it's free. Like everything else on our world.'

'Free?' he said. It wasn't a word he used very often. 'Everything is free on your world?'

'Yes. That's why we don't need money.'

'But . . . nothing is free in the universe.'

'Except on our planet.'

'If you have no money, how do you think you can buy a complete comservice? Who's going to pay for all the equipment?'

'You have agreed to be our supplier, and so you pay for everything.'

'Just hold on. I buy everything, right, but I do it on your behalf. I *buy* but you *pay*. This is a basic translation error.'

'No, William Ewart, this is your basic error.'

His flesh suddenly felt very cold and he shivered.

Because they knew who he was. He glanced quickly around for his security team. They were gone. Everyone was gone. Without him noticing, the whole restaurant had become empty. There was no one left, only him and the three aliens sitting on the other side of the table. Then the one on the left and the one on the right began to fade away, dissolving into the air and vanishing from view. He and the last alien were all alone in the restaurant.

'Who are you?' asked William Ewart.

Since leaving Earth, he'd made his living through buying and selling, and his profit was the margin between the two. Then he discovered how to make even more profit by doing only half the work: by selling without buying.

'Have we met before?' he asked.

This could only be a previous client, someone who had found fault with Ewart's business practices. Even worse, they had now found Ewart. And he was in trouble.

'If,' said Ewart, 'we signed a trading contract and anything went wrong and such things can and sometimes do happen once they're out of my hands I'm the first to admit that I can't control every detail of my operation and if there's any compensation due to you or any problem that needs solving you have my personal guarantee because my reputation is absolutely vital because so much of my business comes from recommendation and repeat orders from satisfied customers and I assure you of my full commitment because if something went wrong . . .'

'Yes,' said the alien, as he shook his head and the hood fell away, 'we've met before.'

Ewart had been cold, but now his blood turned to ice.

He'd thought he was in trouble. But he wasn't. He was in danger. Extreme danger.

Because sitting opposite him was an Algolan.

CHAPTER

EIGHTEEN

There were no days on Caphmiaultrelvossmuaf, no days or nights, evenings or mornings, and Kiru had never had morning sickness. But as she stood in the command cabin of the spacecraft, her stomach suddenly heaved. She opened her mouth and spewed out a fountain of sour vomit.

'Is that what you think of me?' said the pilot.

'Yes,' said Kiru, wiping her chin with the back of her left hand as she raised the axe with her right hand and charged forward to brain the pilot.

Major Diana Travis sprang aside. Kiru allowed her arm to swing down, completing the arc, and the blade sliced deep into the control seat's headrest. She left it there, let go of the handle and took a pace back. The two women looked at each other.

'What are you doing here?' said Kiru.

'It's my ship,' said Diana. 'What are you doing here?'

'Going to Earth.'

'Not in this ship you're not.'

Kiru reached out for the axe.

'Careful with the tomahawk,' said Diana, folding her arms and leaning against the bulkhead. 'It has sentimental value.'

'It's yours? Mandy tried to kill me with it.'

'I know.' Diana glanced at one of the screens in front of the command seat. 'I was watching.'

'Why didn't you stop her?'

'I didn't know what she was planning. And neither did I care. It was nothing to do with me. You handled yourself quite well, not that she was much opposition. Anyway, it wasn't you she was after. We were both expecting someone else. What happened to Candy?'

'Why should you care?' said Kiru. 'It's nothing to do with you.'

'True.' Diana shrugged. 'And that's one reason why I let you kick Mandy off the ship.'

'What's the other?'

'Her *voice* got *on* my *nerves* every *time* she *spoke*.'

Kiru resisted nodding in agreement; Diana was the last person she ever wanted to agree with. Because of her, she'd been deported to Arazon. That was back on Earth, when Kiru made the mistake of going through the door to a police base, and Diana had been a police officer. Kiru hadn't known Diana's name back then, and back then it might not have been Diana – because since that time, Diana had used at least two other names and at least one other body. Maybe she'd never really been a cop, it was just a cover for her career as a cosmic criminal.

'Here we are again, Kiru,' said Diana. 'Just like old times.'

One of Diana's names had been Elliot Ness. That was when she'd been male, and that was when Kiru had shared a lifeboat to Caphmiaultrelvossmuaf with her/him. Kiru realised her life was going in circles. She'd returned to Hideaway, and now she was back on a small spacecraft with Diana/Elliot Ness.

'Are you staying or what?' asked Diana.

'I want to go to Earth.'

'This isn't a taxi. If you want to leave, you can go back to Hideaway.'

That wasn't such a good idea, and Kiru shook her head. A drop of vomit fell to the floor. She wiped her mouth and chin with her sleeve.

'Stay if you want,' said Diana. 'I'll be glad of some *intelligent* company. We got on well during our last voyage, didn't we? I've always thought that if we got to know each other, Kiru, we could be friends.'

'Friends!' Kiru could hardly believe it. 'I ended up on Clink because of you.'

Diana shrugged her shoulders. 'All part of life's rich tapestry.'

And now Kiru's whole life was unravelling.

'Do you ever get a feeling of déjà vu?' Diana said.

This was exactly what Kiru had been thinking a minute ago. She wondered if there was a word – or even two – for that.

'Because,' Diana continued, 'you've blamed me for this before. But if you hadn't gone to Clink, you'd never have reached Hideaway and met Wayne. And where is Wayne?'

'He's . . .' Kiru became silent again. It was best if Diana knew as little as possible. Not that Kiru knew very much.

'You and Wayne, what a romantic story.' Diana waited for some sign of agreement from Kiru. There wasn't any. 'You were the ideal couple for the first wedding on Café World.'

'What about Caphafer weddings?' said Kiru.

'I doubt the locals ever got married. They were too . . .' Diana paused, trying to think of the right word.

'Sensible?'

Diana laughed. 'I don't think the Caphafers have even thought of monogamy, let alone devised some kind of wedding service.' She laughed again. 'What a wedding yours was, Kiru. It's supposed to be the most exciting day of a girl's life. Was it?'

'I've known quieter days.'

'I don't blame you or Wayne for what happened.'

'What! You don't blame us? You give us a wedding cake as a present, then Grawl jumps out to assassinate the guests. What would have happened if the Algolans hadn't arrived to prevent the massacre?'

'Killing tax collectors? That's not assassination, that's pest control.'

'But what would have happened to me?'

'Ah, so that's it. Self, self.'

'Was I going to be Grawl's reward for killing your new partners? And after everything Wayne did for you and Café World.'

'The last thing Wayne did for me,' said Diana, 'was punch me on the jaw.' She rubbed at her chin as if she could still feel the blow. 'Let's forget the past, Kiru. Everything starts from now.'

It was impossible to forget the past, particularly when Kiru had been reminded of the part she had tried hardest to forget: Grawl.

He was last seen being dragged away by a swarm of Algolan warriors, destined to be a sex toy for Empress Janesmith. Kiru was glad about that. It seemed similar to what he'd planned for her. She wasn't certain which would have been worse, her fate or his. Kiru would have been oblivious to everything. Her body would have lived on, but not her brain. Grawl, however, still had his own mind. For a while, at least. He would know exactly what was happening to him. Kiru was also glad about that.

'I've got to get this ship moving,' said Diana. 'This is your last chance to leave. Or you can stay. On one condition.'

'What?'

'You clean yourself up and get changed.'

'That's two.' Kiru glanced at the slime oozing down the front of Candy's spectraflesh suit. 'Candy said she was heading for Earth, that's why I took her place.'

'She thought she was, but I was hired to bring out Mandy so she could team up with Candy again, then take them on to report on a big story.' Diana paused, watching as Kiru surveyed the command cabin. 'Don't get any ideas. You couldn't get this ship back to Earth.'

'No,' agreed Kiru, 'but you could. Candy's not here, Mandy's not here. Your mission is over.'

'My mission,' said Diana, 'is different from theirs.'

'I thought,' said Kiru, 'it might be.'

'I'm leaving. You coming? What have you got to lose?'

'Everything.'

'Yes, but what have you got?'

Kiru had her life, and she had another life within her. She also had no alternative, because returning to Hideaway wasn't an option.

'Okay,' said Kiru. 'Let's go.'

'Good. Glad to have you aboard, Kiru.'

Kiru wondered: why?

What was Diana up to? Major Diana Travis, Terran

cop, who had arrested Kiru; Major Diana Travis, who had changed sex and taken the name Elliot Ness, and who had been on a liferaft with Kiru; Major Diana Travis, who had been promoted and claimed to be her own father, Colonel Travis, and who had recruited Wayne into GalactiCop.

'Are you still Diana?' asked Kiru. 'Or have you got a different name?'

'Diana is fine.' She reached over to the back of the pilot's seat and pulled out the axe. 'For now.' Then she sat down and jerked a thumb over her shoulder. 'Make yourself at home.'

As Diana focused her attention on the controls, Kiru turned and began to make her way back along the ship. It was far larger than the lifeboat she'd shared with one of Diana's alter egos, but it wasn't the kind of vessel she'd expected to travel on. She had imagined a luxury cruise far removed from her previous interstellar voyages as a convict or spacewreck survivor or stowaway, and she'd also thought her destination would be Earth.

Kiru glanced back into the command cabin, watching as Diana prepared to pilot the ship into the unknown depths of falspace.

'Where are we going?' she asked.

Diana told her. One word. Two syllables. Five letters.

Which for Kiru spelled an infinity of fear and terror.

Because it was the last place in the universe she ever wanted to go.

CHAPTER
NINETEEN

All alone on Algol, Wayne Norton kept on waiting. The birdcraft which had destroyed Jay
couldn't have failed to see Norton as it circled the
lander one final time, but it had ignored him and
flapped away. That must have been hours ago, because
the light was quickly fading. At first, there was nothing
he could do but wait and drink. By now, the birdcraft
had long gone – and so had the bottle of Algolan
hooch.

Norton had tried to drink himself into oblivion, but
he'd never felt more sober. The only thing the alcohol
had done was give him a terrible headache. Trapped on
a hostile alien planet, with night about to fall, he knew
he was surrounded by unknown gruesome beasts with
jaws of steel which could tear through the hull of the
lander as easily as he could bite into a hamburger. He
wished he had a hamburger – it was centuries since
he'd had one – he wished he had anything. Searching
the lander hadn't taken long, but there was no food on
board.

He sat on the floor, gazing out across the blue

planet. There had been nothing to see when it was fully light, now there was even less. He'd let his legs dangle from the edge of the hatch at first. The cold wind had made them numb, but at least he wouldn't have felt anything when the first alien predator pounced and ripped through his flesh and bones.

'You!' said a voice. 'Have you got the guns?'

'Jeepers!' gasped Norton, and he fell back inside the lander. He started to reach for the hatch control, but a heavy arm thudded against the deck of the lander, crashing up and down as if calling for service, and he drew himself up against the far side of the hull, staring out at the dark shape silhouetted against the opening.

'The guns?' said the voice. 'The guns!'

Norton wondered what to say.

'It's no use asking her,' said another voice, and a second outline came into view. 'She's an alien. She won't understand our language.'

'How do we communicate?'

'We mime,' said a third voice, and another shape appeared in the doorway.

'How will that work? If she can't understand us when we make a noise, how can she understand if we open and close our mouths in silence?'

'Not that kind of mime. We mime with gestures, we act by movement, we project by body language.'

'If you're so clever, make the gestures for "where are the guns?".'

They were Algolans. Because this was Algol, that wasn't too unlikely. But Norton could recognise their shape, the way they held themselves, from their similarity to Janesmith.

'There's no need for sign language,' he said. 'I can understand you.'

The three shadowy heads turned from side to side as they glanced at each other.

'You speak Algolan!' said one.

It seemed that Jay had told the truth; they knew nothing of translation devices. But they wanted weapons, which matched with what the Taxliens had said about them: Algolans were violent and aggressive. Jay's dissenting argument, that they were a peaceful race, seemed less persuasive in view of the fact they had annihilated him.

'Yeah,' said Norton. If they didn't know about slates, it wasn't up to him to educate them.

'Where are the guns?' asked the first one, again.

This wasn't the kind of question Norton could answer or wanted to answer. The three Algolans had him trapped inside the lander. He needed to take control of the situation. Police training had taught him to get out of his patrol car whenever there was an incident: firstly, because movement was very restricted inside, and in the worst scenario you would be a sitting target; secondly, because if someone was standing outside, they were higher than you and at a psychological advantage. Height gave authority.

Wayne Norton stood up and walked towards the open hatch. His feet were on a level with the Algolans' waists. He towered above them, and they all took a step back, looking up at him. In the gloom, they all seemed very similar to Janesmith. They were bare-chested, which had also been her style; but unlike her, they were flat-chested. (Jay had said: never judge by appearances; but after his previous experience with Janesmith, Norton guessed these three were males.) Their flesh was blue, and they all had wild manes of long white hair. (The talons and fangs, he took for granted.) Despite the cold wind, they wore only knee-length shorts, each of a different colour, plus a matching strap around each elbow.

Norton planted his hands on his hips and stared down at the alien trio. It was time to impose his authority.

'I am a member of GalactiCop, and I am charging all of you with the first-degree murder of the human named Jay . . .' Jay wasn't enough of a name; it sounded as if Norton was accusing them of stealing a pet songbird: '. . . named Jay Edgar Hoover. You're all under arrest.'

'Under what?' asked one of the aliens, thrusting out a clenched fist towards Norton.

'Under arrest,' said Norton. Even in the twilight, he could see the sharp claws, but he stood his ground. 'For murder.'

'What's that?' asked another alien, and a second fist was directed up at him.

'She doesn't speak the Empress's Algolan,' said the third alien, and a third fist was aimed at him. 'She's making up words.'

'Where are the guns?' One of the aliens moved forward and started to lean inside the lander. 'In those boxes?'

Norton spread his legs to block the view of Rajic's drinks cabinets. He quickly raised his right foot, stretched it out, brought it down. But instead of the deck, his foot touched something else. For a moment, he thought it was an alien arm and he kicked down hard. But it wasn't an Algolan arm. It was an Algolan bottle. The bottle was so heavy it must have been glass – and it rolled. Norton slipped, lost his balance and fell out of the lander.

He lay on the ground, his head hurting far more than before, staring up at the three blue aliens who surrounded him and began talking excitedly.

'Look at her beautiful clothes.'

'They're so neat.'

'So smart.'

'Is that what all aliens wear?'

'That's what we could wear if this was a free planet.'

'Lots of unnecessary clothes. How wonderful.'

'This proves we are slaves, denied the latest fashion.'

'Denied any fashion, you mean.'

They all bent down, reaching out to touch Norton's outfit, caressing the fabric, stroking the braid, rubbing the buttons.

'Feel the texture.'

'This material, what can it be, such divine quality.'

'It's so tasteful, so elegant.'

'What's this?'

'It's called a . . . *pocket*.'

'What's it for?'

'To hold things in.'

'It's so small. It can't hold much.'

'It's to hold that stuff you take to a place where they have lots of things. You give them some of the stuff and they give you some of the things.'

'What *stuff*? What *place*? What *things*? What are you talking about?'

'What's the word for the *stuff* you get *products* with?'

'Is it . . . *money*?'

'Money! Yes. Pockets are to keep *money* in.'

'Have you any *money*?'

The aliens became silent, their hands became still. Their claws could have shredded Norton's uniform in a moment. His flesh, too . . .

They wanted money. They were robbers, thieves. They were criminals. The galaxy was full of them. But Norton had no money.

'Let go of me!' he said, forcefully; but not too forcefully. 'I'm a police officer!'

'She's an officer,' said one of the Algolans, and immediately they all sprang up and stood almost in line. 'Salute the officer!'

Two blue left hands shot up to shoulder height, one blue right hand did the same. Each hand had three fingers, one thumb, all tipped by curved claws. The hands waved, the fingers wiggled. Norton had to admit that it wasn't a very military salute; another point in favour of Jay's argument. He rose to his feet gave his best Las Vegas Police Department salute, and said, 'At ease.'

'A what officer?' said one of them, as they lowered their arms. 'What was that word?'

'A police officer,' said Norton.

'She's making up words again,' said one of the others.

'Silence!' ordered Norton. 'I'm not a *she*, I'm a *he*, and I want your names. Now!'

'General Johnsmith, officer!'

'General Joesmith, officer!'

'General Jacksmith, officer!'

The slate's major drawback was its alien name facility; it was very maladroit.

Three Algolan men, three generals. Norton tried hard to remember what outranked a general. He played for time by brushing invisible dirt from his jacket. His outfit was navy blue, and it had always seemed very nautical.

'I,' he said, 'am Admiral Wayne Norton.'

At first, the trio had seemed identical, all solidly built, with broad chests and muscular limbs; but already Norton could tell their faces were slightly different.

'Where are the guns?' asked one of the generals.

'The spaceship isn't very big,' said one of the other generals, 'there can't be many weapons inside.'

'Did you come to Algol alone?' asked the third general.

As yet, Norton didn't know which was Jack or Joe or John, but they seemed unaware of what had happened earlier. He glanced around, and a hundred yards behind the lander there was some kind of vehicle. It looked like a railroad wagon, but with three huge wheels on each side. Two long poles rose up from the body of the wagon. They were masts, and below them were the furled sails.

Norton realised these were different Algolans from the ones in the birdcraft, the ones who had killed Jay.

'If you haven't got any guns,' said one, 'have you any uniforms?'

'Who are you?' asked Norton.

'General Johnsmith, officer!'

'General Joesmith, officer!'

'General Jacksmith, officer!'

'What army are you with?' asked Norton.

'We are the Free Trade Alliance.'

'Bidding for the freedom to trade.'

'And the freedom to ally with other business organisations.'

'Other planets, other markets, other economic communities.'

'Ah-hah,' said Norton.

'What does that mean?' asked one of the Smiths.

Norton didn't know what it meant, but instead said what he did know. 'You were expecting weapons?'

'Yes!'

'Where are the guns?'

Norton couldn't tell them there were no weapons, because that was not what they wanted to hear. If they knew the truth, he'd no idea how they would react. He might start envying Jay's swift exit from the universe.

'What kind of guns did you expect?' he asked.

The generals looked at each other.

'Big guns!'

'Potent guns!'

'Guns to make us free!'

'Have you had much experience of armaments?' asked Norton.

'Yes!'

'Yes, yes!'

'Yes, yes, yes!'

'In the military,' said Norton, 'in most of the universe, it's usually considered the best policy to tell the truth to a superior officer, otherwise there could be serious consequences.' He gazed at them all in turn, staring into their big, blue, sloping eyes. 'You could all be busted back down through the ranks. Sergeants will be giving you orders. Corporals will be giving you orders. Even privates will be giving you orders! Understand?'

'Yes, admiral,' said the three aliens, their voices echoing from the simultaneous linguistic and tonal equaliser.

'So I'll ask you again: have you had much experience of armaments?'

'No, admiral,' came three replies.

'As I suspected,' said Norton. 'That's why there are no guns on board.'

'Oh.'

'That isn't fair.'

'We can't have a revolution without guns.'

'That's for strategic reasons,' said Norton, slowly, as he worked out his own strategy. 'I'm here to carry out a tactical appraisal to discover exactly what kind of military hardware you need.'

'You're a management consultant? Splendid!'

'Superlative!'

'Yes! We need someone who can teach us to . . . what's the word?'

'To inflict serious personal damage on our oppressors.'

Norton gazed over to where Jay had suffered the ultimate in personal damage, then looked back at the Algolans. They were still standing in line, almost, each of them staring eagerly at him. A bunch of amateur renegades, calling themselves generals, they were his best hope of finding Kiru. His only hope . . .

'From now on, you take your orders from me,' said Norton. 'Understand?'

'Yes, admiral!' said three alien voices.

'My first order is: we get away from here.'

'Yes, admiral!' said two alien voices.

'Where to?' said one alien voice.

'First,' said Norton, who had no idea where to, 'we get into your vehicle. Always make decisions one at a time. Understand?'

'Yes, admiral.'

'Yes, admiral.'

'Yes, admiral.'

One of the Algolans moved towards the hatch. 'Is there anything you need from your spaceship, admiral?'

'No,' said Norton. All he had was the clothes he

wore, which was more than he'd had when he first arrived on Caphmiaultrelvossmuaf. The bottles could stay on board; he was never going to drink again.

'What about your *money*?' said one of the others.

'I haven't got any money,' said Norton.

'You must have money. That's one thing we know about the rest of the galaxy. All you aliens have lots of money. You're all, er . . . *rich*.'

'Show us some money.'

'We only want to look.'

'We've never seen any money. We don't have any.'

'No one has any money on Algol. Our repressive regime doesn't allow it.'

'No money?' said Norton.

'No.'

'None.'

'There's no money on Algol.'

'Which,' said Norton, 'is why I didn't bring any, because I knew I couldn't spend it. I didn't bring anything.'

'What about this?' asked the alien who was by the lander, and he held up the bottle Norton had slipped on.

He was about to deny ownership; but if he claimed it wasn't his, they would ask who it belonged to. Wherever possible, it was always best not to lie; but sometimes the truth was impossible.

'It's empty,' said Norton, which was true.

'Yes, but we should return it to be recycled.'

'Recycling saves primary resources,' said another of the Algolans.

'That's right,' said the third of the trio. 'And to encourage the full exploitation of Algol's assets, we must learn to be more wasteful. Long live the revolution!'

'Long live the revolution!' agreed the one with the

bottle. He raised the bottle as if to smash it against the hull of the lander, then hesitated for a few seconds before carefully rolling it back inside the cabin.

'You appreciate our indigenous distilled liquor?'

'Of course,' said Norton. His head began throbbing even more, as if his brain was objecting to the lie. 'Algolcohol . . . I mean, Algolan alcohol . . . there's no word to describe it.'

'Algolcohol?'

'That's a word.'

'It's the word we've been searching for: the perfect brand name!'

'We know it's the best drink in the universe. We could export it to every planet in the galaxy, but our dictatorship won't allow any interstellar trade.'

That was one thing to be grateful for, thought Norton. He could still taste the vile liquor in his mouth, on his tongue and down his throat, while the pounding within his skull went on and on and on.

The Algolans turned and began walking to their vehicle, taking long, easy strides. Norton hurried to keep up with them. They had shown no curiosity about him and hadn't asked where he was from; but they had been expecting a shipment of guns, and they assumed he was connected with that.

'Does Algol have many visitors?' he asked.

'A few.'

'But none who are unauthorised.'

'You're probably the first for a long time.'

'And,' said Norton, 'what happens to unauthorised visitors?'

'That depends if they're discovered.'

'Which they usually are.'

'Later or sooner.'

Norton had already been discovered, but so far he'd escaped the same fate as Jay. 'You mean,' he said, 'I'm here at great risk?' He already knew that but was hoping the Algolans might deny it.

'The reward for risk is profit,' said one of them.

'And you'll be rewarded for your bold initiative in helping Algol win its freedom,' said another.

'We'll work out a full package of incentive payments,' said the third.

'Share options.'

'Performance related bonuses.'

'Deferred dividends.'

'Long live the revolution!' said three alien voices.

They had reached the land yacht by now, which was as big as a gasoline truck, and the strange craft loomed above them in the darkness. The Algolans turned towards Norton.

'Long live the revolution,' he said.

'Liberty!'

'Freedom!'

'And the pursuit of health!'

'Liberty,' said Norton. 'Freedom. And the pursuit of health.'

'Wealth! Not health.' One of the Algolans began to clamber aboard the land cruiser, quickly hauling himself up by a series of rings embedded into the hull. He used only his hands, the muscles of his arms lifting all of his weight. 'The pursuit of wealth.'

'Is it true,' asked Norton, thinking of his own health and remembering what Jay had said, 'that Algol has a very good medical system?'

'That's what the dictatorship would have you believe,' said one of the two Algolans still on the ground. 'But it's very inefficient.'

'What it needs,' said the other one, 'is the imposition of market discipline. Professional managers should be brought in, supported by a properly structured bureaucracy.' He began to climb, effortlessly pulling himself up. 'The health industry shouldn't be run by medical personnel, they have no idea about administration and always give priority to clinical decisions without even considering cost-benefit analysis.'

Norton's slate was having trouble with what was being said. The translation made very little sense to him, but perhaps it was because he'd drunk too much Algolan liquor. Algolcohol. That seemed to have crossed the translation barrier without any difficulty.

'You could argue,' said the last of the aliens, 'that the faults in the medical sector are symptomatic of everything that is wrong with Algol.' He began his own ascent up the side of the vehicle. 'The customer is very sick and the condition will become terminal unless radical surgery is carried out very soon.'

They believed Norton was here to help them perform the emergency treatment, and he had to keep them thinking that he was. The Algolan government, however, was unlikely to be a willing patient. If Norton was found to be part of the rebel operation, the prognosis for his own recovery was very unfavourable.

Jay was already dead. What had he done that Norton hadn't? Was it connected with him being here before? If he had been here before. And had the Algolans really resurrected him?

'I've heard,' said Norton, looking upwards, and it seemed a long way to where the three shadowy silhouettes were gazing down at him, 'that Algolans are peaceful people, not violent, very respectful of life.'

'That's true.'

'And our tyrannical regime has taken advantage of our inherent good nature for far too long.'

'But not for much longer.'

'And if someone is sick or injured,' said Norton, 'they're always given whatever treatment they need, no matter what the cost, and it's free?'

'That's also true.'

'But not for much longer.'

'Because after the revolution, competitive tendering to prioritise best value will be one of the first reforms we introduce.'

'Uh-huh,' said Wayne.

'No customers will suffer as a result.'

'Because of their freedom of choice, we anticipate a much higher client satisfaction index.'

'Everyone will receive a far better service. Long live the revolution!'

'Long live the revolution!'

'Long live the revolution!'

One of the shadowy figures gestured for Norton to climb, and he reached up to the first grips, hoping he could pull himself high enough to get his feet onto the lowest rings. He'd already fallen out of the lander, and his image as military adviser would not be improved if he fell while trying to board the masted vehicle.

'But what if,' he said, choosing his words carefully, 'the revolution isn't quite the great success we all hope it will be? What will happen to . . .' he was about to say 'me' but changed it to '. . . us?'

'Our despotic regime may be a totalitarian dictatorship,' said one of the generals, 'but they aren't barbarians.'

'This is a civilised planet,' said a second general. 'On Algol all life is sacred.'

Wayne Norton was very relieved to hear it.

Then the third general said, 'Although of course that doesn't apply to foreigners.'

CHAPTER
TWENTY

As he sat at the restaurant table, William Ewart looked at the alien sitting across from him. An Algolan. One of the most feared and hostile species in the universe. Not the ideal dinner companion.

The last time Ewart had seen any Algolans, they were trying to kill him, pursuing him through the labyrinthine tunnels deep within Kosmos's not-so-secret pirate hideout.

Ever since, he'd kept as far away from Algol as possible. Because it was one of the most isolated worlds in the galaxy, that wasn't too difficult. Despite being centrally located and close to convenient spacelanes, the planet had deliberately cut itself off from the rest of the universe. Ewart was convinced he'd never had any business dealings with Algolans. If he had done, he would have made certain to keep his side of the bargain. He hated to imagine the penalty clause in one of their contracts.

He was slightly less tense now, and took a sip of his whisky as he looked at the Algolan. One of the greatest assets of a salesman was remembering faces and putting the right names to those faces; but there were some names, some faces, he would never forget unless he had them deleted from his memory.

This face was almost feline, with blue skin and short white hair. It belonged to Janesmith, and she'd been the chaperone to her younger sister, Marysmith.

But years had passed, Ewart realised. She couldn't be Janesmith; she must have changed after so much time. This had to be her sister, now grown up: Marysmith, Empress of Algol – and William Ewart's wife!

'We're not married!' said Ewart. He picked up his glass and drained it. 'We never were married!'

'We know.'

'It was all a mistake!'

'You're making another mistake.'

'What do you want? What have I done? What did you say?' Ewart paused, backtracking. 'We were never married, right? You agree? At last!'

'We were never married to you. You married our sister, Marysmith. We are Janesmith.' She shrugged out of the loose robe, and her outfit was made from fleshide, jet black and skin-tight.

'Janesmith?' said Ewart, and he remembered how she always used to speak of herself in the plural. 'You're Princess Janesmith?'

'No, we are Empress Janesmith.'

'Empress? I thought Marysmith was the Empress.'

'She was, but now we are.'

'You killed her?'

'We wouldn't kill our own sister. We're not barbarians.'

That wasn't what Ewart had heard, but he thought it best not to debate the subject.

Janesmith continued, 'Marysmith —' the slate became silent for a split second — 'abdicated. But because you married our sister, you are always our brother.'

'No!' said Ewart. 'That was never a marriage because there was never any . . . any physical . . . anything. How could there have been? Marysmith was . . . was . . .'

'An alien?'

'No, I wasn't going to say that,' said Ewart, who carefully hadn't said that. 'She was too young. I should have had the marriage annulled.'

'Algol is a primitive and backward world,' said Janesmith. 'There is no divorce, no annulment, marriage is for life — and beyond.'

'You mean Marysmith is dead?'

'Alive or dead, you are our brother now, and you'll be our brother for ever. Marriage is a spiritual union, there's no need for physical contact. That's one of the greatest faults of the rest of the universe, there's too much lust and carnality.'

'What about Algol? What's Algolan for "hello"? "Show us your genitals"!'

'That is a joke, William Ewart.' Janesmith growled, baring her sharpened fangs. 'We invented it for humorous effect.' Growling was Algolan for laughter. 'It's an ironic comment on the universe's obsession with sexual stimulation.'

The waiter came towards them, carrying a glass of whisky in his hand. He had removed his gloves, his patchwork tunic was unfastened, and he walked even more slowly than before.

'You look as though you need this, pal,' he said, as he put the drink on the table. He looked down at Ewart

and winked. 'Cheers,' he added, then turned and
ambled back the way he'd come. Ewart and Janesmith,
Terran and Algolan, were alone again.

Although some of his memories of the *Demon Star*
voyage had never returned, Ewart knew Janesmith had
been on board when they reached Hideaway. He hadn't
seen her from that time till this.

'How did you find me?' he asked, reaching for the
welsh.

If the Algolans could find him, it meant that the
alien tax collectors could also trace him. He didn't
avoid tax, no one could avoid tax, but his revenue
codename wasn't William Ewart. As Ewart, he'd once
endured a very traumatic tax interrogation. That was
on Hideaway, and he'd been there because . . . well, he
couldn't recall that part of his first voyage into space.
He'd arrived at the galaxy's number one pleasure
asteroid, a world of complete escapism and absolute
luxury, and he'd wound up being threatened and
intimidated by the enforcement division of Taxation
Incorporated. But he escaped. And became someone
else.

Until today.

He had postponed his rejuve as long as possible,
hoping that somewhere in the galaxy he could find a
better treatment. Ewart didn't want an extended lifespan; he wanted an infinite life. But until then, he'd
had to make do with the basic body restoration and
renewal service. As an added extra, he could have
altered his entire appearance, but he wasn't vain and
had kept his original facial configuration. He looked
younger than he had done fifty Terran years ago, and
he was also slimmer than he had been half a century
ago. His enemies used to call him 'the fat man', and

during his rejuve he'd taken the opportunity to have his big bones reduced.

Janesmith's head rocked from side to side, an Algolan shrug.

'What,' said Ewart, giving her a question she had to answer, 'do you want from me?'

He realised that the two worlds most feared by the rest of the galaxy, Algol and the unknown home planet which was galactic tax headquarters, were both controlled by females. That wasn't surprising. Women always caused trouble, whatever their species; and if they had any power or authority, they simply couldn't handle it. In the past, females from those two worlds seemed to have singled out Ewart for personal attention. And it wasn't over yet. Empress Janesmith was the president of the board, the chairman of the corporation, the chief executive officer, everything rolled into one. Whatever she was doing here, it meant trouble for Ewart.

'You know what we want,' said Janesmith. 'We've been discussing it. We want a complete new comservice for Algol.'

'Really?'

'Yes, really, and we came to you because you're family.'

'So what you said about there being only one channel, with only five hours' programming every day . . . ?'

'Most of what we told you was all true.'

Ewart looked at her, wondering what part wasn't all true – or did she mean it was all only partly true?

'We,' continued Janesmith, 'the people of Algol, own the SeeV network. But a minority of citizens are unhappy with the current programming. They want more of it.'

'You've got to give the people what they want,' said Ewart, 'not what you want the people to have. You can't ignore consumer demand.'

'That's another great fault in the rest of the universe, thinking of people only as consumers,' said Janesmith. 'However, what we have on our world is "producer demand" because there are a lot of young and apparently intelligent Algolans who want to work in SeeV. Somehow, they've got the idea that media jobs are important and relevant. But because SeeV is so trivial and ephemeral, it's a good way of letting these hotheads occupy their time. Otherwise, who knows what mischief they could get up to? And so it's been decided to allow round the clock transmission.'

'How many channels?'

'One.'

'One!'

'People can only watch one station at a time, and so one station is enough.'

'What about freedom of choice?'

'More channels don't offer more choice, that's an illusion. The only reason most worlds have so many channels is to allow commercial companies to manipulate viewers into buying unnecessary products and services, which it does via the medium of programmes which are themselves unnecessary, and so the parasitic cycle goes on and on, always devouring itself. The greater the quantity of channels, the less the quality of programmes.' Empress Janesmith rocked her head from side to side. 'More means less.'

'But . . .' William Ewart shook his head from side to side as he tried to think of a convincing argument. She was so very *wrong*, but just contradicting her wouldn't have been very persuasive. 'What if people don't like what's on?'

'They have genuine freedom of choice. They can choose when to switch off. And most of the time they will switch off, because they'll be at work or asleep or enjoying quality time with their families. But when they do watch, they can see the best programme there is.'

'If it's the only programme, it's also the worst.'

'There will be no worst. Everything will be superior. Producers will strive to make the best possible programmes for the public, because they know that only top quality results will be screened. The Algolan service will be under no commercial pressure, there will be no chase for ratings, no pandering to the lowest common denominator. Our broadcasting will stimulate the brains of our citizens, not immobilise them, which is yet another great fault in the rest of the universe.'

Ewart let the words from his slate flow around him without listening.

'. . . public . . . service . . . broadcasting . . .'

Who cared about that kind of stuff? He sipped at his drink but said nothing, because he knew there was no point.

'We can tell you're not interested,' said Janesmith, 'and why should you be? Your only interest is in supplying the full range of SeeV equipment we need, and we know you can do that.'

'Right,' agreed Ewart. 'Although I'm not too clear what you meant about the financial arrangements. When you said you had no money on Algol, was that also meant for humorous effect?'

'No.'

Ewart was glad. Money was far too serious to joke about.

'We said it,' explained Janesmith, 'because it's true. We don't have money on Algol. You will supply all our equipment. You will also pay for it.'

'I don't understand you,' said Ewart, who didn't understand.

'But we understand you, William Ewart. In the past, you've been paid to supply communications equipment which you haven't delivered. In this case, the situation is reversed: we will not pay you, but you'll deliver communications equipment to us.'

'I can't do that.'

'Why not? Over the years, you've accumulated a significant financial surplus. You are our brother. What's yours is ours. You're not refusing.' Janesmith's slanted eyes stared at him. 'Are you?'

'No. No.' Ewart shook his head emphatically. 'Not at all.'

'You will do as we ask?'

'Right. Right.' Ewart nodded even more emphatically. 'Certainly. Definitely. Positively. I'll have to go to Earth to make all the arrangements.'

'No,' said Janesmith, as she kept on staring at him, 'you won't.'

Ewart shrugged.

'Is it a deal?' asked the Empress.

'Do I have an alternative?' asked Ewart.

'If you want to continue living,' said Janesmith, 'no.'

'Then we've got a deal.'

'Excellent! Shall we order?'

'Order the equipment, you mean?'

'Order a meal from the menu. That's what you usually do to finalise your agreements.'

'Right, of course. Good. I do feel hungry. Let's order.'

'Only if you want to. We could leave now, head straight for Algol.'

'We?' said Ewart. 'You mean "you"? You could head for Algol?'

'We wouldn't go without you, our brother. Our planet is your planet. You're coming with us.'

William Ewart suddenly lost his appetite.

CHAPTER
TWENTY-ONE

Algol . . .
        Kiru didn't know much about the planet; but one thing she did know was: she didn't want to go there.

'You don't want to go there?' said Diana.

'No,' said Kiru.

'It's either that or out into a lifeboat again. This time you'll be alone, I won't be with you.'

'Sounds good to me.'

'I know two words to convince you otherwise.'

Kiru waited.

'Lifeboat rations,' said Diana.

'I'm convinced,' said Kiru.

'Are you sure you're going to keep this down? I don't want you throwing up again.'

'Why not? It doesn't need saving for recycling, does it?'

Hideaway was hours behind them, the ship was in falspace, and they were about to eat. Spaceship journeys were usually long, always boring. When Kiru and Diana shared an escape pod, they had no idea how long the voyage would be or whether they would live long enough to find out. The highlight of every waking period was the meals, which were stretched out to fill as much time as possible.

At least this ship had a destination, even if Kiru wasn't looking forward to arriving there. It was also a far bigger vessel than a liferaft, which meant she could be on her own when she wanted. And the menu was infinitely better, although it still took only a minute to flasheat and serve.

'Algol is a dangerous planet,' said Kiru. 'It's forbidden to land there. Are you going to tell me why you're going, or will I only find out when we get there?'

'It's only forbidden,' said Diana, as she slid the dishes onto the table between them, 'if you're not invited.'

'And you're invited?'

'Not me, not specifically.'

'You mean Candy and Mandy? They're the ones who were invited? Don't tell me we've *got* to *pretend* we're *Candy* and *Mandy*.'

Diana smiled and shook her head. 'It's the ship that has the invitation,' she answered. 'More specifically, it's the cargo.'

'What's the cargo?' asked Kiru. 'Or should I ask: what cargo are they expecting?'

Diana smiled again, but this time she nodded her head and didn't answer. 'Let's not talk about that while we eat,' she said.

'Okay,' said Kiru, and they began to help themselves to the food. 'What do we talk about?'

'Someone we have in common,' said Diana. 'Someone we both know, someone I've known longer than you, but someone you know better than me.'

Kiru knew exactly who she meant, but she said nothing.

'Where's Wayne?' asked Diana. 'I asked earlier, and I can't remember getting a reply.'

Kiru used her mouth to eat, not to speak.

'I'm going to keep asking,' said Diana, then she also began to eat. 'Have you had a row? Is that why you left him?'

'I didn't,' said Kiru, 'leave him,' as she chewed, 'he left,' then swallowed, 'me.'

'Where did he go? Earth? Is that why you wanted to go there?'

Kiru nodded. There was no way she could keep it a secret. Sooner or later, out of desperation to find something, anything to talk about during the voyage, the truth would come out. It might as well be now.

'Why did he go to Earth?' asked Diana.

'You know about Wayne's finger?' Kiru raised her right index finger. 'The one replaced by a gun?'

'I know,' said Diana, 'because I arranged it. When I recruited him into GalactiCop, I fixed him up with his secret weapon.'

'He's gone back to Earth to find his missing finger.'

'What?'

'It's true.'

'Is it?' said Diana.

Kiru explained how she and Wayne had been on the atoll together, she'd gone for a swim, and when she returned he was just . . . gone. It was only the second time she'd told the story. The first to hear was Jay, soon after it had happened. That time, it had seemed to make sense. This time, it didn't.

Wayne couldn't have left her and headed for Earth to trace his lost finger. He'd left her for another reason, because something had gone very wrong with their relationship – and she hadn't even realised it.

As she listened, Diana kept shaking her head. 'He'll never find his finger. It must have been nixed. There must be something very wrong with him if he left you like that. But of course there is, everything's wrong with him: he's a man. There's not one of them, any race, any species, not a man in the universe who's worth a bent rupan. We're better off without them.'

'*We?*' said Kiru. 'But you're a man.'

Diana ran her pink tongue over her full lips, then ran her palms over her full breasts.

'Some of the time,' added Kiru.

'That's how I know they're all worthless,' said Diana. 'Stick with me, Kiru.'

'What?' Kiru slid back in her seat.

'I mean in a bonding, trusting, non-sexual, best friend sense. We'll make a great team, you and me.' She clinked her cup against Kiru's. 'Galaxy beware!'

Kiru knew that she was the one who had to beware.

Diana ate, chewed, swallowed, took a drink, then said, 'Wayne is the reason you wanted to go to Earth, and the reason you don't want to go to Algol is . . .'

There was no need for an answer, because Diana already knew.

'. . . Grawl.' Diana nodded as if Kiru had told her. 'You don't have to worry about him. You might not even have to set foot on Algol. Even if you did, what are the chances of him being anywhere near? Even if he was, what are the chances of you seeing him?'

'Because he's so small, you mean?' said Kiru. 'What matters is the chance of him seeing me.'

'Even if you and Grawl were on the same planet, the

same continent, the same city, you could be only a block apart and never be aware of each other.'

Logically, Kiru knew Diana was right. But what part had logic ever played in her life? Very little that had ever happened to her made any sense; she'd always been a victim of random chance.

What Diana had said about Grawl also applied to Wayne. If Wayne was on Earth, and if Kiru ever managed to return, he could be as close as a block away and she'd still never find him. And even if she did, that would be the easy part. Because how could she ever make him love her again?

Kiru stopped eating. Most of her food was untouched, and she pushed it aside.

'What's wrong?' asked Diana.

'Nothing.'

'Nothing? There must be something wrong.'

'No,' said Kiru. 'Something isn't wrong.' She leaned forward, folding her arms on the table. 'Everything's wrong.'

'Such as?'

Kiru glanced around the small cabin and wondered where to begin. Every moment which passed took her further and further from the only person she'd ever loved – and nearer and nearer to the one she most feared and hated in the entire galaxy. She sighed, but said nothing.

'What's the problem?' asked Diana.

Kiru looked at her.

'Me?' said Diana. 'I'm not a problem, I'm a solution.'

'Going to Algol, what will that solve? I might be wrong, but isn't Algol the most ruthless, violent and capricious planet in the galaxy?'

'It does have that reputation, yes.'

'And when they discover the ship isn't carrying what it's supposed to, what happens to us?'

'Nothing. I've done this before. It's all a tax fiddle, a way of reducing import and export duties. The cargo isn't what it says on the manifest, there might even be a different delivery address, but someone on Algol has ordered it and is expecting it. I'm a dispatch girl, and this isn't a suicide mission.'

Diana might not have been planning to get herself killed, but why had she been so keen for Kiru to make the voyage with her?

'What kind of mission is it?' asked Kiru. 'Does it have anything to do with the Algolans arriving on Café World and stopping Grawl killing the alien tax collectors for you?'

'I'd almost forgotten about that,' said Diana.

'Really? I thought you'd have remembered losing Café World and might want revenge.'

'It's an idea,' said Diana, as she sipped her drink. 'You and me against the entire Algolan empire.' She nodded her head. 'They wouldn't stand a chance.' Diana laughed. 'Come on, Kiru, cheer up.'

'What have I got to be cheerful about?' said Kiru. 'I've lost Wayne and I'm on my way to Algol, and I don't know why because you won't tell me and I wouldn't believe you even if you did tell me. I don't know who you are or what you are. Back on Earth, you were a policewoman; on Caphmiaultrelvossmuaf, you were running the whole Café World development project. The first time we met, you were female. Next time, you were male, a different colour and much older. Then you were female again. You could be a man or a woman or neither. You could even be an alien. You're devious and untrustworthy, you've lied and cheated and risked my life. Now you're smuggling contraband to the most dangerous planet in the universe – and I'm your accomplice.'

'But apart from that,' said Diana, 'no real complaints?'

'No,' said Kiru, and she almost smiled.

'Always remember,' said Diana, 'it could be worse.'

'How?' asked Kiru, and she did smile.

Diana paused, thinking. 'You could be pregnant,' she said, and she laughed.

She looked at Kiru, and Kiru was no longer smiling.

'Oh,' said Diana. She stopped laughing and glanced towards Kiru's stomach. 'I see.' She nodded her head and took a drink, wiping her lips with her fingertips. 'But it really could be worse.'

'How?' asked Kiru.

'I could be pregnant,' said Diana.

CHAPTER

TWENTY-TWO

Wayne Norton felt very conspicuous as he walked through the streets of the Algolan town with his new companions. He was still wearing the uniform Jay had given him, and his only disguise was the cravat which he'd wrapped around his head and face, leaving a narrow gap through which he could see the alien planet go by. He kept his hands thrust deep into his pockets to hide their colour and lack of claws.

He'd thought of asking the three Algolans about Kiru, if they could be specific about any recent human visitors to their planet. But as they were unaware Norton hadn't arrived alone and didn't even know Jay had been killed, he decided not to pursue that line of enquiry. He was a policeman. If Kiru could be found, he'd find her.

Back on Earth, soon after his renaissance, Norton had been recruited as a member of GalactiCop. Although he'd never had any proof that such an organisation actually existed, it should have done. It would have been the best way of fighting inter-galactic crime,

such as locating people who had been abducted from
one planet to another. But as he was himself an illegal
alien, asking the Algolan police about Kiru probably
wasn't the best policy.

When he'd been very young, Norton had never
understood why the phrase 'police state' was so nega-
tive. The police existed to uphold the law and protect
the majority of the public from the minority of law-
breakers, which must have been a good thing. By the
time he grew up and became a cop, he'd discovered
that a 'police state' was where the police protected the
minority, a ruling elite who made all the laws in their
own favour, laws which oppressed the majority. But it
wasn't the fault of the police if the law was so repressive; their job was only to make sure it was obeyed.

Algol was a police state, but the Algolans didn't
know it – because their language had no word for
'police'.

Norton kept glancing all around, sure that he must
be the focus of countless alien eyes, that the totally
secret police would pounce at any minute, march him
away, torture and interrogate him . . .

No one was paying him any attention, the other
Algolans in the town passed him by without even a
first glance. Joesmith and Johnsmith and Jacksmith,
however, were sticking very close. Norton had to get
away from them before they realised he wasn't a military advisor. How long until they discovered there was
no orbiting ship packed with weapons to start the revolution?

'Are you hungry, admiral?' asked Johnsmith.

'Yeah,' said Norton. He hadn't eaten since leaving
the *Demon Star* and he was hungry, he was thirsty, he
was tired. Sleeping was something else he hadn't done

since boarding the lander, and he wished he hadn't
drunk any of the Algolcohol.

The journey on the land yacht had taken most of
the hours of darkness, and the dawn light brought
Norton his first view of an Algolan town. It was surrounded by a high wall, and at its very heart loomed a
menacing fortress built into a jagged outcrop of rock.
Algol was a warrior world, he saw that immediately,
every town with its own fortified battlements and
dominated by a rugged castle. He and the trio of
apprentice generals had entered the town through a
gateless opening. Within the walls, the incessant wind
died away.

'Take whatever you want,' said Johnsmith, as he
gestured to the array of fruit or vegetables, or some
alien cross between the two, which were piled on rows
and rows of tables by the side of the street. He helped
himself to a few things and began eating. Jacksmith
and Joesmith did the same. By now, Norton could tell
them apart.

Norton couldn't risk eating; he didn't have a bugcollar to make alien food compatible with his digestive
system. He knew that food couldn't be judged by
appearance; but he still tended to believe that if anything smelled bad, then it probably was bad. And the
produce on display absolutely *stank*. It smelled rotten
and putrid, and he felt his stomach heave. Had he
eaten any real food in the last few hours, he'd have
thrown up.

'I don't want to show my face,' he said.

'Good thinking, admiral,' said Joesmith, as he
stuffed his blue face.

Any thinking was good thinking, thought Norton,
because the three Algolans didn't seem to do much of

it. If they really were officers in the revolutionary army, he didn't rate their chances of leading a successful revolt as very high. That was another reason for getting away from them as soon as possible.

Norton watched the trio choosing their breakfast, chewing and swallowing as they walked along the row of stalls. It was as if they were in an open air diner, helping themselves. Other Algolans were doing exactly the same, picking what they wanted from the piles on the tables. Some were eating as they chose, others were collecting wicker baskets full of food.

Algol was the most dangerous planet in the galaxy; Algolans were a violent and deadly race; and Norton was surrounded by alien men, alien women, alien children; this was one of their supermarkets; here, he was the alien.

With its narrow winding streets and small buildings crammed tightly together, the place seemed like a town in medieval Europe. It was also in Europe where they used to have emperors and empresses, Norton realised. Janesmith was his best hope of finding Kiru, but how could he find Janesmith?

Although small, the town was busy and noisy, full of Algolan voices, and his slate worked overtime as it interpreted snatches of conversation. Norton let the words flow through him, not listening, and wished it was as easy to block out the alien smells. Even the smoke from the chimneys stank, as if the basic household fuel was discarded tyres.

A huge animal lumbered by, bigger than an elephant and walking on six massive legs, its feet thudding into the dirt with every step and sending up clouds of dust. Covered with green scales, its enormous triangular head was topped by two intricately curved horns which seemed to be made of chrome. The horns were so highly polished they gleamed and glinted in the light, and sitting between them on top of the creature's skull, with one hand on each horn, was an Algolan child. The kid was riding the animal, or perhaps driving it, because it was a beast of burden – literally. The creature was laden down with boxes and crates which had been piled *into* its back. The animal seemed to have been hollowed out so that it resembled a pick-up truck.

As it pounded past, the beast released a trail of dung into the roadway. Norton quickly stepped away, then paused, and moved closer. The smell of the droppings was far sweeter than any of the other alien odours which assailed his human nostrils.

While the three generals foraged for provisions, this was the ideal time to get away from them. Except he'd no idea where to go. Norton kept watching, wondering what was so odd about the scene. Everything was odd, he knew that, but there was something so completely different that he couldn't quite identify it. None of the food was wrapped or weighed; it was all self-service with everyone simply picking up what they wanted and taking it away. Without paying.

'When we met,' Norton said to Joesmith, 'you talked about money.'

'Yes,' said the Algolan, as he chewed on what looked like a crunchy, grey banana, 'our repressive regime doesn't allow us to have money.'

'The people don't have money, but the regime does?'

'No,' said Johnsmith, as he chewed on what looked like a juicy, black potato. 'There's no money on Algol. It doesn't exist.'

'So everything is . . .' Norton paused. A family

group, father, mother and a gang of blue children, walked by, all carrying a share of their weekly groceries. '. . . free?'

'Yes,' said Jacksmith, as he chewed on what looked like a fistful of purple twigs with spiked turquoise leaves. 'And if anything is free, it's worthless. Only when Algol has a market economy will anything have a marketable value.' He glanced around, then moved nearer to Norton. 'Long live the revolution,' he whispered.

'Long live,' came two echoing whispers from Joesmith and Johnsmith, 'the revolution.'

'There's no money?' said Norton. 'People can help themselves to whatever they want at no cost?'

'There's a great cost,' said Joesmith. 'The cost of progress.'

'Yeah, but the average J – er, the average individual doesn't have a pay a price?'

'It's the price of liberty,' said Jacksmith.

'And who can put a price on that?' said Johnsmith.

'Where everything is free, there can be no freedom,' said Joesmith.

'By everything, you mean . . . ?'

'Everything means everything,' said Jacksmith, as he gestured at the stalls. 'Food.'

'Housing.'

'Fuel.'

'Education.'

'Clothes.'

'Health.'

'Transport.'

'Does that apply to me?' asked Norton. 'I can take anything I want and not pay?'

'Yes,' said Johnsmith.

'Isn't it terrible?' asked Jacksmith.

'You understand why we need your help to over-throw such an inefficient system?' said Joesmith.

The economy seemed to be a mixture of feudalism and communism, but it hadn't held the Algolans back. Difficult as it was to believe when looking at the town, its inhabitants were members of a starfaring race.

'Under this . . . er, inefficient system, can I make my way to the capital quickly, easily?' asked Norton, before adding, 'So I can properly assess the dictatorship's military defences.'

The generals looked at one another.

'This is the capital,' said Jacksmith.

'This?' said Norton. 'I mean the biggest and most important city on Algol.' He glanced around, but the town still looked small and unimportant. 'The capital is where the Empress has her court, where she rules from.'

'We know that,' said Joesmith.

'And this is it,' said Johnsmith. 'You're here, the capital of Algol.'

Norton gazed up at the castle which loomed above the rest of the town, a citadel of geometrically imposs-ible shapes, inverted walls and spiralling turrets, which seemed to have been carved out of the naked rock.

'That's where Empress Janesmith lives?' he asked.

'Yes,' said Jacksmith. 'And we live there.'

'Who?' said Norton, wondering if he meant himself or the three of them.

'We all live there,' said Joesmith.

'All of you?' said Norton, wondering if he meant the three of them or everyone in the town.

'Empress Janesmith is our sister,' said Johnsmith.

Norton was even more confused. Did Johnsmith

mean 'sister' as in having the same parents, or was it simply a phrase like 'all men are brothers'? On Algol, was everyone regarded as equal? How could they be if there was an hereditary monarchy? The more Norton discovered, the less he knew.

'The three of you,' said Norton, 'are brothers?'

'Yes,' said Jacksmith.

'But not these people,' said Norton, gesturing with his elbows to the people in the street. 'They're not your relatives?'

The three brothers growled with laughter, baring their fangs, all of which were speckled with seeds and skin from what they were eating.

'Empress Janesmith,' said Norton, 'is your sister?'

'Yes.'

'Your sibling?'

'Yes.'

'Of the same royal blood?'

'Yes.'

'Oh.' Norton looked at them. The Empress was their sister, but they wanted a revolution? Then he realised they weren't planning a planetary uprising, what they hoped for was a palace coup. They wanted to depose the Empress and replace her with an Emperor, one of them. He wondered if they had agreed which one was to seize the throne. Probably not. 'Okay. Well, er, good. Can I see the Empress?'

'Yes,' said Joesmith. 'If you wait here, you'll see her when she comes to collect her daily bread.'

'No,' said Norton. 'I didn't mean "see" her, I meant . . .' He paused. 'The Empress comes into town to do her own . . . er, shopping?'

Janesmith's brothers glanced at each other. 'We don't understand,' said one of them, but Norton didn't notice who because a distant movement had caught his eye, and he began to turn.

He'd glimpsed something unfamiliar, something which didn't belong on Algol, yet something familiar, something he recognised: a different body shape, a way of moving that wasn't native to this planet, a colour that was strikingly out of place on this world.

The colour was red. It was someone's hair. Someone human.

It could only be one person.

Norton tore the scarf from his face.

'Kiru!' he yelled.

He started running towards her, weaving in and out of the Algolans who were in his way. Some of the natives slowed, paused, stared at him. His disguise was gone, and he'd taken his hands from his pockets. It was obvious he wasn't one of them. They looked for a moment or two, then carried on with what they were doing.

By now, he'd lost sight of her. When he caught his first, unbelieving glimpse of the girl, she'd been crossing the street, perhaps fifty yards away.

'Kiru!' he shouted again, pushing his way through the crowd.

'Foreigners!' he heard his slate mutter. 'Always rush, rush, rush.'

'Admiral!' a voice called, one of the generals Smith.

'Admiral!' called another of them.

'Admiral!' called the third, or maybe it was the first one again, or maybe it had been the first one each time.

Norton ignored them and pressed on, craning his neck for another glimpse of his lost wife.

'Kiru! Kiru!'

'Why do you foreigners have to be so loud?' a translated voice wondered.

Norton reached an intersection where he paused, trying to see which way Kiru had gone. He stood on tiptoe, then leaned to the left, then the right, before leaping up onto one of the street stalls, looking all around and around, his gaze scouring the town, but there was no sign of Kiru. Until he glanced down.

She was on the other side of the table, reaching for a bunch of Algolan weeds and moss. It was her, it really was. Norton relaxed and smiled, stretching an arm down towards the girl.

'Kiru,' he said, softly.

She peered up at him, frowning slightly and showing no trace of recognition, before she looked down again, picked up what she wanted, turned and started to turn away.

'Kiru?' said Norton. Although it was a question, there was no doubt in his mind. It was her, he knew it was her. He jumped down from the stall to go after her.

'Admiral,' said Joesmith, and a clawed blue hand clamped itself around Norton's wrist. The three Algolans surrounded him.

'Let go!' ordered Norton. 'That's an order!' The Algolan obeyed, and Norton added, 'See that alien? Bring her to me, but don't hurt her.'

'What alien?' said Jacksmith.

'The alien like me. A human.'

'A what?' said Johnsmith.

'A human.'

'Where?' said Joesmith.

'Stay here,' said Norton. 'That's an order.'

He'd been watching the direction Kiru took, and he ran to catch up with her. It didn't take long. He stepped around the girl, turned to face her. And she started to step around him.

'Kiru,' said Norton, and he put out his hand to touch her forearm.

A moment later, he was lying face-down in the Algolan dirt, his arm twisted high up behind his back, and Kiru was crouching by his side.

'Do not try to resist,' she said, 'or I will break at least one of your limbs.'

'Kiru.'

'What is this word "Kiru"? Is it all you can say?'

'Kiru,' said Norton. 'It's your name, Kiru. What have they done to you?'

'No one has done anything to me, and my name is not Kiru. I am going to let go of you now and unless you leave me alone I will cause you severe pain.'

'Yeah, okay, I understand,' said Norton. He did understand what she meant, and he waited until she had walked away, then stood up and followed at a distance.

He should have kept his cool, not started running and shouting. This was Algol, the most lethal world in the galaxy. Norton and Kiru were foreigners. They shouldn't draw attention to themselves, they had to be reunited in secret. Then somehow get off the planet.

As he walked along, Norton wrapped the cravat around his face again and put his hands back into his pockets. His wrist and arm were aching, but his heart was no longer broken. He felt so happy, so relieved he'd found Kiru, and nothing else in the universe mattered.

He stopped when he noticed that Kiru had come to a halt. She was talking to someone. From the angle of her head, it seemed her companion was smaller than her, but Norton couldn't see because of all the blue people in between. Kiru turned and looked in Norton's direction, then she pointed at him.

As the crowd of Algolans swirled around, for a moment they all drifted apart and Wayne Norton could see who was standing by Kiru's side, staring straight at him.

It was Grawl.

CHAPTER

TWENTY-THREE

When William Ewart was married to Princess Marysmith, he should have received a dowry, but no payment was ever made. He finally knew why: because the Algolans didn't use money.

The dowry was to have paid for the *Demon Star*, but because no funds were ever transferred, Ewart had ended up with the ship and Hiroshi Larnvik had ended up with nothing.

And now Ewart intended to cheat his old rival again. This time, Larnvik would supply all the necessary equipment to update Algol's entire SeeV system. Once again, he wouldn't be paid. The shipment was already on its way to Algol. As soon as it was all installed, Ewart planned to be on his way from Algol.

'I still don't understand how a whole planet can exist without money,' he said.

'We don't understand why the rest of the galaxy needs money,' said Empress Janesmith.

Algol wasn't what Ewart had expected, but he'd only seen what Janesmith wanted him to see. She was showing him the tourist version of the planet. Except there weren't any tourists. The more time he spent with her, the less he believed. If she really was the Empress, didn't she have a world to run?

This was meant to be the planetary capital, but it looked more like something out of a dataplay: an ancient townscape where the pace of life was so *slow* everything seemed to have stopped, where the people *walked* from one place to another, where there were even *animals* in the streets, where every building but one was so *low* that the whole town seemed two-dimensional. It was as if Janesmith was still trying to persuade him that Algol was a primitive and backward world, although everyone knew the Algolan empire was a threat to the whole galaxy.

Ewart did have to admit that the castle was very impressive. The town had grown up around a steep escarpment, and the fortress was hewn from the sheer blue rock. For centuries, craftsmen had worked with every unique feature in the raw cliff-face, turning each ledge and each crevice, each spur and each fissure, to their advantage. They had created an eerie, intricate structure which seemed so delicate but so strong, an edifice which could neither have been built by sentient beings nor have evolved through the elemental forces of nature, but could only be a bizarre mutation of the two.

The citadel looked fantastic, but the room Ewart had been given was cold and barren, evidently meant as further proof that Algol was a disadvantaged world. No modifications or improvements had ever been made to the original blueprints, and the only way to reach the highest tower where the Empress's emblem flew and where Ewart's spartan suite was located, was by climbing a long, winding stone staircase. Over hundreds of years, the steps had been worn down by generations of exhausted royal Algolan feet.

'Every other planet in the galaxy,' said Ewart, 'is ruled by the laws of supply and demand.'

'Supply and demand aren't laws,' sneered Janesmith, 'not in a legal or scientific sense.'

'Economics is a science,' said Ewart.

Empress Janesmith growled with laughter.

'Supply and demand,' said Ewart, 'control price.'

'The opposite,' said Janesmith. 'Where money exists, supply and demand are controlled by price. Without any prices, without any money, there's enough supply for everyone's demand.'

'No, the universe doesn't work like that.'

'That's one of the great faults of the universe.'

'And you're an expert on the universe?'

'Yes,' said Janesmith. 'That's why we left Algol, to find out if life on our world could be improved. That's why we stayed on Hideaway so long. Because so many different races and species visit the satellite, it was the ideal place to study the customs and habits of other planets.'

'And what improvements did you discover?' Ewart asked, already knowing what she would say.

'None.'

He was right. 'Algol,' said Ewart, stretching out his arms as if to encompass the entire world, 'the perfect planet.'

'Not yet,' said Janesmith, 'but we're working on it.'

Ewart decided not to suggest there might be a long way to go. He was walking through the narrow, dusty roads of the town, with the Empress of Algol as his tour guide. She had no security guards, no entourage, and the other Algolans were not giving her any special treatment. One of the roads was lined with stalls laden down with different sorts of food, and people were helping themselves without paying. Janesmith picked up a large yellow ovoid, her talons quickly stripping the hard shell. She offered it to Ewart, but he declined, and she bit into the fibrous flesh.

Probably the first major discovery of all sentient species was how to make fire. Fire meant heat, and it would lead to the smelting of ore and making of iron knives. With fire, a race could cook; with knives, a race could carve. They were the first steps on the evolutionary ladder towards developing a unique cuisine.

Wherever he went in the universe, Ewart always liked to sample the food and drink, but it appeared that the Algolans had no great culinary tradition. Most of what they ate was raw, so it was fortunate their diet consisted of fruit and grain, pulses and vegetables, fungi and nuts. His bugcollar neutralised the pungent odours of local produce and he'd eaten enough to know what he enjoyed of the native menu – which wasn't much.

'This is all free?' said Ewart. 'People can help themselves to as much as they want?'

'Yes,' said Janesmith. 'There's plenty for everyone.'

'If there's plenty, then there's too much. A free market would match supply with demand.'

'Supply and demand are manipulated by money, by profit, and one person's profit is another person's loss. There's no such thing as a free market. Except on Algol, where everything is free.'

'Anyone on Algol can have anything they want?'

'If it's available, yes.'

'What about your castle? You wouldn't allow anyone else to live there.'

'If anyone wanted to, they could use the empty rooms, but most people have more sense. It's cold, uncomfortable, draughty, and a very long walk to get anywhere. Imagine what it's like to climb up to one of the turrets, then realise you've forgotten something down at ground level.'

'Then why live there?'

'We have to,' said Empress Janesmith, wiping her mouth with the back of her imperial hand. 'It's one of the burdens of office.'

'Every Algolan can have a house? Free? Without paying for it?'

'That's what "free" means.'

'Could someone have two houses?'

'Why would anyone want two houses?'

Ewart was about to say they could live in one house and sell or lease the other, but who would buy or rent a house when every other home was available for no charge?

Algol was not a backward world, it had developed the technology to venture far into space, out towards planets beyond its own binary system. When Ewart and Janesmith had landed here, they came down in the middle of a barren plain. There had been no sign of a spaceport or of any other ships, and they were taken to the capital in a weird vehicle which seemed to be propelled by the wind. At least they hadn't had to walk or ride upon some bizarre creature, just to maintain the primitive illusion.

'You say there's plenty for everyone,' said Ewart, watching as Janesmith paused to sample another unappetising morsel from one of the tables, 'but sometimes there must be shortages.'

'Yes,' agreed Janesmith. 'Take this as an example.'

A clawed blue hand swept through the air. 'Different crops are harvested at different times of the year, and supplies run low out of season.'

'Exactly. Demand outstrips supply. This is where you need money, because price is the perfect way of rationing scarce resources. The price goes up, and fewer people want it.'

'No. As many people want it, but fewer people can afford to pay for it. These are the people you call "rich", and why should they have what "poor" people can't have? On Algol, any shortage of supply is only temporary. In the rest of the universe, products are deliberately kept in short supply to increase their price.'

'That's not true,' said Ewart. 'Producers respond to consumer demand by increasing output.'

'And do prices go down?'

'Er . . . in theory.'

'Prices always go up. It's called inflation.'

'Prices may increase, but incomes go up even more. That's called wealth creation. Everyone benefits.'

'Wealth creation,' said Janesmith, 'is a myth. In the rest of the galaxy, there's only wealth redistribution. And wealth is always transferred from the poor to the rich.'

This was a futile discussion, Ewart knew. It was all part of the charade, the mask the Algolans wore when they turned their face to the universe beyond their own paradoxical planet. Ewart had spent so much of his life hyperblading along the edge where fact became fantasy, it didn't seem too strange that the town was a simulation, its inhabitants illusory.

'In the rest of the universe,' said Janesmith, 'most people work long and hard for very little money.'

'At least they get some money,' said Ewart. 'Here they get nothing.'

'Because they want for nothing. It's one of the great faults of the universe that the few people who own most of the wealth are those who do the least work. Or no work.'

Ewart glanced up at the castle. Prominent location, a house of character. Although it needed some attention, the fortress had to be the most valuable piece of real estate in town. But Janesmith would probably say she didn't own it.

'How's the property market on Algol?' he asked.

'There isn't one.'

'That *is* a surprise.'

'There is no private property. All property is theft. Without property, there is no theft. Theft is caused by greed and need. On Algol, there is neither.'

'There's no crime on Algol? It's safe to walk the streets at night?' Ewart glanced around, wondering why anyone would want to walk through the cramped streets even during the day.

'There's no crime, no crime industry, no lawyers.'

'No lawyers?' That was the best thing he'd heard since arriving here.

'Money is the root of all crime,' said Janesmith. 'You've lived in a universe where money is hoarded and worshipped; but if you thought about it, you'd prefer money not to exist.'

Ewart laughed. 'I always think about money, and I always decide I need more.' He laughed again.

'If there were no money, there would be no taxes.'

He stopped laughing.

'Money has brought so much unhappiness to the universe,' said Janesmith, as she examined another inedible-looking display on a roadside stand.

'Taxation has brought me so much unhappiness,'

said Ewart. One of the main reasons he'd been forced to leave Earth was the extortionate demands of the Terrestrial Taxation Authority.

'Where there's money, there's greed.' Janesmith reached for a small plant covered with diamond-shaped mauve leaves. 'It's a plague which has infected the whole universe, and only Algol is immune. But now we're in danger, and our own brothers are part of the conspiracy.'

'Your brothers?' said Ewart. The Algolan royal family never allowed male offspring to survive, or so he'd heard; but that must have been another lie, like Janesmith having killed her sisters so she could inherit the throne. Unless, of course, she had killed her sisters . . .

'Men,' said Janesmith, as she bit into the stem, stripping the leaves with her sharp fangs, 'they're useless. Our brothers are even more useless. What are they for, except for sex? And they aren't very good at that.'

The Empress must have been talking in general terms. She couldn't have meant that her brothers weren't very good at sex, because how would she know? On most planets, there was still a taboo against incest. But Algol wasn't like most planets. In fact, it wasn't like any other planet.

'And they're not very good at betrayal,' continued Janesmith.

'What do your brothers want?'

'They want to be managers, executives, company directors.'

There was nothing wrong with ambition, thought Ewart. Judging by his apparent surroundings, Algol could do with a lot more of it.

'Our world is facing the greatest threat in its history,' said Janesmith.

'Who's threatening you?' asked Ewart, wondering who would be mad enough to dare.

'The aliens who thrive on extortion and intimidation, the aliens who are taking over the whole universe through bribery and corruption – through money.'

'The Galactic Tax Bastards?' said Ewart, using his own name for the nameless aliens. 'Because you haven't paid your taxes?'

'Because our conflicting ideology is a threat to them.'

'They think that?'

'They know that,' said Janesmith. 'Ideas are far more powerful than any weapons, which is why they want to waste our world. They believe they can use force to annihilate reason, but force can only exterminate flesh and bone.'

'And planets,' said Ewart.

'Ideas and concepts cannot die.'

'But when your body's been vaporised, it makes it that little bit harder to push your point of view.'

'Our armour of truth will shield the pure force of reason.'

'You'll use . . . er, reasonable force to spread your message?'

'We're under threat, we either submit or retaliate. And when we win, we will eliminate the tax invaders and free the galaxy from the dark tyranny of money. Algol doesn't have money, which means no planet needs to have money. Without money, the Taxation Alliance Federation Association has no power. Without money, the universe will be free.'

'So,' said Ewart, 'you're going to liberate the universe?'

'Yes. There will be no more poverty or ignorance or sickness, because without money there's no profit in keeping people poor, uneducated and ill.'

'Right.'

William Ewart had travelled the galaxy, he'd visited many planets, and Algol appeared to be one of the poorest. He didn't imagine the education standards or the level of health care were any higher.

'On most planets,' he said, 'there's not much sickness any more.'

'We agree,' said Janesmith. 'But "not much" is too much. All illness should have been eradicated. There is only one reason why that hasn't happened: without diseases, medical companies are redundant. Why are there so many "alien infections"?'

'I'm guessing,' said Ewart, 'but could it have anything to do with infections from other worlds?'

'That's what they claim, but "alien epidemics" are new diseases created by medical corporations.'

'Why would they do that?'

'For profit. When a planet is infected, people become ill, and the only way to get well is to buy the right medicine. And who supplies the treatment?'

'I don't believe it.'

'It's the law of supply and demand,' said Janesmith, and she growled with laughter. 'The drug cartels create a demand for a cure . . . and they supply that cure.'

'They wouldn't do that.' Ewart shook his head. 'They wouldn't make people ill.'

'Why not? Making people ill makes money, because it creates a greater demand for the new product. Making people very ill makes more money. And if some people die . . .'

'No!' said Ewart, and he shook his head even harder. 'It didn't happen like that. It can't have done.'

'What didn't happen?'

'Nothing,' said Ewart. But it was everything, and he tried to ignore the ancient memory, the ancient pain, to banish it to the lost recess of his mind where it always lay, the one thing in his life he never wanted to remember but didn't want to forget.

He reached into the nearest stack of food, grabbed the closest item, and bit into it. Anything to take his mind off what Janesmith had said. He wished he wasn't wearing his bugcollar, so that the alien morsel would taste as foul as it looked. It was soft and slimy, round and fibrous, and his fingertips became glued to its jaundiced skin. Despite all the gooey juice, it felt very dry in his mouth, lumps of it sticking to his tongue and his lips, and the stringy fibres became wedged in his teeth.

'Del –' he said, managing to swallow some of it – 'icious.'

'When we have conquered the universe,' said Janesmith, 'complete education and total health care will be freely available to everyone.'

They kept on walking through the streets, but Ewart resisted taking another bite of the alien food. When he tried to drop the sticky mess to the ground, it clung to his palm. He picked at his teeth with his fingernails, tugging at the slimy strands.

'When all the sick have been cured,' continued the Empress of Algol, 'anyone who has a minor imperfection can have it corrected if they want. Someone without a voice, for example, will be given the opportunity to speak.'

Ewart would have welcomed the opportunity to speak, because his Algolan snack had sucked his mouth and throat almost completely dry. But he wondered why Janesmith had chosen that as an example. Most people spoke too much, and usually it was those with the least to say. Were there some planets where huge sections of the population had been silenced by ruthless medical corporations?

'William *MegaFat* Ewart,' said a voice from behind him.

It was a human voice, a Terran voice, a voice Ewart could understand without needing his slate.

He spun around, quickly flicking his hand out while he did so, but the half-eaten indelicacy remained stuck to his fingers. The non-Algolan was easy to see, some ten metres away and coming closer, the only non-blue figure amongst the crowd. She looked familiar, although maybe only because she was human. Her hair was long and wavy and red, and she seemed young. He was sure he didn't know her. Who was she? How did she know him?

'What are you doing here?' she said. Except it wasn't her. The girl's lips never moved. But the voice was louder, nearer.

Ewart kept looking, gazing through the aliens, and then he glanced down. Which was when he saw a shape he immediately recognised. Small, squat, bald.

'Grawl!' said Ewart, hoarsely. Whenever he was surprised, and the universe could be a very surprising place, he was careful never to show it. 'I own you.'

'You don't,' said Grawl, and his new voice was like that of a child. 'This is Algol. Everything's free. Including me.' Then he laughed. '*He-he-he, he-he-he.*' Like a child.

'I think you will find,' said the girl, 'that a year and

a day after becoming dormant, bond contracts are no longer valid.'

Ewart ignored her. In any case, he didn't want Grawl back as his bodyguard. After walking out, disobeying a direct order, he could no longer be trusted.

Grawl and the girl had stopped two metres away. They were holding hands. Even after so much time, Grawl seemed hardly a day older. He looked as mean and ugly as ever. Ewart held his ground, and Janesmith came to stand next to him.

'Hi,' said the Empress.

Hi? thought William Ewart.

'Hi, Smithy,' said Grawl.

Smithy? thought Ewart, as he looked at Grawl, then glanced at the Empress of Algol.

'I offered,' coughed Ewart, 'to give you a voice.'

'I didn't want anything from you,' said Grawl, 'not then.' He turned his head and looked up at the girl by his side. She smiled at him. When Grawl returned the smile, it sent a chill up and down Ewart's spine.

'I'm sure you must have a lot to talk about,' said Janesmith.

'No,' said Ewart. He had nothing to say to Grawl, although Grawl probably had a lifetime of talk inside him, but Ewart was careful not to say so. He was also careful not to look too closely at the girl, not while Grawl was watching. And Grawl was always watching.

'Let's go to Rajic's,' said Janesmith.

'Rajic's?' echoed Ewart. 'You mean Rajic Jao Rajic?' That was a name he hadn't heard for a long time. He last saw his younger brother on the pirate planet, which was also the last place he'd seen Grawl. 'Is he here, too? I knew Kosmos wouldn't have killed him.'

'*He-he-he,*' giggled Grawl.

'Rajic's is a restaurant,' said Janesmith. 'The best Terran restaurant on Algol.'

'Ah,' said Ewart.

'The only Terran restaurant on Algol,' said Grawl. 'The only alien restaurant on Algol.'

'Oh,' said Ewart. He ran his tongue across his gummy teeth, over his sticky lips, then shrugged. 'And Rajic runs the place?'

'It's named after him,' said Janesmith. 'This way.' She turned and began walking through the blue crowd.

Ewart looked at Grawl. Grawl looked at Ewart.

'Good to see you,' said Ewart.

'It's not good to see you,' said Grawl.

Ewart glanced at the girl.

'Do I know you?' he asked.

'No,' said Grawl.

'Right,' said Ewart, and he hurried to catch up with the Empress. 'This restaurant we're going to,' he asked her, 'is there anything you recommend?'

'Yes,' said Janesmith, 'there's something perfect for you.'

'Fine. Good. Great. What?'

'The chef.'

'The chef?' said William Ewart. 'Why?'

'Because she's your wife, Princess Marysmith.'

CHAPTER

TWENTY-FOUR

'This wasn't part of the deal, was it?' said Kiru.

'Not exactly,' said Diana.

The ship was in orbit around Algol, but they were on the surface of the planet. Imprisoned in a fortress. But it was the opposite of being chained up in a dark, damp dungeon. The cell was light and airy, thanks to the wide open windows and the constant gale howling through.

There were no bars on the windows because nobody would try to leave that way, or nobody who hadn't evolved wings. They were hundreds of metres above the ground, the room jutting steeply out from the bare blue rock of the mountainside from which it had been carved. Kiru and Diana leaned from a window, gazing down at the alien planet. The world seemed bleak and desolate. Below them was a small walled town, and even that looked desolate and bleak.

Although the prison cell was bigger than the liferaft they had once shared, the food was worse. Kiru would have preferred bread and water.

'Are the Algolans trying to poison us or starve us to

death?' she asked. Despite the wind blowing through the windows, the rotten stench of alien food lingered in the bleak and desolate jailroom.

'Depends how long we're here,' said Diana. She gestured towards Kiru's midriff. 'How long before . . . ?'

Kiru put her hand on her belly. A few hours ago, for the first time, she'd felt the baby move and she thought it was her stomach complaining about lack of food. Maybe the baby was complaining for the same reason.

She knew nothing about babies. But it wasn't a baby yet, was it? It was a foetus, and it would only become a baby when it was born. Until then, it still had to be an 'it'.

To prevent a new generation of criminals being born on Clink, female convicts were given jenejabs before deportation, and so Kiru had thought she couldn't become pregnant. She was glad to have been wrong, but that was on Caphmiaultrelvossmuaf when Wayne was with her. In a cell on Algol, with only Diana for company, it was a different matter.

Her belly wasn't very swollen yet, and Kiru couldn't work out when the baby was due. Back on Earth, it took nine months to produce a child; but without days, without weeks, it was difficult to calculate the passage of time. She was human, the result of millions of years of evolution. Every one of her countless ancestors had been conceived and born to the rhythms of the Sun and the Moon, they were all a part of Earth's temporal microcosm.

Kiru, however, had ventured far beyond the limits of her native world. It was said that the universe was the ultimate chronometer, that every star, every galaxy, pulsed in synchronous harmony. But Kiru had no idea how to tell the time.

'I don't know,' she answered. 'Will we live that long? What's the penalty for smuggling contraband?'

During the voyage, Diana had told her the spacecraft was meant to be carrying communications equipment to refit the Algolan SeeV system. The real cargo was sealed in the hold, and Kiru had opened the seal and discovered the ship was loaded with children's toys and games: all kinds of datakits and technosets and bioware, Play-Deks and MusicMates and ChessPets. Although the contents didn't fit the documentation, the shipment wasn't anywhere near as bad as Kiru had feared.

'All a tax fiddle?' said Kiru. 'Import and export duties? This is Algol. No money means no taxes, no duties. Didn't you know?'

'If I'd known,' said Diana, as she gazed out of the window, 'I wouldn't be here. The Algolans didn't arrive on Café World as paying guests, so how was I to know they live in a cashless society? A planet without money? It's impossible.' She shook her head as she gazed down on the impossible planet. 'I was only the pilot, just doing an honest job.'

If Kiru had to pick a single word to describe Diana, she'd have used the entire dictionary before choosing 'honest'.

'There's no evidence against me,' added Diana. 'I'm completely innocent.'

And the word 'innocent' would have been Kiru's penultimate descriptive choice.

She doubted that the Algolans cared anything about guilt or innocence. Kiru had never been given a trial on Earth, and she also doubted that the Algolans would bother with any judicial formalities. She and Diana had been on the ship, which was more than enough evidence.

'Is that why I'm here?' asked Kiru. 'You wanted me on board to take the blame? Escaped convict, so I must be guilty. You're only a space pirate, down on your luck and ferrying a dodgy cargo to earn a few rupans.'

'What a sad story,' said a voice from inside the cell.

Kiru and Diana both turned away from the window. Standing near the doorway was an Algolan. Kiru suddenly felt very cold, and not because of the icy wind whistling through the cell. She had seen their visitor once before, on Café World.

'And you needed the money for medical treatment for your poor old mother, did you?' continued Janesmith, Empress of Algol, via the simultaneous linguistic and tonal equaliser. Then she growled, and there was no translation for that. 'You should have brought her to Algol, we'd have treated her for free.' She growled again.

Kiru had known Algolans were dangerous, but she hadn't realised they were crazy. It seemed she and Diana had been granted a private audience with the mad monarch of Algol. Empress Janesmith needed no guards, she was a one woman combat squad. Only her head was visible, the rest of her tall body was completely clad in black battle armour; a ring of barbed spikes that circled her short white hair was the imperial crown; an array of knives and swords, clubs and axes, hung from the belts around her waist, her biceps, her shins.

'We know who you are,' said Empress Janesmith. She raised her left arm and four claws sprang from the tips of her gauntleted fingers and gestured at Diana. 'We know who you are.' Her right arm came up and four more claws gestured at Kiru. 'And one of you must die.'

'What have we done?' asked Diana.

'You know what you've done,' said Empress Janesmith. 'You've come to Algol without permission.'

'We've got permission,' said Diana.

'A ship from Earth had permission to bring new infocom technology,' said Empress Janesmith.

'That's us, that's our ship,' said Diana.

Kiru didn't like the words 'us' and 'our'.

'That was not what was on board,' said Empress Janesmith, 'and you know that was not what was on board.'

'But . . .' Diana started to speak, then must have realised denial was useless.

'It's only games and toys,' said Kiru, 'the kind of things children all over the galaxy love to play with. They're all harmless.'

'Harmless?' One of Empress Janesmith's armoured fists reached for the hilt of a short sword, the other gripped the handle of a double-bladed knife, and she glared at Kiru. 'Harmless!'

Kiru stepped back until she was hard up against the rock wall.

'Why didn't you bring poison?' asked Empress Janesmith. 'It would have been a faster, kinder way of infecting and destroying our children.'

'What do you mean?'

'Technoware corrupts and subverts impressionable young minds.'

'No,' said Kiru. 'It's educational. They learn all kinds of things.'

'It's bad enough that children watch two hours' SeeV a day, when they could enjoy singing or dancing lessons, but at least with SeeV we make sure they only watch what's good for them: ballet and opera, classical drama and building renovation.'

'But when they play with—'

'That's not play! Children should use their legs to run and jump, their arms to throw and catch. Children should play with other children. Children shouldn't sit still for hours and hours, ruining their eyesight, exercising nothing but their fingers. Children should sing and dance and play real games where they run and chase and laugh, not have their young bodies degraded and their imaginations perverted by cunningly devised mindtraps.'

The Empress seemed to have strong opinions on the subject, and Kiru decided it might not be such a good idea to advance the opposite point of view. She watched as the Algolan took her hands from her weapons; instead, she began punching her left fist into her right palm.

'Algol is forbidden to outsiders,' she said. She paused, as if waiting for a reply.

'We're only on Algol,' replied Kiru, 'because you brought us here.'

'As we promised, one of you will die.'

'You're going to kill one of us?' asked Diana.

'We are the Empress. We don't do our own killing.' She paused again. 'Except as a special treat.'

'Who's going to die?' asked Kiru.

'That's up to you,' said Empress Janesmith.

Kiru and Diana glanced at each other.

'Only one of you will live,' continued Empress Janesmith, 'because the other one will have died. We don't care who. It's your choice.'

'What, we take a vote?' said Diana.

'I vote for you,' said Kiru, pointing at Diana.

'I vote for you,' said Diana, pointing at Kiru.

They had been standing side by side, facing the

Empress, but now they moved apart. No longer allies, they had become enemies.

'Algol,' said Empress Janesmith, 'is not a democracy. One of you will kill the other, or one of you will sacrifice herself so the other can live.'

'Don't look at me,' said Kiru, as Diana looked at her.

'And don't you look at me,' said Diana, as Kiru looked at her. 'I told you I wasn't on a suicide mission.'

'This is an ancient way of settling disputes on Algol,' said Empress Janesmith.

'By killing each other?' said Kiru.

'Only when it's serious,' said Empress Janesmith. 'Algolans don't go in for that kind of thing any more, it's considered too primitive and backward. But we think it's nice to keep some of these old traditions going, which we can do thanks to the occasional illegal visitors like you.'

'What if we refuse?' asked Diana.

'You'll both die,' said Empress Janesmith, 'which will be a complete waste of one life –'

As she listened, Kiru put both her hands on her belly. Diana noticed, then quickly looked away.

'– although it's only a human life,' concluded Empress Janesmith. 'Here's the chance for one of you to prove what a noble and altruistic species you come from. One of you could surrender her life for the other. Or both of you could, but that would also be a total waste of one life.'

'What happens?' asked Diana. 'We attack and try to kill each other, and the survivor . . . survives?'

'No, nothing so crude. In olden times, the duellists were sent out into the desert with enough food for four days. After eight days, only one of them would return. What happened out in the wilderness, no one else knew. Sometimes, nobody ever knew because nobody came back.'

'You're going to send us out into the desert?' said Diana.

'With food for four days?' said Kiru, who thought her survival chances would be better without any Algolan supplies.

'Maybe not that long,' said Empress Janesmith. 'The pace of life is so much quicker these days. Without weapons or clothing, you each have two opponents: the elements and one another, and you're at the mercy of both. You can use persuasion and logic to reach a reasoned conclusion as to which of you won't return. Or at the first opportunity, one of you can slaughter the other.'

'We each have a fifty-fifty chance of survival?' said Diana, and she looked back at Kiru.

Empress Janesmith was watching Diana. 'Fifty-fifty?' she repeated. Then she glanced at Kiru. 'Not,' she said, 'necessarily.'

'You mean if one of the two is younger and fitter?' said Kiru.

'Or one of them is older and wiser?' said Diana.

'No,' said Empress Janesmith. 'If we remember our history lessons, the parts that didn't involve memorising imperial dynasties . . .' She paused, thinking.

'What?' said Diana.

'There is a way,' said Empress Janesmith, slowly, 'in some cases, of making the competition even more interesting and exciting.'

'But not in this case,' said Kiru, who thought it already sounded far too interesting and exciting.

Empress Janesmith of Algol growled with laughter, baring her fangs, which Kiru interpreted as meaning 'yes, in this case'.

'We must be going,' said Empress Janesmith. 'Nice seeing you again. You're both looking well. So far. It's cold in here. We'll have some extra duvets sent up, because we hope you don't catch a chill.' She turned, paused, and looked back over her shoulder. 'It wouldn't be a good idea if one of you was to murder the other before the contest. That way, you would both die. Another absolute waste of a life.'

Then she was gone, and Kiru and Diana were alone again in their elevated prison. They looked at one another, then at the rough arch which was the doorway.

In her short life, Kiru had been locked up a number of times. But whenever she wanted to, she'd always been able to walk free. All she had to do was open the door and leave.

This cell was different. There was a doorway, but no door. And there was only one reason for a prison without doors: there could be no escape — because there was nowhere to go.

Kiru and Diana stood without a word, lost within their own thoughts, while the alien wind softly whispered its cold threats or screamed its blood-chilling curses.

CHAPTER
TWENTY-FIVE

'I don't think we've been followed,' said Grawl, as he backed in through the cottage doorway, then turned to face Wayne Norton. 'Welcome to my humble abode.'

He wasn't joking, although Norton had never thought he was the type. The walls were made from mud bricks, the roof was turf, the dirt floor was covered with straw. It was very humble.

Grawl had told Norton to stay close as they made their way through the back alleys of the Algolan town; but because every street was so crooked and narrow, they all seemed like back alleys.

'What are you doing here?' Grawl said. 'How did you get here? You shouldn't be here.'

'I've come for Kiru,' said Norton, and he looked towards the entrance.

Grawl hadn't closed the door because there wasn't one. The open doorway was the only source of light in the small, dark room. For Grawl, it didn't matter that it was small.

'That's not Kiru out there,' he said, as he gestured for Norton to move further into the room, deeper into the darkness. 'I'll tell you all about it, but I don't want Zena to hear.'

'That's Zena?'

'My fiancée.'

'She looks like Kiru,' said Norton. 'Exactly like Kiru.' At first he'd been sure she was his missing wife; but after being with her for a few minutes, he was no longer so certain. She acted differently . . . Or maybe that was it: she was acting, pretending not to be Kiru. But was she doing it of her own free will?

Whoever she was, the girl had been left on watch outside the cottage.

'Sit down,' said Grawl.

'I'll stand,' said Norton.

'Sit down,' said Grawl.

Norton sat down in the corner. Grawl wasn't a man to be disobeyed. He remained standing, gazing towards the doorway. Sitting down, Norton was the same height as Grawl standing up. He tried to work out what he was sitting on; some kind of rough stool, or perhaps an upended log.

'What's happened to Kiru?' asked Grawl.

'She's vanished,' said Norton. 'She was abducted from Hideaway.'

'And she was brought to Algol?'

'I thought so.'

'By who?'

'Er . . .'

Norton's eyes were getting used to the gloom, and he saw Grawl glance at him.

'Me?' said Grawl, in a puzzled tone. 'Me?' he repeated. Then he laughed. 'Yeah, me! I get it.' He laughed again.

Norton had never heard Grawl laugh, had never

heard him make a single sound. His voice was like that of a child, high-pitched, almost squeaky; and his laughter was a schoolboy's giggle.

'I thought you couldn't speak,' said Norton.

'I couldn't,' said Grawl. 'Working for William Ewart, I didn't have much time for a social life and I never needed to talk. Until I met Zena. We fell in love, and I'd so much to say to her – but I never got the chance, because she was killed.'

'Killed?' Norton looked from Grawl towards the doorway, where he could make out the girl's shadow, then back to Grawl again. 'I'm sorry to hear it.'

'And I'm so, so, so, so very sorry for what I tried to do to Kiru,' said Grawl. 'Anything I can possibly do to make up for it, I'll do. But I was sick, I was lovesick, and I couldn't be held responsible for my actions. The Algolans cured me. This is a wonderful planet, full of wonderful people. They gave Zena back to me. Zena doesn't know about Kiru, and I'd prefer it if you didn't mention her.'

'But I've got to mention her,' said Norton. 'That's what I'm here for. To find her.' He glanced towards the entrance again. 'Are you sure that . . . ?'

'No.' Grawl shook his head. 'Zena is an android, like the first Zena. And don't *ever* mention the first Zena, okay?'

'Yeah, sure,' said Norton, who knew more than Grawl thought. He'd heard of Zena from Jay.

'Let me explain,' said Grawl, and he did.

When Zena, the first Zena, had her life functions terminated, Grawl removed her identicore and kept it inside a silver pendant, waiting for an opportunity to transfer her essence into another android. Then he'd met Kiru, a fellow convict on Arazon, and decided to

implant the core into her body to create a human/
android fusion. But Kiru had resisted his advances,
and the last she and Norton had seen of Grawl was
when a troop of imperial hailstormers shipped him off
to Algol.

'Janesmith was very young when she first met me,'
Grawl continued. 'It was her first time away from
Algol, and I was the first alien she got to know. She
thought I was exotic and charming, handsome and
mysterious.' Grawl shrugged.

As far as Norton was concerned, none of those words
were appropriate. Grawl had spent most of his life in
silence, but he was more than making up for lost time.

'Can't blame her for having a teenage crush on me,'
he added.

It seemed Janesmith had taken a fancy to all of
them: Grawl, Jay and himself. Did that happen with
every alien she met? Or did she have a special liking for
male Terrans?

Grawl went on, and on, 'I guess Janesmith always
saw me as her ideal hero, charismatic and enigmatic,
and when she found me on Café World she couldn't
resist wanting to take me home and keep me. Like I
said, I'm very glad she brought me here. Algolans are
such a generous people. Everything here is free, you
know that? They gave me a voice and they gave me a
reincarnation of Zena.'

'But why,' asked Norton, 'does Zena look like Kiru?'

Grawl hesitated, and he ran his fingers over his bald
scalp. 'There was a resemblance between Kiru and the
first Zena. I say "the first Zena", but there's only one
of her. It's what's inside that counts. Zena still has the
same personality and character, the same memories,
but her body is different.'

'It's Kiru's body.'

'Yes.'

'Is she Kiru? Did you finally do what you tried on Hideaway, did you erase her mind and steal her body?'

'No,' said Grawl, emphatically, and he shook his head. 'She is not Kiru. It's just that . . .'

'What?' said Norton.

'It was so long ago that Zena's first body was decommissioned, when I had to choose her new body I couldn't visualise what she looked like. I kept remembering Kiru, so I had her made in Kiru's image. But don't tell Zena, okay? Women are funny about things like that. Promise?'

'Okay.'

'Thanks.'

'Does she know she's an android?'

'Of course,' said Grawl. 'We're going to get married. There are no secrets between us. Zena!'

Zena came into the cottage, and Norton's heart beat faster as she approached. Grawl had told a very plausible story, but he wasn't one hundred percent convinced.

'You two haven't been properly introduced,' said Grawl. 'Zena, my darling, this is a very old friend of mine . . . ah . . . what's your name?'

They had spent months together in an escape pod – and Grawl didn't even know who he was.

'Wayne Norton,' said Wayne Norton.

'Wayne, this is Zena, who has done me the infinite honour of agreeing to be my wife.'

Norton stood up and held out his right hand. Zena's hand clasped his – and it felt exactly like Kiru's.

'Pleased to meet you,' said Zena.

'And you,' said Norton. 'I'm sorry about before. I

thought you were someone else.' He kept hold of her right hand, then held out his left. She took his left hand in hers, and in the gloom he felt for a wedding ring. It wasn't there, but that would have been the first step in transforming Kiru to Zena.

Zena drew her hands away and moved to stand next to Grawl. She towered above him, resting her hand on his shoulder, and Grawl turned his head to kiss her fingers.

'Anything you want, Wayne?' he asked. 'Something to drink? Something to eat? You want to watch Algolan SeeV?'

'No,' said Norton. 'All I want is Kiru. The original Kiru. My Kiru.'

'That is who you thought I was?' said Zena. Her voice was slightly different, her tone and inclination not the same; but a voice was also easy to disguise.

'If she was on Algol,' said Grawl, 'I'd know about it. No off-worlders are allowed here. With a few exceptions.'

'I'm an off-worlder,' said Norton. 'I'm here. You didn't know about me.'

'Right,' agreed Grawl. 'How did you get here?'

'Later,' said Norton. 'But if I'm here, Kiru could be here. How can I find out?'

'Why should she be on Algol? I can understand how you thought that I'd . . .' He paused, looking up at Zena. 'If you want to get on with your chores, darling, don't let us stop you.'

As Zena leaned down to kiss the top of Grawl's head, Norton had to look away. The girl faded into the darkness at the back of the cottage.

'When Kiru was taken,' said Norton, 'it seems there was an Algolan ship near Café World.'

'Algolans don't go to vacation planets,' said Grawl.

'They went there on Café World's opening day,' said Norton.

'Because the Empress wanted me,' said Grawl.

That wasn't exactly the way Norton remembered it. Because it was his wedding day, he remembered it very well. But he said nothing.

'After all that's happened,' continued Grawl, I feel I owe Kiru more than an apology. I'll do whatever I can to help you. If she's on Algol, which I doubt, I'll find out where.'

'How?' asked Norton.

'I'll ask Smithy. She'll do anything for me.'

'Who?'

'The Empress. I've got her in the palm of my hand. She knows everything that happens here on Algol.'

'Yes,' confirmed a voice, 'we know everything that happens here.'

Norton glanced around and saw a dark silhouette blocking the doorway, an Algolan in full black combat armour, but without a helmet. Janesmith, Empress of Algol, had to duck down to get into the room, and her spiked crown scraped dirt from the ceiling as she advanced.

'Duke Wayne, how are you?' she said, via Norton's slate.

'Er . . . fine thanks, your majesty,' he acknowledged.

'Hi, Grawl,' said Janesmith. 'What have you been up to lately?'

'This and that,' said Grawl.

'You haven't written a guide book, have you? *Algol on No Money a Century*?'

'No.' Grawl shook his head. 'What makes you ask?'

'We wondered why our lonely planet suddenly

seems to be on the Terran tourist trail.' Janesmith turned her attention to Norton. 'Maybe you can explain. What brings you all this way to Algol? And why haven't you paid us a personal visit?'

'I was going to,' said Norton. 'I'm here on behalf of the Taxliens, and I—'

'And who are they when they're at home?'

'The Taxliens, Empress. It's a name I coined for—'

'A name you *what*?'

'Coined,' said Wayne. On Algol, that might not have been the best choice of a word. 'I made up the name "Taxliens" for the aliens who run the Universal Taxation Bureau.'

'Our greatest enemy? The vermin who have sworn to wipe Algol from the cosmic map? Is that who you mean? You're working for those parasitic excrement-eaters?'

'Yes . . . but no . . . and yes,' said Norton. 'But they want to reach a peaceful agreement. They don't want war. They've appointed me as their ambassador to Algol.'

'You?'

'Yes.'

'Show us your credentials,' said Janesmith, and she growled with laughter.

Norton glanced at Grawl, but he'd started retreating further into the darkness.

'Come with me, Duke Wayne,' ordered the empress. 'You're going to trial.'

'Trial! What for?'

'For illegal entry. On our world, justice is swift. That's one of the faults in the rest of the universe, legal procedure is far too slow. If there was no money, lawyers couldn't cause delays to increase their income.' The empress spun around on her heels. 'Follow me.'

Norton looked at Grawl, then pointed at Janesmith, and he mouthed the word 'Kiru?' but Grawl shook his head. Norton used his only index finger to tap the palm of his right hand, because that was where Grawl was meant to have the Empress. Grawl shrugged his broad shoulders.

'Hurry up, hurry up,' insisted the Algolan, turning as she reached the doorway. 'Everyone else is ready for the trial.'

'What kind of trial?' Norton didn't want to know the answer, but asking the question gave him another few seconds.

'Trial by combat,' said Janesmith, Empress of Algol, and Wayne Norton really wished he hadn't asked.

CHAPTER
TWENTY-SIX

'You will find this interesting,' Empress Janesmith had told him, and William Ewart wondered if that was an imperial command.

He'd also found the visit to Marysmith's restaurant 'interesting' but it was an experience he never wanted to repeat. At first, he wondered if Janesmith intended he should move in with his alien 'bride'. At least by now Marysmith looked big enough to be married. In fact, she was the biggest Algolan he'd seen on the planet. Ewart never liked using the word 'fat' because in the past he'd so often been falsely accused of being overweight, but there could be no denying that Marysmith was fat, very fat. Maybe that was because no one else would eat the food at Rajic's Stellar Restaurant. It was the kind of place where, if the food hadn't already been free, they couldn't have given it away.

None of Ewart's wives could cook, they had no idea even how to flasheat a FastEat, but that wasn't why he'd married them. (It was all a long time ago, and he wasn't really sure why he had married them. Ever since leaving Earth, he'd been careful to avoid the same mistake.) But for someone running a restaurant, cooking would seem to have been the minimum requirement. Not, however, in the case of Marysmith.

As in all marriages, Ewart lied; and this time, he lied about how good the food was. Despite being on Algol, where dining standards were not the highest, the place evidently didn't have much of a reputation. Except for the table where he sat with Janesmith, Grawl and the new version of Zena, the place had been deserted. It was meant to serve a Terran menu, and perhaps the cuisine was so awful because of a lack of genuine ingredients. It seemed that, for some reason, Rajic Jao Rajic had lived on Algol for a while. Ewart knew his brother had always wanted to return to the catering business, but he found it hard to believe that Rajic ever had anything to do with the establishment which bore his name. It just showed how far quality could fall under a different regime.

Marysmith seemed as embarrassed at serving Ewart as he was to be there, and they had nothing to talk about. He was happy to leave Rajic's, although it did seem odd not to have a bill to pay. That was always the final pleasure of a meal, checking the addition and deciding how much to leave as a tip. As he walked out of the open doorway, and every doorway on Algol always seemed to be open, Ewart kept thinking he'd be dragged back into the kitchens and forced to wash the dishes.

Now he was sitting in the back of a wagon which was pulled by a pair of long, scaly beasts whose yellow bodies were fused together. Or maybe it was one creature with two crested heads and six multi-jointed legs which was harnessed to the old cart. Despite being held together with frayed ropes which had been spliced and knotted many times, this was apparently the royal carriage. He was sharing the wagon with the Empress of Algol, who was armed with a varied selection of swords and knives. Encased in full ceremonial white armour decorated with black studs, only her hands and head were visible. Her elaborate helmet was by her side. A black chain encircled the top edge, and from each link a black spike jutted upwards to form the imperial crown.

The cart had no wheels, but was held above the ground by a huge fan which produced a cushion of air on which the vehicle floated, and the ride across the blue grass of the Algolan plain was very smooth. Ewart was on the rear seat, looking towards the direction they were travelling; Janesmith sat opposite, facing him. Although he wondered what lay at the end of the journey, he didn't ask because he might not have liked the answer.

Instead he asked, 'Shouldn't he be at school?' He nodded towards the driver, a child sitting in a saddle at the fork where the animal's two necks were joined together.

'If the rider was a "he", no,' said Janesmith. 'It's futile giving male children anything more than basic education. This is our sister's child, Sharonsmith.'

'Your sister?' said Ewart, suspiciously. 'Which sister?'

'Marysmith.'

'My wife's got a child? How did that happen? Not that she *is* my wife.'

'It happened the usual way, as it does in most of the galaxy,' said Janesmith, then she looked back over her shoulder. 'Sharonsmith, say hello to your father.'

'*What!*'

The girl turned her feline face towards Ewart. She was very much like Marysmith when he first met her, her long white hair tied with ribbons. But of course she looked like her; every Algolan looked very similar. The same oval blue face, the same sloping eyes, the same pointed ears, the same sharp fangs. But the main thing was: the child certainly didn't resemble Ewart. And how could she have done?

'Hello, Daddy,' said the alien girl.

Ewart almost fell out of the wagon.

'Is this something to do with Rajic?' he said. Because he knew it was certainly nothing to do with him. Rajic was Ewart's brother, so did that mean by Algolan custom he could share Ewart's wife? Was Sharonsmith Rajic's daughter?

'William Ewart is from the planet Earth,' said Janesmith. 'That means he's an alien, and you can never trust an alien. Why?'

'Because they tell lies,' said the girl.

'What did you say to Mr Ewart?'

'We said, "Hello, Daddy".'

'And that was . . . ?'

'A lie!' said Sharonsmith, and she growled a childish growl.

'Well done, that's today's first lesson.' Janesmith turned back to face Ewart. 'Education is much more than mere schooling, don't you agree?'

'Right,' said Ewart.

'And Sharonsmith will learn a lot today.'

Ewart wondered what he would learn, but still he didn't dare to ask. Neither did he ask about Sharonsmith's father. There were some things he never wanted to know.

He glanced back, and the town had vanished over the horizon; only the peak of the fortress was still in view. The cart was moving swiftly, and so was the Empress's escort. There must have been thirty of them in total, half on each side of the carriage. Small and broad, clad in plated bronze armour with ridged helmets, they were identical to the warriors who had invaded Kosmos's not-so-secret lair all those years ago.

Janesmith's weapons, although lethal in close combat, were part of her ceremonial regalia; but her troopers all carried more modern, long-range, heavy armaments. And they were all running, jogging in step, keeping pace with the royal carriage.

'Your men must be fit,' said Ewart.

'Yes,' agreed Janesmith. 'We only have sex with young, attractive, fit men.'

'No, I mean . . .' Ewart shook his head and jerked his thumb towards the escort. 'Your men, your troops.'

'They aren't men.'

'Ah, right, I see.'

Algol was a planet run by women, and so the army was also composed of women.

'They're not men,' said Janesmith, 'and they're not women. They're soldiers. In battles, people can get hurt. We don't want that happening to our people, not even the men. Our soldiers are built for war. Because they've never been alive, they have no lives to lose. Their only purpose is to obey orders. If they're damaged or destroyed, they can be replaced.'

'You build your soldiers?' said Ewart. 'In factories?'

'We grow them.'

'What? In fields?'

'No. In flowerpots.'

'What!'

'A joke, my brother. Our soldiers are constructed by an accelerated bioelectronic process. When they reach optimum size for storage and transport, they're also ready for combat. Their armour is an exoskeleton, and every circuit in their bodies is coded to receive orders and implanted with military tactics. They can lose one, two or three limbs, even their heads, but they'll keep on fighting until ordered to stop.'

Algol was even more of a military threat to the universe than anyone knew. The planet had an endless supply of troops, troops who cared nothing for their own survival, troops whose only function was to fight and fight no matter what the odds. These were the warriors who would be in the front line of the Algolan crusade against their great galactic enemy: money.

'Any sign of the new comsystem I ordered?' Ewart asked, gazing up into the green sky.

'The delivery ship has arrived,' said Janesmith.

'Why didn't you tell me?'

'Because they brought the wrong stuff.'

'Typical.' It was the same old story, and it meant he'd be stuck on Algol even longer.

'You don't seem surprised,' said Janesmith.

'Happens all the time,' said Ewart. 'I know what it's like in business. It's difficult to get reliable staff.'

'Perhaps they should pay them more money.'

Ewart looked at the Empress. She growled, very softly.

'Did they give you another delivery date?' asked Ewart.

'Not yet. We destroyed the cargo.'

'Destroyed it! You should have asked for a credit note and sent it back. You don't destroy a wrong consignment. That means you'll have to pay twice.'

'Pay?' said Janesmith.

The imperial cart raced on, and so did the imperial escort, and Ewart watched as another town came into sight.

'The old capital,' said the Empress.

Even at a distance, it looked much more modern than the new capital. The buildings were far taller and wider, the streets much broader and longer. But as they drew closer, Ewart could see the buildings were derelict, the streets deserted. The town was in ruins, drifts of sand and dirt piled high up against the fractured walls of each shattered tower block, weeds and bushes growing through every cracked floor and roadway.

'What happened to it?' Ewart asked.

'We moved out,' said the Empress.

She made it sound as if it had been the previous week, but it must have been the previous millennium – and that was in Algolan years.

'Why?'

'Because of the neighbours.'

'Neighbours, right.' Ewart remembered what it had been like before he'd made his first billion, when he'd lived in the less prosperous zone of a crowded city. 'All the noise, the complaints, the way they borrow things but never give them back. Who needs them?'

'You can't have a community without neighbours. In the old capital, no one had any. The buildings were too big and impersonal, the roads were like barriers which divided the city, children couldn't play out because of the traffic, and it was too far to walk anywhere.'

That all sounded great to Ewart.

'Time to go to work,' said Janesmith. She flexed all

her claws before pulling on her mail gauntlets, then reached for her white helmet, raising it above her, keeping her head rigid, squinting as she turned up her eyes to see what she was doing. As she lowered the helmet, the rim hit the front of her head.

'Here,' said Ewart, and he leaned forward to guide the helmet over Janesmith's head. It was only then he wondered if it was an insult to suggest the Empress couldn't manage on her own; or perhaps it was treason to touch the royal armour.

The rim of the helmet glided into place, neck and shoulder seams melding together.

'Thanks,' said Empress Janesmith of Algol, through the open visor.

Her blue face was in shadow, but a glint of light from the optic sensor array within the helmet reflected on her fangs. Then the visor slid shut, and Ewart returned to his seat.

'Can you hear at the back?' came a stentorian voice from within the helmet.

Ewart clutched at his ears with an exaggerated gesture.

'We'll take that as a "yes",' said Janesmith, in a less amplified voice.

The cart had to slow down as it entered the abandoned town, weaving through the debris of countless crumbled buildings, until it reached a central square. On two sides the buildings had collapsed to create a barrier of jagged, rusty metal and sharp, splintered stone. Throughout the journey, the planet's eternal wind had gusted and howled; but now all was still and silent.

Three sides of the shattered square were lined with genengineered troops. As one, they stood to attention when the Empress stepped down from her carriage, and a hundred gauntleted fists pounded against a hundred bronze carapaces in a single echoing salute. She raised an arm to make Sharonsmith stay where she was, then beckoned to Ewart. He climbed out of the cart, gazing around at the imposing martial array, and he desperately hoped that none of this had anything to do with him. As the Empress strode out into the centre of the plaza, Ewart followed. Their escort assembled in a line behind him, completing the square of bronze armour. Janesmith halted and surveyed her guards.

'Proceed!' her voice ordered.

There was a movement on the adjacent side of the square, behind the row of troops. Ewart saw Zena, Grawl's new android. If she was there, Grawl must have been nearby. Two small soldiers were marching her out into the plaza, towards Ewart and the Empress.

Then from directly opposite, two more troops brought out someone else. The figure looked human, looked female, looked older than Zena – not that Zena could ever age.

Another pair of soldiers appeared, and this time they led a young man, also apparently human. There was something familiar about him, Ewart realised, but he couldn't pin it down.

'Kiru!' the man shouted, and he pulled away from his guards, racing towards the other side of the square.

'Wayne!' yelled Zena, and she also ran across the plaza, heading towards the man.

They reached each other five metres from where Ewart and Janesmith stood. They embraced and hugged one another. They kissed. They held each other as tightly as possible. They laughed. They kissed again.

Ewart glanced around, hoping Grawl couldn't see what was going on. The way the man was behaving with Zena, Grawl would kill him with his bare hands, crushing him till he was no more than the dust which filled so much of the old capital.

Then Zena pulled away from the man and suddenly slapped his face.

'What's that for?' he asked.

'For leaving me,' she said.

'I didn't leave you. You left me!'

'I didn't!'

'You did.'

The older woman slowed down as she neared the couple. She could have been in her mid-thirties, and although there was nothing particularly striking about her, she also seemed somehow familiar.

'Howdy, Wayne,' she said, and threw the young man a casual salute.

The man, Wayne, turned and looked at her in amazement. She kept walking across the square and halted two metres away from Ewart. Then she winked at him.

Zena and Wayne resumed their passionate debate, alternately kissing and arguing.

'Be silent, you two!' commanded Empress Janesmith. 'At least one of you is going to die. Do you want to waste your time blaming each other?'

The escorting troops had retreated, leaving five people in the middle of the square. Ewart realised the three newcomers were all like him, they were human. Despite the Empress's order, Zena and Wayne were still talking; and the woman was still watching him, a slight smile on her lips. Who was she?

'Is this anything to do with getting the wrong SeeV

consignment?' asked Ewart. 'Because that's nothing to do with me. I put in the right order.'

'We know,' said Janesmith. 'We trust you, William Ewart.'

It was one of the scariest things anyone had ever said to him.

Ewart's lips and mouth and throat were very dry as he said, 'You can't kill the crew for bringing the wrong delivery.'

Empress Janesmith turned and looked at him, and he took a step away.

'Because,' he added, 'we'll never get the right shipment. No crew will ever come here if it might cost their lives.'

'These are unauthorised intruders,' said Janesmith, 'and two of them are going to die.'

It must have been Zena who would live, because she'd been specially imported for Grawl. But she seemed to be acting very oddly for an android, and Ewart remembered how her predecessor had become disloyal to him.

'What about me?' he asked. 'Why am I here? I'm not an intruder. You brought me to Algol.'

'You, our brother, are here to witness what happens to illegal arrivals.'

Ewart didn't want to watch anyone die.

'Don't close your eyes,' said Janesmith, 'or you won't see. You three, let justice be done. Get ready. Clothes off. Collect your food.'

'No,' said the older woman.

'If you refuse, you die now.'

'I'm choosing a champion to take my place. That's allowed under the Algolan code.' The woman was still looking at Ewart. 'And I choose him.'

'You can't do that!' Ewart turned to look at Janesmith. 'She can't do that, can she?'

'No,' said the Empress, and she stared at the woman. 'You can only nominate a champion who is your kin, a blood relative.'

'I know.' The woman was still watching Ewart. 'He's my brother.'

'What! No, I'm not! She's lying, I'm not her brother.'

'You are.'

'She's not my sister!' said William Ewart.

'True,' said the woman, and she smiled. 'Don't you recognise me, kid? I'm your big brother. I'm Kosmos.'

CHAPTER

TWENTY-SEVEN

'Kiru!'

She heard his voice before she saw him, and immediately she called out his name.

'Wayne!'

And there he was, running towards her, breaking away from the two Algolan soldiers with him. She also started to run, sprinting free from her guards. They raced towards each other.

Then they were in each other's arms and it was as if there was no one else in the ruined city, no phalanx of squat troops surrounding them, the whole world was theirs, they were alone in the universe, holding each other tight, never wanting to let go.

'I can't believe it,' Kiru whispered, her face pressed against his.

'It's real, Kiru,' said Wayne. 'I'm here, and I'm never going to let anyone take you from me again.'

Take her? What did he mean? Then his lips were against hers, hers against his, and they kissed and kissed and kissed.

They drew apart, looking at each other in astonishment, both laughing, both trying to speak but knowing mere words were not enough, both disbelieving what was happening, holding each other at arm's length, until Kiru freed her right hand, took a step nearer to Wayne – and slapped his face as hard as she could.

'What's that for?' he asked, as he rubbed his cheek.

'For leaving me,' said Kiru.

'I didn't leave you. You left me!'

'I didn't!'

'You did.'

'Howdy, Wayne,' said Diana, as she walked by.

Wayne turned away and stared at her.

'Diana!' he said. 'Was it her? Did she bring you here?'

'Yes,' said Kiru. 'No, don't!' She grabbed hold of Wayne, stopping him from going after Diana. 'But what are you doing here?'

'I came to find you.'

'How did you know I'd be here?'

'I knew you'd been taken to Algol.'

'But . . . how?'

'Because when you were abducted, I went to—'

'Abducted?' said Kiru. 'I wasn't abducted.'

'You were. You were abducted from Caphmiaultrel-vossmuaf.'

'I wasn't.'

'You were.'

'Stop saying "you were"!'

'But you were. You were abducted. That's how you got here.'

'I was *not* abducted. What makes you think that? I was swimming. When I came back, you'd gone.'

'Me? I was gone? Where did I go?'

'Earth.'

'Earth? I didn't go to Earth. Why would I go there?'

'Because . . .' She couldn't tell Wayne why she thought he'd returned to Earth. Instead, she lifted his right hand, kissed his fingers, those that were still there. Wayne took hold of her left hand, his fingertips stroking her wedding ring, then he kissed her fingers.

'I wouldn't go anywhere without you,' he said.

'You did,' said Kiru. 'You left me while I was swimming.'

'I did not!'

'Be silent, you two!' came a translated order. The Algolan was wearing an ensemble of white armour and matching helmet. Because the latter incorporated a spiked crown, Kiru guessed the person within the suit was Empress Janesmith. 'At least one of you is going to die. Do you want to waste your time blaming each other?'

'She's right, Wayne,' said Kiru. 'We'll talk about what happened later.' And she had something else to talk about, something vitally important. 'If there is a later.'

'I don't care,' said Wayne. 'I'd rather die with you than live without you.'

'Oh, oh, oh,' she said, and they kissed again. 'Wayne, Wayne, Wayne.'

They were together again, and nothing else mattered, not even if it was the end of the universe. And for one of them, or both of them, it soon would be.

'Are you okay?' asked Wayne. 'What have they done to you?' He leaned away, looking her up and down.

'What did *who* do to me?'

'The Algolans.'

'They haven't done anything,' said Kiru. She gazed

around at the array of bronze hailstormers, then at Empress Janesmith. 'Not yet.' She put her hands on Wayne's shoulders, pulling him close, and they kissed again. While there was still time.

'Here,' said Wayne, and he gently rubbed at her cheeks. There was so much alien dust in the air, some of it had got into her eyes, making them water.

'Thanks,' she said, giving him a smile.

'Any time,' he said, returning it.

'You three,' said Empress Janesmith, 'let justice be done. Get ready. Clothes off. Collect your food.'

Kiru and Wayne stood gazing at each other, and she could feel his warm breath on her face. They had been apart so long neither of them wanted to look away, and only their eyes turned towards the empress and the other two Terrans: one man, one woman who was sometimes a man.

The man was of average height, more than average weight, about forty standard years old. Kiru had no idea who he was. He'd been speaking to Empress Janesmith, and now Diana was talking with them both, but Kiru paid no attention because she had other things on her mind. She already knew she had to fight an Algolan duel, and originally her opponent was Diana. Her only opponent. Then she'd discovered another person would also be competing. The prize was life. One would survive, two would die. And the third person being forced to fight for life was Wayne.

'We can beat this,' said Wayne. 'We can both live. We *will* both live.'

Kiru doubted it, but that wasn't going to stop her trying. Then she heard the unknown Terran raise his voice.

'She's not my sister!' he said.

'Don't you recognise me, kid? I'm your big brother. I'm Kosmos.'

'Kosmos?' said Wayne. 'I've heard of him. But who's the fat guy over there?'

'I'm *not* fat!' said the man, and he glared at Wayne.

'Not as fat as you used to be, kid,' said Diana.

'And I'm not your *kid*!' the man insisted.

'You are,' said Diana, 'and you're going to fight this duel for me.'

The Empress, the man and Diana all started talking at once, shouting and arguing.

Kiru and Wayne looked at each other, then both glanced at the armoured troops who guarded the square. They were both thinking exactly the same thing, Kiru knew. And they both came to the same conclusion. They looked at each other again, realising they had no chance of sneaking away while the other three were making so much noise. Instead, they had another hug and another kiss.

'Do you think,' said Kiru, 'Diana doesn't want to be part of the duel because she'll be naked, and we'll see what she's made of − if she's really a she?'

'Could be,' said Wayne, and he made himself smile.

'*Be*,' came a slated command, '*silent!*'

'But—' said Diana.

'But—' said the man who said he wasn't her brother.

'One more word,' warned Empress Janesmith, 'and you'll both be in combat!'

'That'll reduce our odds of survival,' said Wayne.

'I wouldn't give much for the fat man's chances,' said Kiru.

'I dunno,' said Wayne, looking at him. 'At least he doesn't have to eat Algolan food, he's got enough already packed in his belly.'

Kiru put both hands on her stomach. As if in response, she felt the baby kick.

'Are you okay?' asked Wayne, again.

'One of us is going to die, the other is probably going to die, and you ask if I'm okay?' She shrugged.

'You're my life, Kiru,' said Wayne. 'I don't want to live without you.'

Kiru thought it unlikely he would. If it came down to a battle between Diana and Wayne, Diana would probably be the winner. Wayne was a man, so he should have been stronger; but Diana had been both female and male, with the advantages of both, because she/he had also spent time as a ruthless criminal mastermind. And if it came down to herself and Wayne, Kiru had no doubt that he'd sacrifice himself for her.

'This is easily settled,' Empress Janesmith was saying. 'The imperial line has been kept pure for hundreds of generations, and we've perfected a method of checking heredity. We can analyse your genealogy, William Ewart, and find out if Diana Travis is really your brother or your sister or neither.'

'William Ewart?' said Wayne. 'That's William Ewart?'

'You know about him?' said Kiru, who had first heard his name from Candy.

'Yeah. He's Jay's brother.'

'Who told you that?'

'Jay did. We came to Algol together.'

'You came here with Jay? Where is he?' asked Kiru, and she looked around.

'You won't see him,' said Wayne. 'He's dead. But he also told me that Kosmos was another of his brothers.'

'Kosmos,' said Kiru, trying to remember. It was a name she recognised. 'Who's Kosmos?'

'I am,' said Diana, as she turned and came to join Kiru and Wayne. 'Or I used to be, back in the old days. How's things, Wayne?'

'How do you think?' said Wayne.

Kiru watched as Empress Janesmith left the plaza, but each row of troops remained in place.

'You're Zena, right?' William Ewart said, with a quick sideways glance at Kiru.

'Wrong,' she answered. 'Who's Zena?'

'You are. You're a zygotically engineered neoplasmic android.'

'I'm not an android!'

'You look like one.'

'What do you mean?' Androids were built to look human. Conversely, she supposed, that also meant humans could look like androids.

'Yes, what do you mean?' asked Diana. 'Is he bothering you, Kiru?'

'Not as much as you are,' Kiru told her – or him.

'Get away from her,' warned Wayne. 'Both of you.'

'Who are you?' William Ewart said. 'And where did you get that outfit?'

'It's my ambassador's uniform,' said Wayne, as he brushed some dust from his lapels. There was plenty of dust and dirt on Algol.

'An ambassador's uniform?' said Kiru. She'd noticed Wayne's outfit immediately, but asking about his fashion choice hadn't been a priority.

'The Taxliens appointed me their ambassador to Algol,' said Wayne.

'Who?' said William Ewart.

'Who?' said Diana Travis.

'The Taxliens,' said Wayne, 'the people who own Hideaway and Café World.'

'The people who *stole* Hideaway and Café World,' said Diana.

'They told you their name?' asked William Ewart.

'No,' said Wayne, shaking his head. 'I invented the name. Taxliens. It sounded right.'

'Right,' agreed William Ewart, 'it does.'

'It does,' said Diana, 'yes.'

'And the Taxliens gave you that uniform?' asked William Ewart.

'No,' said Wayne, 'I got it on board the *Demon Star*.'

'I knew it!' said William Ewart. 'The *Demon Star*, that's my ship – and that's my uniform.'

'It can't be yours.' Wayne glanced down at the uniform he was wearing, then looked at William Ewart. 'It wouldn't fit you.'

'Not mine to wear!' said William Ewart. 'The ship's steward should have worn it, but he refused to.'

'It's a steward's uniform?' said Wayne, and he sounded disappointed.

'Listen,' said Kiru, 'instead of talking about Wayne's clothes, shouldn't we try to work out how we're going to survive?'

'I am going to survive,' said Diana, 'because I'm not in the trial.'

'Kiru's right,' said Wayne, 'and if—'

'Just who are you?' asked William Ewart. 'And don't pretend you're the ambassador to Algol.'

'I'm not pretending. The Taxliens said . . .' Wayne shook his head. 'Okay, yeah, I'm Wayne Norton, and this is—' As he started to introduce Kiru, he was interrupted.

'What were you doing on my ship?' asked William Ewart.

'It was never your ship, kid,' said Diana.

William Ewart stared past Diana as if she wasn't there.

'And this is,' Wayne repeated, 'Kiru . . .'

William Ewart spared her a brief glance.

'. . . my wife,' added Wayne.

William Ewart sighed. 'You poor boy,' he said.

'What do you mean by that?' demanded Kiru.

'Marriage,' said William Ewart. 'The devil's invention. Or maybe it was the Taxliens'.' He chuckled for a moment.

The four humans stood together, as if at the corners of a small square. Around them was a real square, with a platoon of Algolan hailstormers lined up on each side. The Terrans were a long way from home, beneath a green alien sky, trapped by the formation of armour-clad alien warriors. This was their last chance to be allies, to make a stand against Empress Janesmith, to reason with her, to prove it was better to keep them all alive than to allow any of them to die.

'When did you get the uniform?' asked William Ewart.

'On the way to Algol,' said Wayne. 'From your brother. From Rajic.'

'You came to Algol with Rajic?' said William Ewart.

'Yeah,' said Wayne.

'But I killed Rajic years ago,' said Diana.

'Ah!' said William Ewart, and this time he did look at Diana. 'You told me you hadn't killed him.'

'Me?' said Diana. 'You mean Kosmos, don't you. Admit it, I'm Kosmos.'

'Never!' said William Ewart.

'You know I am,' said Diana.

'No!' said William Ewart.

While this was going on all around her, Kiru shook her head, slipped her hand free of Wayne's, turned around and walked away a few paces.

'Where are you going?' asked Wayne, coming up behind her.

'Nowhere,' she said. 'Where can I go?'

'Where is Rajic?' William Ewart called out.

'Dead,' Wayne said quietly, so only Kiru could hear, 'like I told you.'

'Did you?'

'Rajic Jao Rajic was the name Jay used to have.'

'After you went missing,' said Kiru, 'Jay showed me a dataclip of you boarding a shuttle. Ninety minutes later, he said, a ship left for Earth.'

'You went to see Jay? So did I. That's when—'

'Where is Rajic?' William Ewart repeated, even louder.

'He's dead,' said Wayne, without turning around.

'How?' asked William Ewart

'The Algolans blew him up,' said Wayne.

'Why?' asked William Ewart.

'Because he came to Algol to assassinate us,' answered Empress Janesmith.

Kiru looked around. The Empress hadn't returned alone.

Grawl was with her . . .

'No!' gasped Kiru, and her heart began to race. She grabbed Wayne, holding on to him as tight as she could, making sure he was between her and Grawl.

'It's okay, Kiru,' said Wayne. 'It's okay. He's not going to hurt you. He can't get you.'

'He's already got me,' said Kiru, staring in bewilderment at the other member of Empress Janesmith's group: a tall girl, slim, with red hair which curled down onto her shoulders. 'That's me,' she whispered.

Grawl had made a double of her!

Kiru noticed William Ewart looking from the other girl to her, then back again, and she remembered what he'd said about an android.

'He's got an android of me,' she said.

'Yeah,' said Wayne. 'I know.'

'You know?'

'Yeah, I saw them both earlier.'

'So . . . why? Why . . . me? Why . . . that?' Kiru nodded towards the android.

'Ask him. He'll explain. He's got a voice.'

Grawl might have had a voice, but Kiru had lost hers. Not that she wanted to talk to him. She didn't want to have anything to do with him; she didn't even want to see him, but she couldn't stop herself. Still clinging to Wayne, Kiru stared at Grawl. He wouldn't meet her eyes, but his android kept glancing at her. The two of them were standing behind Empress Janesmith. There was a woven sack slung over each of Grawl's shoulders, and the android had both her arms out to hold a deep wicker basket.

'The Taxliens were using you, Duke Wayne,' said Empress Janesmith.

Kiru noticed she used Wayne's word, Taxliens. That meant they had recently talked together. But it might not have been a social occasion, Kiru realised. The Empress had also visited her and Diana in their doorless cell.

'Your role as ambassador,' Empress Janesmith continued, 'was only a cover to get Rajic back to Algol. They were also using him. He was a bomb primed to explode and destroy us. We had to destroy him first.'

'Oh,' said Wayne. 'That's why they convinced me Kiru had been brought here, so Jay could come with me to kill you?'

'Correct,' said Empress Janesmith.

'But Kiru *was* brought to Algol,' said Wayne, and he looked at Diana. 'Are you working for the Taxliens?'

'No!' said Diana.

'Yes,' said Empress Janesmith. 'But you didn't know it. That's their usual procedure. But now you do know. The subversive cargo you carried to corrupt our children was sent by them.'

'You were the pilot?' William Ewart said to Diana. 'You know you brought the wrong shipment? When's the next delivery date?'

'Too late for you, kid,' said Diana.

'Enough of this,' said Empress Janesmith. 'Time for the genetic test.' She beckoned the android, who stepped forward and lifted the lid of the basket. 'You two, over here.'

William Ewart and Diana walked towards the Empress and the android. As Kiru watched, she saw Grawl look at her. When he noticed he'd been seen, he diverted all his attention to the Algolan dust beneath his feet.

'We've all been used by the Taxliens,' said Wayne. 'You, me, Diana, Jay. He paid for it with his life.'

'And now we're going to,' said Kiru.

'No. We can beat this rap.'

'Then what? Even if we both live, we'll be trapped here for ever. You think they'll let us leave Algol? Look at this place, Wayne, look at it. Not exactly Café World, is it?'

'Wherever you are, Kiru, to me that's paradise.'

'And we'll soon be there,' said Kiru. 'You only get to paradise when you're dead.'

They held each other close, and Kiru tried not to think about being dead. She thought of the opposite, of birth, of new life, and wondered whether to tell Wayne.

'No!' shouted William Ewart.

'Told you so, kid,' said Diana – who must also have been Kosmos.

Kiru remembered. Kosmos was the pirate chief who controlled Hideaway when it was a buccaneer base; and he'd been their leader when the Algolans attacked their new hideout. She knew his name because many of the survivors had been on Clink when she was there, but Kosmos wasn't one of them.

'I demand a recount,' said William Ewart.

'He or she is your blood kin,' said Empress Janesmith. 'Total paternal correlation.'

'And I can nominate him to take my place in the duel?' said Diana/Kosmos.

'Yes,' said Empress Janesmith.

'You're using Algolan equipment,' said William Ewart. 'It can't work on Terrans. You've got to run another test as proof. Try him.' He pointed at Wayne.

'Yeah, test me, go ahead,' said Wayne. He lowered his voice, and added to Kiru, 'It'll give us a bit more time.'

Time for what? Kiru wondered. She kept hold of Wayne's left hand as he walked over to the Empress, who took his other hand and slid it into the basket.

'This won't hurt,' said Empress Janesmith.

Grawl was standing close to the android, and by now he was fascinated by the clouds which raced across the green sky.

'Have we met?' asked the android.

'I don't think so,' said Kiru.

'It's as if I know you from somewhere.'

From the mirror, thought Kiru. Grawl was watching her again, and when she looked at him he didn't turn away. Instead, he shook his head slightly. Then Kiru realised.

'I'm Zena,' said the android.

'And I'm not,' said Kiru.

'Sorry?'

'I'm Kiru.'

Zena smiled. So did Kiru. The android had been made to look like her, but a metablock meant Zena couldn't recognise the original from which she'd been copied. And Grawl was worried Kiru would tell her.

'According to chromanalysis,' said Empress Janesmith, her helmeted head aiming down to the basket, 'Duke Wayne is directly related to –' she looked around to William Ewart – 'you.'

'Ha!' said William Ewart. 'He's no relative of mine. Your testing must be nixed. I've never seen him before, never even heard of him before.'

'He's your, let me count correctly,' said Empress Janesmith, 'he's your great, great, great, great, great, great, great, great grandfather.'

'What!' said William Ewart. 'See what I mean? It doesn't work on Terrans. He –' he pointed at Wayne again – 'is not my brother, not my sister, not my anything. Look at him. Even with a rejuve, how could he be my great great grandfather? Your machine's faulty.'

'It's not faulty,' said Empress Janesmith. 'Duke Wayne is an ancestor of yours. He was born on Terra more than three hundred of your years ago.'

Wayne was examining his right hand for damage –

or more damage. 'How do you know?' he asked. 'I'm sure I never told you that.'

'We know,' said the Empress, 'everything we need to know about each of you.'

'You don't know enough,' said Wayne. 'The data *is* faulty. William Ewart can't possibly be my great, great, on and on, great grandson.'

'He is. It says so here. Genetics don't tell lies.'

'They do. They must do. It's a mistake. I didn't . . .' Wayne shook his head, then shrugged. 'I didn't.'

'See?' said William Ewart. 'He knows it's a mistake. He's not related to me, and Kosmos isn't rel—'

'Hey, kid,' said Diana, 'you got it right! Kosmos, that's me.'

'Test her,' said William Ewart, and he pointed at Kiru without looking at her. 'Test the girl.'

'She's got a name,' said Wayne.

'She's the only other human here,' said William Ewart. 'Check her out as well. When you get another stupid result, you'll know your gadget doesn't work.'

'Go on, test me,' agreed Kiru. 'This hand do?' she asked, offering her left. Her right hand was still holding Wayne's left.

Without assuring her it wouldn't hurt, the Empress guided Kiru's hand under the lid and into the wicker basket, and it felt as if it was slipping into ice-cold slime. She tried to pull free, but the Algolan's mailed fist held her firm. Her hand began to throb, and the temperature of the slime started to rise, soon becoming comfortably warm; but the heat kept increasing, and she could hear hissing and bubbling from within the basket. Then Empress Janesmith let go, and Kiru yanked her hand away from the basket. It was dry, normal temperature, but every millimetre of her flesh was tingling. She slid her wedding ring up towards the knuckle, and the skin beneath was slightly different. Her hand had been flayed, she realised, a micron of flesh peeled off for genetic examination.

'Congratulations on your successful fertilisation,' said Empress Janesmith, the voice from within her helmet very soft.

'Thanks,' said Kiru, quietly, and she waited to see if this changed the rules and allowed her to withdraw from unnecessary physical activity. But the Empress offered no more.

'What's the verdict?' asked William Ewart. 'Is she my grandmother?' He forced a laugh.

'No,' said Empress Janesmith, 'she's your grand-daughter.'

'What?' said William Ewart. He shook his head, and his laughter was even more forced. 'That's ridiculous.'

Kiru looked at him, and she hoped it was.

'Did Janesmith say, "congratulations"?' Wayne asked.

'She said "commiserations,"' said Kiru. 'Must be for having him as a grandfather.'

'But he isn't,' said Wayne. 'The test doesn't work. I'm not his ancestor, and –' Wayne suddenly froze, his mouth hanging open, his eyes wide as he stared at Kiru. He began to shake his head, slowly, and he kept on shaking it in an ever-increasing arc. As he did, he closed his eyes, shut his mouth, then let go of Kiru's hand.

'– not *my* ancestor?' Kiru finished the sentence for him.

'No!' said Wayne.

'How can she be my granddaughter?' said William Ewart.

'Because she's the daughter of your daughter,' said

Empress Janesmith. 'Algolan or human, chromogenesis is infallible. Kiru is your granddaughter.'

Diana was looking at Wayne. 'If he's my brother's great, great, and the rest, grandfather, is he also mine?'

'That's how heredity works,' said Empress Janesmith.

'Are you claiming,' said Diana, as she looked from Wayne to William Ewart, to Kiru, 'that we're all related?'

'It's not a claim,' said the Empress, 'it's a fact.'

'Then this is a family reunion?' said Diana.

'Yes, but it won't last much longer,' said the Algolan, 'because two of you are going to die.'

'Two of them,' said Diana. 'I'm sitting this game out.'

Kiru kept looking at William Ewart, but he still hadn't looked at her.

'Who was her mother?' he said. 'Ask her who her mother was.'

'You ask her,' said Diana.

'My mother's name was Maya,' said Kiru.

'Maya?' said William Ewart, and he glanced at Kiru for a moment.

'She died a long time ago,' said Kiru.

William Ewart snapped his fingers. 'I know what it is. Maya was Rajic's daughter. That's why you've got that result. Rajic and me, we're brothers, so my analysis gives the same reading. I'm not her grandfather, Rajic is . . . was.'

'No,' said Empress Janesmith.

'No,' said Wayne, who had opened his eyes and stopped shaking his head.

'What do you know about it?' said William Ewart.

'I know what Rajic told me: that Maya's mother was called Myiko, that she was your first wife, that Maya's father was you, not Rajic, but you refused to take a test which would have proved it.'

'No.' William Ewart put his hands on his head, his fingers interlocked. He looked up, he looked down, then he looked at Kiru. 'It's impossible. You're not my granddaughter.'

'She is,' said Empress Janesmith.

'She is,' said Diana. 'Kiru! I'm your uncle, your great-uncle. I knew there was a reason why I always liked you. I even liked you when I arrested you. You're my favourite niece!'

Kiru looked at William Ewart. True or false, she didn't care. Grandfather or not, what did it matter now? What did anything matter?

When she'd lost her father, when she'd lost her mother, when Kiru had needed a family, William Ewart hadn't been there. He was nothing to her. She'd been on her own most of her life, all alone in the universe until Wayne entered her life. She glanced at him, and he was looking even more confused than ever.

Was he really her great, great, to the power of lots, grandfather? Over so many centuries, so many generations, the branches of every Terran family must have been intertwined.

'Now that's all settled,' announced Empress Janesmith, 'we can get on with the duel. William Ewart, you've been appointed as Diana Travis's champion and will take her or his place.'

'But I'm your brother,' William Ewart protested.

'I know you are,' said Diana.

'Not you!' said William Ewart. 'Empress, I married your sister. We're family. You can't let this happen to me.'

'You're not our brother,' said Empress Janesmith.

'You were never married to Marysmith. We would never allow an alien into the royal family.'

'But . . . but . . . why did you keep insisting I was married to Marysmith?'

'Because Rajic Jao Rajic said it would annoy you,' said Empress Janesmith. 'He was correct. We are amused.'

'And me,' said Diana. 'Rajic always was a joker.'

'But you killed him,' said Wayne.

'Life is a serious business,' said Diana.

'So's death,' said Wayne.

'You'll find out before me, Grandad,' said Diana.

'To continue,' continued Empress Janesmith. 'Only one substitution is allowed in every trial, so neither Duke Wayne or Kiru can nominate their only eligible candidate: Diana Travis.'

Kiru wasn't listening. She was about to enter a contest which could kill her, but she didn't feel frightened. There was only one thing which had ever really scared her, and he was a few metres away: Grawl.

She knew she had to confront him, to rid herself of the fear which had haunted her for so long. Even if she didn't have much time left, she wanted her mind put at rest – before her body was.

Wayne reached out to take her hand, but Kiru shook him off and walked towards Grawl.

'We must talk,' she said.

CHAPTER

TWENTY-EIGHT

The universe was full of paradoxes, thought Wayne Norton. William Ewart didn't look so fat without his clothes, for example; but undressed, Kiru seemed to have put on weight.

As they stood naked in the centre of the ruined city square, Norton found it hard to think of the other two as his descendants. Because they couldn't possibly have been. During his first life, he'd never had any children. He'd never even had sex. If he had, he was sure he'd have remembered.

Kiru had been the first woman in his life. The only woman. And she was all he ever wanted.

It was so unbelievably wonderful to have found her again; he only wished they could have more time together. But the way things seemed, they had no future together. Because at least one of them didn't have a future.

Kiru, Ewart, Norton: Janesmith said two of them must die. She was the Empress of Algol, this was her planet, so it seemed more than likely her wish would be granted.

Janesmith stood motionless within her suit of white armour. Zena was neatly folding all the clothes the prisoners had removed. (A *steward's* uniform! Was that another example of Jay's sense of humour? If so, Norton didn't see the joke.) Grawl was carefully unpacking the two sacks he'd been carrying, making a stack of Algolan food: uncooked and unwashed. Diana, alias Kosmos, was looking very smug because she wasn't going to die.

Or she thought she wasn't going to die. Janesmith must have been up to something, because why else had she lied by saying the other three Terrans were descended from Norton? Was that also for her own warped amusement?

Kiru couldn't possibly be part of Norton's bloodline. He didn't have one. They were completely and totally unrelated, and it was absolutely fine for him to be married to her. Absolutely.

'What did you talk to Grawl about?' Norton asked her.

'Nothing.'

Talking about nothing had taken a while, but now Norton said nothing. He didn't want to waste more precious minutes by arguing. But how many minutes and hours would the three-way duel take?

He noticed a movement over to the side. The row of troops on his right, who had been completely immobile all the time, suddenly broke ranks, some stepping forward, some moving back, some twisting around. Then the soldiers on the adjacent side of the square also fell out of line, followed immediately by the other two rows of hailstormers. They began milling about, forming small groups as if silently talking together.

Janesmith's helmet turned as she looked at what was

happening, and her hands reached for her weapons. Each fist clutching a black hilt, she strode across to one of the crooked lines of bronze warriors.

'What's going on?' said William Ewart.

'Don't know,' said Norton.

They watched as Janesmith marched around the square. The troops slowly returned to formation as she reached them, and they fell into step behind her. She returned to the centre of the plaza, came to a halt, but the long column of soldiers continued out into the debris-strewn road, vanishing behind a pile of fallen and eroded buildings.

'Where's Diana?' demanded Janesmith.

Norton looked all around, but there was no sign of her/him. He shrugged. Grawl and Zena had also vanished. Although they must have gone with the Algolan army, Diana evidently hadn't.

Empress Janesmith crossed her arms and drew a black-bladed knife from each belt around her elbow.

Norton took a step back, so did Kiru. Ewart took two, then another.

'Hold it, hold it,' said Ewart. 'What's going on?'

'You've done this!' said Janesmith.

'I haven't done anything,' said Ewart. 'I didn't even want to come here.'

'You humans!' spat the Algolan. 'It's all of you, you're all part of the conspiracy, you're all in league with the Taxliens!'

Norton said, 'No!'

Ewart said, 'No, never!'

Kiru said nothing.

'You should all die now!' said Janesmith. 'You must all die now!' She raised her weapons.

'AHHHHHHH!' she screamed. The serrated blades

clashed together. Sparks flew. She crossed her arms
again, sheathing the knives. 'We're too soft. That's
always been our weakness.' She twisted around and
headed in the direction her troops had taken.

'What about the tourney?' asked Ewart. 'What are
the rules?'

'There are –' said Janesmith, as she changed course
and stamped up and down on the stack of food with
her armoured boots – 'no rules.' Then she stomped
from the square and climbed into her waiting carriage.

'What was that all about?' said Norton.

Ewart shook his head. 'Look what she's done to the
food,' he said.

'Good,' said Kiru.

Ewart laughed, glanced at her, then turned away.
Earlier, he'd paid very little attention to Kiru; now, it
was as if he wanted to look at her but couldn't.
Although he stood with his back to the other two, he
kept his hands clasped modestly over his crotch.

'My first wife was called Myiko,' he said, looking
over his shoulder to Norton. 'And she had a daughter
called Maya,' he said, looking away from Kiru.

'Maya was your daughter,' said Norton.

Ewart shook his head, looked up at the green sky,
then looked down at the blue and yellow dirt. 'I know.'

Kiru walked around and stood in front of him.
'Why don't you look at me?' she said.

'I can't,' he said. 'You're my granddaughter and
you're naked.'

'I'm not your granddaughter.'

'You are.'

'Forget the genetic test,' said Kiru.

'That's not it,' said Ewart. 'I knew Diana was
Kosmos, knew he was my brother. Or sister. The test

wasn't needed. It's the same with you, Kiru, I *know*.'

'You're *not* my grandfather. The test doesn't make any difference. Genetically, you could be my mother's father. But in every other way, you're nothing to me, you're nobody, you never have been, you never will be.'

'But, Kiru—'

'And stop looking at my tits!'

She spun around and walked away. There wasn't anywhere to go, and she soon came to a halt. She sat down on a chunk of weathered masonry.

Ewart and Norton glanced at each other, and their shrugs were synchronised.

'Women,' said Norton.

'Right,' agreed Ewart. 'But she's a lovely girl, your wife.'

'Yeah.'

'She's got her grandfather's good looks.' Ewart smiled and nodded.

Norton nodded and smiled, and he kept watching the other man. He knew that Ewart wasn't descended from him. Janesmith must have rigged the whole test. But if she had, how did she know about Ewart and Kiru being related?

'Something's gone wrong,' said Norton, as he walked over to Kiru.

'Really?'

'Yeah. Janesmith's plan, something went wrong. The way her troops acted, they shouldn't have done that. It means we've got a chance.'

'Really?'

'Yeah! Come on, Kiru, this isn't the girl I know. You can't sit around here, we've got to get moving.'

'Where to? We're trapped on an alien planet, no food, no clothes.'

'Just like old times,' said Norton.

Kiru shook her head, and slowly she smiled. Norton reached his hands down to her, she lifted hers to his, and he pulled her to her feet. They pressed up against each other, their naked bodies warm against each other.

'That feels good,' said Norton, and they kissed.

'Uh-huh.'

'It's been a long time, Kiru. Why don't we go and find a quiet corner?'

'Is this why you've searched for me all across the galaxy, is that all you want me for?'

'Yeah.'

'Okay,' said Kiru. 'Come on.' She pulled on his arm, and glanced around for somewhere they could go.

Norton looked back, and he saw that Ewart was carefully paying no attention.

'Is he your grandfather?' he asked.

'Maybe.' She also looked back. 'Wayne,' she said.

'What?'

'There's something I have to tell you.'

'What?'

'Something you must know.'

'What is it? Tell me.'

'It's—'

She broke off, she was staring at Ewart, and Norton turned. The other man was watching the sky, his arm raised, pointing. Kiru and Norton looked up. There was a dark shape above them, getting bigger, closer. A lander coming directly down.

'You expecting anyone?' yelled William Ewart, as he backed away.

'No!' shouted Norton.

'What about me?' said Kiru. 'You haven't asked if I'm expecting someone.'

'Are you?' asked Norton.

'No,' she said.

Norton and Kiru retreated to the other side of the square as the lander settled directly onto the remains of what could have become an Algolan banquet. It was the same design as the craft which had brought Norton and Jay down to the surface. The hatch slid back and a biped jumped out. He looked human, he looked male, but looks weren't everything.

'He could be for me,' said Kiru, as she watched him. 'He looks like . . . like . . . I can't remember, but someone I once knew.'

Although he didn't look like anyone Norton once knew, there was something familiar about the man. In a way, he resembled everyone Norton had known, every human male. It was extraordinary how ordinary he was.

'I do hope I haven't kept you waiting,' called the newcomer. 'If you're ready to get on board, we can be on our way.'

Kiru took a step forward, but Norton held out a restraining hand.

'We don't know who he is,' he said, 'or where he's going.'

'Does it matter?' said Kiru.

'Not right now,' said Norton.

Hand in hand, he and Kiru walked towards the lander. Ewart approached the craft from the other side.

'I know you,' he said.

'That's right,' said the man. 'I'm so pleased you remember me, Bill. And Kiru, it's good to see you again. How are you? You're looking *radiant*, my dear. This must be your husband. Wayne Norton, I presume. You're a very lucky man.'

'Why?' said Ewart. 'Because you're here?'

The man laughed and held out his hand. Norton hesitated, then accepted the handshake.

'Who are you?' said Kiru.

'Kiru,' the man sighed, 'I so hoped you'd remember our time together.'

'*******!' said Ewart.

'Who?' said Norton.

'That's right,' said *******. He started to offer his hand to Ewart, but turned away when he noticed Ewart was still keeping his groin covered. 'Kiru knew me as someone else, didn't you?'

'I must have done,' said Kiru, and she took hold of *******'s hand. He bowed his head and lifted her fingers to his lips, kissing the back of her hand. She glanced at Norton and shrugged.

'Shall we go on board?' said *******.

'You first,' said Kiru.

'Certainly,' said *******, and he clambered in.

Norton was very suspicious. He didn't want the craft taking off with Kiru inside and him still on the alien dirt, so he went up into the lander next.

'Ow!' he yelled, as his bare foot stepped on something sharp. He reached down and pulled out a splinter of glass. It was from a broken bottle, a bottle of Algolcohol. The rebel general hadn't broken it, but ******* must have done when unloading all of Jay's cartons to make room for extra passengers.

'Watch your feet,' Norton said, as he beckoned for Kiru to follow him up.

'It's not watching my feet I'm bothered about,' she said, glancing at Ewart.

'Oh, right, sorry,' he said, and he looked away as she climbed the ramp.

'Come on, Bill,' said *******. 'We've got a ship to catch.'

'What ship?'

'The *Demon Star*.'

'My ship!'

'My ship,' said *******. 'You can stay there if you want, it's entirely up to you, but you're most welcome to join us.'

'You've persuaded me,' said Ewart, and he climbed on board with one hand.

'Is that everything?' asked *******, as he looked at his three passengers. 'No luggage or souvenirs? Please make yourselves comfortable. I apologise for the lack of leg room, but this will only be a short journey.'

CHAPTER
TWENTY-NINE

'Thanks,' said Wayne, as the lander took off from the surface of Algol.

'My pleasure,' said *******.

'But what was going on down there? What happened to the Algolan troops? Why did Janesmith suddenly leave?'

'Algol was under attack.'

'Attack? Who by?'

'They don't have a name, which is why throughout the galaxy they're often known as "the nameless aliens".'

'The Taxliens?'

'I believe that's what you've been calling them, Wayne. May I call you Wayne?'

'That's my name.'

'How can anyone, any advanced species, not have a name?' asked Kiru.

'They don't need one,' said *******. 'If you were on your own, Kiru, you would think of yourself as "I" or "me". Names are for the convenience of others, or to establish a personal identity. The nameless aliens have no personal identity.'

'That's why they all have the same name, Dulsedech?' said Wayne.

'Precisely. Or that's the individual name they say they have. For the purpose of this discussion, however, we'll refer to the species by your soubriquet. Algol is at present under Taxlien attack.'

The lander was small and cramped, and all William Ewart could do was sit in silence and gaze at the back of ✱✱✱✱✱✱✱'s anonymous head as he piloted the craft out into orbit.

'We didn't notice any attack,' said Kiru.

Ewart was doing his best not to look at her. She reminded him too much of Myiko. The physical resemblance wasn't very strong, but she was his last link, his only link, with his first wife. Even after so very long, the memory was still painful. He'd nearly lost Myiko to Rajic, but instead she was taken by plague. An alien infection or not, it had made no difference: it had killed her. There was no justice in the world, the whole galaxy was hostile, and the only way to survive was by being as tough and ruthless as possible, stepping on everyone else on the way to the top. That was when he'd broken free from his previous life, when he changed his name and became someone else, someone who would never become close to another person, someone who could never suffer such torture again.

He'd had other wives after Myiko, other children after Maya, and he'd also had grandchildren. None of them had meant anything to him, he wouldn't allow it. He always suspected that Maya was his daughter, not Rajic's; but he wanted to believe otherwise. Without Maya, he had transformed himself into William Ewart. He needed no one, and he wanted no one to need him.

Ewart had travelled across the galaxy, visited

countless planets, eaten the most lavish meals in the universe, but as he stole a glance at Kiru, he wished his life had taken another course, wished he'd spent it with Maya, wished he'd seen her grow to a woman and have a daughter of her own: his granddaughter . . .

'Kiru.'

'What?' said Kiru, and she turned to him.

He didn't realise he'd spoken her name aloud.

'You're right,' Ewart said. 'If there was an attack on Algol, we'd have seen it.'

'It wasn't that kind of attack,' said *******. 'If it had been at all violent, you wouldn't be here now.'

'And you wouldn't be here now,' said Ewart, 'or anywhere close.'

'What kind of attack was it?' asked Wayne.

'An electronic assault,' said *******. 'Algol's entire comtech network is out of action.'

'Their comtech network is out of action?' said Ewart, and he laughed. 'How did they notice?'

'And their spacefleet has been completely disabled,' ******* continued. 'The planet is effectively isolated from the rest of the galaxy. No ship, whether Algolan or not, can come near to the planet without suffering a systems melt-down.'

Ewart didn't like the sound of that. 'What about this lander we're in?'

'DNT,' said *******. 'Different navigation technology.'

'Also known as OLD,' said Kiru, as she gazed around the ancient lander. 'Old.'

'Yes,' agreed *******. 'The same applies to the *Demon Star*. IPS. Incompatible propulsion system – the Rollein-Twist. It means we'll be able to leave Algol's orbit.'

'And the Taxliens are behind this blockade of Algol?' said Wayne.

'That's right. They want the Algolans to stay on Algol. It's only a temporary measure. In a year or a decade or a century, the Algolans will find a way of escaping. And by then, it seems reasonable to suppose, they'll be somewhat annoyed with the Taxliens.'

'How did the Taxliens manage to do all this?' asked Wayne. 'Sabotage?'

'It was the ship Kiru and Kosmos came in,' said *******.

Ewart noticed he'd said 'Kosmos'; he knew who Diana was. Was that why he'd come to Algol, was he still searching for Kosmos?

'The Algolans knew there was something not right about the ship,' ******* continued. 'They thought it was the cargo, which they destroyed. But it wasn't the cargo, that was a decoy. It was the vessel itself which was the danger. As it circled the planet it burst apart, and every fragment of hull took on its primary role as a techbusting orbiter. There are thousands and thousands of them around Algol.'

'How do you know all this?' asked Wayne.

Ewart thought the question was redundant. ******* seemed to know everything.

'I was on board when the ship arrived,' said *******.

'You were not,' said Kiru.

'Because you didn't see me, Kiru, that doesn't mean I wasn't there. I boarded the ship on Hideaway, like you did. In fact, I was with you.'

'Were you?'

'Yes. And when you and Kosmos were taken down to Algol, I was with you then.'

'Why?' said Kiru. 'What for?'

'I had to get to the surface,' answered *******. 'I have many talents, it's true, but reaching the surface of a planet without a lander isn't one of them.'

'Why did you want to get to the surface?' asked Wayne. 'What were you doing on Algol?'

'Nothing much, a bit of sightseeing, waiting until the time was right to head for the *Demon Star*.'

'Because that's the only ship which can make it through the blockade?' said Wayne.

'Yes.'

'And you're going to do something about the blockade? You'll destroy all the satellites?'

'No, not at all. It's part of a small dispute between the Algolans and the Taxliens, there's no need for me to get involved.'

'A small dispute?' said Ewart. 'No need for you to get involved? Didn't you get involved in a dispute between Kosmos's pirates and the Algolans? If I remember right, you even *caused* it by commandeering *my* ship and taking Marysmith to the pirate planet. Or is my memory at fault?'

'Just doing my job,' said *******.

'And where's your job taken you since then? Have you started many rebellions, wiped out many civilisations, caused many interstellar wars, drowned many kittens?'

'No,' said *******, 'no, no, and no kittens. Puppies yes, but no kittens. Things have been fairly quiet since we last met, Bill. By the way, how did you and Kosmos manage to escape the Algolan assault?'

'Wouldn't you like to know?' said Ewart, and he smiled.

'Not particularly, I was only making conversation.

After the Algolans smashed the pirate base, I took a bit of a break and stayed on Arazon for a while.'

'Arazon?' said Kiru, and she turned to look at him.

'That's where I met you. I was there when you landed, remember?'

'No,' said Kiru.

'We left Clink on the same ship. Remember that?'

'No,' said Kiru, again.

For the first time, ******* appeared uneasy. He was an organiser, he planned things, then they happened; but this seemed unexpected.

'The ship docked at Hideaway,' he said. 'You must remember being there, Kiru.'

'I'm not Kiru,' said the girl.

'What?' said Wayne, and he stared at her. 'Who are you?'

'I'm Zena.'

'What!' said Ewart, and he also stared at the girl.

Although he said nothing, ******* looked around.

'You asked what I'd talked to Grawl about,' said the girl, as she looked at Wayne. 'I answered "nothing" because it wasn't me. It was Kiru, she talked with Grawl.'

'Huh?' said Wayne.

'Grawl was very apologetic, saying how sorry he was for his behaviour, that it wouldn't happen again, and if there was ever anything he could do to make up for it Kiru only had to ask.' The girl paused. 'And Kiru asked.'

'I don't,' said Wayne, 'understand.' He spoke slowly, as if he was beginning to.

Ewart already did, and he realised what was coming next.

'Kiru and I swapped places. There was so much

going on, no one noticed. I stripped off my clothes to become Kiru, and she became me. She even gave me her wedding ring.' She held up her left hand, spreading her fingers.

'But . . . why?' asked Wayne.

The girl looked at him.

'Because of the trial?' said Wayne. 'Kiru didn't want to take part?'

'Neither did I,' said Ewart. 'You mean you did?'

'You swapped,' said Wayne, 'and then what was going to happen?'

'As soon as the duel began,' said the girl, 'I was going to kill him.' She nodded towards Ewart.

'What? Me? Why?'

'Because it was a choice between you and Wayne. I'd kill you, then kill myself — not that I'd die, because Grawl could retrieve my infocore and give me another life. Out of the three of us, Wayne, you'd be the survivor.'

'Turn this thing around,' said Ewart. 'We're going back for Kiru.'

'I'm afraid not,' said *******.

'You've got to,' said Ewart.

'Hang on,' said Wayne. 'Let's not hurry this.' He studied the girl by his side. 'It's amazing how you look so much like Kiru.' He ran his fingers through her hair. 'In fact, I think you're even better looking than she is. To tell the truth, Kiru was a bit too skinny for me.' He began to stroke her neck. 'I like a chick who's more curvy, if you know what I mean.' His hand moved down onto her shoulder. 'And I never realised, Zena, that androids are so *authentic*. Even down to every last detail.'

As Wayne's caressing hand began to slide down

from her shoulder, Ewart looked away and clenched his fists. Any more of this, and he'd give him a good beating.

'I think,' Wayne continued, 'this has all worked out very well. You're more attractive than Kiru; and as an android, you'll do what you're told to.'

'You *bastard*!' yelled the girl, and she punched at the side of his head with her fist.

Wayne ducked away to avoid the blow, but it was the wrong move. The first punch had been a feint, and she caught him hard on his cheek with her other fist.

'Ahhhh!' shouted Wayne, but he was laughing at the same time. 'Kiru, don't! You'll hurt yourself.'

'No, I'm going to hurt *you*, you double-crossing . . . double-crosser!' She shook herself free.

'Kiru, I know it's you.' Wayne held up one hand defensively, rubbing his face with the other. 'I knew all along it was you.'

'All along?'

'Yeah!' Wayne laughed.

'You didn't! I had you worried for a minute.'

'Worried? Not at all. I've always wanted an android.'

'Hey!' warned Kiru, laughing as she raised her fist again.

Wayne made a grab for her. In the small lander, there was nowhere for Kiru to escape. He hugged her tight, and after a moment her arms went around him.

******* returned his attention to piloting duties. Ewart relaxed and smiled. Kiru had inherited the family sense of humour, there was no doubt of that. But where had her fabulous red hair come from? It was genuine: granddaughter or not, he couldn't help but notice the secondary evidence. Her colouring must have been from the other half of her family, from her father.

'Careful,' Kiru laughed. 'Mind the baby.'

'Baby?' said Wayne.

Baby? thought Ewart.

'We're having a baby,' said Kiru.

'Are we?' Wayne stared at her in astonishment.

'We are.'

'*We?*' Wayne kept on staring. 'It is, er . . .' He tapped his chest with his palm.

'Don't finish that question,' warned Kiru. 'Don't you *dare*!'

'This is . . . is . . . great!'

'Good.'

'Good? Is that all you can say? Good!'

'Good, yeah, that means I'm pleased you're pleased.'

'Why wouldn't I be pleased? Are you pleased? You don't look very excited.'

'I've had time to get used to the idea. And I am excited, Wayne, very excited. Excited that we're together again.'

'Congratulations, Kiru,' said Ewart.

'Thanks, Grandad.'

'Grandad?' said Ewart.

He looked at Kiru, she looked at him.

'Only my grandad would want to go back to Algol for me,' she said, and she smiled at him.

Ewart also smiled. He'd found a grandchild he never knew he had – and now she was going to have a child of her own.

'I'm not sure about this baby of yours, Kiru,' he said.

She frowned. 'What do you mean?'

'I'm too young to be a great-grandfather,' said Ewart, then he noticed Wayne had turned to look at him.

Because he'd been so involved with part of what Empress Janesmith had revealed about his birthline, Ewart had given no thought to the other direction of his genetic history: Wayne was family, distant family. Without Ewart, Kiru would not exist. But without Wayne, neither of them would exist.

And if having a great-grandchild made Ewart feel old, what was the effect on Wayne Norton? Not only was he going to be the baby's father, he would also be the great, great, great, great, however many greats it was, great-grandfather . . .

CHAPTER
THIRTY

'What do you want?' asked Kiru, once they were on board the *Demon Star*. 'You didn't save us from Algol out of the goodness of your heart.'

'If you have one,' said William Ewart, her grandfather.

'You've heard the phrase,' said ********, '"my enemy's enemy is my friend"?'

'Yeah,' said Wayne Norton, her husband.

'Although I know we're all friends, in any case,' said ********.

'Friends!' said William Ewart.

'We share the same enemy, the Taxliens, and that makes us even greater friends.'

'The Taxliens never did anything to me,' said William Ewart. 'Or not very much. They've taken my money, but they've taken everyone's money.'

'They wiped out Ewart Communications Corporation,' said ********.

'Did they?'

'They did. You remember all your meticulous

planning when you were making a takeover bid for Sol
Global News?'

'Right.'

'And how it all fell through despite every safeguard?'

'Right.'

'That was the Taxliens, they made sure you'd fail
because they planned to buy up Terran assets. Because
of the Crash, they bought the planet at a bargain price.
That's how they operate.'

'Right,' said William Ewart. 'I hate them. Is there
anything to eat?'

'Is there anything to wear?' asked Kiru.

'And where are we heading?' asked Wayne.

'Hideaway,' said *******.

Which was what Kiru had guessed, but was the last
thing she wanted to hear.

'There isn't much choice of food,' said *******,
'but you won't starve. Kiru, if you want to come with
me, we can find you some clothes.'

'And for me, please,' said Wayne.

'Is there another steward's uniform for him,
Grandad?' asked Kiru.

'I wouldn't wear one,' said Wayne.

'Why not?' said Kiru. 'You've got no taste.'

'Except in women,' said Wayne.

They kissed, and it was amazing, astonishing,
astounding, every superlative throughout the alphabet, to be back with him again.

'I'll look for something for you, Grandad.'

'Thanks.'

'How about a drink?' said Wayne. 'I know where
Jay's cellar is.'

'Jay?' said William Ewart.

'Rajic,' said Wayne. 'We knew him as Jay.'

'Right,' said William Ewart, as he gazed around the total mess of what had once been his stateroom on the *Demon Star*. 'People don't look after anything these days,' he said. 'There's no respect for other people's property.'

'That's the Taxliens for you,' said *******. 'It's the same with Hideaway. They're making a fortune from the place, but they won't spend anything on it. That's one reason why we've got to get them out of there.'

The other three all looked at him.

'We?' said William Ewart.

'Yes,' said *******. 'I'm planning to evict the Taxliens from Hideaway, and I was hoping you might assist me.'

'Is that why you rescued us from Algol?' asked Kiru.

'Yes.'

'If we refuse,' said Wayne, 'will you make us go back again?'

'You're not going to refuse,' said *******.

'How about that drink, Wayne?' said William Ewart.

'Yeah,' said Wayne. 'I could do with one.'

'So could I,' said Kiru.

'No alcohol for you,' said William Ewart.

'Go try on some clothes,' said Wayne. 'That's what women like doing, isn't it?' He grinned and tried to give her another kiss, but Kiru turned away and went out into the corridor with *******.

She didn't know much about trying on clothes, she'd never had much chance to practise. But the *Demon Star* had a vast selection of outfits, and she began to teach herself.

One cabin was jammed full of brand new clothes,

all still wrapped and sealed. It was as if she'd discovered a lost hoard of couturier treasure, forgotten cargo once destined for a chain of interstellar boutiques. Most of the garments were for aliens of various species, which meant the lengths and widths, the collars and sleeves, the openings and fastenings, were the wrong ratios and locations and angles for a human – but the colours and designs and fabrics were irresistible. It took Kiru hours to decide on suitable shipboard attire, then one minute each to find something for Wayne and her grandfather. As she was leaving the cabin in her tailored red bodysuit and matching ankle boots, she noticed a multivisor and picked it up, then she went back to join the others.

'Just the four of us,' said Wayne, 'we're going to eject the Taxliens from Hideaway?'

'We'll have some help,' said *******.

'The Algolans?' said William Ewart.

'No. The whole purpose is to leave Hideaway intact. It's important that the outer shell isn't damaged.'

'Why?' asked Kiru.

'Because over the millennia, that's what has attracted so many different species to move in. They live there for a time, sometimes a very long time, then another alien race takes over the tenancy. It's a very hospitable environment.'

'Which is why the Taxliens don't want to move out, I guess,' said Wayne. 'Cheers.'

'Cheers,' said William Ewart, and two glasses clinked together.

'Who's going to help us?' asked Kiru.

'I've got people on Hideaway,' said *******.

'A whole legion, I hope,' said William Ewart, sipping at his drink.

'I could hire a gang of mercenaries if that's what I needed,' said *******, 'but there must be a minimum of violence.'

'Who are these people on Hideaway?' asked Wayne.

'There's someone called Terry who's been very useful to me over the years.'

'Terry?' said Kiru. 'The boy whose body's bent almost double?'

'It's a shame he's like that,' said *******. 'We've been in contact for a long time, but until recently we'd never met and I didn't know how bad he was. When this is all over, if he wants to be fixed, I'll take him to Algol. Then maybe he can meet up with his father.'

'Who's that?' asked Kiru.

'Kosmos,' said *******.

'Kosmos?' said Kiru. 'Kosmos is Terry's father?'

'Yes,' said *******. 'But neither of them know, not yet. Perhaps Terry shouldn't meet his father yet, not while he looks more like his mother.'

'If Terry is Kosmos's son,' said Kiru, slowly, as she looked at William Ewart, 'that means I'm related to him.'

'Who's this?' asked William Ewart. 'Another new relative?'

'I wonder,' said *******, 'if I should go back to Algol now. Kosmos could be useful.'

'Leave him to rot there,' said William Ewart. 'I hope Janesmith catches up with him.'

'While he was pirate chief,' said *******, 'he did a good job of looking after Hideaway, took care of the place, kept it on the move.'

'He threatened to kill me,' said William Ewart.

'Executive stress. He was under a lot of pressure at the time. He also tried to kill me.'

'But he did kill Rajic,' said William Ewart. 'Or did he?'

'Temporarily,' said Wayne. 'The Algolans put him back together again.'

'If I went back to Algol,' added *******, 'I could also collect Grawl and Zena.'

'What for?' asked Kiru.

What Kiru had said to Wayne about Grawl was true: he'd been full of apologies and remorse. He was the one who did most of the talking, saying he could-n't excuse or justify what he'd tried to do to her, and then he'd attempted to excuse and justify himself. Then, suddenly, he said he had been wrong – and Kiru was astonished, because men never admitted they were wrong. That was all she'd needed from him. It was over. The fear was lifted. But she still never wanted to see him again.

'Because I promised Zena a wedding,' said *******. 'I hear the service on Caphmiaultrelvossmuaf is excellent, although I've never visited the place. Do you recommend it?'

'No one should get married,' said William Ewart. 'Not even Grawl.'

'But it's too late to get back to Algol,' said *******. 'We're on the move now, and soon we'll be slipping into falspace. Before that, I'd better contact one of my correspondents on Hideaway.' He glanced over at William Ewart. 'Either Candy or Mandy.'

'Candy and Mandy!' William Ewart drained his glass in a single gulp. 'They betrayed me.'

'They were working for the Taxliens,' said *******.

'They were working for Hiroshi Larnvik,' said William Ewart.

'He was working for the Taxliens,' said *******.

'But none of them knew it. You don't want me to pass on your compliments to Candy and Mandy?'

'No.'

'Mandy?' said Wayne. 'Is that the same Mandy I met?'

'Yes,' said *******. 'How about you, Kiru? Want me to give your regards to Candy and Mandy? Or one of them in particular.' As he spoke, he touched the bottom of his left eye.

Kiru closed her eyes, both of them, and tried not to remember what had happened between her, Candy and the Ipralan with the extra anatomy. But what she did had to be done, it was the only way she'd been able to leave Hideaway. When she took Candy's place on the ship, she'd left the woman and the alien tied together with the filament from her dress – the dress Terry had given her, in fact. That was before she knew about Candy's opticam.

'You'll be pleased to know,' added *******, 'that Candy and Mandy are ecstatic with the way everything worked out. When you threw Mandy off the ship, she went looking for Candy – and found her with her new friend. The three of them have been inseparable ever since. They're going to get married. As for that –' he touched his eyelid again – 'it's been erased.'

'Good,' muttered Kiru.

'What's all that about?' asked Wayne.

She looked at him, and he was wearing the eye visor she'd found. It was pulled down over his forehead, and he was experimenting with different colour shades and lens patterns.

'Candy and Mandy getting married?' William Ewart shook his head. 'I made them, you know. Or rather, I paid to have them made.'

Wayne lifted his glass to his lips, but missed, and poured his drink down his chin. He pulled the multivisor around his neck and wiped at his face.

'Aren't we getting away from the point?' he said, and he stared at *******. 'Who are you? What are you? What do you do? And what do you really want from us?'

'I take care of Hideaway,' said *******.

'You're the caretaker?' said Wayne.

'Yes.'

'What is Hideaway? Nobody knows who built it.'

'I know,' said *******.

And he told them.

Hideaway had been built a million years ago, he said. Kiru thought that a suspiciously convenient number. A million years by what calendar?

The asteroid was constantly being renewed, rebuilt, reconfigured. It was a living entity – and it was designed for living, an attractive home for every kind of alien. The atmosphere, the gravity, the shape and dimensions of every room and corridor, all could be altered. The satellite was also a spaceship, it could be flown from one end of the universe to the other. If the universe had an end.

The name 'Hideaway' was the latest in an alien lexicon. Everyone who had inhabited the unique world had given it a different title. Only the Taxliens had kept the previous name. To save expense, they used the same one the pirates had when the planetoid was their galaxy-reaving base.

At its core lay a small star which burned with brilliant white radiance, providing all the energy for the world which encircled it. And deep within the star was where Hideaway's true owners lived – assuming the word 'lived' could apply to such a strange existence.

Wayne had been frozen in suspended animation for three hundred Terran years; but Hideaway's creators had been dormant in the heart of their stellar inferno for far, far longer. Compared to the infinite existence of the universe, it was nothing. But compared to most species, most races, they were immortal. They were asleep, but they would awake. They might remain in hibernation for another million years, or ten million, or a hundred million.

'Or they might wake up next Tuesday?' said Kiru.

'Yes,' said *******.

'And you have to keep everything neat and tidy, in case they do?'

'In a way.'

'And the Taxliens are bad tenants?' said William Ewart.

'In a sense.'

'What way?' asked Wayne. 'What sense?'

'The Taxliens are hated and loathed across the galaxy,' said *******. 'As well as accumulating vast wealth, they've quickly accumulated more enemies than any other race in recorded time. Because they've hidden their origins, their homeworld cannot be invaded.'

'You must know where it is,' said Kiru.

'Certainly,' said *******. 'But no one else knows, and only the elite in the Taxlien hierarchy know the location of their home planet. If anyone plans to attack them, they'll attack them on Hideaway. That can't be allowed. They have to go.'

'And we're going to make them?' said Kiru.

'I can't do it alone,' said *******. 'I'm not the man I used to be.'

Kiru doubted he ever had been a man. His current appearance was probably only for their benefit. They were human, and so he looked human.

'It's time for me to retire,' he said. 'I need to find a successor.' He looked from Kiru, to Wayne, to William Ewart. 'Or successors.'

'You're offering us . . . *jobs*?' said William Ewart.

'Yes.'

'As . . . *caretakers*?' William Ewart laughed, then drained another glass.

'It's a job for life,' said *******.

'I've got better things to do with my life,' said William Ewart.

'That depends how long your life is,' said *******.

'Are you threatening my grandad?' said Kiru. 'Because if you are . . .'

'Not at all. All I'm saying is: being the trustee of Hideaway is more than a job for life. It's a job for more than life, longer than life, far longer than your brief human lives.'

CHAPTER
THIRTY-ONE

Wayne Norton sat holding Kiru's hand, opposite them was William Ewart. There was a table between them, with plenty of bottles and glasses. No one was drinking, no one was speaking.

Ever since Kiru had told him she was pregnant, Norton had been thinking of where the baby had been conceived – on Caphmiaultrelvossmuaf – and wondering if the child would be born with gills and webbed fingers and toes. He knew the idea was crazy, but he couldn't get it out of his head.

When people moved to another world, they came under the influence of that planet and its star, and their bodies began to alter. It happened slowly, very slowly, over years and years, and the changes were barely perceptible. After a few generations, the children would become slightly different, their bodies adapting to the new gravity, the variations in atmosphere and climate. It took a long, long time. But it had to begin somewhere – and what if this new genesis began with their first-born . . . ?

Kiru squeezed his hand, and she smiled at him. He

ran his fingers over hers, feeling the red wedding ring and hoping that was the only thing they had brought with them from Café World. Kiru's other hand was resting on the table, and her grandfather was loosely holding it.

Norton had been worried about their child not being fully human, and now ******* had offered them something else: the chance of becoming more than human.

'Is it true?' Kiru had asked.

'If it isn't,' Norton had said, 'it's a great way of getting us to help him shift the Taxliens.'

'I think it is true,' Ewart had said. 'This isn't a spur of the moment offer. ******* came to Algol to get us, but it goes back longer than that. I first went to Hideaway because of him, when he commandeered my ship. Kiru first went to Hideaway because of him, when he organised the great escape from Arazon.'

'But I didn't go to Hideaway because of him,' Norton had said. 'Or at least I don't think so. I went because of Kosmos.' Although he hadn't known him as Kosmos at the time.

'You only met Kosmos,' Ewart had said, 'because ******* had chased him away from his pirate lair.'

'And we met, Wayne,' Kiru had said, 'because we arrived on Hideaway at the same time.'

'It all fits together,' Ewart had said.

'That's what bothers me,' Norton had said. 'Why us?'

'Why not?' Kiru had said.

And now they sat in silence, waiting for an answer, while ******* had gone to get an answer of his own from one of his contacts on Hideaway.

'I've never wanted to die,' said Ewart.

'Who has?' said Norton.

'I want to live,' said Ewart. 'I want more out of life. I want . . . more life.'

'Forever is a long time,' Kiru said.

'It isn't forever,' Ewart said.

'Near enough,' said Norton.

'I wonder if there's a pension?' said Kiru.

Wayne Norton laughed, William Ewart laughed, Kiru laughed. They laughed as they contemplated eternity.

Then ******* returned. His face had always been expressionless, he never hurried, but not any more. The other three stopped laughing.

'What's wrong?' asked Ewart.

'The Taxliens are leaving Hideaway,' answered *******.

'Good,' said Kiru. 'That means we won't have to kick them out.'

'I should have realised this might happen,' said *******. 'I'm losing my touch. Getting . . . old.'

'What's happened?' asked Norton. 'What are the Taxliens doing?'

'The blockade of Algol, it's not just to keep the Algolans trapped there, it's so they can't protect themselves when the Taxliens attack.'

'But you must have thought of that?' said Ewart.

'Yes. Even if the Taxliens destroyed Algol, it was only significant because they use Hideaway as their headquarters.'

'What's different now?' asked Norton.

'The Taxliens are going to attack Algol *with* Hideaway. The stellar core will obliterate the entire planet *and* Hideaway.'

'There goes the job,' said Kiru. 'And the pension.'

'Can you stop them?' asked Norton.

'If we can reach Hideaway in time, yes.'

'What are we waiting for?'

'We're not,' said *******. 'I've started the Rollein-Twist sequence.'

'You should be able to save Hideaway, right?' said Ewart. 'But if not, so what? Algol's demolished? No great loss to the universe. And if Hideaway's core gets destroyed, does it matter? Except to the immortals – who won't be.'

'It's more than that, it's worse than that. The core is no ordinary star, not a single atom is from this universe. It belongs to another continuum, and detonation in this strata of existence could cause a chain reaction that would . . .'

'What?' said Norton.

'. . . destroy the galaxy,' said *******.

'That bad, huh?' said Kiru.

'Perhaps worse,' said *******.

'Worse?' said Ewart.

'How could it be worse?' said Norton.

'It might destroy the universe.'

'Yeah?' said Norton.

'In your time, Wayne Norton, remember the power of a nuclear bomb? Atomic fission is caused by the splitting of an atomic nucleus. Now think of a whole star, even a small star, and imagine how many nuclei there are in that star. And that would be only the beginning . . .'

The *Demon Star* shook. The lights shimmered, the walls of the cabin appeared to dissolve for a moment, the entire ship becoming transparent, but beyond the hull there were no stars. The cosmos was a kaleidoscopic maelstrom of scarlet and gold, purple and orange, emerald and crimson.

'I get the idea,' said Norton. As the cabin returned to normal, he added, 'That's a good trick. How did you do that?'

'I didn't,' said *******. 'If it's not one thing, it's another.' He sighed and shook his head. 'That was the Rollein-Twist. It's malfunctioning.'

'What?' said Norton.

'No!' said Ewart.

They were all on their feet. ******* was still by the door. The other three stood near the centre of the stateroom, Kiru in the middle. Norton held one of her hands, Ewart held the other.

'The Rollein-Twist,' said *******, 'is about to roll us into another space and twist us into another time. That's what happened to all the other ships that vanished.'

'No one knows what happened to them,' said Ewart.

'I know,' said *******. 'Falspace is another dimension, but the missing ships slid even further out of true space and real time, through into a dimension beyond that.'

'Can you fix it?' asked Kiru.

'Given enough time, yes,' said *******. 'And for me, there will be enough time, far more than enough to memorise all the manuals and strip down the engines to their last neuron and capillary. But there's one thing I can't fix.'

'What?' asked Norton.

'Your lives. You'll have to do that yourselves.'

'How?' asked Ewart.

'The Rollein-Twist affects the ship and everyone on board. Because there are only four of us, there are fewer permutations of potential catastrophe. No other ship ever made it back. But we can. We have to.'

The other three watched him and waited.

'Each of you,' said *******, 'is about to return to a key moment in your own history. The further back in time you go, the longer you'll be there. If each of you makes the right decision, does the right thing, we'll all be back here at precisely the same moment. Objectively, no time will have elapsed, and we can reach Hideaway and stop the Taxliens destroying the satellite and starting a cataclysmic reaction which could eradicate all sentient life in the galaxy.'

'Easy,' said Kiru.

'We all make a decision?' said Norton. 'What do you mean?'

'I don't understand,' said William Ewart.

'You will,' said *******.

Norton squeezed Kiru's hand – and felt his fingers start to melt into hers . . .

Her body was dissolving, fading.

She vanished.

And Ewart was also gone.

Then Wayne Norton blinked out of existence.

So did the *Demon Star*, taking ******* with it.

CHAPTER
THIRTY-TWO

As soon as he saw himself, William Ewart understood. And he knew what he had to do.

He remembered that day so very clearly, the day he should have become the richest man on Earth. Instead, he'd been taken to court and ended up having to escape from Earth.

Ewart hadn't set foot on his native world since then, and now his mission was to ensure that he left in the first place.

Grawl and Zena, the original Zena, had sprung him from the court room, and they had all been chased across the city by police and security squads. There were three skimmers waiting to complete the getaway, two of them decoys.

Although Grawl was shooting at them, the police were drawing closer. Zena was standing by one of the skimmers, which was painted in police colours. She gave the signal, and it took off.

That was when William Ewart first caught proper sight of his younger self. It was true, he realised, he was fat . . .

Or he had been, back in the days before his galactic wanderings began.

And the only way to begin his misadventures in time and space was by scheduling a repeat of this original day. A decoy had distracted the police, he remembered, a human decoy.

The decoy, he now knew, was himself. His older self. His slimmer self.

If his earlier self escaped, his life would go on, until finally it looped back across the years and through the cosmos to this very moment, when again he'd be standing here, waiting to act.

Ewart's other self was fifty metres away, on the other side of the wide street, where Zena was getting ready to send off the second decoy skimmer.

Now was his moment.

'Right!' he yelled, as he ran out from the shadows. 'I'll hold them!' He angled across the road, and some of the cops turned and came in his direction.

He looked around and saw his unreconstructed self staring straight at him.

'Get going, you fat bastard!' he shouted.

William Ewart kept on running, and he was laughing, laughing because he was slim and fit and could run, and because he'd played his part so well.

He saw a skimmer streak into the air high above him, and he knew it was himself, his younger self heading for the future and his rendezvous with destiny.

CHAPTER

THIRTY-THREE

Kiru looked in horror at the man standing on top of the building, the man holding the little girl, the man holding her . . .

He was going to jump!

She ran forward, grabbed his arm, pulling him back from the edge and seizing the child from his grip. The man reached for her, but she dodged aside. He overbalanced and fell, fell screaming, down down down, down to the ground far below.

He was her father.

Then the girl also began to scream, staring in absolute fear at the demon in red who was clutching her.

'It's alright, it's alright,' said Kiru. 'Everything will be alright,' she said, even though she knew it wouldn't be.

The girl screamed and screamed.

She would have nightmares for years and years, but at least she'd live. It wouldn't be much of a life, not until she reached the stars. But when she finally met Wayne, at last it would all be worthwhile.

Wayne Norton ran, ran from the police car being driven by Wayne Norton, ran along the sidewalk, then ran down into the alley that led to the casino basement. He halted, ducking behind a row of trashcans. There was a squeal of tyres, and the patrol car sped down the alley. Norton caught a glimpse of his other self as he drove by.

He stood up and gazed down the slope, and he could see Susie's red Jaguar parked by the loading bay. His other self would also see the convertible, and that was why he'd go into the building. He would never come out again. Not fully alive. Not dead, either.

Down in the basement was the cryonic chamber where Norton would begin the next three centuries. And the man responsible for him being there was Mark Ash, Susie's father. As well as putting Norton into suspended animation, Mr Ash was about to commit murder.

Once a cop, always a cop, and Wayne Norton planned to make sure Mr Ash was arrested. A phone call, a tip-off, it had to be done fast while the bodies were still warm. Meanwhile, his earlier self would remain hidden away and frozen.

Norton walked back up to the street. The first part of his job was done: by making his earlier self follow him, he'd completed the circle. Now he had to get his hair cut, go home and change into his twentieth-century clothes to make himself look like he did in this era — although there was nothing he could do about his missing finger. Then he had to marry Susie Ash.

She was over twenty-one, she didn't need her father's consent. Her father would be in jail by then, but it would probably be best if Susie didn't know that. A secret wedding, that's what it would have to be. This was Las Vegas, they could get married any time they wanted.

He felt bad about this, because he was already married — although maybe 'already' was the wrong word. Norton hadn't married anyone. Not yet. Kiru, his future bride, hadn't even been born. And she never would be unless Norton became a father. All of this had to be done fast, because he didn't know how much time he had.

Marrying Susie was the honourable and decent thing to do, even if he would be whisked back over the centuries and across the galaxy soon after. It was better than abandoning her as an unmarried mother, it must have been.

Wayne Norton glanced up at the sky. It was blue. Somewhere up there, watching the planet, he knew there was a Taxlien observation drone.

'We'll get you!' he shouted to the stars.

But saving the universe would have to wait.

Because first he had to propose to Susie, get married, go on honeymoon, start a dynasty.

Then, after everything, there would be time for eternity.

The author's thanks go to:

Everyone at Orbit, past and present, for out-standing devotion to editorial duty, in particular:

Colin Murray, for starting it all by saying *Yes* – and even for saying *No* . . .

Lisa Rogers, for saying 'are you sure about this word/sentence/paragraph . . . ?'

and Tim Holman, for saying the right things at the right time; and for seeing this epic through to its fabulous, stunning conclusion . . .

David Garnett

Orbit titles available by post:

❏ Bikini Planet	David Garnett	£5.99
❏ Sten	Chris Bunch and Allan Cole	£5.99
❏ The Burning City	Larry Niven and Jerry Pournelle	£7.99
❏ Knight's Dawn	Kim Hunter	£9.99
❏ The Empire Stone	Chris Bunch	£6.99
❏ Nothing But Blue Skies	Tom Holt	£15.99
❏ A Shadow on the Glass	Ian Irvine	£6.99
❏ Ender's Shadow	Orson Scott Card	£6.99
❏ Guilty Pleasures	Laurell K. Hamilton	£5.99
❏ Hunting Party	Elizabeth Moon	£5.99

The prices shown above are correct at time of going to press. However, the publishers reserve the right to increase prices on covers from those previously advertised, without further notice.

orbit

ORBIT BOOKS
Cash Sales Department, P.O. Box 11, Falmouth, Cornwall, TR10 9EN
Tel: +44 (0) 1326 569777, Fax: +44 (0) 1326 569555
Email: books@barni.avel.co.uk

POST AND PACKING:
Payments can be made as follows: cheque, postal order (payable to Orbit Books) or by credit cards. Do not send cash or currency.

U.K. Orders under £10	£1.50
U.K. Orders over £10	**FREE OF CHARGE**
E.C. & Overseas	25% of order value

Name (Block letters) ....

Address ....

....

Post/zip code: ....

☐ Please keep me in touch with future Orbit publications

☐ I enclose my remittance £ ....

☐ I wish to pay by Visa/Access/Mastercard/Eurocard

Card Expiry Date
